Brian,

Good luck in your new adventures......

GREEN SHADE$

ACCOUNTANTS AREN'T SUPPOSED TO DIE THIS WAY

by

GREG D. ADAMS

Enjoy the Journey !! :)

TELEMACHUS PRESS

Warning: This book includes violence, numbers, accounting equations, and sexual tension.

Disclaimer: Green Shade$ is a combination of fiction, accounting edutainment, and a resource guide. Names, characters, places, and incidents either are the product of the author's experience, imagination, or are used fictitiously. Any resemblance to actual persons, living or dead, events, or locales is entirely coincidental.

GREEN SHADE$
Copyright © 2024 GREG D. ADAMS
All rights reserved, including the right to reproduce this book, or portions thereof, in any form. No part of this text may be reproduced, transmitted, downloaded, decompiled, reverse engineered, or stored in or introduced into any information storage and retrieval system, in any form or by any means, whether electronic or mechanical without the express written permission of the author. The scanning, uploading, and distribution of this book via the Internet or via any other means without the permission of the author and publisher is illegal and punishable by law. Please purchase only authorized electronic editions and do not participate in or encourage electronic piracy of copyrighted materials.

The publisher does not have any control over and does not assume any responsibility for author or third-party websites or their content.

Cover designed by Telemachus Press, LLC

Illustrations by: Kristine M. Kammerer

Cover art: Copyright © shutterstock_2254626895_bright

Publishing Services by Telemachus Press, LLC
7652 Sawmill Road
Suite 304
Dublin, Ohio 43016
http://www.telemachuspress.com

Visit the author website:
http://www.CPA-Author.com

ISBN: 978-1-956867-92-3 (eBook)
ISBN: 978-1-956867-91-6 (Paperback)

Version 2024.05.15

To Kris and Olivia, who made it a better book.
And to my family and friends for their endless support
and encouragement.

Author's Note

All their adult life accountants, auditors and finance professionals are asked—"What do you do?" Being polite they would answer, "I'm an Accountant" or "I'm in Finance." Then the awkward silence would happen. They would have to quickly restate their answer with "I'm in finance, BUT…" providing further details of their stimulating roles, responsibilities, and personal playbook to navigate the uncertain waters of business. The "BUT" answer was also to assure their audience that they were cool and not your typical boring numbers person.

GREEN SHADE$ explores a variety of different worlds and settings, it's the earnest and guarded public accounting profession which provides the darkly humorous main backdrop for this exciting financial crime thriller. I invite you to join Dex McCord on his fast-paced global quest while uncovering secrets of the Big Four public accounting firms and everyday concepts of the Fundamentals of Finance ($\Gamma \emptyset \Gamma$). You will not only be entertained but also be provided with a provocative resource-oriented guidebook to help you expand your own financial lexicon as well as diagnose that Accounting and Finance is like a language: we need to understand it, communicate it, and embrace it.

Hopefully this book will help in some manner develop many of the skills needed in your world. Have fun with the journey and let the exploration begin!

Table Of Contents

Chapter 1	1
Chapter 2	19
Chapter 3	35
Chapter 4	48
Chapter 5	70
Chapter 6	85
Chapter 7	114
Chapter 8	147
Chapter 9	177
Chapter 10	200
Chapter 11	214
Chapter 12	231
Chapter 13	256
Chapter 14	280
Epilogue	286
Letter to the Reader	294
Index of Exhibits	295
About the Author	329

GREEN SHADE$

Chapter 1

"The significant problems we face cannot be solved at the same level of thinking we were at when we created them."
—*Albert Einstein*

- Tony Young
- Sydney's Northern Beaches, New South Wales, Australia
- The Aquariva
- Accounting Equations

New South Wales, Australia

"I'M ROOTED," Tony Young thought.

He was being pulled by his feet behind a new Aquariva Super, an Italian speedboat capable of 41 knots. The ski rope was taut. His hands were tied behind his back and his head was bouncing off the water. He felt powerless. Tony's mouth was wedged open by an old fishing net stuffed down his throat. Salt water was steadily flowing into his windpipe causing him to gag, and he felt himself getting asphyxiated.

Boat weight plus body weight times horsepower = speed. "Boat weight of 1,000 kilograms *plus* my 15 stone *times* 200 HP," Tony thought to himself. "We're going 30 knots." His mind on autopilot, he knew that if the intake of salt water is two milliliters per second and a person's lungs hold 240 milliliters, he had about 120 seconds before he drowned.

Tony was good at physics and math. Most accountants are. As a partner in a public accounting firm, Tony's instinct was to calculate the probability of events, and his impending death was no exception. Using statistics and constants to calculate solutions to problems was second nature. But this time solving the time of his death with linear algebra and a diminishing mind was stretching his mathematical abilities. He thought about the knots in the ski rope.

Young was well trained in knot theory, a rich area of mathematics. He learned from sailing that knots are based on the crossing number. There is only one knot with a crossing number of three, the cloverleaf knot. The figure-eight knot is the only knot with a crossing number of four. He tried to untie the ski rope around his wrists. It didn't work. He knew it wasn't a clover or figure-eight knot. Trying two other methods for untying five crossing knots didn't work. Time was running out. From there the number of knots increased dramatically. Tony kept trying to solve the problem, "There are over 12,000 knots with 13 or fewer crossings and 1.7 million with 16 or fewer crossings." His knowledge of knot theory wasn't going to save him.

"This is a sick form of waterboarding," he thought, "and definitely not the peaceful slow death described in *The Perfect Storm*." Drowning is a horrible way to die. Water fills your lungs until your chest feels like it's going to explode. First there is surprise, then panic, followed by fight-or-flight, and then calm. As the airway begins to close to prevent more water from getting into the lungs, a person will start to hold their breath involuntarily until they lose consciousness. In 2007 it was reported that the U.S. Central Intelligence Agency was using waterboarding on extrajudicial prisoners and the Department of Justice had authorized the procedure. Government officials said they did not believe waterboarding to be a form of torture. In 2009, President Barack Obama banned the use of waterboarding. Tony Young's captors were not from the U.S., nor did they care about treaties banning torture. Besides, their technique was entertaining and produced results—death or declaration.

Tony could feel his lungs starving for oxygen. He was getting dizzy. The force of the water was pounding his bones. Eyes shut, ears whistling, and neck extended. "It's too much pressure," he thought. His collar bone started to tear from the clavicle while his sternum was pulling apart interconnected ligaments and tendons. Young's short-lived hope was quickly fading away.

Accountants aren't supposed to die this way.

~~~

Tony "Youngy" Young was an ethical accountant and a devoted surfer. He headed to the beach religiously before work whenever wave alerts sounded over the wireless. Starting a workday in Australia after

10:00am was not unusual for Tony. "Work to live" was his motto. Youngy knew how to work and play hard, a stand-out and stand-up bloke.

In grade school Tony was a strong student and leader, captain of the cricket and swim teams. A smart and personable guy who was loved by many. After high school, and a six-month walkabout with friends in Europe, he attended the University of New South Wales in Kensington. He earned a Bachelor of International Commerce undergrad degree and continued with postgraduate coursework obtaining a Master of Professional Accounting. Shortly after graduation and a three-month backpacking excursion in the United States, Tony started his public accounting career in Sydney at KGO (Australia) Limited.

At the firm Tony quickly climbed up the ladder. After 12 years of hard work, and fun times, he was promoted to audit partner. Youngy appreciated that his success was due to a talented group of co-workers. He advocated the concept that accounting and auditing is a team sport. He also preached personal accountability, often saying, "Culpability does not begin with you, it begins with me." He believed it's all about holding oneself accountable, setting goals, defining consequences, and coaching people toward an agreed-upon finish line.

Tony took his role as a public accountant and external auditor seriously. As an independent Chartered Accountant (known in the U.S. as a Certified Public Accountant—CPA) he was responsible for auditing and reporting on his clients' financial statements. His primary responsibility at KGO, besides finding new business, included issuing an opinion on whether his clients' information was presented fairly in all material respects and in accordance with generally accepted accounting principles. Tony was ethically bound to deliver his opinion on whether his clients were performing financially well or poorly. And if they were conducting their business in a lawful manner.

Above and beyond his professional life Tony fully enjoyed his friends and community. He was a steadfast member of the Manly Beach surf club and rescue boat rowing team, and he'd spent many hours as a volunteer lifeguard growing up on Sydney's Northern beaches. As a partner and leader, he knew how fun it was to achieve a challenging goal with a group. He would often present his staff with the analogy of saving 15 panicked swimmers out of the surf after a sandbar collapses and the rip current pulls them out to sea. Just like his fellow lifeguards, Youngy's team of accountants was required to work together to save the day.

Tony was in his fourth year as audit partner when he was contacted by his friend and colleague at KGO New York to conduct a simple internal control review for one of their clients. The request was to perform an audit of a data processing facility in Bangalore, India, NSG Global. It wasn't an unusual request, and Tony had been to India many times, including Bangalore. The city was officially renamed to Bengaluru in November 2014, though it was often still referred to as Bangalore. Young instructed senior auditor Jiemba Abbot to visit the facility in India, perform test work, and complete a detailed internal control report on the company's policies and procedures and their effectiveness. He informed Jiemba, who was recently hired by KGO, that he would visit him in India at the end of the week to review his report. Tony noticed the young accountant was excited to be involved in such an important assignment.

Young arrived in Bengaluru five days later, exhausted from the 15-hour journey. Mechanical problems had resulted in a three-hour delay prolonging, already long 12-hour flight. After waiting over an hour in customs, Tony headed straight to his hotel for a desperately needed rest. Though Tony was a partner at a large accounting firm, he didn't like to waste partnership income sleeping in first class, he preferred staying awake in business class and saving his spend on premier accommodations. In Bengaluru Tony was staying at the majestic Leela Palace.

Early the next morning, Tony waited in Leela's lobby restaurant to meet with his young auditor. He ordered his traditional tea and biscuits at a table next to a large statue of Shiva overlooking a lush garden. Jiemba came into the café wearing a wrinkly suit and white shirt, fully looking like the part of an auditor.

"Good morning, sir," said Jiemba reaching his hand out with a smile.

"Gidday mate, sit down, sit down, wannacuppa?"

"Yes, please."

Young motioned to the waiter wearing a white dinner jacket, who in turn promptly summoned another wait staff to bring a fresh pot of tea.

"Is this your first time in Bengaluru?" asked Tony.

"Yes. I haven't seen a lot of the city, but it appears very different than Sydney."

"Struth mate, after a while you get used to this place. But I don't think I could ever stay here for more than a week."

"How many times have you been to India?" asked Jiemba.

"Hmmm. Too many times to count. At least 20. The benefits of being in KGO's technology practice," said Young as he pointed towards the empty plate of biscuits on the table and again motioned to the waiter. "This will be a quick trip. I'm meeting a friend tomorrow and then heading back to Sydney on Sunday morning. That being the case let's go over your report then head over to the facility. Were you able to set up a meeting with the Managing Director?"

"Yes. We have an appointment in her office at 1:00pm."

"Her? A Sheila?"

"I believe so, though I haven't meet her yet."

"You usually don't see the pitch-and-toss being a woman. It used to be forbidden in Indian culture."

"They have many women on staff, too," commented Abbot.

"That's good. How's it going? Are you learning about the nuts and bolts of the big data industry?"

"Trying to, Mr. Young. The NSG staff seem hesitant to share facts about their XML tagging process. The developers say it is driven by proprietary software that was created in the U.S. The analyst stated that their main task is to check their XML tags for accuracy."

"Have you documented the workflow?"

"Yes. But there are still a few open items and question marks that I need answers to. Finding the right person has been a challenge."

"Doesn't sound very Indian of them."

"I agree. One person said that he believes there is a final quality assurance review performed offshore somewhere. But he didn't know where."

"A QA process in another location?" asked Tony.

"Yes, but when I follow up the conversation goes back to the process of actuarial computations that they do for the parent company in Sydney."

"What's the chance of getting other NSG staff to open up?"

"Honestly. Buckley's. I've been in front of several project managers with very limited success."

"Well, then, mate, what do Aussies do best?"

"Surf?" replied Abbot knowing that Tony was a keen surfer.

"That's close, but no. Aussies drink heaps of beer. Take the project team out. Get them pissed on a few schooners. Indians can't hold their beer. Then they'll open up to you, mate."

"Got it, Mr. Young."

For the next three hours the two accountants reviewed workpapers. Young posed prodding questions as Abbot went through his structured internal control review approach: assessing the organizational structure; documenting key processes; reviewing business transactions; performing diagnostic tests; and identifying areas for improvement. Young was satisfied that the appropriate audit work was completed, and with the details Abbot documented in the report. But he was concerned about the control environment and the additional unidentified steps in the quality assurance process. He instructed Abbot to stay through the weekend to complete a critical task—getting the NSG Global staff to open up through alternative means. In other words, get them drunk and uncover the material weakness in their process.

Later in the day the two men visited the data processing facility and met with the company's Managing Director. The meeting was cordial enough, but Tony was unable to gain further insight into the processes surrounding the data services that were being provided to the firm's client in New York. He had significant concerns and a hunch that management in the facility was intentionally hiding something. He decided to leave his senior auditor behind for a few days to try and uncover the facts, to identify the weaknesses surrounding internal controls. Tony believed that Jiemba Abbot would be able to uncover additional information by utilizing his suggested tactics.

Tony returned to Sydney two days later, after visiting a former co-worker who was working in Bengaluru, landing at Kingsford Smith International Airport on a sunny Sunday afternoon. He was worn-out from his 12-hour flight and getting impatient waiting the usual 45 minutes at the Australian Border Force gate. The ABF were one of Oz's most critical law enforcement agencies, reporting to the Department of Home Affairs, responsible for offshore and onshore border control enforcement. They took their job seriously as they were the final stand for keeping the "undesirables" out of the country.

Eventually Tony made his way through customs and to baggage claim. After retrieving his luggage, he headed outside to his town car where his chauffeur was waiting patiently in a black livery BMW. On the way home he noted that the Sunday afternoon traffic in downtown Sydney was thicker than normal, due to the pride parade that was taking place in the popular Rocks neighborhood. Eventually his driver broke out of traffic and onto the Harbour Bridge's ramp, heading over the "coat hanger" as the locals would say. They continued driving through Neutral Bay then the city of Mosman and over the Spit Junction bridge towards Manly Beach. The driver at last arrived at the beach town and carefully drove his sedan through a disembarking crowd of tourists who were just off the ferry. At 5:30pm, Tony's sedan arrived at his Manly Beach flat.

"We made it, Mr. Young. Let me get your luggage from the boot."

"Thanks, mate," said Tony as he looked in his wallet to tip the driver, something most Australians don't do.

"No worries, any time. I'm glad you made it home in time to see the sunset," said the delighted driver.

"Hopefully I can stay awake for the colors. But doubtful, I'm tuckered," noted Tony as he handed the happy driver his tip.

"Thanks again, Mr. Young, and let me know when your next trip is."

"Sure will. See yas later," said Tony, throwing his bag over his shoulder.

~~~

After walking up three flights of stairs into his harbour view flat and heating up a tasty frozen meat pie, Young was ready to go through his pile of mail. Amazing how a week of bills and junk mail can accumulate, he thought to himself. The Day Four England versus Australia cricket test match was on television, but it wasn't even competitive. The Aussies were thrashing the English again. Tony couldn't keep his eyes open watching the lopsided match. He quickly dozed off to sleep on the couch.

At 10:00pm Tony's cell phone rang out, waking him from a sound slumber. The name Nauti appeared on his phone.

"Tony here."

"Hey, Youngy, welcome back. How was your trip?" It was Nigel Metcalf, CEO of his largest client.

"She was all right, but it's a bloody long flight home. And the food was horrible in Bangalore. I was getting tired of eating Pulihora and Curry Chicken."

"Sounds awful, I hope it was productive. Did you uncover anything?"

"I believe so mate. There may be a few internal control issues at your facility, but we'll sort them out," Tony proclaimed.

"Superb. The reason for my call is that I need your help with two recruits tomorrow morning."

"Ah, Nauti, I just got back this afternoon. I'm spent." Nauti was the nickname Tony called Metcalf. "Why can't you do it?"

"I'm stuck up in the Gold Coast trying to win a new client," replied Metcalf.

"Losing at the casino again?" kidded Tony. "Seriously mate, I don't think I have time. There is heaps of work waiting for me at the office."

"Come on, Youngy, these guys will bring me another Premiership."

"What do you need another trophy for?"

"Really, you'll have fun with these blokes," pleaded his client. "They will be in my Aquariva at 6:00am, docked at Carrel Bay Marina," asserted Metcalf.

"But I haven't been home for over a week, and I was planning on getting into the office early tomorrow morning," explained Tony.

"She'll be right. Take the two of them fishing for an hour and then for a paddle off Avalon beach. You'll be back by 11:00am."

"You're killing me, Nauti."

"Sorry, mate. The blokes are excited to get out on the water. They'll be waiting at the dock ready to go."

"But I don't know if…"

Metcalf interrupted, "Ahh, you need to get that Indian pong off you anyway."

"It wasn't that bad, but I guess an ocean breeze would help." Tony decided to cave in and keep his client happy. "OK, I'll meet your blokes. You'll owe me for this one."

"Good on ya, Youngy. Put extra hours in my bill," demanded Nigel.

"No worries, mate."

"I have fishing poles in the hull but bring two surf boards. I don't think they hired any."

"These blokes surf?"

"Don't know. But if they'll play for the Ocean Hawks I'll buy those boys boards, lessons, and Sheila's."

"Are they that good?" asked Tony.

"Good enough that the Penrith Panthers put out an offer."

"All right Nauti. I'll give you a call when we get back to the marina."

"Great. Cheers and thanks again!" Metcalf said jubilantly.
"Cheers, mate."

~~~

It wasn't unusual for Tony to receive last-minute entertainment requests from clients. He was the go-to guy to entertain one of KGO's largest clients and their important international guests in return for add-on business and referrals.

SYDNEY AND ITS NORTHERN BEACHES

Map showing Sydney and its Northern Beaches, with labels for Avalon, Carrel Bay Marina, Mona Vale, Narrabeen, Manly, Sydney, and Bondi.

Tony was exhausted and quickly fell back to sleep. His alarm went off at 5:05am. He felt like he hadn't slept at all as he dragged himself into the shower. After a quick rinse and before he departed his two-bedroom flat, Tony booted up his laptop to take a peek at the Avalon Beach web cam and surf report. The surf height was only one to two feet. Small rideable lefts with NW offshore winds at 10 to 14 knots. Challenging enough for beginners, he thought. The surf report also noted some schools of sharks had been migrating off Palm Beach point. They shouldn't be a bother, he deliberated. The water temperature was 20-22°C. Perfect conditions for the blokes.

After backing out of the garage Young loaded a couple of surfboards in the passenger seat of his convertible blue Mazda Miata. He left his Manly Beach flat driving north. Normally Pittwater Road through Narrabeen and up to the northern beaches would be chockablock with traffic but at 5:30am the roads were empty. Tony stopped at the 7-Eleven in Mona Vale for a coffee and bought four buttered rolls for his guests. He then jumped back into his convertible and continued north on Barrenjoey Road, turning left past the Careel Bay cricket oval, then right shortly thereafter, arriving at the marina at 5:55am. A blue Holden Commodore sedan was the only car in the shell-covered parking lot. The marina's main office was already open, the dockmaster busy inside reading the newspaper, drinking his morning coffee, and eating vegemite on toast.

Two athletic-looking dark skinned men were in Metcalf's boat and greeted Tony with wide smiles. The larger man was wearing a blue faded muscle shirt and red speedo. The other man was shorter and wearing a white golf shirt and colorful board shorts. Upon greeting them, Tony could hear from their accents that they were from the West Indies. "You two blokes must be Carrol and Frazier," confirmed Young. The men looked eager to get going and happy to be on such a beautiful boat. The Aquariva Super had been purchased by Metcalf for the bargain price of A$2.1 million. Its sleek retro look made it a cult yacht for collectors worldwide. The speed boat was an example of both beauty and performance. The Aquariva was 17 meters long and round on the bottom to displace its weight for improved aerodynamics and speed. The hulls were designed in a way that the boat's power pushed forward towards the bow, displacing water from the craft, while simultaneously allowing water to close in behind the boat, pushing it faster and increasing its velocity.

Shortly after Tony's arrival the men unloaded the surfboards from the Miata into the Aquariva. They promptly untied the boat from the dock and pulled away from the marina, heading east towards the bay's inlet. The trip through Pittwater Bay at sunrise was sensational. The out-of-town guests were gleaming with anticipation. The water in the harbour was a deep aquamarine. Palm trees lined the bay. Magpies and kookaburras were chirping as they woke from their nighttime slumber. Wood ducks were searching for food along the banks. The air was still and quiet. No other boats were in sight.

The Aquariva cruised at 15 knots past Coaster Retreat on the left, then past the Great Mackerel Nature Reserve where the Currawong Beach cottages lined the shore. There were no signs of early morning movement. It was dawn and the sun was rising quickly on the rose-pink eastern horizon. The temperature was 25°C. The day was going to be hot and balmy inland but cool and refreshing at sea. Tony slightly increased the vessel's speed, staying below Pittwater's inner harbor maximum of 20 knots. The Barrenjoey Lighthouse and headlands were coming up on the right, one of the must-see Sydney northern beaches hikers' destinations. The headlands were part of Australia's many national parks and home to countless other attractions, including ocean caves, protected marshlands, rocky cliffs, and native Aboriginal sites.

The speed boat was quickly approaching Lion Island and Broken Bay. Another eight minutes and they would be out to sea. The remainder of the cruise from the bay into the Tasman was smooth and uneventful. The men were heading out into the infinite ocean, leaving behind the landscapes of sandy beaches, rocky shores, and steep cliffs. The seas were calm. Young was proud of his country and loved to share its natural beauty with his guests.

Tony opened up the Aquariva to 40 knots. He felt the power of the boat and was now grateful to Nauti for the opportunity to spend one more day out of the office. In less than 30 minutes, the three men were 20 kilometers off the New South Wales coast ready to fish for barramundi.

"This should do it lads," said Tony as he turned off the engine. "My finder says there's a school of fish right below us. Get the poles from below and let's catch us some tucker," Tony directed.

The man in the white collared shirt went down into the cabin but didn't come up with the fishing poles. Instead, he was holding a large pump-action shotgun. The larger man who had opened a small locker at the back of the boat was holding a ski rope. Youngy was puzzled.

"Hey lads what's going on here?" The men said nothing. "We're not going fishing for sharks today," kidded Tony.

"Shut up and stay still," said the smaller man with the shotgun.

"We don't need a gun today, mate. Wait a minute. Did Nauti put you up to this?" There was no reply. "OK this must be some kind of joke," said Tony as he turned away from the larger man who was approaching him with a serious look on his face.

"No, mon," said the smaller man in charge. "Stay still and don't move."

"Listen, we don't fish with guns," said Tony as he backed up towards the stern.

"We're not fishing or surfing today, Mr. Young."

"Then what's going on?"

The men didn't respond. Unexpectedly the larger man lunged forward and gripped Tony with a strong bear hug. He then tossed him against the port side of the boat and Young went down, hitting his head on the polished wood of the Aquariva. Tony immediately felt pain and became dizzy as he tried to stand up and fight back, but the large man had the size advantage and strength over the concussed Young.

"Come on, mate. This is no way to treat your host. What do you want? The boat?" asked Tony as he was hurled to the floor again.

"We don't want the boat. Relax, mon, and we won't harm you."

The smaller man placed the shotgun on the driver's seat and retrieved the rope. The larger man in the speedo was holding Tony down while his hands were being tied behind his back. His legs were then tied together at the ankles. Young was unable to move or fight back.

"Keep him down on the floor," directed the smaller man, picking up the gun as he stepped down into the hull of the Aquariva.

Seconds later he emerged with a scaling knife and dirty brown fishing net. The man cut the net into a 12-inch square and stuffed it down Youngy's throat. Tony was grunting and snorting as loud as he could. There we no rescuers within miles to hear his call. One of the men grabbed the rope that was tied to Tony's ankles and secured it to a cleat at the back of the boat. The two men picked up Young in unison, the larger man from behind, underneath his armpits. The other man lifted both his legs and they tossed him overboard.

Tony was thrashing in the water trying to stay afloat. The engines of the Aquariva roared as the boat started to push forward. The ski rope immediately became taut with a body in tow. Three minutes later the water intake was increasing down Tony's throat. His hurried calculation of 120 seconds to live was not going to prove correct. He was dying. The salt water was now streaming into his mouth more rapidly than two milliliters per minute. The speed boat was going faster and faster. Tony's mind was exploding with pain and then without warning his body entered a state of hypoxic shaking.

Just before the convulsions, Tony's thoughts turned to Olivia, his 12-year-old daughter. He could see her face looking up from her iPhone. Her long blond hair, green eyes, and everlasting smile brightened his heart. He wished and reflected. Was she going to miss him? Will her mother be sad? He should have tried harder to make his marriage work. He knows he is loved. He can't breathe anymore. Hold on, hold on. Peace.

The men on the boat reeled in the lifeless body and cut the ropes from his hands and ankles. They started up the vessel and headed back towards shore with the corpse. At their backs, the sun was quickly rising in the east. A lone fishing boat was anchored five kilometers off to the southwest, anyone onboard unable to see any wrongdoing. On the Aquariva, a kilometer from shore, one of the men attached the surfboard's ankle strap to Tony's leg. From the beach the glare of the rising sun made it impossible to see his body being dumped over the side of the boat. The men maneuvered the surfboard and secured Young's body on top, keeping him afloat on the board with his ankle strap firmly attached. The body slowly drifted away in the Tasman Ocean currents. The engines roared with the push of the throttle and the speed boat pulled away. The sky was changing from pink to deep blue.

The two men arrived back at the marina. It was less than an hour and a half after they left. A man at the marina was cleaning the underside of his 35-foot sailboat. He was fully engaged in his task, not taking notice of the idling engines and the jolt of the speedboat bumping into the pier's buoys. The quartermaster was still in his office, engrossed in the sports section of the *Herald Sun*, reading about yesterday's Australia vs. England Test Match and an exhibition rugby union result from a competition in Perth. The men tied the boat to the dock at the same slip they left from earlier in the morning, retrieved their backpacks, and carried out one surfboard. They left the fishing poles and shotgun in the cabin of the boat. One man stepped into a Holden Commodore and the other into a convertible Mazda Miata after placing Tony's remaining surfboard in the passenger seat. The cars pulled out of the shell-covered parking lot and headed south towards Sydney.

It was another beautiful New South Wales summer day.

~~~

Tony Young loved accounting since taking a course in Year 11 at age 16 in secondary school. He loved the fact that there was always a right answer. The accounting equation was a powerful concept. The balance sheet had to BALANCE. The basic formula was simple and just worked:

$$Assets = Liabilities + Equity$$

The left side of the equation represented what the company owns, and the right side of the equation represented how the assets were financed. The income statement equation was just as simple:

$$Revenue - Expenses = Profit\ or\ Loss$$

The income statement represented the organization's net profit achievement during a period of time. It described the revenues earned and expenses incurred, with the difference being profit or loss.

Young's beloved accounting equations were simple enough concepts. However, he understood that most students interested in majoring in accounting got left behind when the concept of double-entry was introduced. This concept was the number-one reason Tony's professor at university asserted on his first day of class, "Look to your left and look to your right. One of your classmates will be gone by the end of the year."

All students struggle with the double-entry concept. It leads to "accounting anxiety," the jitters that make smart students stay away from accounting as it became increasingly difficult. Turned off by spending too much time studying debits and credits without knowing why they learned them. Many students believe that accounting courses fail to connect what they are learning with the larger world. The commonly asked question what's a widget?

Tony's profession since university was in public accounting. He appreciated the fact that most companies and organizations had to follow standardized accounting rules whose financial statements were either prepared or audited by an external, certified public accountant or chartered accountant. This was how Tony Young made a good living. He enjoyed providing advice, interpreting accounting rules, and examining his clients complete set of financial statements:

- Income Statement (or Statement of Profit & Loss—P&L)
- Balance Sheet

- Statement of Retained Earnings
- Statement of Cash Flow

Young believed that all people should cultivate a good grasp on the Fundamentals of Finance (**F Ø F**). He felt that financial skills and gaining an understanding of the dynamics of dollars and cents would take the guesswork out of their decision-making. Tony loved his profession and his job. He was going to be missed.

If interested see Exhibit 1: Purpose of Financial Statements and Double-Entry Accounting

Chapter 2

"An investment in knowledge always pays the best interest."
—Benjamin Franklin

- Dex McCord
- Trivia Night
- The Big Four Public Accounting Firms
- Public Accountants Org Chart and Salaries

New York, New York

DEREK "DEX" McCORD was a manly accountant. A dependable man. His excellent academic background along with a six-foot-five frame and sculpted body, results of his collegiate football career, made Dex a sought-after candidate for the large accounting and auditing firms. McCord attended the College of William & Mary in Williamsburg, Virginia, west on Route 84 from his hometown of Newport News. The College of Knowledge, also known as the Ivy League of the south, was a perfect fit for Dex. A hometown boy who had done good.

McCord's size and 1650 SAT score made him a sought-after recruit for an academic Division I-AA or II football program. He played tight end, but his stone hands made him a blocking specialist and curtailed his boyhood dream of being drafted by the NFL. At W&M he studied hard enough with the support of the athletic department's Teacher Assistants who served as tutors to the football players. With assistance and encouragement from several subject matter experts, McCord focused on graduating with a BBA in Accounting.

Dex could not recall when he first liked math. Most accountants like math. He also enjoyed solving puzzles of all kinds—number puzzles, relational puzzles, logic puzzles, even jigsaw puzzles. McCord's real joy came from solving serious mathematical problems that were contrived in a puzzle. Like figuring out the right way to account for a unique transaction or just conducting an audit, most accountants enjoy the challenge of a puzzle.

McCord had always had a keen sense of moral principles. He instinctively knew right from wrong and exhibited integrity and ethics in his actions, perhaps the result of constant reminders from his parents to always do the right thing. He had been raised in a lower-middle-class household. His family wasn't poor, but his parent's median income fell below the Census Bureau's PEW calculator. Growing up McCord never felt like he needed more than he had, but he knew he wasn't wealthy either. He wanted to get a job and someday earn enough money to help his parents get out of debt and enjoy life without burdens. He also wanted to own a house with its own dock and fishing boat.

Becoming a public accountant wasn't the first profession McCord dreamed of, but he knew it was one of the highest paying jobs out of college. His goal was to be part of the rising upper-middle-class, obtaining a job offer in a valuable profession and capital rich location could help him attain that goal. Midway through his junior year it was becoming evident that he would achieve his objective, since every W&M accounting student was assured an interview with all the large public and regional accounting firms. McCord believed the odds were good that a recruiter would be impressed with his personality and extracurricular activities. After all, there weren't many BBAs in Accounting that could run a 4.9 second 40-yard dash and play college football. McCord was earmarked by recruiters as a high-quality candidate, a well-rounded leader. The petty things he had learned from his college counselors—what to wear to an interview, how to differentiate himself, sending a thank you letter—did not elude him. He also followed the STAR method when writing his resume, in which each of his previous jobs outlined a Situation, a Task at hand, an Action, and a Result, as opposed to simply listing his high school and summer activities.

In the spring of his junior year, McCord was interviewed by the major players in the public accounting world, every firm offered the young superstar an office visit. The recruiting tours included lavish dinners, five-star hotel accommodations, and excursions to local attractions. He was happy to accept the all-expenses paid trips, which were not too dissimilar from his football recruiting trips. McCord had also interviewed and was recruited by the Federal Bureau of Investigation. Apparently, the FBI needed accountants. The growth in cyber and white-collar crimes had led to an increase in demand for recent college graduates in their fraud detection units. The life of a special agent was a great opportunity and sounded exhilarating. But the paper shuffling for racketeers and double-entry detective work sounded boring. Working at Quantico, the FBI headquarters in northern Virginia did seem cool. But at the end of the day McCord decided against a career in law enforcement. Most FBI agents had to carry a gun and he didn't like guns, despite growing up in conceal-and-carry Virginia.

The decision of where to work in the real world wasn't easy. After listing his pros and cons McCord decided to pursue a firm in the financial capital of the world—New York City—because, after all, if he could make it there, he could make it anywhere. New York was miles away from his childhood home in Chesapeake Bay, and auditing was much different from his clamming and crabbing jobs in the silty waters of the Virginia marshlands. But working in Metro New York offered a rich adventure. He liked one particular accounting firm, KGO LLP, from his first campus interview. The firm had sent a W&M alum who worked in their Washington, DC office to meet with interested students. She was blunt and honest. McCord appreciated her candor. She noted that her firm had a reputation for being more casual than the Big Four firms but like the other firms they had long hours and demanding clients. As a new hire McCord would be working very lengthy days at the beck and call of his managers, but he wasn't concerned about the effort required and was looking forward to making the big bucks. He was also happy to hear that they put a lot of money behind their corporate sports programs like softball, basketball, and ultimate frisbee.

Fast forward to ten plus lightning years later, on a cold evening in mid-January in New York City. McCord was now a KGO senior manager hosting a social gathering for winter interns and first year staff accountants in a conference center overlooking Times Square. He had been one of the elite few that stayed over 10 years in public accounting. Over the years McCord earned his way up the organizational chart harvesting more responsibility, bigger clients, and a bigger paycheck. The winter reception was full of enthusiastic accounting recruits, interns, and whiz kids steeped in technical skills but a tad boring and dull. McCord didn't recall being perceived as that same green candidate 10 years earlier.

KGO required their senior employees, like McCord, to host a number of the firms' social events. They recognized that many of their accountants were introverted and just not good at people skills. If they were going to take the next step in their career, these team members would need to learn the skill of networking and fostering relationships. McCord did not embrace these events, especially in the middle of the January to mid-April busy season. Hanging out with a bunch of eager college seniors and first year accountants wasn't the most thrilling experience. He wanted to leave this uninteresting party but understood his role: impress the recruits. So, after a few college football stories, three IPAs, and the courtesy group tequila shot, he determined that he spent sufficient hours entertaining and summoned the courage to text his most recent crush.

McCord decided to reach out to a beautiful accountant he had run into while in Central Park the previous summer and coincidently at an accounting conference in the fall in DC. He was a little nervous being so bold, and a few months had passed, but he decided to send out the Hail Mary text anyway.

"Do you want to meet me at the Four Seasons Bar?" He continued his thread, "The KGO partners and managers are celebrating a new six-figure client win."

Five minutes later a response lit up his cell: "Sure. Be there in 30 minutes ☺."

McCord instantly texted back, "Great! Do you know where the bar is?"
"Yes."
"Perfect. I'm on my way, Stacy."
"Can't wait—see you there," she replied.
McCord was eager to see his friend, so he quickly retrieved his coat and left the intern reception without saying goodbye to anyone. It wasn't a

good policy for the host to leave his own reception, but he didn't care, he had more essential matters to attend to. The Four Seasons was a 10-minute walk crosstown. He wanted to ensure he got there before Stacy Atchison arrived.

~~~

Stacy Atchison was a scholarly accountant. She enjoyed learning. Not only academia but learning about new people, places, and things. Her life as an accountant meant she was always listening and learning about something new—whether it was a difficult transaction, the ins and outs of a client's industry, or discovering new cities and personalities. Stacy had a thirst for learning.

Ms. Atchison was a product strategist manager at Ernst & Young's Foundry Group. The New York-based consulting team was comprised of entrepreneurs, industry experts, and strategists who endeavored to turn ideas into successful new growth businesses, acting more like venture capital employees than public accountants. Their primary purpose was to build and launch new businesses for EY. Stacy was responsible for framing solutions, breaking them down into component parts, and evaluating each methodically and thoroughly. She fit right in as a former high school salutatorian and alum of the University of Pennsylvania. McCord appreciated her brilliance and success—and also saw her as one of the most beautiful (and sexiest) accountants in New York.

Dex first laid eyes on Stacy at the annual JP Morgan Chase Corporate Challenge in Central Park. The event's intended focus was on raising money for charitable causes and promoting "fitness in the workplace." The competition to win was fierce among the accounting firms, and one that KGO and its partners took seriously. The footrace portion of the Challenge was a 3.5-mile-long sprint through Central Park. McCord was not a great long-distance runner, but he'd be damned if he lost against any "non-athletic" accountants.

When McCord reached the 2.7-mile marker on a warm summer night he was starting to tire, the long gradual hills of the park were wearing him down. But he was able to block out the pain with mind over matter after a stunning woman passed him by. He became fixed on her athletic physique and stride, and he had to push himself to keep up with her pace. Pursuing her from behind, the bounce and shape of Stacy's bottom became spellbinding—up, down, left, and right. In his hypnotic state McCord had a newfound energy. Several minutes later Ms. Atchinson willed McCord across the finish line, ahead of his teammates, salvaging his athlete-celebrity status with his co-workers. After the race Dex went up to Stacy, thanked her and said goodbye with a long bear hug. She wasn't sure who he was or what he was thanking her for, but she enjoyed the squeeze from the big burly stranger.

The following December McCord and Atchison met again at the annual American Institute of Certified Public Accountants (AICPA) conference in Washington, DC. After several technical presentations McCord got up the courage to approach Stacy. He thanked her again for the motivation in Central Park. The two confident professionals laughed about the Corporate Challenge, engaged in flirty conversation, and were immediately attracted to each other. There was an instant romantic connection, but since co-workers surrounded them the two new friends did not have a chance to sneak away and be alone. They exchanged phone numbers and promised to meet again in New York. Dex added her number to his favorites.

~~~

After leaving the intern reception McCord briskly walked through the midtown crowds and streets on the way to the Four Seasons on 52nd street. He was looking forward to seeing Stacy again. His bulky frame dashed between pedestrians on the sidewalks and around slow-moving cars in the streets while ignoring the illuminated Do Not Walk signs. He arrived at the

Four Seasons less than eight minutes after leaving his uninspiring event in Times Square. The KGO celebration was in full swing with the heavy buzz of conversation, the clinks of glass on glass, and fist bumps. The private room was filled with enthusiastic accounting professionals in dark blue suits, white shirts with skinny ties, stunning dark dresses, and sheer nylons. The space was accented by a wall of windows draped with metal beaded curtains and a long table under a colorful cloth loaded with sparkling glasses of wine, imported beer, and variety of cocktails. The bartender was serving at a steady pace, not bothering to measure his pour. Everyone was drinking and toasting each other. Dollars were overflowing from the tip jar.

Stacy arrived towards the end of the celebration. A little longer than 30 minutes but Dex didn't mind. She was in the perfect black spaghetti strap cocktail dress with a conservative string of pearls around her neck. Her figure slender, elegant, and defined. All eyes in the room turned towards her as she entered, and McCord went from the other end of the room through the crowd of professionals like she was a magnet. Stacy saw him walking over and flung her arms around his shoulders. She liked Dex and was happy he reached out. Stacy had just left her girlfriends at a nearby restaurant and building on an earlier buzz, was excited to be playing a game that accountants deemed forbidden, crashing a competitor's party.

An hour later in the Four Seasons bar under the dim light of incandescent bulbs McCord was kissing her neck. The last of the hors d 'oeuvres were finished, and they were ready to leave. Stacy promptly invited him to join her to meet up with a few associates. Dex was tired and it was getting late, but there was no way he would say no and disappoint. He wanted to be with her. They walked down the stairs of the restaurant, past the impressive Bogoievic oil on canvas, out the double doors, and into an Uber Stacy had ordered. The car drove down 52nd Street towards the East River and turned left onto First Avenue heading uptown. McCord was hoping they would ditch Stacy's friends and head back to her place on the Upper East Side. This would not be the case. After a couple of turns and driving north 31 blocks they stopped in front of an old-style Irish bar, *The Five Lamps* on 83rd and York Avenue.

"Where are we?" asked McCord who was a little disappointed the car was not in front of Stacy's apartment.

"Well, it's trivia night at The Five Lamps. My team is going for first place. I had to come here and help," responded Stacy.

"Trivia night? I'm not very good at trivia."

"Don't worry if you don't know the answers, you just drink."

The two jumped out of the car and walked into the pub. The place was packed. Patrons were crowded around tables with beer and oversized pretzels in front of them. All listening intently to a person sitting on a small stage who was reading a question over a microphone. Stacy spotted her three friends at a table left of the host. On the wall written in chalk she noticed it was round 12 of 16. "Only four rounds left," she told McCord. Stacy immediately answered the question that was asked over the microphone as they approached the table.

"It's Thomas Edison! Edison, Edison!" she lunged toward the table and murmured to her friends in a frenzy.

"That's it," one of them replied. "Thank god you're here."

"Okay where are we at?" asked Stacy.

"Third! We only have three questions left. But it's so close, I think we can take them," said one friend.

"How many teams this time?"

"Fourteen."

"I want that money, not just the free shots this time," said the other woman at their table. "Alright let's do this," said Stacy.

"So, who are you? Actually, it doesn't even matter, are you here to help us?" the third woman asked looking in McCord's direction now.

"I'm not sure but I'll try," said Dex.

"OK good, get us another pitcher of Guinness. And a few pretzels!"

McCord left the group and headed to the bar. He didn't know a lot about trivia nights but recognized that the questions covered a wide range of topics from history to sports, from movies to music—something for everybody. And that the questions asked by the host were usually to test the knowledge of a drunk person. McCord didn't let Stacy's friends down. He returned with a pitcher of beer and two pretzels. The team was cheering and high fiving after just answering the 14th question. Dex was consumed by the team's energy and excitement. Shortly thereafter the engaging and funny host read the 15th question. It was something to do with movie trivia and Harry Potter. He didn't have a clue, but Stacy leaned over to her teammates and dispatched the correct answer. Something to do with Hagrid's beloved boarhound Fang. She was correct.

"This is it, team. We have 92 points," said Stacy as she put her arm around McCord.

"We just need this last question!" said one teammate.

"I can count the money now," stated the other women.

Stacy's team was banding together in the spirit of competition getting ready for the last question. The host announced the category: sports trivia. Everyone at the table looked at McCord. He started to get nervous. The host read the question: "In 1972 the Miami Dolphins were the first and, so far, only team in NFL history to win every game in a season. Who was the fullback of that undefeated team?"

The team was waiting for a response from McCord. He was frozen and dumbstruck. He had no idea what the answer was.

Stacy smiled and whispered in her new boyfriend's ear, "Larry Csonka."

"That's it!" Dex exclaimed.

The team huddled and submitted the answer. It was in fact Larry Csonka. Team Atchison was the only group at Five Lamps to submit the fullback's name correctly. Stacy even knew the correct spelling. McCord's group of new friends hugged and cheered. Dex was swept up into the moment.

The host came over to the table and gave the team their cash prize winnings. They all agreed to divide it evenly. McCord put his share on the table for another round of drinks. He was keenly aware that since arriving at trivia night, Stacy had answered every question correctly with an adept degree of grace and poise. Dex was in awe of Stacy's knowledge of a broad range of subjects. Her friends bragged to McCord that she was the best player in the league. He noticed that Stacy made people around her feel comfortable, she didn't look to impress or be impressed, she just enjoyed the moment. She was certainly a change of pace from most of the women he dated. He wanted to be with her more than ever.

When several celebratory pitchers of Guinness were consumed and banter with the trivia crew ended, it was time to leave. McCord volunteered to walk Stacy back to her apartment on 74th street. She accepted the invitation. The couple walked out of the bar and turned left onto York Avenue and headed south. It was past 1:00am on a Tuesday. The city was silent and forlorn darkness owned the streets. The couple passed by 400-feet high apartments stacked in the air with sleeping residents. They sauntered along quietly holding hands. McCord enjoyed her hand in his. The sexual tension was rousing.

After a five-minute brisk walk, they turned right onto 74th street, crossing First Avenue. They arrived in front of a five-story pre-war brown brick building. Stacy pulled her keys from her purse. She turned the key in the lock, pushed open an old wooden door, and they floated up three levels of stairs, unlocked the bright red metal door marked 3D, and in they slipped.

Stacy took off her jacket and tossed it on the chair in the entryway. She made her way over to the couch. Without offering McCord a drink she invited him to follow her there. As she got comfortable, her dress slid up above her knees revealing her perfectly shaped athletic thighs. She felt exposed but didn't bother to fix it. Ms. Atchinson enjoyed flirting with McCord.

It wasn't going to take long before they couldn't keep their hands off each other. Stacy removed her pearl necklace and pinned up her hair into a loose bun inviting him to gaze at her soft white neck. McCord started softly kissing her. First behind her ear then slowly, softly, traveling down her neck around to her chest, continuing to discover her. She took a long slow breath, signaling that she was right there with him. Dex whispered softly in Stacy's ear, "I'm so glad we're here tonight."

He realized that his kisses and now his words were giving her chills and causing her to arch her back, pushing herself hard against his chest. They stood up with their bodies intertwined. She slid her hands under McCord's shirt and pulled it up over his big shoulders and off his strong arms to reveal his bare chest. Her hand then slid over his belly, taking all the blood from his brain to below his waist. Dex slowly slipped Stacy's thin black straps off to expose her bare shoulders, continuing to gently tug until her dress fell to her belly. All remaining clothes were now being quickly ripped away. He was appreciating her body, gently kissing it. They moved into the bedroom and fell onto her queen-sized bed into piles of down. They needed the larger bed to continue their exploration. McCord was 100% devoted to the moment and thought that Stacy was feeling the same. He wanted his partner to walk away satisfied with the experience. The couple played through the remainder of the night exploring each other's bodies... and then they fell off to sleep. And a great sleep it was.

The morning arrived much too soon for McCord's liking. It was late and he needed to get to the office as soon as possible. He jumped out of bed and headed into the bathroom, leaving the bathroom door open and wishing that Stacy would join him. McCord was ruminating alone in the shower, remembering the amazing connections they made. He heard Stacy's voice from the kitchen.

"Better step it up, you're going to miss your staffing meeting!" Stacy shouted. "And save me some hot water."

"Where are my pants?" He shouted back.

"I hung them on the back of the door to get the wrinkles out. The steam from the shower works wonders," she said as she popped her head into the bathroom handing him a much-appreciated hot cup of coffee.

McCord smiled sweetly as he took the coffee from her hand. He kissed her once more before she disappeared out of the steamy room. Shortly after Stacy entered the bathroom naked and joined Dex under the hot water. He could feel Stacy's heart beating as their bodies intertwined under the shower head. They became wet with soap and shampoo. Bubbles slithered off their bodies. They couldn't keep their hands off each other. Connected lovers.

Just the start of another day in the life of an accountant.

~~~

Across the globe the Big Four accounting and audit firms are massively influential. Together they earn over $130 billion annually and employ over one million people. McCord was happy to get an interview with all the Big Four in order to compare them verses the smaller accounting firms:

- Deloitte.
- Ernst & Young
- KPMG
- PricewaterhouseCoopers (PwC)

McCord observed slight differences between firms. Deloitte (Deloitte & Touche) had a reputation for being meritocratic, conservative, valuing prudence and perfectionism while being genteel in appearance. Ernst & Young (EY) was wrapped up in the middle of the pack, enjoying a reputation for exacting standards, competence, and being identified more as collaborative specialists. KPMG, the smallest of the Big Four, was recognized as the symbol of an accounting establishment, however, they had a reputation marked with repeated scandals. Their people tended to be less uptight, and more relaxed and candid compared to the other firms. PricewaterhouseCoopers (PwC) image was a vibrant, modern-thinking, buttoned-up white shirt firm. Their partners had a reputation for ironing their own underwear, but the firm's reputation was tarnished by their colossal mistake at the Academy Awards when actors Faye Dunaway and Warren Beatty announced the Best Picture award incorrectly, sparking the chaotic ending of the 2017 ceremony.

During his interview process McCord noticed that there is no love lost among the Big Four. All the public accounting firms used regimented recruiting procedures and guidelines to ensure they were getting the best and brightest. All compete vigorously for talent; all are out for themselves. The most intractable problem for the Big Four and the second-tier public accounting firms was that, as investment banking and software coding became lucrative professions and more baby-boomers flooded into retirement, there was never enough talented or promising people to go around.

McCord was concerned that he would be lost in the shuffle at one of the Big Four. He also heard that over the last decade the largest firms have been moving out of the small business marketplace. For most of the Big Four firms, if a top mid-market or large multinational client is not generating over one million dollars in audit, tax and consulting fees, it's not worth their effort nor risk. And thanks to the extra Sarbanes-Oxley internal-controls work, they appear to have decided it's better to trim their client lists and move away from smaller clients. McCord wanted to stand out at a firm, to have a bigger impact, more variety, less politics, and more personalized interaction with his clients. So, in his senior year he accepted a winter internship in New York with a smaller more personal firm, KGO LLP.

His short month and a half of winter internship validated KGO's collaborative and open culture; and his employment experience didn't disappoint as he was assigned to projects on interesting clients and introduced to the firm's audit philosophy. He also thought it cool being taken to the corporate box to watch Rangers and Knicks games with a few of the firm's managers and partners. McCord appreciated that the smaller public accounting firm wanted to impress their star intern, so after an exciting six weeks in the city and a nice paycheck for second semester spending money, the choice of which accounting firm to join was easy: McCord decided to stay away from the Big Four firms and be that big fish in a smaller pond at KGO (an acronym for Kristof, Garvey and Owens). He also liked their tagline, *Those Who Know, Know KGO.*

After graduation McCord began his professional career as a staff accountant with a starting salary at the high end of the bell curve, plus a guaranteed 12-month retention bonus. Early on he was exposed to a wide spectrum of clients and industries, all different and all interesting, after a few years of diversified audit engagements McCord was assigned to his preferred industry practice: information technology. As his responsibility increased McCord was getting a better picture of how his career might progress. He saw that with consistently strong performance he could move up into future senior positions. This meant a lot more opportunity and exceedingly more pay than what he earned growing up as a clammer in Chesapeake Bay. As he came to appreciate, public accounting had a hierarchy:

THE TRADITIONAL AUDIT ENGAGEMENT TEAM:

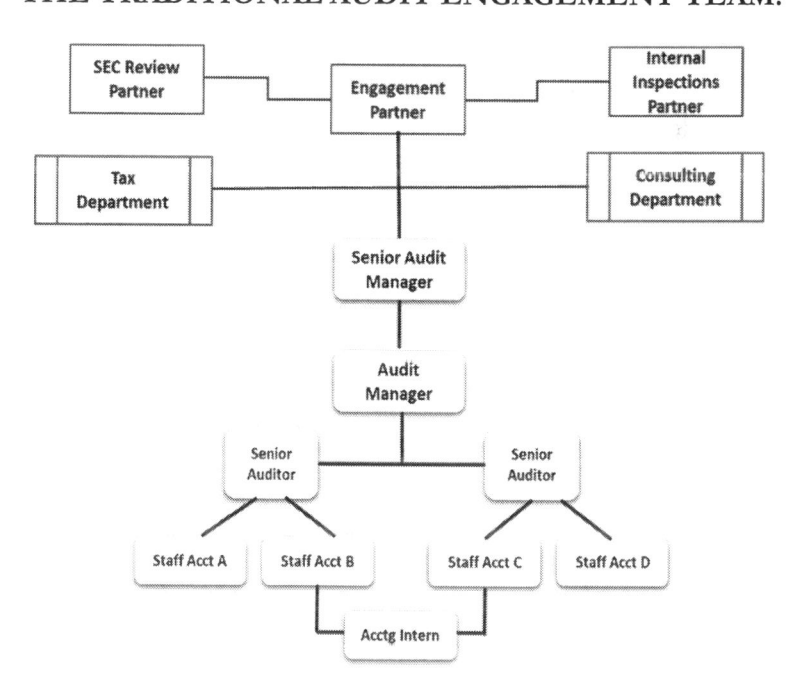

```
SEC Review Partner ─── Engagement Partner ─── Internal Inspections Partner
Tax Department ─────────────┼──────────────── Consulting Department
                            │
                    Senior Audit Manager
                            │
                       Audit Manager
                        ┌───┴───┐
                  Senior         Senior
                  Auditor        Auditor
                  ┌──┴──┐        ┌──┴──┐
            Staff Acct A  Staff Acct B  Staff Acct C  Staff Acct D
                          └── Acctg Intern ──┘
```

~~~

McCord understood that the basic audit function and starting salaries didn't differ much from firm to firm. The accounting firms try to draw distinctions, but there are more similarities than differences and depending on the city location, the work performed at each firm was relatively constant.

To be surprised see Exhibit 2: The Fall of the Bog Eight, Public Accounting Roles and Annual Salaries

Chapter 3

*"Try not to become a person of success, but rather,
try to become a person of value."*
—*Albert Einstein*

- Don Borovina
- The SEC's EDGAR System
- Types of Public Company Filings
- The CPA Exam

MAJOR ACCOUNTING FIRMS IN NEW YORK CITY

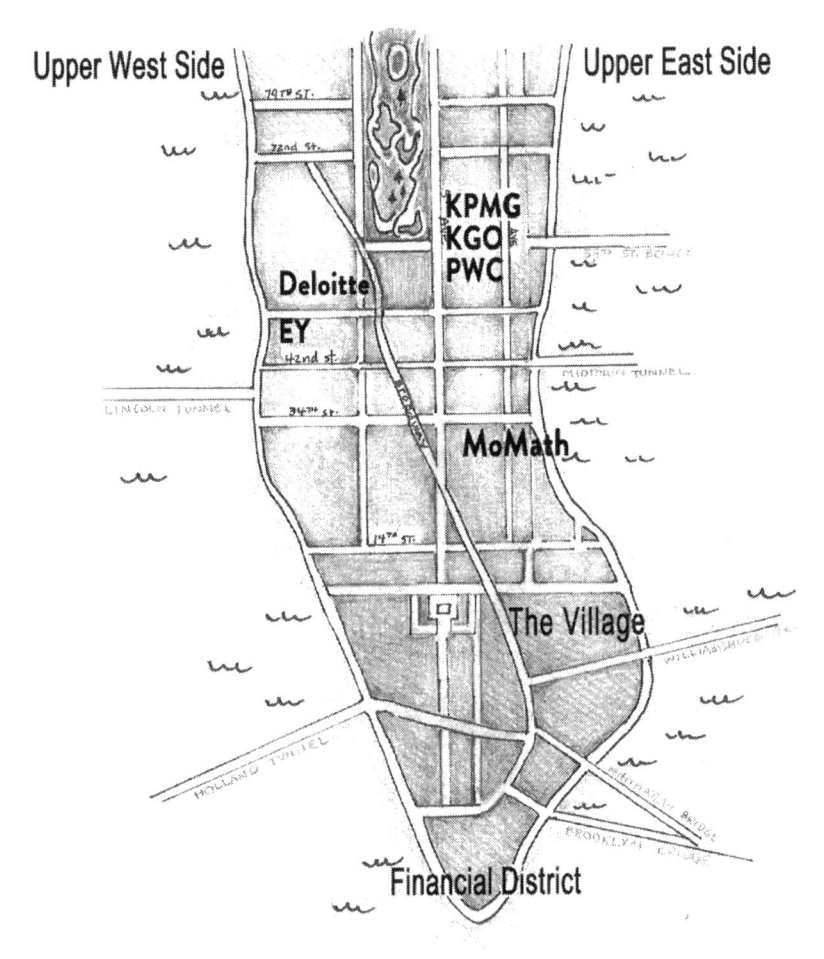

EY – One Manhattan West (33rd and 9th)
Deloitte – 30 Rockefeller Plaza (49th Street and 6th)
KPMG – 345 Park Avenue (51st Street)
KGO – 250 Park Avenue (45th Street)
PWC – 300 Madison Ave (42nd Street)

Upper East Side, New York

STACY ATCHISON'S BROWNSTONE walk up apartment was on the Upper East Side between First and Second Avenue on 74th street. A long journey to the KGO offices at 250 Park Avenue on 45th Street. McCord rushed out the doors and down the steps in a sprint. It was 8:20am and he was already late for his staffing meeting. The streets were filled with people headed to work and children strolling to school. McCord had to do his best high school football moves to avoid taking down a few innocent pedestrians.

The three city blocks to the 77th Lexington Avenue subway station from First Avenue were longer and steeper than McCord remembered. Most visitors don't realize heading from the eastside to the westside of Manhattan is difficult: the city blocks are long, and the hills are steep. The new Second Avenue subway construction was finally complete, but its sheer stairs and intermittent trains would put more time on the clock. McCord decided it would be faster to go for the #6 train on Lexington Avenue to reach his Park Avenue destination.

The subway platform at 77th and Lex was packed with a mosaic of humans. McCord muscled his way to the tracks to ensure he was able to get into the next car. The #6 train pulled up and it was more crowded than usual, earlier delays had the crowds of people smashed up against each other. As the doors opened his tactic of hollering "excuse me" or "coming through" didn't seem to be working, but a seam opened as a select few departed the arriving subway car. McCord made himself slim and pushed his way in as the doors shut behind him.

Subways are generally the best way to get around New York City if you're traveling more than a half mile and need to make good time. This is especially true if you're going from one part of the city to another. Eight hundred and forty-two miles of tracks, carrying millions of people on thousands of subway cars, 24 hours a day, every day. The subway is still undeniably safe—most of the time. Major felony crime on mass transit (buses and subways) represents just two percent of overall NYC crime, not sure-thing odds but worth the risk.

Standing closely next to McCord on the subway was a woman, he assessed to be in her early 40s. He could tell she felt comfortable and somehow safe in his shadow. After two stops of being firmly pressed against the women the subway doors opened at 59th street, and a group of self-focused commuters pushed their way out of the crowded train making it now easier to breath. McCord anxiously thought "one more stop before my office." As the door's closing bell sounded a beast of a man made a late entrance before the doors closed behind him. The rotund man purposely leaned his body forward pressing up against the woman standing next to McCord in an attempt to intimidate her. The woman was not happy to have this smelly overweight guy pressing up against her, with his sour breath coming down upon her head. She instantaneously pushed him away, shoving with both arms showing her disgust. The lout did not take the hint and took his stance once again dominating the woman.

McCord had never been present for such a scuffle in the subways, but then again, he had only been back in New York for a few years. In his sports life, though, he had "seen things escalate and quickly get out of hand." He needed to act. As the train started to move McCord picked up the woman and whirled her body around to his back landing him directly between the two with him now facing the intruder. McCord didn't say a word, he just kept staring down at him with his steely blue eyes. He had formed an impenetrable barrier. The skirmish dwindled, with the woman yelling at the man from behind, "Don't mess with me. Do not mess with me."

A few minutes later the #6 train was slowing down approaching its next stop. With a poker face McCord whispered to the man, "You Are getting off at this stop, and You Are taking the next train, Correct?" The surprised man looked up and nodded in the affirmative. As the train doors opened the man exited, disgruntled but clearly intimidated. McCord was happy that the situation didn't escalate. No weapons, no visible bloodshed, and the problem solved.

McCord left the subway station and the man behind at the 51st Street platform while he dodged the crowds running up the stairs. He hustled through the streets and stormed through the revolving doors at 250 Park Avenue, ran up the escalators, and arrived at the 8:00am audit staffing meeting at 8:45am to the applause of the group. His red face from the morning's sprint and extracurricular activities exacerbated his embarrassment. McCord just smiled and waved to the group of senior managers who were already fatigued from the early morning staffing battles and trade negotiations. Fighting for human resources was a non-contact sport that all managers dreaded. If an audit partner didn't get the right staff for his client, the rest of your day and week became a long mêlée of complaints.

McCord was paying his dues as staffing manager. The partners in the New York office believed a staffing assignment was an effective way to get him acclimated after spending three years abroad in KGO's Sydney office. They saw it as a way to return him to a New York state of mind after his plum expat assignment. McCord's planned rotation in Australia was originally for 18 months but it ended up being over 30 months. The partners Down Under liked Dex and wanted him to stay longer, however, a few of the New York partners were annoyed by McCord's length of overseas service. When McCord returned, his payback was to fulfill the duties of staffing 325 accountants to audits while managing two demanding clients of his own. He was responsible for assigning billable hours to first and second year accountants and senior auditors for the firm's Technology Practice. McCord found that his staffing responsibilities, albeit painful, provided him with needed exposure to several partners and, more important, first dibs on talented personnel.

"McCord. What was it this time?" barked the partner-in-charge of staffing, Don Borovina. He didn't appreciate his tardiness.

"You know Don, day games after night are always tough," quipped McCord.

"Well sit your ass down and let us all know, how you are going to staff Accenture?"

~~~

Don Borovina was a competitive accountant. Don believed serving clients and completing timely audits required a team of highly committed professionals. He emphasized that when assigning employee talent, his group of staffing managers apply critical thinking and common sense. Borovina wanted his team to work as a single unit to achieve their fellow employees' aspirations and the firm's customer goals, that they coordinate projects with their stakeholders and most prominently with the firm's partners. Otherwise, their ass will be thrown out on the street.

Besides proudly being the self-proclaimed biggest prick in the office, Don was partner-in-charge of staffing for all New York Office audit engagements. However, the responsibility he took most pride in was coach of KGO's softball team. Borovina slow pitched for the company team even though he wasn't the best high arc pitcher. But it was his bat and ball, and no player would dare to complain. Defense and hitting usually compensated for his lack of talent. The other partners did not challenge Don's exorbitant outlay for such extracurricular firm activities, nor could they argue with the success of the NYC team. Everybody likes to be part of a winner. At the annual partner meetings in Orlando, Borovina was quick to point out which office had the most national softball championships. However, many of the partners feared the risk associated with national tournament weekends. The New York office reputation of beer-filled bathtubs and damaged suites didn't sit well with the other regional offices.

McCord had earned Don's respect on the ball field and especially in the batting box. During the previous summer Borovina's softball team won the national KGO Championships in Washington, DC thanks to McCord's two home runs in the finals. Borovina lived for these tournaments. The New York Office was the perennial winner. They had a seven-year winning streak and McCord was a big part of those championships. As a result, Don liked and supported McCord by securing him favors that few other received, including a coveted international assignment in Australia.

The KGO NY staffing meeting continued its talent negotiations for another 75 minutes after McCord arrived. It ended promptly at 10:00am, the mandatory deadline for Borovina's weekly meeting. The cut-off allowed enough morning time to return emergency phone calls before the obligatory client and/or partner lunches.

As McCord was walking out of the conference room Borovina pulled him aside, "Dex, Walsh called from EDGAR."

"Why didn't he call me?"

"He couldn't find you this morning, asshole, and called me. Where were you?"

"I was busy promoting inter-firm activities," grinned McCord.

"What indiscreet activities would that be, conflict resolution?"

"You could sort of say that," Dex smiled.

"Well, Casanova, give Walsh a visit and see what he wants. He's an important client so don't screw things up," Borovina demanded.

"What's he looking for?"

"He wants an update from the Australian partner you sent to India. Something about a review of his vendor's internal controls."

"Tony Young? In Bangalore?"

"If you say so. What's going on over there, McCord? I hope he doesn't think I am going to jump on a 24-hour flight and stay in some grimy Indian Marigold Hotel," said Borovina.

"No worries Coach I'll have it taken care of," asserted McCord.

"You'd better Sherlock. They are a good client. Take care of this. And hotshot, our meetings start at 8:00am. Not 8:45am," noted Don.

"I had a good excuse, but I get it," he smiled.

"No more excuses, mark it down, Wednesdays 8:00am."

"Sure will."

McCord walked away no longer concerned with the repercussions from his tardiness. "It's good to have friends in high places," he thought.

~~~

McCord understood that if he was going to continue to rise through the ranks of KGO he needed to piss off as few partners as possible. In addition to internal staffing responsibilities McCord had two significant audit clients—Dr Pepper's International Division and EDGAR Data & Intelligence Inc. McCord dreaded working with the partner on Dr Pepper's account. He was a transfer from KGO Boston and kind of a dick. No interpersonal or soft skills and never played softball.

The Dr Pepper audit work and McCord's responsibilities were limited to the review of foreign joint ventures and complex accounting transactions, a proficiency he learned while in Australia. Pepper was doing business in more than 190 countries worldwide, including Thailand, Turkey, Azerbaijan, or any other unusual country a person could think of. It took 12 in-house accountants in their New York headquarters just to figure out the appropriate US GAAP for international joint ventures. The accounting treatment was always subject to interpretation and ultimately boiled down to substance over form or, better yet, common sense.

The NY partners considered McCord's past international rotation as a qualification to formulate substantive accounting recommendations. But he preferred to be out in the field inspecting production lines, evaluating business models, and discussing strategy with operational executives. His work hours were long, especially before quarterly review presentations and his clients' regulatory reporting deadlines. More often than not he found himself in Dr Pepper headquarters past midnight with his prick audit partner trying to come up with creative solutions. However, he was a good soldier and thought of the assignment as putting in his dues until a more attractive engagement presented itself.

EDGAR Data & Intelligence ("ED&I") was McCord's favorite client. ED&I was a business information company that sliced and diced public company filings that were then submitted electronically to the Securities and Exchange Commission ("SEC"). In the late 1990s ED&I created an electronic interface to the SEC reporting database that simplified access to public company filings for investors and the public at large. The company leveraged its proprietary application programming interface to disseminate reported information around the globe in real time.

"EDGAR" was an acronym for Electronic Data Gathering, Analysis and Retrieval. Prior to the introduction of the EDGAR system, SEC filings were only available on a delayed basis in expensive paper or CD-ROM format from a limited number of document providers or by visiting the SEC's public reference rooms. Annually and quarterly public companies were required to file reams of reports with the Securities and Exchange Commission disclosing a wealth of information. Among the juicier tidbits contained in the SEC submissions were earnings release, information about company growth, or lack of it, disclosures of pending litigation, investigations by government agencies, default of bank covenants, compensation figures, and, of course, details on game-changing transactions. Before the EDGAR system and the Internet company filings were made available in paper format. This was a huge advantage that the large investment houses exploited for decades.

In 1994 the SEC began accepting electronic filings of compliance documents and, since May 1996, they required all U.S. and foreign public companies to make their information available in an electronic format through the EDGAR system. Since then, and over the past few decades, timely data and accurate information about public companies have become increasingly necessary for investors and money managers to gain a competitive advantage and to protect their investments. The speed on private trading platforms based on extracted financial information and other "8K" Fair Disclosure (Reg FD) events meant the difference between investment success and financial ruin.

McCord and his audit team became experts on the major categories and corresponding forms filed into the SEC's EDGAR database:

Filing Category	*Filings Included in SEC FORM's:*
Annual Reports	10-K 10-KSB (Small Business)
Quarterly Reports	10-Q 6-K 10QSB (Small Business)
Special Events (Reg FD) – including: ✓ Earnings releases ✓ Material Events	8-K 10-C 6-K
IPO Filings	S-1 SB-1 SB-2 F-1 (Foreign) 424B
Insider Trading	3 4 5 144
Ownership	13-F 13-G 13 D
Mergers & Acquisition	S-4 14D-1 14D-9
Secondary Stock Offerings	S-2 F-2 S-3 F-3
Mutual Fund Filings	N-1A N-30D 497
Proxies and Information Statements	DEF-14A

Since the inception of the EDGAR system in the 1990s the SEC has continually increased the requirements on public companies to disclose more timely information electronically. The tailwinds of democratizing information, along with government mandates to increase both the number of people who can gain access to EDGAR-derived data and the amount of data going into the EDGAR database, led to a growing demand for real-time information. McCord's client was one of the few technology providers that was able to deliver financial information to employees, customers, and shareholders in real time. Their unique process of XML tagging SEC filings became one of the primary sources of public company information on customers intranets, private networks, and websites.

ED&I also had tailwinds from the early rapid growth of the Internet. The open delivery method allowed them to provide customers with data and financial information in a more efficient and less expensive manner. Almost overnight ED&I became known as the experts in extracting and delivering timely and actionable information. McCord understood that those investors, companies, and individuals who were clever enough to use his client's machine-readable EDGAR information would have a significant advantage over the less informed.

~~~

In McCord's first year at KGO, he knew he had to turn his attention to passing the CPA exam, becoming a certified public accountant was not a trivial task. McCord took the exam in Norfolk, Virginia so he could stay at home and avoid the distractions of New York City life. On his first try Dex passed each part with a 75 minimum. "No need to get any higher," he thought. "After all the highest paid physicians are the ones that just barely got through medical school while the high honor roll students end up with low paying research jobs." As a reward for passing the CPA exam KGO paid McCord a $5,000 bonus. It came in handy when making his student loan payments.

Of course, McCord knew his work experience at KGO was going to be vital and that credentials matter, too. For the future partner or CFO, an MBA is good, but a CPA is gold. In the post Sarbanes Oxley world that is the capstone credential, most firms and executive recruiters wanted to see that box checked. Even with formal training in accounting the lack of a CPA seems like a sign of unfinished business.

McCord was happy that he chose the path to become a certified public accountant. CPAs had become suddenly intriguing in 2002 with the spectacular collapse of Arthur Andersen. This added unwanted color to the accounting profession, but it has remained a breeding ground of capable people. It's not just that the large accounting firms collectively employ millions of people around the world; unlike big companies in other industries, the accounting, tax, and audit firms really mean it when they say that people are their biggest assets. Their product is their employees' knowledge, and their distribution channels are the relationships between their staff, alumni, and clients. More than most companies, they have to worry about how to attract, retain, and stay in touch with their brightest workers.

And, of course, there's the problem of supply shortage; there are never enough skilled or promising "bean counters" to go around. McCord knew this all too well; the pool of his available talent was sometimes shallow due to several major factors: a CPA requirement for a fifth year of higher education, early retirement, and turnover rates.

In the late 1990's the American Institute of Certified Public Accountants (AICPA), in its infinite wisdom, decided to increase the educational course requirements for CPAs from the standard 120-hours of course credits to 150 hours. The new "150-hour" rule mandates the equivalent of a fifth year of higher education. The rules change caused a significant decline in students taking accounting courses at university. The number of students going on to sit for the CPA exam continues to fall to new lows. The talent shortage hasn't significantly impacted the large accounting firms yet, who still have their pick of talent, but even these firms are starting to question the necessity for a fifth year of schooling.

Turnover rates at the Big Four and large accounting firms are historically high, roughly 15-20% leave each year compared with as few as 5% in other industries. It was especially true in McCord's technology group where thousands of start-ups were poised to steal his finance talent. The profession's biggest staff exodus comes after three years, once trial balance top dogs pass the CPA exam and gain the required experience to be certified as accountants. Most public accounting professionals intend to stay longer than three years, then quickly come to realize that they can parlay their qualifications into a new job and fatter paycheck somewhere else. However, something McCord preached to his staffers was to consider that the habitually loyal accounting professionals who stay five to six years rather than two or three, will have a much higher likelihood of obtaining a better position with higher pay. Not to mention the added benefit of an expanded alumni network.

By the tenth year, employee turnover is greater than 95%. Even so, the public accounting firm's goals are more subliminal than simply increasing retention rates. Instead of fighting the turnover problem, they embrace it. And for good reason, as they have detailed programs that keep the firm in touch with their former employees, who tend to be future clients. Not everyone will become a senior partner, but they can still be extremely valuable to their former firm.

McCord was aware of the turnover statistics at the larger accounting firms. He had fortitude and an appreciation of the big picture that went well beyond number-crunching. Such experiences were essential for his professional development and, indeed, may lead to a future CFO-track job. Or perhaps he'd stay for partnership riches—time would tell. For now, McCord was happy at KGO. He wanted to live a rewarding, comfortable life and understood that making partner could take him there, but he was also keenly aware it may take longer than he wanted to stay.

He was endlessly torn between a safe climb up the public accounting ladder or deciding to take a chance. Perhaps it was just the fear of failure that was keeping him from pursuing a different less prestigious course.

See Exhibit 3 for a significant change to the CPA Exam.

Chapter 4

*"I'm tired of hearing it said that democracy doesn't work.
Of course it doesn't work. We are supposed to work it."*
—*Alexander Woollcot*

- Jiemba Abbot
- Big Data and XML in Bengaluru, India
- Nigel "Nauti" Metcalf
- The Bajans

Sydney, New South Wales

JIEMBA "ABBO" ABBOT was a resolute accountant. Jiemba is a Wiradjuri word, the name for the planet Venus or "the laughing star." His ancestors were from the Wiradjuri tribe, the largest Aboriginal group in New South Wales. They once occupied a vast area in central New South Wales, on the plains running north and south to the west of the Blue Mountains.

Since the European invasion of Australia in 1788, the Aboriginal people have been oppressed into a world unnatural to their existence. The early Europeans took a dim view of the Aboriginal way of life when they first encountered it. To most settlers, the Aboriginal people were considered akin to kangaroos, dingoes, and emus—a strange society to be eradicated to make way for the development of farming and grazing.

The new arrivals carried with them infectious diseases that decimated the immediate population of the Sydney tribes. It struck a fatal and extensive blow to the Aboriginal people, who until that point had been isolated for thousands of years. They had no resistance to the deadly viruses carried by the sailors and convicts—smallpox, syphilis, and influenza. In less than a year, over half the indigenous population living in the Sydney Basin had died from disease. Further ignorance and colonialism led to thousands of Aboriginal people being killed by white settlers, and attempts were made to "breed out" their culture through assimilation. The region, once alive with a vibrant mix of Aboriginal clans, now fell silent. Within six months, the colonists had destroyed a way of life that had outlasted British history by tens of thousands of years, and the people soon realized that the trespassers were committed to nothing less than total occupation of the land.

What Jiemba Abbot's ancestors had to overcome was a testament to their fortitude and strength in character. His grandparents and their families left the bush in the 1960s after the formation of the Australian Aborigines Progressive Association, escaping the government-controlled stations and reserves. The association called for an end to the forcible removal of Aboriginal children from their families that had almost erased their culture.

Abbot's parents were raised in Sydney. His father graduated from secondary school, but he still faced fundamental barriers to finding a good paying job. Eventually he found work as a laborer with the help of new formed unions for indigenous citizens.

Abbot's mother stayed home and raised two children, Jiemba and his younger sister Kalina, the feminine name for love and affection. His mum was an artist who leveraged grants from the federal government and local community. She started painting in earnest when the children were teenagers, and her paintings became immensely popular. As an Indigenous woman, she could create Aboriginal art. A non-Indigenous Australian does not have the authority to paint an Aboriginal piece of artwork, and only artists from certain tribes are allowed to adopt the dot technique. It is considered both disrespectful and unacceptable to paint on behalf of someone else's culture. As the market for native Australian art saw greater demand, Abbot's mother was able to raise her prices. She was now able to pay for her children's education. Abbo so loved his mother's art that he got a colorful dotted lizard tattoo on the side of his neck.

At the University of Technology Sydney (UTS), Abbot completed a cooperative education program in accounting and earned a bachelor's degree. The program was an intensive course offered in conjunction with major local employers. Its students complete a compulsory first major in accounting and full-time work training. Abbot's first job out of UTS was with Grant Thornton, a smaller public accounting firm. He was excited to be an auditor on day one. Abbot was a sponge gaining valuable work experience in different businesses and industries. One day he was at a beach umbrella manufacturing company, the next at an electronics plant, then at a pharmaceutical company. The work was both challenging and rewarding. He was able to get a behind-the-scenes look at a wide array of businesses, making Jiemba a sought-after commodity.

After five years of dedicated service at Grant Thornton, Abbot was recruited by KGO as a senior auditor. The large accounting firm was criticized for its lack of diversity and needed to employ more minorities. The preoccupation with image-making was symptomatic with all public accounting firms. For too long, the accounting industry celebrated white men in buttoned-down shirts, but it was time for a new look and Abbot checked that box. Abbot at five foot four with darkskin, heavy brow ridges and broad nose checked the box. The reason for his recruitment didn't matter to Jiemba, he was thrilled to be joining the premier league of the accounting world.

During Abbot's first few months at KGO his initial tasks were limited to self-paced training on the firm's audit procedures and internal administrative projects, but that changed when Tony Young, an audit partner, called the young accountant into his office. When Jiemba walked into the office the first things he noticed behind Tony were a University of New South Wales master's degree and Chartered Accountant certificate hanging on the wall surrounded by action photos of professional surfers. He hadn't expected to see such colorful and vibrant pictures in a public accounting office. Jiemba was eager to receive his first assignment out in the field.

"So, you are the young Mr. Abbot," Tony said as he reached out to shake his hand.

"Yes, Mr. Young, but you can call me Abbo. Everyone else does," answered Jiemba.

"OK, mate. I appreciate that. Your first name is too bloody hard to pronounce anyway," smiled Tony.

"What can I do for you, Mr. Young?"

"First, stop calling me Mr. Young. You can call me Tony. Or Youngy if you really want to get my attention mate."

"OK. Yes sir," confirmed Abbot.

"We have been requested by our friends in New York to kick some tires at a facility up in Bengaluru, India. They want us to document their internal controls and workflow. The organization is NSG Global. They are an actuarial consulting and data services firm," explained Young.

"No problem, sir. I did plenty of internal controls reviews on pension plans when I was with GT."

"Good. Ignore the actuarial stuff. I need you to look at their controls surrounding the XML data tagging of documents coming in from the States."

"When do you want me to leave?" asked Abbot.

"Tomorrow, mate. I cleared it with the partner on the project you were working on. I'll probably need you up there for a week or so. After you complete the controls testing, I'll come up to India and review your findings. You'll have five days. Are you good with that?"

"Yes, definitely, sir."

"Great. Now, Abbo, go home early and rest up, I'll have my assistant book your flight. She'll send you an email with the details. I will see you in Bengaluru late next week."

"Thank you, Mr. Young," Abbot said as he got up to leave.

"Call me Tony, mate," said Young as the eager professional walked out the office.

~~~

Jiemba was excited about the opportunity. His first audit assignment at KGO, and it's an international account! His family was going to be immensely proud of him. He'd have to call his Mum and Dad and give them the big news. Abbot missed his family as they no longer lived in Sydney, having moved away after the success of his mother's art career. They went back home to open up a gallery in the tourist town of Katoomba, at the foothills of the Blue Mountains amongst a backdrop of rugged sandstone tablelands, dramatic peaks, waterfalls, and canyons. A good place for Mrs. Abbot's art gallery.

Early the next day Abbot boarded a flight to Kempegowda International Airport Bengaluru. While on the 12-hour flight he studied the KGO training manual on internal control reviews, had business class tucker, and took a nap. Abbot's Qantas flight arrived on time at 4:55pm, and he was able to quickly retrieve his luggage, pass through customs, and board a taxi in less than 30 minutes. The traffic to the hotel was thick and slow. Abbot's rush-hour journey of 10km was going to take him over two hours. Traffic woes are a well-known fact across India, and Bengaluru was the most traffic congested city in the world in a report released by TomTom. In fact, the southern Indian city expects their visitors to spend an average of 71% extra travel time stuck in traffic. After two and a half hours Abbot finally arrived at his hotel, checked in, and immediately went up to his room. He wanted to get a good night's sleep and start his first meaningful assignment well rested.

The next morning, Abbot took the short walk to NSG's facility and arrived promptly at 8:00am. His engagement was considered simple. Plan A: Assess the likelihood of errors in the client's process and document and test controls, including five interrelated components of internal controls:

1. Control environment assessment
2. Detailed risk evaluation
3. Identification of control activities
4. Information and communication processes
5. Ongoing monitoring of controls

Abbot would then need to complete two types of testing before Tony arrived:

1. Observation
2. Compliance test of transactions

Abbot's first step was to flowchart the entire control process surrounding the XML tagging of documents. As an auditor he had to gain familiarity with NSG's business to identify the key transactions and their importance in the overall business. It took Abbot several days to find the right employees to explain the data tagging services outsourced to NSG from the United States. He noted that most of the employees were not forthright in sharing their job description or processes, but they were excited to discuss actuarial assumptions. Abbot's findings on the XML tagging of documents were not going to be conclusive. There were still question marks surrounding workflows, including lack of segregation of duties, timeliness of management exception reports, and controls over the dissemination of the information. Abbot's initial discoveries: NSG had excellent control documentation around their actuarial data services, which their employees loved to talk about, but very little controls surrounding XML data tagging. There were still many open audit items that needed to be cleared. Abbot would need to perform additional observations tests as there wasn't sufficient documentary evidence of effective performance controls.

Abbot then went to internal control review Plan B: gain intimate familiarity with the client's data tagging process. He needed to identify all the key types of transactions and their importance in the overall business. From his experience at Grant Thornton, he learned that most people, when asked what they do, loved speaking at length about every aspect of their job. This did not seem to be the case at NSG. The employees appeared nervous when Abbot asked his standard internal control questions. Tight lipped but, in Indian fashion, very polite. In short, they were unwilling to open up and discuss what they were doing. After three days he still didn't have all the facts and controls documented for his final report. Tony Young was arriving the next day and Abbot was getting nervous that his findings and workpapers would not be acceptable. He worked almost all night to put them in order.

The next morning Abbot left his modest hotel to meet Tony in the lobby of the imposing Leela Palace with its opulent fabrics, dark wood, and marble floors. A stark contrast to his hotel and the world outside. Tony was waiting with tea and biscuits at a table overlooking a lush garden setting. Jiemba came into the café wearing a navy-blue jacket, black slacks, and a white shirt. The uniform of a good auditor.

The two accountants spent the morning reviewing Abbot's internal control workpapers and drinking tea. While reviewing the audit papers Abbo walked his boss through the construct of his internal control documentation, his diagnostic test work, and the overview of the company's information systems. Along the way Tony asked thought-provoking questions but lingered when he examined documentation surrounding information systems and processes on XML data tagging. Abbot noticed he was focused on NSG's software tools and data protection controls when final documents were being returned to the United States. He was surprised when Tony shared his thoughts on the client's technology and software-as-a-service product line. Partners at his old firm never spent time getting into the weeds with him.

Tony appeared satisfied with Abbot's audit work and the details included in his workpapers, but he was concerned about the control environment and an unidentified quality assurance process. Before the men left the hotel, Tony instructed Abbot to get the NSG's employees to open up on the final steps of their XML tagging process, to stay through the weekend and complete one critical task: "Uncover the material *weakness*."

Before leaving the hotel to visit the NSG facility Abbot had informed Tony that he had scheduled an appointment for 1:00pm with the Managing Director, Purvi Singh, but that she only had 45 minutes to meet with them. Tony thought that would be enough time for him to assess the business environment and was looking forward to speaking with her. Abbot was concerned that the meeting wouldn't go well.

~~~

NSG's facility was led by Purvi Singh. As a child of the 1970s she grew up in the garbage-lined streets of Chickpet, a suburb of Bengaluru, the capital and largest city of the Indian state of Karnataka. Since the late 1980s Bangalore—now officially Bengaluru—became one of the world's preeminent software development locations. The city's identity was tied to technological innovations and the fact that firms like Infosys and Wipro were among the first to set up shop there. Bangalore was regarded as the "Silicon Valley of India" because of its role as the nation's leading information technology exporter.

Purvi's early childhood was a product of the local society. The children of Chickpet were even more likely than adults to live in poverty. India still accounts for approximately 30% of all children living in extreme poverty globally. Despite growing up in a slum, Purvi was able to find her refuge in books that she received through the free elementary education system. This access to education provided Purvi with the knowledge and life skills to realize her full potential. With the assistance of the government's "Gati Shakti" subsidy she enrolled at the competitive Ramaiah Institute of Technology (RIT) in the Department of Computer Science and Engineering, one of the preeminent technology programs in India. Ms. Singh wanted to pursue a career in software engineering. She was able to overcome all barriers.

In university Purvi excelled and graduated at the top of her class with a degree in Computer Science. Ms. Singh stayed two more years at RIT and received a post-graduate diploma in Statistics & Analytics, a degree focused on enabling students with skills in data analytics that drew heavily from the disciplines of mathematics and computer science. After graduating with honors, Purvi landed a highly sought-after job overseas at a Caribbean software development company in Barbados. The company halfway around the world was offering free housing, food, and travel allowances at an eye-popping US$15,000 per year. She would essentially be living for free and be able to send money home to help her family escape poverty. As her career progressed Ms. Singh became the poster child of women empowerment in India. She was now part of the established 35% of women in the Indian IT labor force a cohort instrumental in radically powering the industry's rapid growth over the past several decades and profoundly changing the landscape of the information technology workforce in India.

~~~

Jiemba Abbot and Tony Young, were escorted past rows of cubicles and into NSG Global's executive row where Ms. Singh was sitting in her corner office. Jiemba noticed she was not wearing the traditional Indian sari like most of the other female employees at the office, but rather a crisp tailored business suit, a grey Dior jacket and slacks with a white fitted shirt. Her appearance conveyed credibility and competence.

Ms. Singh's office was comprised of a simple ergonomic desk and chair. Her desk was facing the door to create an inviting and accessible vibe.

There were plants in each corner and a long teak credenza under the window. Behind her desk were numerous awards and a large display of colorful opals. On the wall her multiple diplomas from the Ramaiah Institute of Technology were surrounded by an actuary certification and various technology certifications.

"Good day, Mr. Young. I am Purvi Singh. You can call me Purvi."

"Gidday, Purvi. It's a pleasure to finally meet you. Senior management back in Sydney has spoken very highly of you and your team here. And you can call me Tony. This is my associate Jiemba Abbot."

"Hello, Mr. Abbot. I have seen you speaking with my team. I hope they have been hospitable to you."

"Yes, very hospitable, thank you," replied Abbot.

"What do you think of our facility, Mr. Abbot?"

"Excellent. Extremely high tech."

"We've made a lot of investments in the past few years. You'll find our data analytics and artificial intelligence capabilities cutting edge. We are implementing many interesting, automated processes."

"I can see that everything is state of the art. It must have cost heaps."

"Yes, Tony. We invest all our profits back into technology," added Purvi.

"One issue we are having is completing our review around your XML content validation process. Your team doesn't seem too eager to provide many details," stated Tony.

"Well, gentleman, it is an extremely complicated process that a lot of the staff are having problems understanding. You see traditional XML languages do not express enough meaning. Our XML approach is immensely powerful, with all the necessary rules embedded within the applications."

"I'm not sure we follow you Purvi. Can you expand?" asked Tony while Abbot was taking notes.

"Well, the XML rules are written application by application and in different proprietary ways that are impossible to exchange across business systems. We are trying to develop one standard approach that will enable such an exchange." Purvi continued, "With XML data tagging you can manage both the information itself and the business rules that support creating accurate actionable intelligence. Thus, allowing you to seamlessly communicate business information."

Abbot was shaking his head, making believe he understood what Ms. Singh was saying, but he noticed that his boss was intently listening to Ms. Singh.

"Ah yes, I understand," said Tony. "We were just surprised that your staff didn't provide us with all the details. They also mentioned a final QA process at another location?"

"I am not aware of that. But I can tell you that our processing software is very accurate. Most of our project team have Actuarial Science degrees, it's our core business. In fact, we have many actuaries on staff and it's a known fact that unless you're the boss, being an actuary is one of the least happy careers. So don't be offended by their lack of cooperation."

"And why do you suppose that is Purvi?" asked Tony.

"Primarily due to the fact that most actuaries spending much of their time on the maddening details. Not all of them take to it so well."

"Strewth," agreed Tony. He had recently read that, based on surveys, actuaries rate their career happiness 2.5 out of 5 stars, putting them in the bottom 5% of careers.

Ms. Singh, continued, "But our actuaries are well compensated, which makes crunching data more palatable. In your country experienced employees have the potential to earn from A$150,000 to A$250,000 per year, and many of our actuaries earn more than that."

Abbot could sense that Purvi was changing the subject away from the control environment, just like the other employees he tried to interview. He stayed quiet and watched Tony's reaction.

"Mr. Young, our actuaries play a crucial role in the psychological, physical, and financial stability of society. I understand that chartered accountants like yourself, who have tried their hand with actuary talents, agree that it is way tougher than being a CA. Unlike accountants, actuaries need to pass a series of difficult exams. Our test is seven parts verses your four parts. And our pass rate is typically only 30-40%."

"Yes, we understand the challenges actuaries face, Ms. Singh. I believe we have the information we need," said Tony as he rose from his chair.

"Oh, I hope I didn't go on too much about our actuarial capabilities. I get very passionate about what we do here, Mr. Young. We are people who deal with the measurement and management of risk."

"No not at all. We are always happy to learn new things. I have just two more simple questions. Where did you get all those opals?"

"From Australia of course. We have a very generous owner."

"I am well aware of Nigel's generosity," smiled Tony. "I think I will get some for my daughter as well."

"Certainly."

"My second question—is that you with your Uni class in Goa? It's incredibly scenic," said Tony as he pointed at a picture on the wall behind Purvi.

"Oh, no. It's my data analytics team when I worked in the Caribbean."

"Looks beautiful. I'll have to hear more about that someday."

After shaking hands and exchanging niceties the two auditors promptly left the office, as Ms. Singh assured the men that she would be happy to meet again if they had any open questions. While Tony walked away from the corner office and out of the building, he looked over at Jiemba and winked, appearing satisfied with the meeting. Before Tony boarded his taxi, he instructed the auditor to keep probing and questioning the staff about the extra quality assurance steps, that he would connect with him in Sydney next week. Abbot was happy that Tony was satisfied with the visit and his workpapers. He walked back into the facility to finish his test work and invited members of NSG's XML project team to an evening of free dinner and drinks.

Ms. Singh closed her office door behind Tony and Jiemba, walked over to the credenza, and clutched one of her opals as she gazed out to the parking lot. Watching Tony get into his taxi she picked up her cell phone and called Nigel Metcalf, her boss in Australia.

~~~

Nigel "Nauti" Metcalf was an enterprising accountant. Nauti developed his numeracy skills by balancing the books at his father's sporting goods warehouse in North Sydney. His experience in bookkeeping led to a predictable major in accounting at the University of New South Wales. After Uni and before entering the workforce, he attended business school in America to pursue a master's in finance. He was accepted into the highly competitive Dardin School of Business at UCLA. While living in California, Nigel was a good student but excelled at networking. His new circle of friends spanned the globe—from future wealthy businesspeople to Saudi Arabian princes to influential gentlemen from the West Indies. These were important relationships he would be able to leverage in the future.

When he returned from the States Metcalf joined Ernst & Young in Sydney. Starting a highly sought-after position at a premier public accounting firm made his working-class family proud. EY was the perfect fit for Nigel as the firm stressed over and over again that quality service is deeply rooted in their history and tradition. The original founders of Ernst & Young held themselves as the accountant's accountant, emphasizing their image as "Old Reliable." With this reputation EY took steps after the Big Eight consolidations to assure its place as a large international firm by adopting several modern marketing tactics to dust off the boring quality image by securing clients like Coca Cola, General Motors, and Hilton.

During Metcalf's brief career in the public accounting profession, he thrived in statistical sampling and analysis. He was a methodical and logical thinker who paid strong attention to detail with an uncanny ability to influence and persuade others with facts—a skill set essential for his future success. He understood that he had something different from everybody else, everyone was smart and hardworking, but he was a lot more imaginative with numbers than others. Metcalf also had an outgoing personality, and, despite his slight build and small size, he played on EY's rugby team, where he developed solid friendships. But Nauti's most valuable expertise was the ability to analyze data, build complex business models, and configure business algorithms into actionable items. This would serve him well in the private business arena.

Three years after Nigel enlisted at EY, his dad was diagnosed with prostate cancer. He quickly succumbed to the disease, dying just two months after diagnosis. Nigel was devastated and lost interest in providing quality service in accordance with EY standards. Seeing her son's unhappiness, Metcalf's mother encouraged Nauti to leave EY and be an entrepreneur like his father. Mum sold the family's wholesale sporting goods business and provided him with seed money to start his own business. This was his golden ticket out of public accounting, and he could now be his own boss.

Leveraging his local relationships and knowledge of statistics Metcalf started an actuarial company in Sydney, Metcalf Consulting Ltd. Nigel had a talent for working with copious amounts of data and creating meaningful spreadsheets. For his swiftly growing client base Metcalf was able to create unique risk management and investment plans that best suited each enterprise's financial condition. His group of actuaries possessed skill sets that Metcalf valued most: delivering a statistical look into the future using data and numbers. By delivering logical results and dependable financial mathematical models, his firm was able to calculate the probability of events occurring in each month, quarter, and into the future.

Metcalf became a natural at studying uncertain events, especially those of concern to insurance and pension programs. He surrounded himself with mentors in the industry, including the CEO of one of the largest pension and insurance experts, Buck Consulting. Nigel became effective at leveraging all his relationships and desperately wanted that next level. He would say, "you give me a chance on your account, and I promise you will never meet a more creative problem solver." While he was known to be a tough businessman, his clients loved him as he provided increasingly effective solutions in evaluating risk and protecting them from economic loss. Over time Metcalf's actuarial business expanded into selling investments, insurance products, and pension-related funds.

In a matter of five years Metcalf's empire grew to over A$150 million in revenue, proving that being blessed with excellent math and analytical skills is good for the wallet. During the company's period of accelerated growth, Nauti purchased a small data analytics and software development company in Bangalore, India. He named the company NSG Global (Nigel Software Group). Their developers and actuaries were experts in data mining and leveraging immense amounts of information. NSG's managing director, Purvi Singh, was a highly respected leader in the industry.

One of Metcalf's pension clients was an under-producing gold mine in Krakow, Queensland. It was an ignored property of Newcrest Mining Limited, a stagnant mining division producing negligible amounts of gold in Australia's outback. Newcrest also had a majority interest in an opal mine. Nigel believed, based on his statistical analysis and a certain combination of proven liquid solvents, that both these mines could increase production three-fold. After strategizing with the local Queensland geology team over countless Four-XXX beers, he orchestrated a management buy-out with their parent company. The transaction made him the largest shareholder. Then by leveraging solvents and an underutilized mineral extraction device, combined with longer production hours, the mines literally struck gold, producing over 900 ounces a day. Metcalf's educated guess was correct.

Eighteen months later and correctly timing a gold futures surge, Metcalf was able to cash out, orchestrating a sale of the Krakow gold mine for A$350 million, of which he owned 80% (through various acquisition triggers). Metcalf ended up clearing over A$200 million after tax proceeds. Not bad for 18 months of work. Also, as part of the transaction he was able to carve out a majority interest in the opal mining business and use lapidary methods to produce flawless polished stones. That company was for Nauti's mother. She loved opals.

Shortly after the sale of the gold mine business, Metcalf had a serious off-road Jeep accident while on vacation in a rainforest north of Cairns. The accident left him with two metal screws in his back that made him unable to walk or sit down for extended periods of time. The physical therapy was difficult and painful. Nigel had to give up his beloved weekend sport of rugby, but he was driven to overcome his handicap. The simplest way for him to continue to be in the game was to own the game. So, to offset his feeling of inadequacy, he bought the Manly-Warringah Ocean Hawks, a perennial loser in the National Rugby League. The purchase price was at a premium and cost Metcalf tens of millions. He became obsessed with winning the rugby league Premier Championship. He knew that his dream would be costly, but he didn't care how much cash the Ocean Hawks would need to achieve his goal.

Like its owner, the sport of rugby is a mix of hardness and ferocity, a fast-moving game supported by enthusiastic fans. Metcalf believed the future of the National Rugby League was bright and, similar to American football, would become Australia's most popular sport. During the first three seasons Metcalf spent millions to turn his "footy" club around. With his investment the Ocean Hawks became competitive again. Metcalf was at last able to put behind him his physical handicap after his team won their first Premiership by beating the perennial champions Brisbane Broncos. The Ocean Hawks never looked back and kept on winning, thanks to Metcalf's continued support and significant capital outlays.

~~~

Nigel was waiting patiently at a small table on the second-floor marketplace in front of Sydney's Queen Victoria Building Tea Room. Sipping on his late morning tea while preparing his scone with preserve and clotted cream. He was wearing a gray suit and black crewneck shirt, a Steve Jobs look. The

QVB, as known by locals, is a famous 1898 historical building located in Sydney's central business district that is home to boutique stores and cafes. The spacious and ornate building of Romanesque design was created as a produce market and functioned as such for decades. It became Sydney's most elegant shopping environment, almost too beautiful to be called a shopping centre. Perhaps the most exciting and mysterious of the displays in the QVB is a sealed letter written by Queen Elizabeth II. The letter is to be read in 2085 by the future Lord Mayor of Sydney. No one knows what the letter says, as it is hidden somewhere in the off-limits dome at the top of the building.

Australia's constitutional parliamentary system of government angered Metcalf. He believed that the country should simply drop its relationship with the British monarchy, it was archaic, and gives control of his country to a foreigner. He wanted Australia to become a republic with a parliamentary appointed head of state, a nation where its government formally gets all its power from its people, not from some ancient royal family. The majority of Aussies supported and agreed with his position. Nauti had made it his mission to actively pressure his parliament connections for a new referendum, he also wanted political power.

At the Royal Automata Clock, which was about to chime at the hour of 12 noon, Metcalf was staring out. He could see walking through the crowds two dark skinned gentlemen in pre-washed jeans wearing designer t-shirts, one white and the other navy blue. As they approached, he observed the crowds dispersing as the barrel-chested men walked with athletic purpose. The two men confidently sat down next to Metcalf.

"Hello, gentlemen. Did you take care of the problem?" Nigel inquired without getting into formalities.

"Sure did, Mr. Metcalf, he won't be using his surfboard anymore," boasted the man in the white shirt as he sat down.

"OK, well done. I hope you were respectful to my friend," remarked Nigel.

"As respectful as we could be, but he needed some persuading to get into the water," grinned one of the men.

"Did anyone see you in my boat when it returned to the marina?"

"No, sir, there wasn't a soul at the dock except an old man inside the office reading his paper. I don't think he even looked up."

"How about Mr. Young's belongings?"

"We left his backpack on Avalon Beach like you said. And his car is off the street parked in our garage," confirmed the man in the navy shirt.

"OK, good. We'll get rid of the car at the right time. Were you able to find out anything about the location of the Aboriginal bloke?"

"We saw him arrive at the airport this morning and followed him after he got into a hired car. His taxi was driving down M1 highway and we were right on his tail. They were making lefts and rights all over Kings Cross. The traffic was really bad on Darlinghurst Road, but we always had them in our sights."

"Keep going."

"When his car stopped in front of the Potts Point Hotel, the porter opened the door to let him out, but no one got out. He vanished, mon!" exclaimed the white shirt.

"What do you mean vanished?" questioned Nigel.

"Nobody was in the car, mon. He must have gotten out somewhere in Kings Cross when we were stuck in traffic."

"An Aboriginal in Sydney doesn't just vanish!"

"Did we mention traffic was really bad?"

"You did, and I don't care. How can you remain part of the Ocean Hawks organization if you can't eliminate an Aboriginal in Sydney?" challenged Metcalf.

"We'll find him, Mr. Metcalf," declared white shirt.

"Keep looking for him. Search around Kings Cross. Ask around. Find him and take care of the problem," instructed Metcalf.

"We'll track him down," said the confident blue-shirted man.

"Call me when you do," said a concerned Metcalf.

"Sorry to let you down. It won't happen again."

"It better not," his face could not conceal his impatience with the men clearly not viewed his intellectual equal.

Metcalf finished eating his scone as he watched the men get up from the table and walk away from the tea room. The two hired assassins left with purpose as they were engulfed by the lunchtime crowd.

~~~

Douglas Carroll and Errol Frazier are <u>not</u> accountants. They are rugby players from the Caribbean. They were introduced to Metcalf by his good friend, Master Teague, from the UCLA Darden business school. The gentleman from Barbados recommended that Nigel give the lads a chance to play for his Manly-Warringah Ocean Hawks rugby club. The men had a reputation of being tough physical players when they represented The Wahoos, the West Indies national rugby league team. Metcalf wanted quality inexpensive players and these two men filled the void.

Douglas Carroll was from Jamaica. He had a happy childhood growing up in the capital city of Kingston and was not aware of his family's or community's poverty. The luxurious tourist destinations on the island did not represent the reality of the country and its 2.8 million residents many of whom were poor like Douglas' family. His parents had eight children, six boys and two girls. Douglas was the sixth. His parents were strict without being cruel. He went to primary school but did not go to high school even though he was a good student.

In Jamaica, primary schools were free, but most families had to pay for secondary or higher education. The fees were too high for the eight Carroll children and for the majority of Jamaica's citizens. Douglas was normal sized but extremely strong, quick, and athletic. His build and talent enabled him to get out of the ghetto to pursue a career in rugby. As a child he often went to rugby and sprinting championships at the National Stadium, which was just half a mile from his shanty. He played footy with friends every day, perfecting the sport he loved while staying away from the street gangs that his brothers had joined. Through rugby Carroll had an outlet that enabled him to avoid the crime and violence that persisted on the streets.

When he was 18 years old, Carroll's athletic skills were sizable enough to leave the island to attend a prestigious rugby union training facility in Barbados, joining the considerable number of Jamaican immigrants that left their homeland to go overseas. There he met Errol Frazier. The men became instant friends and teammates playing together for the West Indies Rugby Union that represented the countries of Bahamas, Barbados, Bermuda, British Virgin Islands, Cayman, Guadeloupe, Guyana, Jamaica, Martinique, Saint Lucia, Saint Vincent, and Trinidad & Tobago.

Errol Frazier grew up in Barbados, the most prosperous country in the Caribbean region. Education was free and compulsory for children, unlike Jamaica. There are approximately 270,000 people in Barbados (compared with 2.8 million in Jamaica) and roughly 80% are descendants from slavery and came from Africa. Barbadians (or Bajans) are generally warm-hearted, thoughtful, generous, proud, and confident people who live life to the fullest. Frazier was no exception. Family values and friends were an integral aspect of his life. He grew up as an only child with an air of protection that surrounded him as the island is small and most people knew him, or he knew someone who knew someone else who knew him.

Frazier was head and shoulders above most Bajans in physical stature. A big boy who became a bigger man. At age 16 he joined the Junior U18 National Rugby Union team and two years later represented Barbados in international play at the Caribbean rugby union championships, joining legends of the island who had been playing international rugby union since the mid-1990s.

The two friends, Carroll and Frazier, were stars in their prime and at the peak of their careers when they were selected to play in the global seven-a-side tournament at the annual Deloitte Sevens, the longest running club rugby sevens tournament in the Caribbean and around the world. Rugby Sevens was a lightning-quick version of normal rugby. Instead of 15 players per team playing 40-minute halves, rugby sevens involved seven-a-side athletes in seven-minute halves. The two mates played on the Sevens team for over six years before leaving for the newly created and faster-paced Rugby League. They were enjoying successful careers playing for the Wahoos when it all abruptly ended. Their team was supposed to play in the World Cup qualifying in the United States but was forced to pull out due to lack of funds—and the squad was disbanded.

The men were now in their early 30s and unable to return to the younger union and seven-a-side teams, past their prime but potentially useful to Metcalf. He understood that most rugby players and athletes start losing their abilities at age 30 and are done with their athletic careers by age 40, being passed by the younger generation. The men had nowhere to go until Metcalf, supposedly as a favor to his close gentleman friend from Barbados, employed Carroll and Frazier to play for the Ocean Hawks. They packed their bags and headed Down Under, expecting to play in the popular Australian Rugby League, but their talents would be leveraged by Metcalf for other malicious motives.

Chapter 5

"Try not to become a person of success, but rather, try to become a person of value."
—*Albert Einstein*

- Steve Walsh
- Finding the *WAVE*
- The Role of a CFO

Stamford, Connecticut

AFTER THE KGO staffing meeting Dex McCord headed to Grand Central Station on 42nd street. He was catching a train on Metro-North Railroad to Stamford, Connecticut to visit his client. EDGAR Data & Intelligence was a new audit engagement for McCord. He wanted to ensure that his staff was on track with their tight timetable for completing the year-end audit. More importantly, he was anxious to see Steve Walsh, the company's Chief Financial Officer. Borovina had told him to get his ass up there and visit Steve to make sure he was happy with KGO's service. Specifically, he needed to answer his question regarding the status of the engagement by McCord's Australian team in India.

Dex had been handpicked as senior manager on the ED&I account after his predecessor was dismissed by KGO. The former manager was disliked by both fellow employees and, more crucially, by Walsh. He declared that "the guy just wasn't a good fit." So, with little debate the manager was removed from the engagement and told to pack his belongings. A very swift termination after years of service. McCord was immediately named as the new guy on the ED&I account. He had only been on the job for six months completing one quarterly review audit. Walsh had taken a liking to McCord, acknowledging that he was way better than the former manager. He already considered himself a mentor to Dex after lengthy discussions about business and sports. Walsh was quick to provide advice and his thoughtful opinions. He also had the Irish gift of gab.

~~~

Steve Walsh was a specialist accountant. He inherently had the unique ability to obtain an intimate expertise of an industry's playing field. McCord had observed that as a finance leader in technology Walsh was remarkably conversant in a broad range of cutting-edge disciplines and subjects. In particular he had a thorough understanding of the SAAS (software-as-a-service) industry, acquired from his years of experience in the private sector and on multiple audit engagements during his time in public accounting. While Steve's basic financial reporting responsibilities remained the same, he passed the everyday tests that were expected of CFOs—effectively execute business models, guide operations, and on the way, navigate corporate ambitions.

Walsh was quick to remind Dex that he started his career at PricewaterhouseCoopers (PwC). At the time PwC had the best reputation out of all the Big Four, their commitment to quality was one of the highest, and their clients the largest. PwC was deemed to have leading technical competencies and an outstanding reputation for professionalism. After the fall of Andersen, they became the new button-down white shirt guys, keeping a tight hold on marquee clients like ExxonMobile, IBM, and Disney.

While working in public accounting was exciting, the grueling hours at PwC were taking a toll on Walsh's family life, and he was getting burned out. After seven years at PwC, Steve left to take a finance position with his client IBM as a divisional controller at their headquarters in Armonk, NY. The move into private worked well for Steve as it was closer to home, and he wanted to be near his growing family after the birth of his second child.

For nine years Walsh moved around IBM performing various finance roles in different departments, including internal audit, then he left to find CFO gold during the Internet boom. He heard from a recruiter that Stamford, CT based EDGAR Data & Intelligence, a small Internet startup, was preparing to go public. Walsh wanted a change from working at a behemoth company where his role didn't have much influence. He was eager to make a job change to a company where he would have a significant impact. ED&I was his chance to cash in on all the years of hard work. At IBM Steve saw firsthand, the early investments made in the Internet and its global potential, he wanted to be part of the dot-com craze.

The company was founded by a husband-and-wife team, Marc and Susan Strausberg. Before starting this new venture, Marc was president of a company selling computer-based trading platforms for hedge funds and brokerage firms. Susan was a consultant to the Internet Financial Network and a successful movie producer. A golden couple for the late 1990s dot-com IPO frenzy.

When Marc uncovered this business opportunity, he was publishing the Livermore Report, a newsletter that focused on the valuation of initial public offerings. The newsletter was named after Jesse Livermore, considered the pioneer of day trading. Livermore was the original Wolf of Wall Street. He used what is now known as technical or quantitative analysis as the basis for his trades in a time when accurate financial statements were rarely published. Some of Livermore's trades, such as taking short positions before the 1906 San Francisco earthquake and just before the Wall Street Crash of 1929, were legendary within investing circles. At one time, Livermore was one of the richest people in the world; however, at the time of his suicide, he had liabilities greater than his assets.

While penning his weekly hedge fund bulletin, Marc had the idea of creating ED&I when researching a story on the SEC's new EDGAR pilot program. The consultants at the SEC told Marc that he was the first guy from Wall Street to ask about this new electronic filing system. The light bulb went on and ED&I was created. Marc recognized that the EDGAR regulatory filing system, coupled with the rapid growth of the Internet, would be a game changer for investors.

Susan, as a former movie producer and board member of RKO Pictures, was the perfect asset for the sizzling IPO market. She hired a talented group of investment bankers to produce and direct the IPO roadshow. As CEO she would be the star in ED&I's Hollywood story. With Walsh as CFO, the company successfully sold 3,600,000 shares of common stock at $9.50 per share, raising over $34 million. The valuation was an eye-popping $120 million, despite reporting a meager $2 million in revenue and incurring significant losses the year before. Yet the institutional investors all wanted an allocation of shares in this sexy IPO. Steve was happy to join Susan and Marc on the wild roadshow ride.

~~~

Walsh often reminisced to McCord about his humble beginnings and long hours at the Big Eight and IBM.. He liked Dex and was usually pleasant to his audit team. He considered himself a mentor and was always quick to provide career advice.

"Dex, you have to find a new WAVE and RIDE IT," Walsh proclaimed.

"Is that how you ended up at EDGAR?" asked McCord.

"Yes. They were the first to disseminate and parse electronic SEC filings. Their software engineers leveraged an innovative technology that at the time was the most cost-effective in extracting business information in real time." Walsh continued, "Our programmers developed very sophisticated Application Programming Interfaces (APIs) for the daily fire hose of thousands of filings coming out of the EDGAR System."

"That's very cool," commented McCord, ensuring his client that he was excited to be working with his company.

"Literally nanoseconds after an 8K or 10Q was filed with the SEC, our software delivered it to the world. We would stream over a company's Management, Discussion and Analysis to Yahoo! Finance, extract financial statements for analyst at Thompson Reuters, and pass on 8K special events to reporters at The Street.com. We even calculated red flag ratios for public accounting firms and auditors at the SEC."

"All without human intervention," confirmed McCord.

"Yes, our extracted company data was being disseminated directly into desktops and laptops in a flash," Walsh proudly explained.

"That's why Yahoo! keeps sending me SEC alerts."

"Probably, and we were having fun doing it until Falcone Capital, Mitt Romney's beloved venture capital boys, invested in us through a series of expensive secured convertible notes."

"The accounting gymnastics on those debt instruments is hard as hell to figure out," complained McCord.

"Agree. And they may lead to our downfall. The interest alone from the notes are causing us to incur losses and bleed cash."

"I know. I saw the latest financials. It's not pretty."

"I think our dot-com party may be over Dex. It might be time to sell the company."

"Why is that?" McCord knew the answer but like a good auditor he wanted to listen to his client explain the facts and circumstances surrounding a potential sale.

"Well, for our vulture capitalist we are the perfect buy-n-flip target. We have unique disruptive technology, a major opportunity to steal additional market share, and a reorganized cost structure to improve profitability. Plus, we have considerable tax loss carryforwards that can be utilized by a larger profitable company," declared Walsh.

"Sounds like you guys will be forced to make a move."

"Yes, I don't think we have a choice. We're facing a lot of headwinds and Falcone's management team wants to force us into a sale that we may not want."

"That sucks," sympathized McCord.

"It does. Our board is desperate, and cash is running on fumes. We've been trying to cut costs without sacrificing quality but our friends at Falcone Capital have taken that initiative a step further. They are gutting our tech and quality assurance teams. Moving most of the jobs and activities overseas to a third-party vendor in India," explained Walsh.

"Your current low-cost solution provider."

"Yep. The group your Australian friends are looking at."

"A total restructuring of the organization," acknowledged McCord.

"And since Falcone controls a majority of ED&I they have the power to squeeze every dollar out of overhead until the organization is primed for a sale," said Walsh.

"I guess they came in as short-term investors."

"Yep. Churn out revenue growth and generate positive cash flow. The venture capitalist divine treasure of growth and Earnings Before Interest, Tax and Depreciation," noted Walsh.

"Has Falcone hinted that they are going to sell the company?"

"No news yet. But I know my days here may be numbered. If we're acquired, they won't need two CFOs," added Walsh.

"What are you going to do if that happens?" asked McCord.

"Well, I have an air-tight change of control provision in my employment agreement. So, I could retire but probably won't. I guess I'll try find the next wave," Walsh announced.

McCord in jest started singing a line from a Beach Boys song: *"Catch a wave and you're sittin' on top of the world."*

"Don't lose your day job, McCord," mocked Walsh. "But yes, just like a surfer an accountant should rely on skill and intuition to meet the wave at just the right moment, speed, and angle. Then maintain balance and ride it to shore."

"So, what do you think the next wave will be?" asked McCord.

"Looking at history over the past half a century the successful person—and excuse me if I measure one aspect of success as getting extraordinarily rich—is able to attach themselves to a new disruptive wave. In the 1970s it was telecom, in the '80s software development, in the 90s the Internet, in the 2000s green tech, and in the 2010s streaming digital content."

"Where do you think you'll end up?"

"I'll probably explore joining a company that has a product attached to some digitized subject matter. Perhaps a new ChatGPT approach to business analytics coupled with metadata and artificial intelligence.

Delivered in a manner that we don't even know about yet. Like a hologram or something."

"Sounds like you believe it will be a new form of content with a unique delivery method?" asked McCord.

"I think so. Remember brother, if you control information, you control the world," Walsh exclaimed.

"Got that right," nodded McCord while he continued to flatter his client. "But that's obvious coming from you."

"But not all content my friend. Actionable behavior-changing information. Data that causes a shift in human behavior, that's what you need to embrace," said Walsh convincing himself that it may be time to make a move.

"Like your EDGAR data back in the day?"

"Correct, especially intelligence around numbers. They don't lie. As a green eye shade accountant, you should know that."

"For sure. So, Steve if I understand you correctly, you're going to look for a company with actionable content delivered in a unique way—like porn transported in a hologram?" McCord kidded.

"Yeah, smart ass a 3D Avatar. But no worries, I'll find something crazy. Remember Dex there are no straight lines in life. Look for the curling wave."

Walsh was always quick to point out to McCord that his role as CFO was often misunderstood. While it's true that he was charged with optimizing the company's profitable performance—from financial reporting to returns on investments—his duties extended well beyond that of the stereotypical bean counter. He also had to stay on top of technology, regulatory compliance, shifting economic trends, changing supply chains, international trade agreements, evolving tax laws, and even the global impact of pandemics. Each of these macroeconomic factors could potentially alter his company's overall business strategy and his career as a CFO.

It was not very hard for McCord to admire Walsh's business acumen, and the man figured out a way to showcase his impressive skills. Dex was starting to appreciate more and more that senior finance positions were less about reporting and the rear-view mirror and more about bringing strategic insight into how the corporation should be running. If he was ever going to make any future moves between companies and move up the corporate ladder, his timing was going to be extremely important. He knew that a common mistake young finance professionals make early in their careers was putting too much emphasis on salary, benefits, and a flexible work schedule. He had seen firsthand that job-hopping every two years or languishing in one department for too long was not good, it was a warning sign to recruiters and potential employers that could show a lack of loyalty or laziness—a common complaint he heard from CFOs towards the next generation of finance professionals.

Walsh wanted to help McCord become successful. He knew that if his mentee was going to profitably advance in his career, he would need to develop the right combination of business acumen, financial skills, and industry knowledge. The attainment of financial perks could be made up later.

"Dex, remember business is a series of competitions. The finance profession is still a slow-and-steady culture and winning a series of wieldy situations is the best way to move up."

"I'm a proven competitor."

"You're also a proven asshole. But besides that, don't be stagnant and unimaginative. This is among the biggest offenses that accountants commit. Keep it fresh. If you work hard and pay your dues, you'll eventually find the right opportunity. And Dex, most importantly, trust your instincts and your gut!" Walsh advised.

"Eyes and ears open, got it."

"And make sure you build a network. Leverage organizations like The Financial Executives Network Group (FENG). Establish relationships and foster them. Many accountants are so introverted and just not good at people skills. They hate networking."

"That's true," agreed McCord, endeavoring to stay on Walsh's good side even though he had heard this speech before.

"Networking will get you ahead in business. That and work ethic."

"Wise words, Steve."

"Yes, they are. And master the soft skills," Walsh continued. "How to lead outsells how to manage."

"Sure does," said McCord trying to keep up with Walsh's preaching.

"Lead by example and be positive, Dex. Good leaders provide energy and communicate hope. Be the steady and trusted voice in the room. Especially when it's time to get in front of boards, investors, and fellow employees."

"Your stakeholders?"

"Yes. And when you speak to the Wall Street sharks and anxious analysts, you will have to be the proxy for your CEO." Walsh continued, "In these situations, you must be comfortable speaking in public to win over your audience."

"I'm ready for the challenge," confirmed McCord.

"You're on the right track," confirmed Walsh. "If you keep your ego in check and continuously improve, good things will happen."

"I hope so."

~~~

Walsh enjoyed talking about business and educating McCord about his company and the thousands of Word documents their clients send to ED&I to be 'XML' or 'XBRL' tagged before they are filed with the Securities and Exchange Commission. He explained that their tagging process and data storage infrastructure needed to be 100% bulletproof. ED&I's reputation depended on it. But their success brought forward unintended consequences, as additional SEC reporting mandates came into effect and the number of draft regulatory filings sent to Walsh's company increased exponentially. Satisfying their clients' demands with its current U.S. resources had become almost impossible, and their majority stockholder Falcone Capital recognized this.

Shortly after their initial investment the venture capital firm directed ED&I to employ offshore resources. They introduced the company to NSG Global in Bengaluru, India, the experts in Data as a Service (DaaS). Shortly after signing the NSG outsourcing agreement, ED&I's programmer, analyst, and quality control teams were sent to India. Their mission was to train the local NSG Indian team on their proprietary XML processors and content validation tools. Almost overnight NSG became an extension of the company.

"In fact, Dex, of the 43,000 public companies worldwide, over 20% outsource the XML tagging of their regulatory filings to us. Our guys have been flooded with work."

McCord appreciated getting educated again about Walsh's industry and the challenges they were facing in India. He had already sent an audit team to NSG in Bengaluru to assess the operations and control environment.

Regardless Walsh continued to explain the current state of the business, "Putting software tags on financial statements is not the core competency of most finance teams. Besides with outsourcing, if a deadline is missed or if there is a mistake, it's the outsourcer's problem not the CFO's."

"I guess your clients' finance departments decided to shift the burden to you. Sounds like a real CYA move," acknowledged McCord.

"You got that right. Dex, has your team from Australia completed its review of NSG's internal controls in India yet?" asked Walsh.

"No, not yet. We're still waiting for the final internal control report from our Sydney office," apologized McCord. "I'll check with the partner Down Under and get back to you."

"Please follow up, my friend. Something doesn't look kosher. Our Indian friends have been completing our customers' data tagging jobs and their work is solid, but they understate their invoices and rarely ask us for price increases," Walsh noted.

"Sounds like a good thing" McCord stated.

"It's too good," said a puzzled Walsh. "Something doesn't feel right."

"I'll follow up with my guys immediately."

"Good, I need to know if I can't trust the management team in India. Our tech and quality assurance teams love these guys, but you know when something is too good to be true…" Walsh expounded.

McCord finished his sentence, "Then it usually is too good to be true."

"I believe the employees in India may be getting pressured from somebody to take short cuts. NSG's finance team wants to share something. I can feel it. I'm hoping they might share that something with your friends from Sydney."

"No worries. My mates from Sydney will find out what's going on," McCord assured him.

~~~

A few weeks earlier McCord had asked his buddy and former Aussie flatmate, Tony Young at KGO Sydney, to find out what was going on in Bengaluru. Tony immediately sent an accountant to inspect NSG Global's control processes. McCord noted to Walsh that during his last conversation with the Australian partner, he had relayed that he was going to personally make a visit to India to inspect the facility and join the senior auditor on location. Knowing that he was going to see Walsh, McCord had reached out to Young earlier to get an update on the work in India but only got his voicemail.

When McCord was living in Sydney three years earlier, he had become close friends with Tony Young. He was there when Tony was promoted to partner, and he was also there when Tony split from his American wife after seven years of marriage. During their breakup Tony moved into McCord's flat in Manly Beach. It was a tough time for Young, and he was a bit lost. Dex helped him get through that difficult time by keeping him physically active and off the booze, since at the end of the day it was too much liquid sauce that got Tony in the doghouse with his ex-wife.

After Young moved in with McCord the two men were inseparable. Commuting in the morning on the Manly to Circular Quay ferry, playing touch footy after work, lifeguarding on weekends, and on most evenings pursuing beautiful women. A Yank and an Aussie having the time of their lives. The two men lived together for six months until it was time for McCord to go back to the States. McCord remembered their experience together as one of the best times of his life and a fun way to end his sweet expat rotation.

The rotation to KGO's Sydney office was a coveted spot in the public accounting firm. The overseas assignment had been requested by McCord after five long years of excessive hours on very difficult but profitable audit engagements. He was handed the favor by KGO's "partner in charge of softball," Don Borovina. With Don's seniority and influence he called the firm's national office in Montvale, New Jersey to ensure McCord's request for an international assignment was brought to the top of the list. Shortly after hearing from Borovina the principals in Montvale officially offered McCord an 18-month rotation in Australia. He had been selected as one of the fortunate few for an overseas assignment, so without hesitation he accepted the offer and could not pack his bags fast enough for the adventure Down Under. Some resentful candidates believed McCord earned the assignment on the softball field, but that didn't matter as there was no challenging Borovina's desire.

McCord appreciated spending time abroad and thought of his overseas experience as one of the most important facets in his professional journey. All the large accounting firms publicized international expatriate rotations when attracting new graduates and during most interviews their recruiters were quick to point out that candidates could have the opportunity to work overseas. McCord, like many college recruits, wanted to work in a foreign country at some point in his career. In fact, it was one of the reasons he joined a global accounting firm. He appreciated the sweet expatriate packages while on rotation, which included, among many other benefits, housing allowances, travel reimbursement, cost of living adjustments (COLA), and tax gross ups. It's a tough job, but somebody has to do it…

~~~

McCord knew that if he kept his clients happy and paid his dues at KGO, he had what it takes to reach his ultimate prize: the Chief Financial Officer slot. He also understood that while taking the road less traveled may make for nice poetry, choosing certain well-traveled roads like his accounting and auditing journey could make all the difference for someone with their eye on the CFO's office. And that working at a large firm would hone his business skills and provide him with an avenue that would put him face-to-face with top executives at major corporations, an excellent network to have. Already McCord's life as an auditor was more interesting and exciting than he imagined. Every day was different. Especially the years when he was living Down Under with Tony Young on Sydney's northern beaches.

Dex wasn't blind to the fact that the CFO career path would be a challenging one, and his self-proclaimed mentor Steve Walsh constantly reminded him of that fact. McCord understood that his undergraduate accounting degree, CPA license, and tenure at a large accounting could lead to attaining a senior role as a finance executive, but it may not be enough as many prodigious corporations wanted additional experience, such as:

- Controller
- Divisional VP of Finance
- General Manager
- Treasury Executive
- Investor Relations Executive

McCord was also aware of the fact that if he wanted to be a CFO someday, he had to check many of the boxes, and he'd most likely need at least 12 to 15 years of hands-on viable finance experience to even get on a recruiter's radar. While Walsh's stories were sometimes repetitive, he appreciated his mentor's advice and sermons on the fundamentals of the CFO job.

For some of Walsh's guidance, see Exhibit 4: T-Account Finance Education Model—WIDE and DEEP SKILLS

Chapter 6

"Prepare. The time to win your battle is before it starts."
—*Frederick W. Lewis*

- *OZ As She Is Spoke*
- Harry's Café de Wheels
- The Speedo
- Youngy's Funeral

THE CELL PHONE on McCord's night table rang at 3:00am. "Gidday Mate," it was Austen Perrin, a friend of McCord's from his days on rotation in Australia.

"Austen, couldn't you wait until my day starts?"

"Apologies. I have some shocking news. Youngy died."

Dex was silent for a few moments trying to wrap his head around the news. "Wait, what? Tony's dead? How the fuck did that happen?"

"Surfing accident, mate. Or maybe a heart attack. They found him not too far from Avalon Beach last Tuesday morning," explained Austen.

"He's surfed off Avie a hundred times before. Where did they find him?"

"On the rocks by Caves Bay. Some day walkers in Bouddi Park were trekking to an old paddle steamer wreck and saw him lying there. Body wrinkled and chewed up from being in the ocean for a few days."

"That's pretty far north of Avalon. How did they know he was surfing off Avalon?"

"The police found his backpack on the beach. The currents must have taken him up north, about 15 kilometers or so. Surprised the sharks didn't eat him up first, somewhat nasty waters out there."

"Did you see him?"

"No, not me. His Mum took a look. Tough old Shelia she is. I heard it wasn't a pretty sight. The only thing she could identify was the puka shell choker around his neck."

"How about Warren?"

"His dad was out of town on business."

"That's sad. I'm sure he was devastated when he found out."

"Yeah, mate. It was the day after Youngy arrived back from India. Maybe the return flight made him a little crook and caused a heart attack or something," said Austen.

"He was up in India doing an engagement for me. Did he go into the office after he got back?" asked McCord.

"Nay—left a message with his secretary. She said that Youngy's voice sounded a little crook. Thought he was taking a sickie."

"Sick? I guess that makes sense, the plane food back from India sucks," McCord recalled.

"Fair Dinkum."

"Alright Austen, thanks for calling. I'm going to book a flight and get my ass down there for the funeral. I think it would mean a lot to Nancy, Olivia, and his Mum and Dad."

"You sure? It's a bloody long flight."

"Youngy would do the same if it was me," stated McCord.

"You're a good bloke, Dex. I'll pick you up at the airport. Email me your flight details."

"Great and thanks. I appreciate you letting me know about Youngy. I'll see you in a couple of days."

"Hoo Roo," replied Austen.

McCord couldn't get back to sleep. He thought about his last few months in Australia hanging out with his friend Tony Young, their adventures and shared conquests. He logged into his laptop, updated his Australian ETA Visa application, and booked a flight to Sydney. He wanted to be there in person to say goodbye to his good mate. Early the next morning McCord went to the Australian consulate to secure his expedited visa. He arrived at 7:30am to ensure he was first in line, but he was fourth. After obtaining his "super rush" visa he tended to the business of clearing his work schedule. He boarded a subway to his New York office to notify a few partners and staff that he wouldn't be back from Australia until late next week. Around 2:00pm, after emailing a few clients, McCord returned to his apartment and started to pack. His flight was scheduled to leave that evening.

A feeling of sorrow was darting through McCord's body. He was going back to Sydney again but for all the wrong reasons. It wasn't for vacation or to reunite with friends, it was his buddy's funeral, an exact miserable moment in time. But he wanted to be there, he needed to be there, and he wasn't going to let the year-end busy season interfere with his devotion to the Young family and his friend.

McCord quickly finished packing and left his apartment in Murray Hill two and a half hours before his flight, he thought plenty of time before departure. The allotted travel time was needed as his taxi to JFK airport got caught in late afternoon traffic. It was raining in Queens, which meant the Van Wyke Expressway was a parking lot. He was only seven miles away and had another hour and a half before his flight, but he was starting to doubt that was enough time. McCord's taxi arrived curbside at Terminal C 50 minutes before take-off, but the check-in line was short and he had only one suitcase, which contained a few summer clothes and a dark suit for the funeral. He promptly darted over to the snail-paced security line. He calculated that it would take another anxious 35 minutes to get through, but it should be enough time to get to his gate. McCord stayed distracted in the slow-moving zigzag line by answering emails and texts. There were still a few loose ends in the office that had to be wrapped up before his flight as a high-profile audit engagement was without a senior. He rotated assignments and solved the staffing puzzle before arriving at the front of the line.

The TSA agent at the security desk checked McCord's passport and ticket in their customary slow motion. He cleared the uninterested agent and quickly pulled his laptop out of his backpack, placing it into the bin on the conveyor belt. McCord passed through the full body scanner without a hitch. He quickly put on his sneakers and jogged down to the gate passing hundreds of arriving fatigued international travelers. At the departure gate McCord was happy to see two young Virgin Airlines attendants smiling at their last guest before closing the plane's door. He made his flight and was now able to breath.

The flight time from New York to Australia typically took over 23 hours, but including layovers the trip was closer to 30 hours, assuming everything went well: two hours early to the airport; six hours from JFK to LAX in Los Angeles; five-hour layover; 17 hours direct to Sydney from LA (2+6+5+17=30 hours). His Virgin Atlantic flight left JFK at 6:00pm EST and arrived in Los Angeles at 9:00pm PST. His next flight to Sydney was not leaving until 11:45pm, plenty of time for McCord to grab a burger and a few beers. Other airlines had faster planes, but McCord loved the service on Virgin. He also had enough sky miles to upgrade to first class on the long flight to Sydney, and he needed leg room. Plus, in first class Virgin offered free massages, pedicures, and manicures. "Richard Branson was a smart man," McCord thought.

When McCord was sent to the Land of Oz six years earlier, he had studied international accounting standards, reporting regulations, and Australian sports. He was captivated by the Australian culture and language. The Aussies had their own unique lexicon, complete with quirky slang words. During his flight he would have to refresh his knowledge of the dialect and its meaning. The "shrine" or language as spoken by Aussies had its distinct cadence and accent. While Australians spoke English, the intricacies of the dialect and jargon used in everyday affairs was difficult to pick up. Most locals spoke in rhymes and had expressions or names for everything. The KGO Sydney office was no different. McCord did not want to be the ugly American arriving overseas and instantly alienating the locals. He pulled out of his backpack what he read years ago on his first 24-hour flight, the *Unofficial Dictionary of Australian Dialect*. McCord studied and memorized heaps of choice words and phrases:

> ROOT – Having sex, a naughty, a bang, throw the leg
> ROOTED – Tired, one being fucked
> GIDDAY – Greeting, hello
> OWSHEGOING – How is everything?
> SHE'LL BE RIGHT – All will be well regardless
> NO WORRIES – OK, no problem
> BEWDY! – Exclamation of approval

BUCKLEY'S – You've got no chance at all
DJAVAGOODWEEGEND – Greetings on Mondays
TO DYE – The day between yestiddy and tamarra
ARVO – Afternoon
WANNACUPPA? – Would you like tea or coffee?
TUCKER – Food or grub
BRECKIE – Breakfast
HEART STARTER – First drink of the day
MIDDY, POT, SCHOONER – Beer measurements
TINNY – Can of beer, tube
PISSED – Tipsy, drunk, elephants' trunk
CROOK – Not well, ailing, butchers hook
SICKIE – Taking a day off when you're a bit butchers
ESKY – A cooler, ideal for loading up drinks and frosty treats
CAUSSIE – A women's swimsuit
BUDGIE SMUGGLER – A man's swimsuit, Speedo
DUNNY – Bathroom, outhouse, loo, thunderbox, toilet
THE BILLY LIDS – Kids, children
NIPPER – Small child, junior lifesaver
POMMY – A person from England
POME – Prisoner of Mother England
FAGS – Cigarettes
BLUDGER – One who doesn't pay his way
SHOUT – Your turn to buy
FIAR DINKUM – Honestly, genuine, true
GO TROPPO – Crazy; the heat going to one's head
STREWTH – The truth or exclamation of disgust
CHOCKERS – Anything that's jam-packed or full
PITCH AND TOSS – The boss
RIPPER – Excellent or admirable
HOO ROO – Bye or so long

A lot of the words and phrases did not have much to do with business, but they sure were important for McCord to learn. He did not want to show up at a local sporting event PISSED and ROOT for his colleague's daughter.

McCord was also aware that understanding the culture and work ethic was just as important as the vernacular. During his second month in Australia six years earlier, he made an outsider's mistake when requesting an audit team to come into the office on a weekend to finish up workpapers and clear his review notes. The request was rebutted with: "No, mate, we don't do that here, you know "work to live, not live to work." McCord never made another overtime request while in Sydney.

In the course of his expatriate rotation years ago, McCord was assigned to KGO's U.S. desk in Sydney, which meant that all U.S. audit reports and memorandums had to pass his quality assurance. He was to ensure that reports heading back to America were 100% correct, a last set of eyes to confirm the reports were accurate and did not expose the Australian partners to ridicule. As part of the job Dex had to gain a critical knowledge of how business was accounted for and transacted in both Australia and the United States. He needed to become financially bilingual and directly gain an understanding of international accounting standards. At the time McCord understood that this knowledge would be critical for his ex pat role and success, however this was easier said than done.

The goal of achieving a single worldwide accounting financial reporting model had been espoused by both the International Accounting Standards Board (IASB) and the U.S. FASB (Financial Accounting Standards Board) but that progress stalled. McCord's job was to figure out the proper reporting and highlight the key differences to his colleagues back home.

Usually, his recommendations and advice were deemed brilliant by the local partners but most of the time he thought he was just making up new accounting rules. Over time McCord learned to fully appreciate the importance of gaining an understanding of not only the accounting difference of opinions but also the cultural workplace expectations.

For something arbitrary see Exhibit 5: The Major Differences Between GAAP and IFRS

~~~

SYDNEY, NEW SOUTH WALES

McCord left New York for Youngy's funeral on Friday afternoon and arrived in Oz Sunday morning, 26 January, Australia Day. The country was gearing up for celebrations. It was their July 4th, the official National Day of Australia. The celebration commemorated the arrival of the first fleet at Sydney Cove in 1788 and the proclamation of British sovereignty over the eastern seaboard of Australia. At the time the English settlement was seen as necessary because of the loss of the thirteen colonies in North America. In the early 2000s Australians were asked if the date of Australia Day should be moved to one that is not associated with a European penal settlement. The survey found 79% favored no change.

Sydney Airport was full of light at 9:30am, rays from the morning sun reflecting off the 747s sitting on the runway. McCord was held up in the customs line for 30 minutes, a relatively brief time compared to most international airports. As he rounded the corner out of customs McCord found his two mates, Austen Perrin and Mark Warburton, enthusiastically waiting for him—each one holding three cans of Tooheys beer, Dex's favorite brand. The men started chanting, "OZZY, OZZY, OZZY – OY, OY, OY."

"Take it easy boys, you're going to scare the children," whispered McCord, surprised the boys were so happy to see him. He expected a somber hello because of the circumstances but understood that his friends must have been excited when he turned the corner.

"Ah the little nippers will be right," said Warburton.

"You look like shit, mate," added Austen as he grabbed his bag.

"I feel worse than I look. It's a long bloody flight."

"Here's a heart starter, you need to catch up," said Mark as he handed him a tinny of beer.

"Thanks. I feel a little rooted, but I'll rally," said McCord practicing his Aussie slang.

"Stop your whining mate, we have a chockablock day." Perrin continued, "There are a lot of people who want to see you. It's been too long since your last bender mate."

"Yeah, especially some of my sisters' friends," smiled Warburton.

"OK, let's go but I'm starved. Can we stop at Harry's?"

"No worries," his mates agreed in unison.

McCord wasn't in the mood to celebrate with his friends given the circumstances, but he recognized that Warburton and Perrin needed to release their sorrow. The three men walked briskly out of the airport terminal to the car park. As they approached Austen's new black Mercedes four-door luxury coupe, McCord walked towards the left side of the auto, keenly aware not to make the mistake of entering the driver's side on the right. The men jumped into the car and headed towards downtown Sydney.

Austen and Mark were two of McCord's good mates during his days in Sydney. They both worked at KGO but subsequently moved on to other companies after McCord's return to the States. Since his departure, Perrin went to Toll NZ, an International Shipping Company, and Warburton left for Macquarie Bank to work in their investment banking division. McCord appreciated that despite both men being knuckleheads while 'off-duty' they took their careers seriously.

Austen Perrin was a trustworthy accountant. It was no surprise to McCord that Austen became a finance leader in the international shipping industry as it was his industry specialization while he was in public accounting. He knew Perrin's management skills would call on his integrity to ensure that information remained secure as he dealt with the financial health and condition of his organization's vessels. He also recognized that when Austen was serious, he could leverage his exceptional organizational skills to deal with the deluge of complex bills of ladings for his container ships that were carrying infinite supplies of goods to ports all around the world.

Mark "Warbo" Warburton was a critical-thinking accountant. McCord was surprised to hear Mark landed a job in the investment banking industry. He knew he was a good problem solver when crunching his digits, and that he had the capability to present fresh ideas, but he didn't realize the extent of his critical thinking skills around complex banking transactions. He thought that since Warbo was extremely sociable and distracted he could, from time to time, misplace a digit or a comma that would potentially result in huge financial consequences, especially in mergers and acquisition transactions where a mistake could result in millions of dollars left being on the table. But McCord recognized Warbo's ability to focus when needed and presumed the checks and balances on his work would lead to sound investment banking solutions for his clients.

~~~

The Mercedes pulled out of the airport and headed North towards Sydney city central. The drive from the airport was always longer then desired, especially after a long intercontinental flight. There were no major highways from the airport to the center of Sydney so driving from the airport to Southern Cross Drive or the M1 was a perpetual challenge. McCord always laughed at the idea of the M1 being called a highway, as the city's roads were littered with heaps of bicycle lanes, pedestrian crossings, and shrubs. It was not like the highways he was accustomed to in the States, but he appreciated the city's attempts at being aesthetically pleasing and green.

The natural fragrance of the Eucalyptus trees filled the air while the men drove by Centennial Park and The Lakes Golf Club. Passing the golf course reminded McCord of his many fun afternoons out on the Australian links, in particular with Tony Young. His memory of the route towards downtown and Manly was easily recalled, having made the trip with Tony countless times during his three-year rotation. Finally, after 45 minutes in heavy Australia Day traffic, the hungry men arrived for lunch at McCord's beloved eating spot, Harry's Café de Wheels. The unique setting instantly brought back memories of drunk evenings and stained shirts. He was looking forward to eating his favorite item on the menu, a meat pie topped with mashed potatoes, mushy peas, and extra gravy.

Harry's Café de Wheels was a landmark in Sydney that had been serving customers for over 80 years. Frank Sinatra, Sir Elton John, and Prince Harry were among the many celebrities to sink their teeth into their iconic "Tiger" meat pie. The idea of a moving food truck all began with Harry "Tiger" Edwards, whose frustrations in finding a good late-night snack led him to open a caravan café near the front gates of Woolloomooloo naval dockyard in Sydney. He named it Café de Wheels, as the local city council laws at the time required him to move the caravan a minimum of 12 inches a day.

The three mates ravenously downed a few of Harry's tasty meat pies at a nearby picnic table and then headed next door to the Woolley Bay Hotel to grab a few pints. An ABBA cover band was playing on stage while they sat at the bar with VBs (Victoria Bitter beer) in hand and rocked to the music. The crowd of 20-somethings were singing and dancing to "Money, Money, Money." McCord thought to himself, "The Australia Day celebration is definitely in full swing." Warbo left Austen and Dex at the bar to join the dancing.

"Did you see Youngy before he passed?" asked McCord.

"Nah, I haven't seen him for a few weeks. He had been getting pissed too often again. Probably depressed," added Austen.

"Why's that?"

"Ah you know, Youngy was still going through tough times with Nancy. She wasn't letting him see Olivia but once a month."

"That's not good."

"Yeah, mate. She really spins his head around. Those American Sheila's are tough to figure out. Too demanding."

McCord didn't know how to reply to Austen about his comment about American women, so he left it alone. He instead wanted to hear Austen's understanding of the circumstances around Tony's death.

"I spoke with Youngy just last week. He sounded fine," explained McCord. "He was doing me a favor, taking a peek at a client's operation in Bengaluru. An easy internal control review."

"Maybe it was jet lag or something," replied Austen.

"What do you mean?"

"Well, mate, you know they found his body not too far from Avalon. Maybe he was just too tuckered to be surfing. He's not getting younger and from what I hear he was burning the candle on both ends."

"That's just it. Why Avalon? It's at least a 30-minute trip from his flat. If he was totally exhausted why not surf near home at Manly Beach?"

"Better surf up north, I guess," said Austen.

"I looked at that day's surf report. The swells were small up and down the northern beaches. Plus, Tony surfed off the northern beaches hundreds of times. And he was a great swimmer. Almost made the Aussie Olympic team. Just doesn't make sense that he would drown in small surf," McCord reflected.

"Yeah mate, you know better than most that he used to surf almost every morning and then arrive at the office by 10:00am," said Austen.

"Yes, but that was after a morning of surfing at Manly Beach. Just doesn't make sense he would be surfing off Avalon."

"I don't know. It's just too fucking sad," shouted Austen as the crowd sang "Mama Mia" in unison.

Perrin didn't seem to want to discuss the subject of Tony's death. McCord sensed he was also very sad but unsure of the facts and wasn't ready to go there. Instead, he and McCord watched Warbo stagger around the dance floor a few times before grabbing him. It was going to get ugly and Warbo had a long Australia Day celebration in front of him. The three traversed their way out of The Woolley and through the crowd of midday partiers to Austen's car parked by Harry's. McCord was expecting the next stop to be at his hotel for some much-needed sleep. It would not be the case.

Austen's diesel Mercedes crossed over the Sydney Harbour bridge and 15 minutes later pulled into the d'Alboroa Marina at Spit Junction in Mosman. It was only 2:00pm and despite the purpose of McCord's visit to Sydney, they wanted to treat their friend to a fun day. The marina was located at the gateway of Sydney's Middle Harbor, and it had all the facilities and services needed for Warburton's family boat. The dockmaster had already tied his Bay liner to the pier for an easy turnaround. Warbo jumped out of the car before it stopped. His younger sister Lisa and her boyfriend Griffen were already in the boat moving coolers, towels, and backpacks into the boat's hull.

"Where we heading, Warbo?" asked McCord as he climbed out of the car.

"We're going to a barbie at Shore Beach with my sister and her fella."

Dex sighs, "Really?"

"Ahh, don't be a poofta mate. Plus, we're going to meet a few of Lisa's girlfriends. I hope you're not too tired. Its gonna to be bloody ewge," said an enthusiastic Warburton.

"No worries, Warbo. I'll just sleep later."

"Do you have a Speedo packed?"

"No, I don't. I kind of was packing in a hurry and for a different occasion," answered McCord.

"I expected that. The boys at the surf club heard you were coming and got one for you. Here you go."

Warbo tossed a used Speedo across the top of the car.

"Are you going to fit into that budgie smuggler?" mocked Austen.

"It's a little tight but it'll work," replied Dex as he slipped into the speedo underneath a beach towel.

"Bloody beautiful, it fits. Look at you mate, still a mountain of a man," commented Warbo.

"Strooth," laughed Perrin.

"I haven't lost it yet," declared McCord.

After 15 minutes of Warbo struggling to complete a pre-voyage checklist, the group powered away from the dock in his Bay liner, Warbo's sister at the helm. They had two hours to kill before meeting Lisa's friends at Shore Beach. Warbo wanted to treat McCord to a little Australia Day hospitality and directed Lisa to head towards the Sydney Opera House.

Hundreds of boats were already in the harbor gathered for Australia Day festivities. The Ferrython, the race from Fort Denison around Shark Island to the Harbour Bridge in dragon boats, had already started. Lisa was navigating her way past the steady flow of party revelers while fireboats were spraying green and yellow streams of water in the air. The Bay liner ended up in a crowd of boats across from a floating music festival adjacent to the Opera House. The stage's performances were in full swing. Lisa turned the motor off and drifted towards the Tarronga Zoo ferry terminal on the north side of the harbor to join up with 25 or so boats that had been anchored and tied together since early morning. Griffen threw a rope to one of the boats in the flotilla. After the front and back of the speed boat were secure, Warbo yelled out, "We're not here for a haircut!" The party was on.

Conversation flowed, drinks were consumed, and there was no mention of Tony Young while the revelers were enjoying a sunny day in the Harbour. McCord was now catching a second wind and feeling like he had never left the country. After an hour of tales, good music, and hoots the group's liquid supplies were quickly being depleted, and there was a look of concern on Warbo's face. He waved down a small power boat that read Sammy's Convenience Store. A burley 20-something bloke with a dark tan, six pack abs, and a sock-packed Speedo was selling beer, soft drinks, and snacks. Griffen and Lisa appeared to be good friends with the store owner. The tanned stud quickly unloaded a case of Victoria Bitter and pre-mixed daiquiris in the Bay liner's hull while telling a story about a scantily dressed woman trying to coax him onto her yacht. "Be careful mate, those types of ladies are aggressive. They want to get into your speedo," warned Austen.

After a few more songs by a local Australian band on the floating stage, the crew untied the boat and headed east back towards the Heads and the mouth of Sydney Harbour. Everyone was hungry and ready to go to Store Beach and light up the barbie. In less than 15 minutes the Bay liner and its crew arrived at their destination. A sign there read "Boat Access Only." There were only two other parties on the beach, heaps of room to spread out their beach accessories.

The men carried the coolers, charcoal, and barbeque up onto the beach, while Lisa tended to the blankets and beach chairs. The roles and tasks were choreographed perfectly from years of practice. Ten minutes later four young women arrived at the beach in a large rubber Zodiac. It was Warbo's sister's girlfriends, all looking excited and ready to start a fun day at the beach. The girls were representative of Sydney's cultural mix—two Aussies, one Australian Asian, and an English POME on a working visa. The 20-somethings had firm, tanned bodies, except for the girl from

England who looked like she didn't get out in the sun too often. McCord was no longer tired. "Four guys and five girls, good odds," he thought.

Dex recognized a few of Lisa's friends from his days in Manly. He could not believe his eyes when he saw how they'd grown into adult women in just three short years. He was greeted with extended hugs and kisses, followed by questions on what he had been up to the last few years and if he had a girlfriend yet. After McCord updated his audience on his New York City exploits, a delicious barbie of shrimp, bangers, and burgers were consumed. A few more Victoria Bitters were chugged down, and sunblock was applied. McCord had several requests to apply lotion on the backs of Lisa's friends and happily complied. After lying on the beach for some time the group set up a volleyball net and picked squads. Austen and McCord teamed up with the Asian looking girl and one Aussie. Warbo, Lisa, and Griffen were paired with the other Aussie and the POME. Five against four, but no one was complaining.

The men walked over to the makeshift volleyball court in their Speedos, McCord feeling a bit foolish in his faded used swimsuit. The girls had taken off their bikini tops for sunbathing and didn't bother to put them back on. None of the young women appeared to be concerned or bashful. "Topless volleyball, this is great," Dex thought. "I love this country." Just like beer and potato chips, and most other things in the world, he loved breasts. McCord considered himself an expert. "Not a single man in the history of this earth should ever complain about a heavenly pair," he preached. McCord did his best not to look at Warbo's sister's breasts.

The match was close and became competitive. McCord was the most athletic player, but his concentration simply wandered. The three women on the other side were a colossal distraction, their boobs bouncing up and down in unison with every jump. As McCord became preoccupied with the sights, the ball kept ricocheting off his head. He couldn't take his eyes off the sweaty and sandy topless girls. Lisa's friends made fun of him, but he didn't mind the ridicule. After three keenly contested sets the match ended, and the host team won despite Warbo's intoxication. But unlike most defeats, McCord wasn't upset. He had thoroughly enjoyed the beach volleyball competition.

The topless girls were first to run into the cove's aqua blue water followed by the men. The group spent another 20 minutes frolicking, splashing, and having chicken fights. After McCord and his partner were finally brought down, the revelers reluctantly returned to the beach and started gathering their items. It was getting late. They each had plans and needed showers— nighttime activities surrounding Australia Day had to be prepared for. Lisa's friends jumped into their Zodiac and headed towards the nearby Manly skiff club. Warbo's crew pushed off from Store Beach and headed back to d'Alboroa Marina. Within minutes the Bay liner was weaving between vessels just 200 metres offshore, an armada of boats from North Harbour Sailing Club had already set sail heading towards the Harbour Bridge, racing for preferred positions to see the annual fireworks show. For McCord, the national holiday celebration on Sydney Harbour was a memorable one, but his trans-pacific flight, two Toohey's, and ten VBs were catching up to him. He was tired and needed sleep.

The Bay liner eventually made it to the marina and was promptly emptied. Warbo left with his younger sister who was driving while Griffin stayed behind to hose down the vessel with fresh water. Austen departed with Dex. The Mercedes diesel merged onto Spit Road and headed east towards the Pacific Ocean. Within twenty minutes the two friends pulled in front of the Manly Pacific Hotel, and McCord climbed out to unload his luggage from the auto's boot.

"See ya in the morning, Dex."

"Thanks for picking me up. Fun time today."

"Are you sure you don't want to go out for a drink? It's an ewge night in the city mate."

"No. I'm tuckered, and my body clock is still on New York time. I'm looking forward to just crashing on a soft bed."

"Alright then, I'll pick you up at 10:00am and we'll head over to the church."

"I'll be ready to go."

"See you then, Yank, Hoo roo!" said Austen while driving away singing along to an old Jimmy Barnes tune on his playlist.

~~~

McCord checked into his oceanfront hotel, made his way to the room, unpacked his bag, and quickly fell into a long deep sleep. He woke up at 9:30am to the ring of his cell phone, still in his Speedo. He had slept a solid 14 hours. Austen was on the other end of the phone heading towards the hotel. McCord's body felt jet-lagged, but his mind said get up. He leapt out of bed and went directly into the shower, but not before hanging up his crumpled black suit and white dress shirt in the bathroom. He turned the shower water on hot and steam promptly filled the bathroom. After finishing his shower McCord noticed that his suit came out wrinkle free, the trick he learned from his new girlfriend in New York.

~~~

The traffic to the church was light as most of the population was sleeping off a fun night of reveling. The funeral was being held at The Garrison Church in the Rocks, Sydney's oldest historical area, located under the Harbour Bridge. The Rocks was the original site of the first European settlement, established in 1788 when convict-bearing ships arrived from England. The name itself came from the original buildings, which were made of sandstone.

As McCord and Perrin pulled up to the church, lines had already formed to get inside. There was a crowd of funeral-goers—it was clear that Tony and his family were well loved and respected. Dex was not expecting such a tribute for his friend. The entrance to the church was impressive. The Garrison Holy Trinity Anglican Church was located at the intersection of the cobblestoned Argyle and Lower Fort Street, its architecture a mix of

Gothic style constructed with sandstone, and its contents demonstrating the nineteenth century importance of the harborside. Outside the church were historic Georgian and Victorian late-nineteenth century residences, art galleries, cafes, and restaurants.

The Garrison filled up quickly. Rows of pews were filled to capacity while other attendees stood in the back. Tony's closed casket rested in front of a large stained-glass window, depicting the Angel of Death sheltering a small child, in the nave under two high arcades formed by five horseshoe arches and supported by solid stone columns. The Monsignor of the parish started the funeral service with the typical Christian prayers and sermons. Nearly all his audience prayed along with the reverend as Christianity was the predominant religion in Australia. After the prayers, several members of the Young family delivered readings and hymns. Tony's sister read a tear-jerking elegy that shared the joy her brother's life brought to family and friends. His dad delivered a powerful eulogy that talked about his son's compassion, great heart, and achievements. He concluded with an assertion, while trying not to break down between sentences, that he looked forward to seeing him again when the time came. The priest ended the service with:

May God give to you and all whom you love His comfort and His peace, His light and His joy, in this world and the next; and the blessing of God Almighty, the Father, the Son, and the Holy Spirit, be upon you, and remain with you this day and forever. Amen.

The Young family slowly walked out of the church first followed by the throng of funeral-goers. The receiving line outside Garrison was long and slow as friends of the family stopped to hug, kiss, shake hands and pay their respects. Much of the dispersing crowd headed towards the reception after the service. It was being held down the street at the Museum of Contemporary Art (MCA). The museum was closed for the holiday but opened for a private reception for the family and their guests. The Youngs were big supporters of the MCA.

Located at one of the world's most spectacular sites on the edge of Sydney Harbour, the MCA is dedicated to exhibiting, collecting, and interpreting the work of Australia's greatest artists. The reception was held in the MCA's Foundation Hall. An impressive ballroom with a terrace overlooking Sydney harbour, Circular Quay, and the Opera House. No expense was spared.

Warren Young, Tony's father, was the Chief Executive Officer of Buck Consultants, the HR services firm that provided management and business operations consulting, including actuarial services. Warren grew up on Bondi Beach, a fifth generation Australian. He started his career as a traveling insurance salesman and then after earning a great reputation joined Buck's pension advisory group in his mid-20s. He quickly became an expert on structured pension plans and moved up the proverbial corporate ladder. First as vice president of process and work design for human resources clients, then to Buck's executive wealth practice and, penultimately, the corporation's strategy and leadership team before taking on the role of CEO.

Like his son Tony, Warren was well liked by everyone he met, a larger-than-life character with a big frame that supported his affability. He was a master networker and his clients respected him. For his employees he believed in a culture of well-being. Warren's theory was that, as a service organization, when your people thrive, your organization soars, which in turn leads to excellent customer service. It made good business sense to him to help his employees be their physical, financial, and professional best. Warren was ahead of his time. Because of his simple well-being philosophy, he was adored by his customers, employees, and community, which of course led to a high-performing company and his great financial success.

The reception at the MCA was fairly reserved except for the circle of friends that gathered around McCord. His former colleagues were happy to see him and wanted to hear what he had been doing since he left Oz. McCord was discussing the differences between the NYC work environment and Sydney's when he was tapped on the shoulder. It was Tony's ex-wife.

"Hi, Derek. How are you?"

"Nancy. I'm good, how are you doing?" said McCord as he embraced his close friend's former partner.

"Barely hanging in there. It's been difficult for everyone. Especially Olivia," said Nancy while pointing at her young daughter speaking with friends in the corner of the ballroom. "I don't think it has set in that Tony won't be around anymore."

"It just sucks. I think about him and all the great adventures we had together. He was such a good friend. If there is anything I can do to help, just let me know."

"Thank you, Derek."

Youngy's ex-wife, Nancy Leigh, was raised in Southampton, New York, a posh Long Island beach town. A confident, energetic, and smart American woman, an unusual match for a genuine Aussie man. Nancy met Tony 13 years ago when she was taking a vacation from her expatriate engagement in Shanghai, China. She was teaching English as a second language to the locals. The couple ran into each other in Hong Kong, enjoying a once-in-a-lifetime experience: The Hong Kong Sevens Rugby tournament, one of Asia Pacific's biggest national springtime sporting events with over 120,000 spectators jammed into Hong Kong Stadium. It's a time when the city turns into a three-day carnival.

Attendees know the HK Sevens and debauchery go hand-in-hand, and nothing catches the spirit of the Rugby Sevens as much as the South Stand at Hong Kong stadium. The South Stand is the only place where the general public can drink alcohol in their seats and, in famous tradition, don costumes like it's Halloween. Rugby fans and visitors from around the world go there expecting to have a great time. Nancy and Tony were no different. They met in the South Stands fully engaged in the festivities at the Sevens and openly fell in love.

Nancy was dressed as a sexy flight attendant, in a blue low-cut shirt with gold strips, satin skirt, a pilot's hat, and black fish net stockings. Youngy was dressed as a Royal Australian Air Force (RAAF) WWII pilot, sporting the RAAF blue tunic jacket with open lapels, and two box pleated breast pockets, a visor cap of blue wool cloth, and a thin black patent leather chin strap. Tony wasn't classically handsome nor the suavest gentleman in Hong Kong that week, but he was pretty muscular from surfing his whole life and able to charm Nancy with his nonchalant and playful spirit. She instantly became enamored with Tony. The couple were drawn together in craziness and never looked back. Just two weeks after they met, she left her teaching job in Shanghai and moved in with him Down Under.

The relationship was challenged from the beginning. Nancy, the strong American woman, trying to tame the wild Australian. Tony the outgoing, fun-loving man, but not a high-level achiever in the romance department. However, Nancy got pregnant and the two stayed faithfully together. Their marriage lasted eight years until they couldn't make it work any longer. At that point Tony moved out and into McCord's flat in Manly while Nancy stayed nearby in Sydney's northern beaches to raise Olivia.

Nancy and Dex spoke for a few minutes longer before she was pulled away to receive condolences from other mourners in attendance.

"It was good seeing you again, Derek. You really helped Tony when we split."

"It was a tough time for both of you."

"Yes, it was. He really appreciated your friendship and loved you. There weren't many times when I saw him that he wouldn't mention your name and wonder what you were doing in the States."

"It was mutual."

"I know. Thank you again," Nancy smiled, gave McCord a hug, and slowly walked away.

McCord returned to his circle of friends. The stories about Youngy's life continued, a combination of a few tears and some laughs. Dex was encouraged to tell the story of when Tony and he ran Sydney's 17K City to

Surf race. Four years ago, Dex and Tony had run the race wheeling a shopping trolley loaded with medicinal supplies of ice on beer. Six kilometers into the run they saw a fit beautiful blond-haired person standing on a platform attached to a light post. She shouted over to them, "Hey boys can you give me a lift?" They immediately b-lined the cart over to her and she jumped in. After a couple of kilometers, they heard a helicopter hovering overhead. They were being followed and cheered on as they passed by the crowds, but they couldn't figure out what was going on.

McCord continued to explain to his eager audience that they were told the girl they picked up was the number-one seed, Australian Tani Ruckle, the Commonwealth Games marathon gold medalist. She had had enough and pulled out of the race after cramping and being physically and psychologically unable to continue running. Tony and Dex ran with Tani the last eight kilometers of the race. At one-point Youngy jumped on the back of the trolley, and they were flying down the hill in Bondi. Her agent was freaking out. He obviously thought his "golden ticket" on the cart of beer was going too fast. Dex and Tony had downed numerous heart starters that morning and had no concern for the matter. It took them 119 minutes to propel Tani to the finish line, despite their best efforts to reduce the trolley's load by consuming all the beer.

Some of McCord's friends were laughing out loud at the tale, but he noticed a few were fighting back tears. The story was probably not appropriate for the occasion, but he was positive Tony would have wanted the funeral reception to be a celebration of a life well lived. So, McCord continued with his story. "Well, we were all over the media wearing our KGO blue and yellow neon shirts. The photo-op press loved our performance. Interviews on Channel Nine and Fox Sports news, a cover picture and feature in the *Sydney Moring Herald*. I think we made everyone at the Sydney office proud. We just hoped we didn't embarrass ourselves. I guess we didn't because Tony and I immediately became somewhat local celebrities with the ladies. Even the female newscaster noted that she wouldn't have minded being with those burley guys. It was good fun," concluded McCord.

Dex finished the story with a few "good on ya, mates" from his former colleagues and the conversation continued with more Tony Young stories. Since his departure from Australia, McCord had come to appreciate the friends he made during his time in Sydney, a great group of accountants, he thought. While one of his former audit seniors was "taking the piss" out of McCord's regained New York accent, he saw Warren Young in somber conversation with a gentleman wearing an expensive tailored suit. He looked sad and Dex wanted to say hello and try to cheer him up, if just a little. The last time McCord had seen Youngy's father was at a dinner party during his last week in Sydney. Tony's mother had wanted to prepare Dex a proper Aussie meal before he went back Stateside, and the dinner was a memorable one.

Warren had been away on business in Saudi Arabia, arriving just a few hours before dinner from Dubai. He came down the stairs in a full Arab sheik outfit. A large white thobe robe complete with the traditional red and white checkered kaffiyeh headdress held on by a black agal cord. It was quite a sight to see, a large Caucasian man with a red face and bulbous nose in an XXL sheet. At dinner Warren informed everyone that he was wearing nothing underneath. A very scary thought to have while eating.

McCord excused himself from the group and headed over to Warren to give his condolences. As he approached, Tony's father stopped his conversation and opened his arms, engulfing McCord, which only a few men could do.

"Hello, Derek. Thank you so much for coming all this way."

"I wouldn't have it any other way, Mr. Young," replied McCord. "Your son really had such a positive impact on my life and everyone around him."

"You're a good man, Derek. Are you going to stay in Australia for a while?"

"No. Unfortunately I'm just in town for another two days. We're in the middle of busy season and my team needs me back in New York."

"That's truly unfortunate. It's such a long flight mate. Are you sure you can't stay longer? We have a few rooms open at our house."

"I wish I could. But I have a client commitment and I think some of the partners are concerned that I may never come back."

"You should stay in God's country. After all, you certainly made good friends and Tony shared with me a few of your memorable adventures."

"We certainly did. And a few that I shouldn't repeat."

Warren smiled. "I'll have to hear about them on your next visit or when I get back over to New York for business, hopefully soon. Where are you staying?"

"At the Manly Pacific Hotel," said McCord.

"Ah, yes. Your old stomping ground," replied Warren.

"It was a great time living with your son in Manly. I think we left our mark on that town."

"I bet you blokes did."

"I'm going to stop by the surf club and see a few of Tony's mates before I leave."

"Great. They will be happy to see you," said Warren.

"Knowing those guys, I'm sure it will be a memorable visit. Always is."

"Oh, wait. I'm being rude. Let me introduce you to my friend. Nigel Metcalf, this is Derek McCord. He came here all the way from America."

Nigel Metcalf was a close friend of Warren Young. When Nigel started his actuarial consulting firm Warren became his mentor. He didn't hesitate to take Nigel under his wing, doing a favor for his late dad that Warren knew from a North Sydney sporting goods warehouse. Nigel's father had provided Warren with all the uniforms Buck Consulting purchased to sponsor the local area little league teams in boys' and girls' rugby, cricket, and field hockey. The two men had a solid business relationship. So, when Nigel left public accounting to start his own business, Warren did not hesitate to provide guidance and pass along customers to his favorite vendor's son. After Metcalf achieved enormous financial success, Warren continued to provide advice and support. Besides referring business and other opportunities, he made Buck a significant sponsor of Metcalf's Manly-Warringah Ocean Hawks Rugby League team. In turn, when it came time for Nigel to pay back some of Warren's favors, he ensured Metcalf Consulting's lucrative accounting, audit, and tax work went to his son Tony at KGO Sydney. The engagements became some of the more profitable ones at the firm. A major reason why Youngy was fast tracked to partner.

"Good to meet you, Mr. Metcalf."

"You must have been a good friend to come all this way," said Nigel.

"Tony was a great man. He would have done the same."

"Derek lived with Tony in Manly Beach while on assignment from America. Those boys had a little bit of fun together," added Warren.

"No doubt. Manly is a fun place to live."

"Yes, very," McCord said with a wry smile.

"Who do you work for now?" asked Metcalf.

"I'm still with KGO in New York."

"Ah, good firm. Your blokes in Sydney do a lot of work for my firm."

"Thanks, Mr. Metcalf. They're the reason I was able to live down here and get to know a great guy like Tony."

"Yes indeed. He will be missed," agreed Metcalf.

"It's still hard to believe he is gone," said McCord while looking at Mr. Young.

"Yes, it is. I'm still trying to understand how it happened. As you know, Tony was a great swimmer and surfer," said Warren.

"I know. That's bothering me, too."

"I was told by the police that he had a contusion on his head. I guess he hit a reef or his board or something and it knocked him out. A fluke accident I suppose," said Warren, sadly shaking his head.

"Horrible, I'm really sorry," replied McCord also shaking his head.

"Well, it was a pleasure meeting you, Derek. I hope you enjoy the rest of your visit," said Metcalf, trying to change the subject.

"I will, thank you."

"Again Derek, thank you so much for making the trip. It means a lot to our family," said Warren.

"Your son was a great man, Mr. Young. My sincere condolences."

"Thank you, Derek. I'll pass on your thoughts to the family."

"It was nice meeting you Mr. Metcalf."

"Yes. A pleasure," replied Nigel.

McCord walked away happy he had a chance to speak with Tony's father. Somehow, he felt a little better that Warren found his son's relationship with him as one of the best experiences in Tony's precious life. As Dex headed back towards his circle of friends he was intercepted by a man in a wrinkled blue jacket, white shirt, and khaki pants. On his neck was a dotted lizard tattoo. He appeared anxious and jumpy, turning his head from side to side when he spoke.

"Sorry to bother you, Mr. McCord. I am Jiemba Abbot."

"Hi, Jiemba. Nice to meet you."

"I am the audit senior who went to NSG Global in India with Mr. Young."

"Ahh, you must be the guy that Youngy mentioned was working on the internal control review," said Dex.

"Yes, sir. Sadly, Mr. McCord, I may have been the last one to spend time with him before his tragic accident."

"Most likely, Jiemba. My apologies for sending you up there last-minute. Our client in the U.S. had some concerns. How did it go?"

"Mr. Young came up and we reviewed the workpapers before he returned to Sydney. He wasn't completely satisfied and told me to perform additional field work before I left the NSG facility," said Abbot as he nervously looked around.

"Did you finish everything?"

"Yes. All the workpapers are located on our network. I think I uncovered something unusual. A material weakness."

"Material. What was it?"

"I can't explain in detail here, Mr. McCord."

"Why is that?"

"I'll have to show you in the report that I put together. Plus, I think my life may be in danger."

"Danger?"

"Yes. When I walked out of the airport I noticed two strange men closely watching me. Then when I pulled away in a taxi, I saw them jump into a large blue auto and follow us. They stayed right behind me for a few kilometers. So, I asked the driver to let me jump out when we got into heavy traffic. I lost them but I hear two men have been in Kings Cross asking questions about me. Like where I live and do they see me out at night. I'm worried Mr. McCord."

Abbot looked around. He didn't want to speak in public anymore. He asked, "Mr. McCord where are you staying?"

"The Manly Pacific Hotel," replied a bewildered McCord.

"OK but I don't think we should meet in the hotel."

"Where do you want to meet?"

"How about 9:00pm in North Head? At Fairfax Lookout? It should be quite and safe there at sunset. Do you know where it is?"

"Yes, it's a good spot. 9:00pm works for me, Jiemba."

"Great. I'll bring the workpapers and highlight what I think might be a significant issue for your client."

"OK, thanks. I'll see you then."

"Thank you sir. See you later, Mr. McCord."

The nervous accountant walked away in a hurry. Moving quickly through the crowd like a Bondi bound train. McCord could see in Abbot's face that he believed he was in real danger, a feeling he knew many Aboriginals still have living in Australia. But this sense of fear was for a different reason. McCord started thinking again about Tony's death. Murmuring to himself, "I knew something wasn't right. An accident? It couldn't be, he was an excellent surfer."

A few meters away Nigel Metcalf was observing the conversation between McCord and the Aboriginal. Shortly after their discussion Jiemba hurried through the crowd and out of the MCA into the local Sydney streets. Metcalf walked onto the terrace of the museum and looked out, searching for Abbot among the bustling day trippers at Circular Quay. After a few unsuccessful minutes he pulled his mobile phone out from his jacket pocket and called the Ocean Hawks practice facility.

Chapter 7

"Do not dwell on the past, do not dream of the future, concentrate the mind on the present moment."
—*Buddha*

- The Heads
- Holden Commodore
- Shark Nets
- Kendall Cove

TONY YOUNG'S FUNERAL reception at the MCA ended shortly after Abbot's departure. The crowd of well-wishers disbursed from the museum and away from Circular Quay, except for McCord and a group of his former colleagues. Since Dex was in town only for a short time, the group decided to head back onto the cobblestone streets of the Rocks and visit the Lord Nelson Pub for a few pints.

As everyone singled-filed into the Nelson, Warburton made the call, "It's my Shout." At that moment McCord realized he'd just been caught in a five-man shout. Warbo enthusiastically threw down an A$50 banknote on the bar. The "shout" under local accountant's rules refers to an act of spontaneous generosity where one person in a group elects to pay for a round of drinks. Dictated by etiquette this meant that no one could leave the pub until all participants purchased and consumed a minimum of five drinks. McCord wanted to stay sober for his meeting with Abbot but knew he could easily handle the five-man shout. It was the 10+ shouts that were truly difficult to survive.

After an hour at the Nelson the shout obligation was fulfilled by all participants, except for Austen as he was the designated driver. Warbo volunteered to fulfill Perrin's drinking contract without hesitation.

"Hey Dex, do you need a ride back to Manly?" asked Austen.

"Nah, I'll take the slow boat home," replied McCord.

"No worries, mate. Suit yourself. You still need to blow that Yank stink off you anyway."

"Very funny. It's a nice afternoon and I need the air. So, I'll just walk over to the ferry."

"Whatever you say. See's ya later," said Austen as he walked away from the pub.

Dex wanted to enjoy the picture-perfect summer afternoon on the 35-minute ferry ride out of Circular Quay back to Manly Beach. The trip brought back fond memories of surveying the harbor's sights and remembering the many late nights on the ferry's outside deck, gazing up at the Southern Cross. Especially the drunken trips back home with Youngy while eating messy midnight gyros.

McCord arrived back at the Manly Pacific Hotel just before 6:00pm. Enough time for a much-needed power nap before his meeting with Abbot in North Head Park. Before he even got out of his suit, McCord lay on his king size bed and fell into a deep sleep. Nearly two and a half hours later he woke up in the exact position that he fell off in. He had slept longer than he wanted thanks to his participation in the afternoon shout at the pub. His head was still in quite a haze—understandable given the events of the last few days. McCord needed the nap to recharge his batteries, and now felt well rested and ready to start his evening. He also thought it necessary to go for a good run to sweat out the excess consumption of beer. Rather than order an Uber he decided to get a little exercise and jog up to Fairfax Lookout. Dex put on his gym shorts, a muscle shirt, and laced up his running shoes.

MANLY AND NORTH HEAD PARK, NEW SOUTH WALES

McCord burst out the hotel doors setting out from the Manly Pacific a little after 8:25pm, ready to start his three-kilometer run to meet his KGO colleague at the North Head bluffs. Dex was to connect with Abbot at 9:00pm and thought a half hour was more than enough time to navigate the crowds and steep hills of Manly Beach. He passed through the hotel gates, crossed South Steyne Street, and ran along the brick oceanfront esplanade heading southwest.

Metcalf's two hired hands from the West Indies, Frazier and Carroll, were patiently waiting outside the Manly Pacific Hotel in a blue Holden Commodore, on the ready for their newly assigned person-of-interest to make his next move. Their automobile's badge was a known entity in Australia. The sporty look, wide stance, and big footprint gave the car some real visual aggression. Combined with Holden's propensity for doing fleet deals, its cars led very hard lives. In its first two years this auto in particular had covered extensive kilometers, as the NSW police force took a shine to its powerful V-8 engine. The six-speed manual gear box and worn-out clutch made it a bit noisy. The two men had been informed by Metcalf that sooner or later McCord would lead them to the Aboriginal.

The Manly Beach promenade was lined with 45-foot-tall Australian pines filled with lorikeets chirping at six octaves. The noise was deafening as the birds discussed their escapades of the day. McCord's stride was long and agile, his body straight with the speed of a Division 1 athlete, his build powerful and confident. Several tourists were in his path, walking and gazing at the rolling waves of the Pacific Ocean. Many, especially the ladies, quickly turned their heads and watched this awesome mountain of a man as he passed by jogging effortlessly towards the sunset. Out in the water local surfers displayed their tricks on perfect waves while the boat crews of Manly Surf Club were running practice drills, navigating the last few five-foot swells before the dark made it much too dangerous to go out in the surf.

After a few hundred meters on the promenade McCord turned right off the brick boardwalk onto the Corso, the local pedestrian mall, connecting the Pacific Ocean with the Manly ferry terminal. The 300-meter Corso passage was filled with shoppers who had just finished spending a leisurely day at the beach. The walkway was filled with a cadre of cafes, boutique clothing stores, surf shops, and street entertainers. Jugglers on unicycles were entertaining crowds along the corridor while the excited tourists peered into their iPhones ready to catch that magical moment. At the opposite end was the Ferry Terminal Wharf, accepting its array of late afternoon vessels arriving from downtown Sydney and its suburbs. McCord was now jogging through thick pedestrian traffic. He was doing his best Rob Gronkowski imitation, weaving in, out, and around the oblivious vacationers. The blue Holden following him was unable to make the right turn into the Corso shopping district. Barriers had been erected that read Pedestrians Only. Frazier and Carroll were frantically driving around the streets of Manly Beach looking for their target. McCord was blissfully unaware that his turn down the crowded open-air shopping area made him lose his followers.

Dex eventually made his way to the other side of the Corso as the latest ferry docked and released another hundred or so residents and visitors onto the peninsula. He quickly turned left to avoid the crowds and headed south. After distancing himself from the masses and his pursuers, McCord continued his trek up the long steep hill of Osborne Road towards North Head. The charming southern hills of Manly were lined with three-story brick flats and interspersed intermittently with large stately houses, perfect for the transient population of a beach town. His run up the incline passed lush gardens lined with tall red hakea, swatches of black-eyed Susans, blue hydrangeas, and other plants Dex couldn't identify. McCord's difficult uphill climb with its combination of left and right turns continued for two kilometers until he came upon a sign to the park entrance that read:

North Head
Sydney Harbour National Park
Gate Locks one hour after Dusk.

Another three-quarters of a kilometer to his destination, he thought to himself. North Head consisted of 150+ hectares and was home to a variety of native animals and plants, as well as historic buildings and structures dating as far back as the 1800s. The National Park was one of the finest places along the Northern Beaches to watch the sunset. It offered a remarkable panoramic view of Sydney Harbour and the city skyline. At the end of the park were the Heads, majestic sheer cliffs that formed a two-kilometer-wide entrance to the harbor.

On the eastern side of North Head facing the ocean lay North Fort, built to protect Sydney from air and sea attacks. Completed around 1938 it played a pivotal role as an enemy deterrent during World War II. During the war, Aussies were on high alert for a Japanese assault. It happened in May 1942 when a Japanese midget submarine snuck into Australia's Sydney Harbour for a daring suicide attack. It had not gone far when one of the vessel's propellers became entangled in anti-submarine nets. The submarine's crew, realizing they could not free the midget's propellers, chose a warrior's death and fired demolition charges that destroyed several anchored vessels. There were many other enemy attempts made to enter the harbor during WW II, but they were detected and promptly depth charged repeatedly by Australian patrol boats.

On the western side of North Head was a facility originally set up in 1837 to quarantine new arrivals to Sydney to minimize the spread of communicable diseases such as smallpox and whooping cough. Previously it was used as a cemetery and ceremonial site by the native Camaraigal people before the whole area of North Head was set aside for the quarantine station. The station was closed in 1984 and the site became part of Sydney Harbour National Park.

McCord continued his jog on a walking track passing swathes of dry bushland, flora bandicoots, and darting blue tongue lizards. He remained on the side trails past the North Fort Barracks and Hanging Swamps, keeping a lookout for poisonous snakes. After seven minutes of running on dirt and barren rock McCord reached his destination, the bluffs at

Fairfax Lookout. Standing on a large boulder he took in the extraordinary view across the harbor entrance over to South Head and Balmoral. "This view never gets old," thought Dex. Roughly 40 meters below the harbor spilled out to the ocean creating huge swells and glistening whitecaps. There were no other remaining tourists visiting the lookout. Nobody there to appreciate one last panoramic view of Sydney before sunset. And there was no sign of Abbot.

His waterproof Tag Hueler watch hands pointed to 5:55am, still set on U.S. eastern standard time, Dex quickly did the math—8:55pm in Sydney. The sun was starting to set. Breathtaking colors were gleaming from the horizon. McCord sat down on his boulder admiring the view for another 15 minutes until he heard the squeal of old bicycle brakes. "It must be Abbo," he thought. He then heard another sound off in the distance. It was the grinding sound of an automobile transmission, which McCord presumed was a tourist arriving for the sunset. Looking into the setting sun he could barely make out the body of a person awkwardly jumping off a bicycle onto the walking track. The dark figure was a black blur outlined by the blinding glare of the sunset in the west.

"Hey, Jiemba, is that you mate?" McCord shouted out.

"Yes, Mr. McCord, it's me," replied an exhausted Abbot as he walked down the sandy path toward the boulder where McCord was standing.

"I wasn't sure this was the right location."

"I thought it would be a great place to meet. Mr. Young told me you used to go here when you were living together in Manly," said Abbot.

"Ah, yes. Youngy and I would come up here with a few VBs and discuss the differences between Aussie and American sports, work ethic, and women. Man, this place brings back memories."

"Very complicated subjects I assume?"

"Yes, very. So why the secret meeting?" McCord queried.

"I don't feel safe, Mr. McCord. As I told you there are two men looking for me and I think its because we uncovered something while Tony and I were in India reviewing NSG's controls."

"Are you sure?"

"Yes. They asked one of my neighbors if I was back from India yet. Nobody except for my parents knew I was in India."

"Go on."

"While conducting the audit I came across an issue in the company's quality assurance controls. The staff became very anxious when I pointed out an unusual extra step in their process."

"Who were you questioning?" asked McCord.

"I was speaking with a few employees on their finance team and some developers over a few beers. Tony suggested I do that."

"I figured as much," added McCord.

"Yes, and that was when they opened up and I uncovered the irregularities," said Abbot.

"Go on mate. What were the problems with NSG's controls and data tagging processes that concerned you and Youngy?"

"It wasn't necessarily the data tagging process that concerned us. It all looked in good order. Their clients' earnings releases, Form 8Ks, 10Qs, and 10Ks were very accurate. What bothered us was the fact that some of the filings were being funneled to another location before heading back to EDGAR's U.S. office for final submission to the SEC." Abbot pulled out his internal control report to show McCord what they had found and continued. "Also, the developers and NSG's assistant controller appeared to have concerns surrounding the internal controls on data management," stated Abbot.

"How confident are you that there's an issue?"

"Very. I was able to flowchart the extra process and confirmed with the senior project manager that this was correct. There is definitely an unexplained additional step that doesn't make sense."

"So where are the SEC documents being directed?" McCord probed while looking concerned.

"At first, I couldn't find out where the documents were going but then one person during my last night mentioned a location. I jotted it down. The location is noted in our audit workpapers," said Abbot while handing Dex a binder clipped set of papers. McCord started flipping through Abbot's workpapers. "After Mr. Young headed back home, I completed my documentation and uploaded the report for his review. I am not sure he had a chance to review them before his surfing accident."

"I don't think it was an accident, Abbo," shared McCord looking up from the workpapers. "It doesn't make sense he would go surfing up north so early in the morning after returning from India."

McCord was deep in thought flipping through the pages of Abbot's report when he saw the shadows of two men approaching behind Abbot from the bush. He had a hard time distinguishing the figures as the sunset behind them was only permitting him to see shapes. Dex saw the flash first before hearing the loud bang. In an instant Jiemba fell into McCord's arms with a pained look on his face. Abbot had been shot and now the dark shapes were heading towards him.

Dex dove to his left, dropping Abbot and landing behind a large boulder as a single shot ricocheted off the rock above his head. "Holy shit," he thought to himself. "These guys are trying to kill me." McCord was trapped and could hear the sound of footsteps slowly approaching. He heard people whispering to each other in accented English that sounded Caribbean. On the left and right sides of his hiding place was open ground. He would be an easy target. Behind him was the ocean with South Head across the way. McCord had nowhere to run. There was only one escape path—three strides downwards and a leap off the 130-foot North Head bluff. He peered over the boulder, barely making out the shadowy figures that were advancing, one to the left, one to the right. The waning sunset was still obstructing his vision. He could hear the men slowly moving forward. McCord quickly weighed his options. Two men with guns who didn't appear to want to negotiate or a dive to almost certain death. He decided to embrace his only getaway. McCord turned around and accelerated as fast as he could, then took the leap.

~~~

Earlier the two hired men in the Holden Commodore were unable to turn down the Corso pedestrian walkway in pursuit of McCord. Dex was weaving his way in and out of the late afternoon crowds.

"Turn right here!" yelled Carroll at Frazier who was driving the former police car. "He'll come out on the other side."

"It's one way!" retorted Frazier.

The Holden headed south on North Steyne Road but could not make a right until four blocks later. The Pacific Ocean was on their left. All possible turns were either one way or closed for water main repair. A frequent occurrence due to the salinity in Manly's public water system.

"Right here, mon," Carroll directed.

The auto's clutch grinded its way up and down the back streets of Manly Beach looking for Derek McCord. He was nowhere to be found. The rugby players from the West Indies were getting increasingly desperate. Pedestrians, tourists, and bicyclists cluttered the streets. They continued their crisscross of Manly for ten minutes, continuously heading south and uphill towards North Head.

"He's got to be out here somewhere, mon," said a frustrated Carroll.

"Perhaps we go back to the hotel and wait?" recommended Frazier.

"It's not an option. I am not telling Mr. Metcalf we had him in our sights and lost him."

The two men were desperate and getting discouraged. They went back down the northern hills of Manly and parked on the west end of town on East Esplanade Road. The assassins were overlooking Manly Harbor contemplating next steps. A new crowd of visitors had just disembarked the ferry and was moving past their old blue automobile. It was getting close to evening as the sunset was starting to bloom. They were running out of alternatives. Waiting all night in front of the Manly Pacific Hotel for

McCord to make his next move was not a preferred option. At that point a bicyclist quickly raced in front of their Holden Commodore.

"Ovadayso!" exclaimed Carroll. "It's the Aboriginal on that bike?"

"No way, mon. Yes, I think it is," said Frazier elatedly. "Shall we take him out?"

"No. Give him some distance and let's follow him," instructed Carroll. "Let's see where he is heading. If we can eliminate both the Aboriginal and the American, the boss will be pleased."

Jiemba Abbot was riding his bicycle feverishly after disembarking the Manly ferry that arrived from downtown Sydney. He wanted to meet McCord before the sun went down and the park closed. The hill up Osborne Road was steeper than he remembered. Abbot took his mind off pedaling by recalling every part of his India visit with Mr. Young. The meetings, people, processes, systems, workpapers, and flow charts. He wanted to provide McCord with all the information he needed to complete the engagement and ensure his promotion to senior auditor. Jiemba wanted to make his family proud.

After making it up the hill and turning left on Marshall Steet and right on Darley Road, Abbot made his way to the park entrance. The sun was still up but sinking fast. The old blue Holden was not far behind but kept its distance so as not to be noticed.

"He's headed into the park, stay back some. There's no way out," noted Carroll.

"Jah, mon. This is the perfect place to make our move," said Frazier excitedly.

The Holden rolled slowly through the park entrance proceeding around turns and past thick bushes, keeping a safe distance behind their target. The men would occasionally lose sight of Abbot and then find him again peddling forth toward the end of the park. The passengers, remaining hidden in their auto, watched their target finally reach his destination. Abbot maneuvered his bicycle into a narrow walking path. He then leapt off the bike and rushed towards the bluffs. "We have him now," thought both men.

"Keep back and park here," ordered Carroll while reaching into the glove box and pulling out a Glock 17A handgun. "Let's wait a minute to ensure he connects with the Yank."

The Holden's transmission grinded as Frazier backed into a parking space. So as not to be detected he parked at the furthest end of the lot. The sun was setting behind them making it, they thought, even more difficult to be noticed. After waiting three minutes the hired assassins got out of their vehicle and headed east towards McCord and Abbot. Carroll had the handgun in his hand. Frazier grabbed a ski rope from the vehicle's boot so he wouldn't be empty-handed. At this point no other vehicles were in the parking lot. No bystanders. No one to witness the ruthless deed that was about to occur. The walk across the lot was less than 35 meters onto the walking path. Shortly after entering the trail Abbot and McCord came into view. The assassins saw them standing next to two large boulders. Carroll was leading the way forward carrying the Glock, ready for action. Both men could hear their targets talking.

"Stay low and behind me," commanded Carroll.

Frazier followed behind the trained gunman at the ready. "Let's take them out, mon," whispered Frazier.

Then no more words were spoken, just hand signals. As the two men got closer to their targets their walk became more upright. From 15 meters away and now in full sight Carroll raised his Glock and fired one shot at the smaller open target. He saw the Aboriginal fall into the larger man. He didn't have a clear shot at the American. Not yet. Moving slightly closer he was ready to unload his second shot, but the huge figure began moving sharply to the right. At the same time Frazier with his rope in hand, not wanting to miss the action, clumsily pressed forward to keep stride with his teammate. Not realizing his partner stopped and was about to pull the trigger, Frazier bumped into Carroll. He fired wildly. The single bullet missed the intended target, bouncing off a boulder and out into the salt air.

Despite their uneasiness, the two men cautiously pushed forward towards the large rocks. Still 10 meters away. Carroll motioned Frazier to move left to encircle the cornered man. Both pushed slowly forward trying to deter their target from making any wild moves. As they approached the American the sun was setting behind them. Darkness was coming quickly. Frazier was now five meters away. On the left he glanced at the body on the ground in front of him. Carroll held up his hand to signal stop. Then he headed forward to the right. He was prepared to shoot whatever moved. The stillness was palpable. Hunter and hunted both silent. As he approached the enormous boulder, he expected to encounter a desperate and aggressive giant. To his surprise no one was there.

Looking at Frazier, Carroll shouted, "Where is he?"

Frazier approached the hiding place, stepping over the Aboriginal's body. "He had nowhere to go," exclaimed Frazier with an equally puzzled look.

They stared intently at each other, and then gazed out towards the ocean.

"You don't think he jumped?" queried Frazier.

"Mon, that is one crazy Yank," responded Carroll. "Do you see anything below?"

Both men cautiously looked over the bluff so as not to not slip and fall to their own death. The assassins leaned over searching for any sign of life 40 meters down. The water below was choppy and violent, whitecaps and darkness made it difficult to see signs of life.

"I guess he's gone," said Frazier.

"Yeah, he couldn't survive that jump. Too high," concluded Carroll.

The two men continued to look out to the water as nightfall quickly approached and stars replaced the colorful sky.

"What do we do with the Aboriginal's body?"

"Get some rocks and lets toss him over the side," instructed Carroll.

"Really, mon?"

"Yes, shark bait."

The two men gathered several large stones and strategically stuffed them down Abbot's shirt and pants. They used Frazier's rope to anchor the heavy stones to the body. Making sure to erase all signs of blood in the dirt and the surrounding area, they picked up the body and on the count of three tossed the evidence over the cliff and out towards the sea. The men then spent another five minutes cleaning up the crime scene to remove any potential evidence. Carroll picked up a stack of papers, one sneaker, and an empty beer can. He threw them over the edge and out to the cascadian tide below. They returned to the Commadore, stored Abbot's bicycle in the uts's large boot, and headed back to Pittwater.

~~~

McCord had nowhere to run. Crouching down in a three-point stance like an NFL tight end Dex was ready to make the leap. It was his only alternative as his pursuers were moving closer and closer towards his cover. McCord was thinking about the cliff divers in Acapulco that he used to watch on ABC's *Wide World of Sports* as a little kid. "I could do this," he thought. Feet first, stay upright and hold onto your jewels. The slight decline towards the cliff's edge was now in-front of him. His eyes were focused on the other side of the harbor entrance so as to not look down. Then he subconsciously began to count to three. McCord started his sprint on the count of two. He couldn't wait and stormed out of the blocks sprinting down the short ledge and silently leapt into the air.

Dex was airborne, plummeting full throttle in a blitz of pure fear and adrenaline. Going too fast to even scream. His mind was focused on keeping his body straight and upright. "Feet first and hold your breath," he mumbled to himself. The wind rushed past and into his eyes with a feeling of an insane natural high. The free fall continued for what seemed like a long time. McCord stiffened for impact. BAAMMM!! The open water enveloped him as his sneakers exploded off his feet. Hitting the water felt like smashing though a wall of sheetrock with wooden studs. He felt a severe pain in his side and then a sudden increase in pressure in his eyes. He was now decelerating underwater, anticipating the impact of the sea floor rocks. McCord didn't feel anything hard or sharp undersea. His privates and legs were intact and unbroken. McCord's body progressively submerged deeper and deeper until finally coming to a slow stop under 15+ meters of water. He was still alive!

McCord felt the pull of the inlet's high tide currents. They were strong and swiftly flowing out to the open ocean. He could feel his body being pulled in one direction, east. McCord needed to get to the surface and overcome the weightless feeling of being deep underwater. "Keep kicking and pulling," he thought, remembering the buoyancy factor. He had to overcome any fears of sinking deeper into the unknown with little air in his lungs. For what seemed like minutes Dex kept pulling upwards, continuing to hold his breath, determined to reach the surface. He was starting to see a faint light above the water's surface. He had hope now. With a few strong kicks McCord burst out of the water and into the air. He could breathe.

Floating on his back and out of breath he could barely see the cliffs of North Head off in the distance. The undersea currents had pulled his body out toward the sea. The spindrift from the waves was making it difficult to get his bearings. Waves were now cresting and splashing over his head. He was floating up and down two-meter swells created by the Sydney harbor waters meeting the ocean. The currents were still pulling him out to sea as the high tide was draining form the harbor. McCord stayed still and floated in the currents. He understood that if he didn't splash around in the choppy waters his attackers would not be able to spot him. McCord had been swept 200 meters away from land and it was twilight.

Dex was familiar with these waters. As he floated, he recalled the last time he was in the rough surf off North Head as a member of the Manly surf boat team. A fellow crew mate had lost his father who was an Australian Navy veteran. McCord had been invited to take part in the tradition of scattering a veteran's ashes out to sea. He took it as a privilege. While the late sailor's family watched from the bluffs of the Heads, McCord and his crew members held their oars up vertically, in traditional Navy fashion. The crew did their best to hold the surf boat steady in the rough surf while their friend released his father's ashes. Mission accomplished but not without a tear or two.

The rip tide was still pulling McCord rapidly out into the South Pacific Ocean. He knew he shouldn't fight it as the current would eventually stop. Dex conserved his energy and continued to float on his back heading further out to sea. As the darkness from the night sky came, he gazed at the radiating pattern of stars arranged in the sky. For a moment his mind drifted to what might be lurking below the water's surface in the deep. He didn't have a fear of the ocean and knew he had to remain calm and still. In time the ocean currents would come to a stop. Slowly the waves subsided, and the waters became calm. His thoughts switched to swim and survival mode.

McCord needed to head northeast for over 2,500 meters (1.5 miles) to get around North Head and return to land. Before starting his swim, he confirmed his direction by identifying the Southern Cross star constellation. Composed of five stars forming the shape of a cross, it was the most distinctive feature in the Australian sky. Like the Big Dipper of the northern sky, navigators utilized the Southern Cross to indicate the direction of the south pole. McCord thought it was a glorious sight. With the constellation in his sights, he began swimming.

The first few strokes were painful. He was barely able to raise his left arm due to an agonizing discomfort on his side. He thought a sign of a broken or bruised rib. McCord fought through the pain and continued his slow and steady strokes. He didn't want to stop and break his rhythm nor shift his mind towards the pain. McCord was an above-average swimmer. As a child he rode waves for hours at Virginia Beach. When he landed in Australia six years earlier, he trained to become a weekend volunteer lifeguard, a prerequisite for being a member of the Manly surfboat rowing team. To compete for his club McCord had to pass a grueling lifesaving examination. The training included long hours of swimming and performing rescue drills off the beaches of Manly. A passing grade would make him an official volunteer lifeguard and earn him the coveted Australian Bronze Medallion. He succeeded and was able to spend his summer weekends on the beach saving lives—a commitment he enjoyed and an invaluable skill that just might save his own life today.

The ocean waters were dark, but the half moon and stars were illuminating the way. One mile had passed since he started his journey. McCord's landing target was in reach around the rocky cliffs of North Head. The calm shore of Shelly Beach was his destination, a comforting thought. The ocean swells had settled down and the seas became quiet. That's when he heard the sound of splashing in the water. The slapping sound startled him. "What the fuck?" thought Dex. Then he saw it—a shark fin whipping from side to side in the water. It was only 10 meters away. The sound was terrifying, but Dex then remembered that during his long surfboat rows he would often pass by small sections of nets.

New South Wales shark nets were commonly found off the busy local beaches. They did not form a complete barrier for bathers but did give everyone a little peace of mind, especially swimmers, surfers, and divers. The nets used off the beach were between 150 and 160 meters long and hung 6 meters down. The submerged fishing nets had a mesh size of around 50 to 60 centimeters. The New South Wales nets have killed thousands of sharks before they are able to visit their breeding ground in Sydney Harbour. When a shark or other large fish is caught, they frantically try to escape and get tangled in the nets. The nets were checked every two to three days. Tonight's fish was a fresh catch. McCord's concern was that the beast thrashing in the net was bleeding and attracting other sharks to the area. He was on the lookout for fins.

Fifty minutes after jumping from the cliffs, McCord saw the lights of Fairy Bower. He was getting close to his destination. Every stroke now had significance and value. He was going to make it. As he approached Shelly Beach, Dex could hear voices above on the surrounding cliffs walking track. It was too dark to signal to them. Almost to his destination, a fully exhausted McCord felt the water getting warmer as he swam around the final corner of North Head towards the beach. That's when he saw the coral reef illuminated below him with its adjoining white sands. He thought this must be the phosphorescent glow that he had seen years before radiating up from the ocean's floor, but then McCord started feeling bubbles hitting his body as they surfaced around him. He knew there was only one rational explanation, night divers. A group of scuba divers were making their way around the reef with torches in hand. Unaware that above them was a sole swimmer who just escaped an encounter with death. Then suddenly in front of McCord rose two divers. The buddy system. Startled at the sight of this large human swimming alone in the night ocean the divers were hesitant to approach the awkward ocean mammal. But then they quickly recognized the person was exhausted and hurt. The two divers reached out and started to guide McCord to shore. He was rescued.

~~~

Kendall "Kenny" Cove's favorite open water lesson was night diving. Her class of seven novice divers had finished a session earlier in the day in Sydney Harbour. Now they were ready for their last required dive before receiving a PADI certification. That night the dive team unloaded their gear, went through the pre-dive checklists, and in pairs headed into the water from the white sands of Shelly Beach. Kenny teamed up with the weakest student of the group to ensure he would not panic. Night dives could be scary. At the beginning it's a daunting thought to dive in the dark. The diver experiences a smaller field of vision. Only the area illuminated by your and other torches are visible. Everywhere else is in the dark and everything looks and feels totally different. They would encounter creatures of the night not often seen during the day.

The dive team slowly made their way out into the dark water, submerged above a large coral reef. Brilliant extra illuminated colors of coral started to appear in their torch lights and cyalume sticks. The class found a different underwater environment at night. The presence of nocturnal sea life was somewhat minimal compared to the students' dive earlier in the day. Most daytime fish sleep inside the coral reefs, hiding away from predators like sharks and stingrays that feed at night.

Kendall Cove had completed hundreds of dives without incident. When she first looked up from the ocean floor and saw the shadow of a dark figure, she suspected that a large stingray or sea turtle had invaded her class. Not a huge man splashing in a ripped muscle shirt above. Seeing a swimmer coming from the open sea to invade her class at night was something new. Kenny clutched her partner's hand and cautiously ascended to the surface.

At first Kenny was hesitant to let go of her shaky partner, but she could see that this intruder was in distress. McCord was exhausted and stopped swimming when he came face-to-face with Cove. He was treading water and confused until he realized it was night scuba divers. Kenny directed her buddy to go behind the man and motioned to grab his left shoulder as she reached under the arm pit of the right shoulder facing McCord. She spit out her respirator.

~~~

"Are you alright, mate?" asked Kenny.

"I am now. Help me to shore," requested an exhausted McCord.

"What are you doing out here?"

"It's a long story," he said while holding onto Kenny and kicking slowly, careful not to hit his rescuers. "I'll tell you when I'm safely on land."

"We'll get you there. Try to relax mate. Our team will help you along."

The rest of Kenny's class rose to the surface, equally curious as to what came out of the sea. Kenny directed the divers to encircle McCord but kept their distance until instructed. Each pair of buddies participated in the rescue. Kenny recognized a good teaching moment. The group started supporting McCord's exhausted body 50 metres from shore. Their circle rotated as they took turns tugging his 235-pound frame back to the beach.

After several starts and stops to change rescuers the dive team made it to their destination with their prize in tow.

"You are all PADI certified now!" exclaimed Kenny as the team arrived at shore. Her group of divers cheered out loud as they moved onto the beach.

McCord sat down on the sand completely exhausted resting his head on his bent knees. He was having trouble breathing due to a bruised rib suffered from the jump. He was slowly getting his breath back to normal. A few of the newly certified PADI students went to the van and retrieved medical supplies. Kenny was handed a rescue blanket from one of her students and put it around McCord's shoulders. She then called out for someone to fetch a bottle of water. The dive team kept their distance so as to not smother the injured beached giant. Kenny handed him water.

"Thank you," said Dex looking up at his rescuer. He was surprised to see such a stunning heroine. Kendall's super woman body was muscular and tight from years of scuba diving and carrying tanks while building her business.

"You're welcome, mate," replied Kenny. "So, why is an American bloke like you swimming at night alone in the open ocean? Don't you know sharks like to eat at night?"

"I didn't give it a thought. I was just trying to get to land and survive," explained McCord.

"Where did you come from?"

"North Head."

"Wait, what? How did you get out there? Did you swim from the harbour?" queried Kenny.

"No, I jumped from the cliffs."

"Jumped? So, you are telling me that you pulled a Peter Pan right off The Heads?"

"Well, not as graceful as Peter Pan. More like someone jumping out of plane without a parachute," stated McCord.

"Are you a stubbie short of a six pack?" asked Cove.

"Nah, it was my only option. I was being chased by two men who shot the guy I was with."

"Shot? Yank, you're sounding a little irrational now."

"Seriously. One moment I was speaking with my friend and the next he was lying in my arms."

"That's crazy. We were loading up the van earlier at the dive shop near the wharf. I didn't hear any Blue Heelers or ambos flying up the main road to North Head," noted Cove.

"It was only the two of us up there. I guess nobody reported anything," answered McCord.

"What happened next?"

"After my friend was shot the two guys were moving towards me. The sun was behind the blokes so all I saw was shadows. Then a flash. That's when I dove behind a boulder at the edge of the bluff."

"Did you try to speak with them?"

"No, I don't think they wanted to talk. My friend was lying face down on the ground. The blokes were waiting for me to show myself," continued McCord. "What was weird is that the guys hunting me down sounded Caribbean, not Aussie. And looking at Abbo lying lifeless next to me with blood pouring out didn't give me a sense that these guys wanted to discuss reggae music."

"Who is Abbo?"

"The guy who got shot. My colleague from work. We called him Abbo. Anyway, he was not moving, and I didn't want to end up like him with my face in the dirt. I looked behind me and knew I only had one option."

"Jump?" confirmed Kenny.

"That's right. I ran down the embankment and went full flight. Feet first holding onto my jewels. It hurt a bit when I hit the water. I lost my breath and my sneakers. Maybe bruised a few ribs but I'll be alright," winced McCord.

"Do you need to go to hospital?" asked Kenny.

"No. No. I want to find out if Abbo is OK."

"Alright. I'll call my mate at the police station. She'll be able to see if your friend is still up there. Stay down and I'll get my phone."

Kenny got up from McCord's side to retrieve her cell phone. The dive class was watching from a distance while removing their scuba gear. Occasionally glancing over at the large man sitting in the sand while they brought their gear up to the van in the parking lot. McCord noticed the PADI students talking amongst themselves. Most likely telling stories of when they first sighted the night swimmer and trying to guess where he came from.

Ms. Cove located her backpack amongst the pile on the ground and pulled out her phone. McCord could see Kenny explaining the situation twice to the person on the phone. He noted her conviction describing to the police all the facts. Going back and forth with additional details as questions were being raised at the other end, while all the time sending over a few smiles at Dex. The back-and-forth conversation came to an end. Kenny walked down the beach and sat back down in the sand next to McCord.

"The police are going to send a car up to North Head to see if they can find your friend. They want to listen to your story. I know the officer. Her husband is friends with my brother. A good woman but sometimes she can get mad as a dead dingo's donger. I guess she has to deal with a lot of crazy tourists in Manly so don't be shocked if she doesn't believe your story," explained Kenny.

"That's alright. My story is a bit nuts. You believe me, right?" Dex asked while gazing into Kenny's blue eyes.

"Mate, the look on your face when we pulled you from the water is all I had to see," stated Kenny while staring right back into Dex's eyes. "An escapade like yours is hard to make up. Although I have never heard of anyone taking a dive off the Heads before. Or at least live to tell the story."

"Always a first time," confirmed McCord.

~ ~ ~

The two continued their conversation for a few minutes exchanging details before Kendall put on a t-shirt over her one piece and left to tell her class what had happened to Dex. They stood quietly in disbelief, glancing towards McCord, who was still sitting on the beach. After taking a few questions from curious students, she informed them that the police were coming to interview the Yank, that it would be a little while before they headed back to the dive shop to drop off and wash down their gear. No one asked further questions as they were still trying to comprehend the situation. At that point McCord got up from the sand, walked over to the van parked in the Bower Street lot, and thanked the class for pulling him out of the water. He noticed the group appeared thrilled to be a part of such an unexpected rescue and none seemed anxious to leave. Adding in unison that they had an Esky full of VBs to celebrate their well-earned night diving certificate and that it was a sensational ending to their week of PADI dive instruction.

After five minutes in the parking lot listening to scuba diving stories, a white and checkered blue police car pulled into the Shelly Beach lot. There were no sirens or flashing lights as the driver did not want to alarm the patrons dining at the adjacent Boathouse restaurant. An officer dressed in her blue uniform struggled to get out of the car. She was weighed down by a bullet proof vest, taser, expandable baton, pepper spray, ammunition magazines, and handgun.

Officer Karen Beveridge was a sergeant in the Manly Beach Police department. She was wearing navy drill pants with side pockets; general purpose GP boots, and a navy baseball cap. Kenny didn't know Karen that well but knew her reputation. A tough Sheila with a short temper, someone to be careful around. They both grew up on the Northern Beaches of NSW and would periodically run into each other at surf carnivals, bars, and footy games. Beveridge had been a Manly resident her whole life. A person that never left her comfort zone. As a young athlete she was a fierce competitor on the field hockey circuit. She played for her hometown Manly Warringah Junior Hockey Club. Her husband Peter grew up in Narrabeen. He was a few years older than Kenny and still friendly with her brother. Peter was a premier player on the men's field hockey team. That's how he connected with Karen. He was so good that he played four years for the Aussie National team until younger talent forced him to retire. He was now repairing refrigerators up and down the NSW coast. A good tradesman with a lot of free time.

Officer Beveridge glanced over to Kenny with a nod and greeted McCord with a firm handshake. Her eyes were going up and down, checking out McCord's massive body while looking for signs of injury.

"So, Kenny tells me her dive class found you swimming out by the Heads. That they pulled you out of the water. Something about an incident with an Aboriginal and you jumped off the bluff into the harbour's channel?" questioned the officer.

"Yes. Two men were approaching us. One of them fired a gun and shot my friend."

"Wait. Wait, mate. What's your name?"

"Derek McCord."

"Profession?"

"I'm an accountant but that's not important right now!"

"Calm down. OK, start again," requested officer Beveridge.

"I believe the two men were dark skinned. They had a West Indies sort of accent."

"The men pursuing you at the Heads?"

"More like hunting us down, but I couldn't make them out so well. The sun was behind them."

"The funny sounding dark men?"

"Yes. Then suddenly, they fired a gun, and my colleague went down in my arms. Then they fired another shot at me. I dodged behind some rocks."

"Shot at you?" asked a confused Beveridge.

"Yes. The men started to get closer and closer. I had no choice but to jump off the cliffs. We need to get up there to see if my friend is still alive," demanded McCord.

"OK, hold on Yank. You're telling me there is a wounded person up in the Heads? Right now? Are you sure or just a bit delirious from your late-night swim?"

"I'm sure. I feel fine. I'll show you."

"Hold on, mate. Sit down and rest a bit. We already sent a patrol car up there," said the officer. "Where did you say you were?"

"We were on the bluffs. Fairfax Lookout. Just down a bit from the parking lot," explained McCord.

"I know the location."

Beveridge walked away from McCord shaking her head and pulled out her two-way radio. He could hear the officer explaining the situation and instructing the listener to walk around Fairfax Lookout in search of a body. The person on the other side of the radio had her repeat the request and then signed off without further questions. Officer Beveridge returned to McCord and asked him to explain in detail what happened on the Heads. For 15 minutes McCord provided a play by play of events surrounding the encounter and his journey back to safety. Dex was describing the sound of a shark caught in nets when a voice came over the two-way radio.

"Seargent Beveridge, this is Officer Dopel," cracked a voice from the other end.

"Chip, what did you see up there?"

"Nothing, Seargent. No sign of any disturbance. It's still fairly light around here with the moon being so bright tonight. I also used my torch, but we saw no signs of dead bodies nor evidence of any struggle. I did find some empty beer cans, but they look a little old," reported the officer.

"Alright, Chip, come back to the station and we'll take another look in the morning," ordered Beveridge.

"Righty'O," responded Officer Dopel.

Beveridge gazed at McCord, "We'll take another look first thing at the crack of dawn. Yank, you look buggered. I suggest you get some rest."

"Shouldn't we go up there? What about some kind of all-points bulletin? My friend is still missing!" shouted McCord.

"Easy there, mate. She'll be right."

"Why not tonight?"

"Nah. My boys didn't find anything unusual. No need to spend any more time up there. We'll take another look in the morning. In the daylight. We'll take your report then. For now, stand down, McCord."

"I'm just eager to find out what happened."

"I understand. But the park is closed. Where are you staying? Do you need a ride?" offered Beveridge.

"I'm staying at the Manly Pacific but I'm not going back there. Whoever was trying to get me may be waiting back at the hotel."

"Well, you can stay in the police station. The holding pen is not very comfortable but you're welcome to do so."

Kenny jumped in, "You can stay at my place, Derek. I have a big couch you can sleep on."

"Better than a prison cell," confirmed the officer.

"Are you sure it's not a bother?"

"No problem at all. I have lots of pillows and blankets," added Kenny.

"I appreciate that," said an exhausted McCord.

Officer Beveridge returned to her vehicle while looking at the dive students drinking their celebratory beer. "You be careful out there," she instructed the lot. The group waved back with a smile. The blue checkered police car pulled out and headed back towards Manly's city center. Kenny's students finished their drinks and packed the last of the diving equipment in the van. Everyone climbed in, including McCord whose ribs and entire body were still hurting from the escape. They headed back to the shop to unload and rinse off the dive gear.

~~~

By the time Kendall Cove closed her dive shop it was past midnight. Dex and Kenny drove off together arriving at her Balgowlah flat in less than five minutes. She couldn't afford the rents in Manly but her large one-bedroom apartment a short distance away from her storefront worked well. Her flat was on the second floor of a two-family home. McCord struggled to climb the stairs, hurting and exhausted from the day. Kenny opened her door and directed Dex towards the couch. She went into her room and came out with a large t-shirt that belonged to her brother.

"Here, this should fit you," said Kenny tossing McCord the clean shirt.

"Perfect," replied Dex as he struggled to pull his ripped muscle shirt over his head.

"I don't have any shoes that will fit you, but I can drive over to the hotel in the morning and get your bags. I'll be discreet," asserted Kenny.

"That would be great."

"Yeah. I know a few people who work at the Pacific. I should be in and out in a flash."

"Thanks again, Kenny, I really appreciate you helping me out. I wasn't looking forward to sleeping in Beveridge's prison cell."

"No worries, mate. Let me get you some water and something to eat."

Kenny went into the kitchen to get a glass of water and make a vegemite sandwich. When she returned McCord was already fast asleep on her couch. She placed the snack on a side table and gently placed a blanket over Dex's body, being careful not to wake him. Before heading to her bedroom, Cove took a moment to admire the specimen of a man sleeping soundly on her couch.

~~~

Kendall Cove is an energetic accountant. During university she sailed through accounting but wanted more. She was gregarious, competitive, fun-loving, and sociable. Always up for an adventure. Growing up she worked at a local surf shop in Narrabeen on the Northern Beaches of Sydney. Best known for the world famous North Narrabeen Break, Kendall's hometown coastline was a breeding ground of some of the best surfers, and home to several world champions. While Kenny herself was a good surfer, her passion was scuba diving. She loved the freedom of being underwater, the sense of absolute serenity that subconsciously transferred her to mother's womb. It was her escape from the pressures of everyday life and provided her with the proper conditions for redefining personal limits.

Kenny was extremely comfortable with new people, places, and experiences—not a typical trait in an accountant. While she loved the ocean, she wanted a career that was not a job for the sake of earning a living but rather to follow her passions in a bid to help society. Generally, people who are not following their passion pick up any job for the sake of earning a living. Not Kenny. Cove appreciated her accounting ability to assist clients with identifying options towards an ultimate course of action. She wanted to leverage her expertise to help companies succeed. After university Kenny decided to leave her local surf shop bookkeeping job and explore the consulting industry.

At age 23 Cove landed a position at Deloitte's consulting practice in Sydney, a Big Four audit firm with a very strong technology consulting capability. She found Deloitte's advisory practice to be unstuffy compared to the other consulting firms that made her offers like Bain & Company and McKinsey. In addition, Deloitte was famous for supporting and developing its new female employees, an important initiative that could lead to Kendall's success. But after 18 months out in the field assisting numerous Australian start-ups, she found the work not as impactful as she'd hoped. The engagements were more technical in nature and not strategic. At the time Deloitte was making money off the hundreds of data analysts and systems engineers whose main purpose was to support information technology systems. Not the strategic consultative track she wanted. So, Kendall explored going out on her own. She was confident she could start a business and exclusively work outdoors instead of being confined inside an office all day.

With her consulting experience in hand Kendall left Deloitte and started Cove Dive Shop in Manly Beach. Her prior expertise working at a local surf shop along with Kendall's enthusiastic drive couldn't be stopped.

She was confident she could use her energy to attract customers and build a profitable business. Based on her accounting experience it became innate for Kenny to set priorities and constantly think of performing tasks that yielded effective results. From the beginning selling dive equipment and managing inventory was Kenny's sweet spot. As her business grew, she quickly expanded into the more lucrative business of scuba diving instruction, leveraging the shop's product sales and reinvesting profits into scuba excursions. In addition to day trips around the New South Wales coastline, the Cove Dive Shop introduced thrilling three-day diving expeditions to places like Queensland's Great Barrier Reef and Gold Coast.

Cove's most popular diving location was just around the corner at Shelly Beach. The site became a very desirable destination for customers. Only two kilometers from Kenny's shop in Manly, its access was adjacent to the popular North Head Park as the only west facing beach on the eastern coast of Australia. The beach's sandy shores were protected from the ocean swell with a maximum diving depth of about 12 meters. A perfect spot for dive instruction and an excellent spot for beginners. And ideal for repeat business.

Kenny and her staff were certified PADI dive instructors. The PADI System of diver education was based on progressive training that introduced skills, safety-related information, and local environmental knowledge to student divers in stages. Cove Dive Shop's new students would practice using scuba gear in a local rock pool until they were comfortable diving in the ocean. Waves regularly crashed into the pools filling and replenishing them with seawater. A defining feature for open-water dive instruction. The Australian coastline had an abundance of rock pools for her students that were carved out along the coastline from cliffs at the ocean's edges. In Australia's prudish Victorian-era daytime swimming was banned at the beach, prompting wealthy individuals to build pools on the rocky surf coast. The first rock pools were hewn from stones hoisted by convicts in the mid-1800s as a bathing spot for the privileged residents and police officers keeping guard. Young and old swam, splashed, and played there with protection from the ocean waves.

Nestled into Manly's gentle bend of rocks and the pathway to Shelly Beach sat the Fairy Bower rock pools. The perfect site for Cove Dive Shop's PADI "mini dive." The shallow dive helped new divers build confidence and underwater abilities before making the required four open water dives. Kenny and her staff were certified master scuba diver trainers. She had the best and most experienced divers from NSW ocean beaches, great for business and reputation. To qualify her instructors had to:

- Pass a test to become an Open Water Scuba Instructor
- Certify at least 25 new PADI divers
- Hold Five PADI Specialty Instructor Certifications
    - Underwater Navigation, Deep Diver, Boat Diver, Wreck Diver, and Night Diver

After just two years in business, Cove's passion and dream became the most successful dive shop in the Northern Beaches.

~~~

Metcalf arrived at the Ocean Hawks practice facility on Pittwater Road at 8:30am. He was eager to meet with his henchman. The expensive multipurpose training facility was built and maintained with Nigel's personal funds, primarily from the sale of his gold mine and significant gains on trading stocks. The state-of-the-art grounds were complete with a pool, gym, athletics track, rehabilitation facilities, fitness testing equipment, and administrative offices. He wanted to ensure that his footy club was at optimal performance and always in the running to finish first in the league premiership.

Carroll and Frazier were already in the gym throwing around weights with a few other players and coaches. It was off season, but the guys were committed to their personal workout regimen. Metcalf walked into the gym and motioned the two men to follow him into his office. Metcalf was behind his massive mahogany desk, which was void of any paper, when the duo walked in. The office was decorated with championship trophies, silver cups, wooden plaques, rugby memorabilia, and numerous action photos. Metcalf was seated in a wine-red leather chair, which was tufted with buttons and trimmed with brass nail heads. He rose from his chair, walked over behind the two players, and closed the door.

"Sit down, gentleman. Did you find the Aboriginal and our friend from America?" asked Metcalf as he walked back around his desk and sat down.

"Yes, mon. We took care of everything. Well, sort of," said Frazier eager to tell the events that unfolded the night before.

"What do you mean sort of?"

Carroll jumped in. "We waited outside the Manly Pacific like you told us. The American left the hotel and went for a run. So, we followed him."

"Go on," said an impatient Metcalf.

"We were right behind him making sure he didn't see us. But he ran down the center of town where no cars are allowed to go."

"Did he know you were following him?"

"No, sir. We drove around to the other side of town and looked for him near the exit of the ferry terminal. We expected to see the Yank run by. But there was no sight of him. It was crowded and the ferry had just let out. There we people everywhere crossing the street. That's when we saw the Aboriginal."

"You saw who?"

"The Aboriginal bloke, Mr. Metcalf. You were right. The American led us to the Aboriginal. So, we followed him. He was on a bicycle and went up into North Head. We were careful to keep our distance waiting for the right time to take him out."

"Did anyone see you following him?"

"No, the park was empty. No cars were in the lot except ours. We saw the Aboriginal go up a dirt path, so we got out of the car and followed. It was getting dark, and we didn't want to lose him. That's when we saw the American and Aboriginal together," said Carroll.

"What did you do then?"

"We took them out, mon! Shot 'em dead," said Frazier.

"Both of them?"

"Not both of them," continued Carroll.

"Go on."

"Well, we had taken the gun you gave us. As I mentioned to you, I'm a pretty good shot."

"Yes, as you have told me."

"The sun was at our back. So, they weren't able to see us sneak up on them. I had a clean shot on the Aboriginal. I took it and his body fell into the American's arms. I then aimed at the big guy but when I fired, he ducked behind the rocks. We thought he would come out and make a run for it. But there was no movement. By the time we surrounded him, he was gone. He must have jumped."

"He what?"

"I think he jumped, mon. Like a flying bird," exclaimed Frazier.

"Did you see him in the water?"

"No, by the time we got to the edge and looked down he was gone."

"No signs that he survived?"

"There is no way he could have survived. Too high and too many rocks," added Carroll.

"Are you sure he didn't escape you blokes?"

"No way, mon. Nowhere to go. Must have cracked his head on the cliffs and drowned in the water. No signs of anything, mon."

"How about the Aboriginal?" asked Nauti.

"We took care of the body. No one will find it," Carroll assured him.

The two men went on to explain how they got rid of the evidence by weighting down the man's body with rocks, throwing him off the edge of the cliff, and watching the body sink into the ocean. They then provided further details of cleaning the area, sweeping away blood in the dirt, and putting Abbot's bicycle in the boot of the Commodore. Metcalf sat quietly listening to the story. The details appeared so accurate that it must be true.

"Alright, boys. Make sure the American is dead. Go back to the Manly Pacific and see if he returns. I want to make sure this bloke is really gone."

"Yes sir," replied Carroll.

"Don't speak with anyone. Just stake out the place for a day. We don't want people noticing you two hanging around the hotel. If you don't see him by the end of the day, go back to your flat in Pittwater and pack. We need to get you blokes out of the country."

"Where we goin'?"

"You are joining me on a trip back to your homeland."

Chapter 8

"Courage is more exhilarating than fear and in the long run it is easier."
—*Eleanor Roosevelt*

- Darling Harbour
- The NSG Flowchart
- McCord's Last Night in OZ
- Sally Sasso

IT WAS CLOSE to 11:00am before McCord woke up, propping himself up on the couch as a cool steady blast of salty air hit his face. He could hear birds chirping through the open window. Kenny had already retrieved his bags from the hotel and was there for him with a fresh cup of coffee, her face still glowing from being out in the morning sun. She was wearing a cropped teal blue Ocean Hawks t-shirt with the neckline and sleeves cut off, revealing her bikini straps tied around her neck, white seabreeze shorts, and a scuba red Cove Dive Shop hat. Her stomach was tight and tan. McCord didn't remember Kenny looking so stunning, a golden ray of sunshine.

"About time you woke up from your kip," said Cove.

"I'm still breathing," replied Dex, rubbing his eyes open.

"How you feelin'?"

"My ribs are hurting and it's a bit tough to breath, but she'll be right," said Dex as he reached for the coffee and chocolate croissant Kendall had bought him earlier.

"I spoke to Officer Beveridge this morning. They went back up to The Heads but still didn't see any sign of your friend. She wants to meet you up there at 1:00pm."

"Nothing?"

"Nah, mate, she was sharp with me. Like we are wasting her time," explained Kenny.

"Do they think I just swan dived off the cliff and swam with sharks past North Head for my health?"

"Don't mind her. She can be a bit of a gash sometimes. Always has been since we were young," explained Ms. Cove.

"I'll set her straight later. Did you say 1:00pm?"

"Yes, she said don't be late. The Manly Beach PD is a busy department in the summer. You know all the crime that takes place on the peninsula," said Kenny sarcastically.

"OK, thanks. And thank you for the coffee and breakfast, I owe you one. Can I borrow your phone?"

"No problems."

Kenny pulled a cell phone out from her shorts and passed it over to McCord, firmly holding onto it before finally releasing so she could feel his strong touch. She enjoyed having a guest and was happy to help in any way she could. McCord walked outside onto Kenny's balcony and started touching numbers on the phone. He closed the sliding door behind him. Kenny could see McCord explaining to someone on the other end details of yesterday's adventure. She stayed busy fluffing up pillows on her couch, putting away sheets and cleaning, trying to tidy her one-bedroom flat before Dex returned.

After 10 minutes McCord returned inside though the sliding glass doors, deep in thought planning out his day. Dex sat down at the kitchen table and helped himself to another fresh croissant that was lying on the table. He told Kenny he had to meet a friend in Darling Harbour later in the afternoon, then asked her for a ride up to the Heads to meet with Officer Beveridge, a task she was more than happy to perform. They continued with idle chat about McCord's expat assignment in Australia and what he did while living in Manly, finding out that they had mutual friends at the Manly Surf Club. The conversation flowed easily, and Kenny was getting comfortable with her new friend.

The couple left for North Head National Park at 12:15pm, as McCord wanted to get there early to re-trace his footsteps. The traffic in Manly was already thick with tourists arriving for a day at the beach. It was Monday, but the extended holiday weekend was still in full force. Boogie boards and bright towels were overcrowding the streets and walkways. Before leaving Manly, Kenny had stopped by her dive shop near the ferry terminal to ensure her staff was good to be left alone for a few hours. McCord stayed in the front seat of Cove's Jeep. He noticed several customers entering the dive shop. In a few minutes Kenny returned to the Jeep and proudly informed Dex that her store was already buzzing with activity.

They arrived at the North Head parking lot adjacent to Fairfax Lookout less than seven minutes after leaving Kenny's shop. The lot was already a quarter filled with tourists who were blissfully unaware of the previous night's events, and Beveridge was waiting on the bluffs at Fairfax Lookout. McCord and Kenny walked through the paved lot and down the dirt path to meet the MBPD officer, who was alone and looking puzzled.

As the couple approached officer Beveridge shouted, "You mean to tell me you ran and jumped from here to down there?" pointing towards the white-capped ocean below.

"Yes. I started right behind that big rock over there," replied McCord.

McCord led the officer over to the boulder he was hiding behind just 17 hours earlier. There were no signs of the assassination or the assailants, no proof to confirm his statements.

"Right from here?" Dex nodded. "Did you Go Troppo?" asked Beveridge.

"I'm not sure what that means, but no."

"Crazy mate."

"No, I'm not crazy and I am not making this up."

"Well, I'm not sure I believe it."

"See the chip on the rock," noted McCord pointing to the boulder. "That's where the bullet hit, right after they shot and killed my colleague."

"The Aboriginal bloke you talked about?"

"Yes."

"Well. My crew was here all morning, and we couldn't find a trace of any shooting."

"We were right here," said McCord as he was also trying to find any evidence of the assassination.

"OK, and you said you heard the voices of two blokes? But you couldn't see them?"

"That's right. They were speaking some sort of Caribbean, a West Indies accent, maybe Jamaican."

"Were they dark skinned?"

"I assume so."

"Mr. McCord, do you know about Australia immigration laws?"

"Only that it's difficult to get a visa to stay in the county."

"That's right. And there are very few Black men with Caribbean brogues in our town."

McCord was keenly aware that the population of "Non-White" immigrants in Australia was fairly insignificant in numbers. The Australian immigration laws made it difficult for outsiders to enter and stay in the country for any long period of time or as a permanent resident. Most people who weren't indigenous tended to be Asian, Indian or American tourists on vacation, or basketballers and other athletes brought in to improve the local teams.

"OK, I don't really believe your story Mr. McCord, but I'll take down your information in case we have more questions."

"How about a missing person report? I guess you're going to tell me there is some kind of waiting period, like 24 or 48 hours, before I can file a report."

"That's only in the movies, Yank. The waiting period doesn't exist for real police officers. In our country as soon as we know an adult or child is missing, we report it to our local police."

"My misunderstanding, officer."

McCord went on to provide a complete description of Abbot to the best of his recollection. He had only met him twice, at Youngy's memorial service and last night. He provided approximate details of Jiemba's height, weight, and age—and highlighted the Aboriginal design lizard tattoo on his neck. He described what Abbot was wearing, although he couldn't exactly recall the type and color of the bloodstained shirt or pants on the victim. McCord did not know where he lived or who his parents where. He told

Officer Beveridge he'd ask a colleague at KGO to contact the family and have them send the MBPD a photo.

Before the officer left the bluffs, McCord asked about the investigation into the death of his friend Tony Young. Beveridge was taken off guard that he knew about the accident. Dex tried to explain the connection between Abbot and Youngy, but the officer didn't want to hear about it.

"Leave it alone, mate. It was a surfing accident," said Beveridge.

"Yes, I understand, but I believe what happened last night in North Head is related to my friend Tony Young's death."

"Mr. McCord, drowning deaths happen every year to surfers. They happen as a result of heart attacks; head strikes or just an overconfident swimmer. It was just a freak accident." Beveridge didn't want to get into the details of Young's death as there was no autopsy performed on the body. She was informed that the police in Avalon didn't have much to work with. The body had been found covered in jellyfish and masticated, most likely by a school of strong jawed bonito fish.

"Listen, as I said, I don't believe anything happened up here. Have you found any new evidence that my team didn't uncover?"

"No, but how can you be so sure my friend Tony wasn't murdered? It couldn't have been a surfing accident. There was little to no surf that day."

"Because we obtained a closed caption video of your friend at a 7-11 in Mona Vale around 6:00am on the day the body was found. It was clear that he was going for an early morning paddle. His car was loaded with surfboards. We also found his backpack and personal belongings on Avalon Beach."

"Where is his car now?" questioned McCord.

"We never found it. Probably pinched from Avo by some local delinquents."

"You mean stolen?"

"Yes, there's a lot of that going on at the northern beaches. Keeps me up at night," said Beveridge sarcastically.

Officer Beveridge finished taking details from McCord and handed him her card to forward to Abbot's parents. She walked back to her police car even more convinced that McCord's "episode" was some made up incident by a crazed drunken Yank who just went for a late-night swim off Shelly Beach. McCord was angry and feeling isolated from the reality of the situation.

Kenny walked over to Dex and put her hand on his back. "You OK mate?"

"I don't think she believes me."

"She can be a bit stubborn."

"This is real. My friend was murdered, and a man was shot right in front of me. What else do I have to prove?"

"Not sure. I guess she hears all sorts of crazy stories from the visitors on this peninsula," replied Kenny.

"Well, mine is not crazy. It's the truth."

"I know."

The two walked back to Kenny's Jeep in silence, not knowing what else to say about Beveridge's dismissal. They drove out of the park and swiftly headed down the hill to Manly Wharf, where McCord needed to catch a ferry to Sydney to meet the managing partner of KGO at his office near Darling Harbour. Cove's Jeep pulled up to the ferry terminal.

"I'll see you later, right?" asked Kendall.

"Yes, I owe you a nice dinner. It's the least I can do."

"I'm not sure about that, mate. But I'll take you up on the offer."

"Pick someplace nice."

"OK. I have a harbor dive for a small class this afternoon that should be done by 7:00. Let's meet at 7:30," suggested Kenny.

"Name the spot."

"How about we meet at the Steyne and then we can go to dinner from there?"

"Sounds good. Make a reservation somewhere expensive. At least for the price of a hotel," Dex said with a smile.

"Sure will, Derek. Have fun with your accountant friend," said Kendall.

Kenny leaned over and gave McCord a kiss on the cheek before he got out of the Jeep. He smiled and sauntered his way over to the entrance of the ferry terminal.

~~~

The ferry service between Manly Beach and the city has had a range of high-speed vessels, some more successful than others. In the late 20th century, the hydrofoil ferry service, travelling at 32 knots to Circular Quay covered the 10-kilometre journey in 15 minutes, compared to 35 minutes for conventional ferries. The problem was, the daily hydrofoils were travelling at such great speeds that when they entered into rough waters where the Pacific Ocean and Sydney Harbour converge, the impact from waves was causing extensive damage to the rear foil. That coupled with poor management and multiple sea wall collisions made the hydrofoils unreliable. The Sydney JetCat was then introduced as a new class of high-speed transportation.

The Jetcats were custom designed and built for the Manly run. The catamarans were promoted as superior to the larger Hydrofoils on the basis of being lower cost to purchase and more dependable. After a few years in service the Labor government then wanted to cancel the Jet Cat, a bureaucratic order from the result of an inquiry into the business practices of Sydney Ferries. The findings: "if a private operator can deliver better service outcomes than the Government, then Sydney Ferries must be franchised," As a result, in 2014 the Manly Fast Ferry Company secured the contract as sole provider of ferry commuter services from Manly to Circular Quay.

McCord preferred the larger Slow Ferry. The three emerald class slow ferries were named Clontarf, Balmoral, and Fairlight, paying homage to the suburbs of the northern beaches. Dex boarded the Balmoral shortly after 2:00pm.

The harbor ferries were made for daydreaming. To McCord there was something very relaxing about passing Sydney's isolated beaches, colorful coves, beautiful boats, and ending a trip with the spectacular view of the Opera House. He loved the harbor and Sydney for its aesthetics and physical enjoyment. Few great cities in the world offered such unrivaled opportunities for the Four S's: sightseeing, swimming, sailing, and surfing.

DOWNTOWN SYDNEY, NEW SOUTH WALES

EY – 200 George Street (near Essex)
Deloitte – Grosvenor Place – 225 George Street (near Bridge Street)
KGO – 2 Margaret Street (Central Business District)
PWC – One International Towers, Watermans Quay (near Darling Harbour)
KPMG – Three International Towers – 300 Barangaroo Ave (near Darling Harbour)

~~~

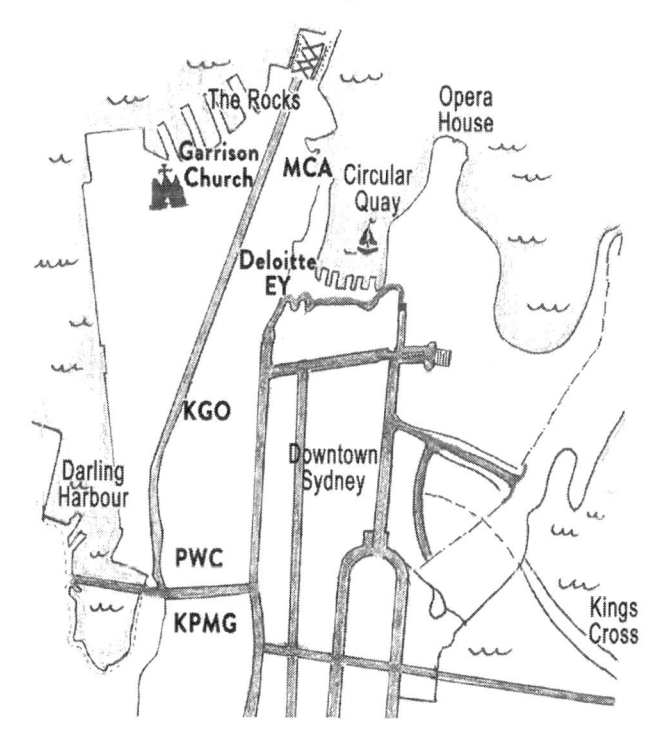

McCord disembarked the ferry in Circular Quay and dodged his way through the crowded streets of downtown Sydney to meet his former colleague, Mark Epper, at KGO's office in the Central Business District—near Darling Harbour. His walk to his old office was longer than normal due to the city bustling with heaps of tourists and shoppers, trying to take advantage of the post Australia Day sales.

For many years Darling Harbour was the working port for Sydney, home to a myriad of finger wharves, shipyards, factories, and warehouses. In 1984, with Australia's bicentennial pending and the country primed to celebrate, Darling Harbour was "returned to the people." The neighborhood was given a massive facelift with public spaces and welcoming attractions. The precinct was formally opened by the Queen of England as part of bicentennial celebrations in 1988. After the 200-year party further attractions were added to its résumé and the area became one of the city's premier entertainment districts, with shops, restaurants, and plazas. At the beginning of the century Darling Harbour played a major role in the 2000 Olympics, hosting five sports events.

McCord arrived at KGO's office before Epper. He presented his New York business card and was escorted by security onto the elevator up to Level 11. McCord was surprised to see a few junior staff members in the conference room working during a long holiday weekend. He recalled six years earlier, during the first month of his expat assignment, when he made an outsider mistake of requesting his staff to work the weekend. The reply was unanimous: "Nah. We don't do that here, mate. She'll be right."

This time there was staff in the office on a holiday weekend. They were working on a significant coordinated international customer proposal. McCord was keenly aware that when a large accounting firm sets its sights on winning a new client, personal schedules were disrupted, even in Australia. The routine audit and tax work is cast aside, and all parties are swept along in the effort. The accountants are turned into commando units planning a raid. Teams gather up-to-the-minute intelligence and check on competitors' capabilities in key cities, trying to find a weakness in their plans. Charts had to be prepared, illustrations completed, and performances videotaped that would be played back to an independent audience. The client presentations had to be smooth, structured, and credible. With a potential lucrative account up for grabs, a client that could generate millions of dollars in fees globally, nothing was left to chance.

McCord enjoyed seeing the activity but stayed away from inserting himself. He sat patiently in the lobby waiting for Epper. He noticed on the table in front of him was a brochure from AMA Australia promoting a Certified Professional in Management program (AMA CPM®). McCord wasn't aware that his favorite training company had a presence in Australia. The 100-year-old American not-for-profit had effectively preached their way of leadership education Down Under. Early in his career McCord had made a conscious decision to train with the American Management Association International. He wanted to become a great manager of people that could drive business results through AMA's proven power skills education: professional effectiveness; relationship management; business acumen, and analytical intelligence.

McCord recognized the value of these skills. He knew all too well from his staffing duties that partners pick people and clients pick professionals they want to work with. His firm and their client management hitting it off could be the deciding factor in one's career, and in winning or losing proposals. McCord understood that at the end of the day accounting is not a numbers game; at its heart it's a people business.

Marc Epper arrived at the office lobby 25 minutes after McCord, a little flustered but happy to see Dex again. Epper had been out of town at his beach house in Nelson Bay, unable to leave his young grandchildren to attend Tony Young's funeral. But when McCord called in the morning and told Epper what happened to him and Abbot, he told his wife that he had leave and go straight to the office. The pitch and toss understood.

~~~

Marc Epper was a process-driven, edgy accountant. When McCord was with Epper, he noticed that everyone around him was having a good time. That philosophy seemed to serve him well through the ranks at KGO and ultimately to the partnership. McCord heard his technical skills were adequate but what separated him from the pack was not only his joviality but also his ability to identify key process improvements that made his clients more efficient, thus more profitable. Even within his own firm he was able to find ways to squeeze cash out of operations and into the hands of his fellow partners.

Epper recognized that, like most public accounting firms, KGO was finding it increasingly difficult and expensive to hire local talent for the daily grind of administrative work. He convinced his partners to delegate all the back-office tasks to nearshore and offshore teams while letting their local employees focus on what they do best—delivering exceptional value to their clients. In the span of three years the offshore staffing solution provided his firm with time for innovation, a renewed focus on profitable activities, and ensured a better work-life balance for all their professionals. As a result, the partners' average work week decreased from 45 to 32 hours. Based on his ability to squeeze out additional profits and other client victories, Epper was ultimately named managing partner of KGO's Sydney office.

"Dex! Owshegoing," bellowed a happy Epper walking into the office.

"I'm hanging in there, Marc. Good to see you again."

"Apologies I didn't see you yesterday. But, you know, family commitments."

"No worries, Marc," stated McCord.

"Sad thing about Youngy. Fuck me dead," exclaimed Epper while shaking his head.

"Yeah, it sucks. He was a good man."

"Hey, I heard you had a good day with Warbo and Austen. Those guys are a bit dangerous," said Epper, trying to change the subject.

"Yes. It was great to get right back into it. It felt like I never left."

"God's country."

"Sure is," replied Dex.

"When you told me what happened last night, I dropped everything. What can I do to help?"

"Well, you know the staff member that I told you about, Jiemba Abbot?"

"Yes, the young Aboriginal bloke."

Marc had only meet Abbot once at one of his traditional weekly lunchtime gatherings for invited staff. The luncheons were a way for Epper to get to know office staff, especially new hires. He would take them to his favorite Malaysian restaurant, Malay Malay. He loved the authentic dishes, especially the spicy noodle dishes of Laksa and Mie Goreng. Marc would order the unsuspecting group the hottest dishes to see which staff member sweated the most. He believed that an individual's personality shines when they are put in awkward situations. Plus, he thought it was funny. Often his super-hot dishes would end with footy club songs and noodles being flung across the table, a by-product from the significant consumption of beer to cool one's mouth down.

"I need access to his workpapers in the network," requested McCord.

"We can do that, mate. After all, you were the one that sent him up there."

"Thanks, Marc. I'm hoping to see something they may have found in India. Before Jiemba was shot he said he uncovered something. I'll like to know what that something is."

"Follow me to my office. I'll log you in on my computer."

"Perfect."

While walking to Epper's office McCord handed him Sergeant Beveridge's card with instructions for Abbot's parents to contact her. Marc confirmed he would have human resources follow-up on this sensitive matter.

"Here, I'm logged in to Abbot's files," said Epper pointing towards his computer. "Go ahead and have a look."

"Thanks, Marc."

"I'll close the door and give you a bit of privacy. Those guys out there can get loud practicing their pitch. Besides, I have to head out and buy a few opals for my wife."

"That's nice of you."

"Ahhh. Our anniversary is next week. It'll keep me out of the doghouse, mate. She loves opals."

"I'm sure her jewelry box is chockers," said McCord.

"Sure is. Actually, we can buy them at a significant discount. One of Youngy's clients owns an opal mine. I get them at his retail shop in The Rocks. Yep. The ole' ball and chain is starting to build up a bit of a collection."

"Nice."

"I guess I'm going to have to figure out who is going to take over the account," said Epper looking down in thought. "Before I go, Dex, do you wannacuppa or a cold drink? The team over there has plenty of liquids to go around. I believe they have a few VBs as well."

"Not yet."

"Well help yourself. And, mate, be careful out there."

"I'll try, Marc, but I can't promise anything," stated McCord with a wry smile.

"All right. Come see us again soon, it's been too long between visits."

"Yes definitely. Marc, thanks again for coming down to the office from your holiday. I appreciate the help."

"No worries."

Epper left his office and headed back towards the elevator bank. McCord turned his attention to the files in the firm's network. He started to read through the workpapers on the computer screen. Abbot's internal control documentation was tight and in accordance with firm guidelines. His draft report on NSG included the standard sections:

- Background and Overview of the Organization
- Scope and Approach
- The Review Period

- A Findings Summary
    - Positive and negative findings
    - Open issues
    - Significant problems
- Final Observations and Conclusion—the 5Cs
    - Criteria, Condition, Cause, Consequence, and Corrective Action with remediation plans and recommendations

The IC report was thorough with very few material weaknesses identified. All was in order until McCord scrolled further down to Exhibit 7 and reviewed NSG's XML data process flowchart that Abbot had prepared. He printed out the flowchart and emailed Abbot's file to himself. McCord looked out the window towards Darling Harbour, muttering to himself, "Barbados?"

INTERNAL CONROL REVIEW: EXHIBIT 7

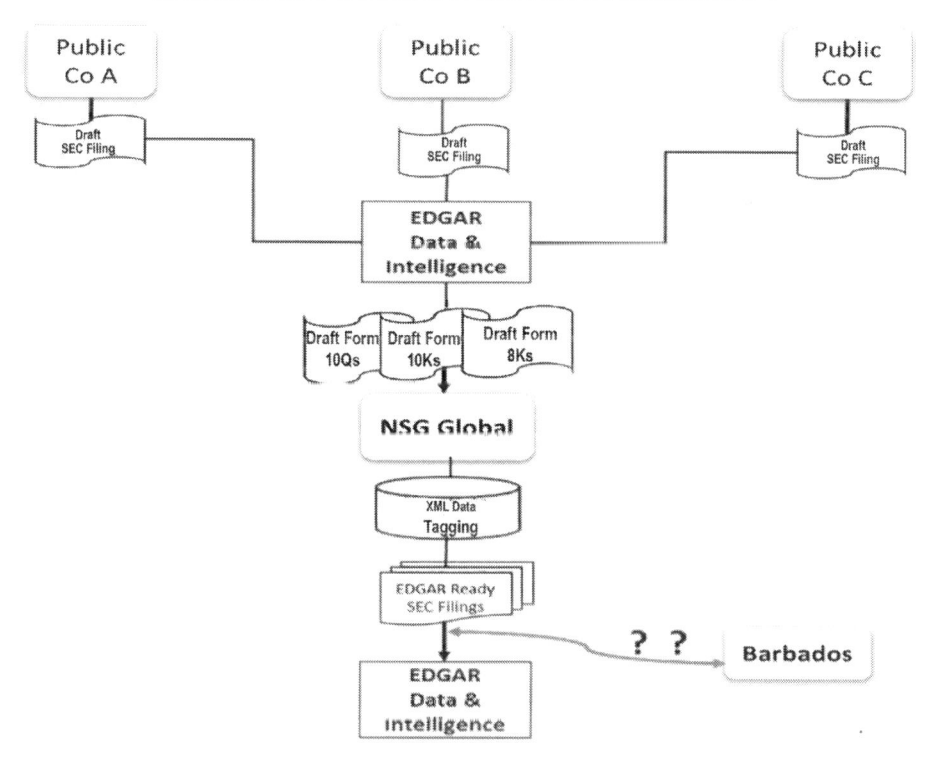

WATSONS BAY, SYDNEY HARBOUR

McCord returned to Manly on the slow ferry rather than the Jet Cat, as he wanted to enjoy one more cruise down memory lane before heading back to the United States in the morning. He arrived at the Hotel Steyne at 7:15pm and headed up to the rooftop bar, securing a good location to enjoy the spectacular view of waves crashing onto Manly Beach. On the televisions were lawn bowling and snooker matches. McCord ordered a Tooheys. Shortly after his first sip two young women moved up beside him. They were on holiday from Melbourne. McCord wanted to start their night off in a hospitable fashion, so he paid for their drinks. They chatted for a little while and then the two women left the bar. A local bloke in a torn t-shirt, old cargo shorts, and work boots sitting next to McCord leaned over.

"Hey, mate. We don't do that in Australia."

"What do mean?" McCord replied.

"Buy Sheilas a drink."

"Why not?"

"They might get used to it."

"I'll remember that for next time."

"That's just the rules, mate. You don't want to make us blokes look bad," stated the local Aussie as he turned his attention back to the snooker match on the tele.

From his days living in Australia McCord knew there was an unwritten rule that you don't buy Aussie girls drinks. God forbid you would even light a woman's cigarette. But he routinely broke from that rule to let his American charm shine through. He understood that most Australian men were chauvinistic, it was just part of their DNA.

Kendall walked into the Steyne a little late at 7:45pm wearing a white sundress, her blond hair flowing in the ocean breeze. Many of the patrons turned their heads and a few of the locals waved hello. McCord noticed she was wearing makeup that accentuated her blue eyes. He was still wearing his NY Athletic Club collared shirt and golf shorts from earlier in the day when he met Officer Beveridge at the Heads. On his large feet were new white Nike sneakers that he purchased on sale in Darling Harbor.

McCord got up from the bar stool and greeted Kenny with a gentle hug, "You look nice."

"Thanks. Sorry I'm a little late. My dive went longer than expected."

"Can I buy you a drink?" offered Dex as he glanced at the local bloke next to him.

"That's OK, I'll wait. I made dinner reservations for 8:30pm and it's a bit of a trip to get to the restaurant."

"Where we going?"

"Well, you told me to pick somewhere nice. So, I did. But let's keep it a surprise. All I can tell you is we need to catch a water taxi."

"I'm game," said Dex excitedly.

McCord tipped the bartender generously, again breaking one of Australia's unwritten rules. The two left the Steyne Hotel in a hurry and headed down Manly Corso towards the ferry terminal. They arrived at a small dock between the wharf and the Skiff Club, where a line of water taxis were docked. Kenny motioned to one of the small boats and the captain immediately started up his engine.

"Where are you going, Kenny?" shouted the driver as the couple walked down the dock. He appeared to know Cove well.

"Watsons Bay, Doyles on the Beach."

"Excellent choice."

"Thanks, Johnny, this is Derek McCord. He's from New York."

"Wow. Nice to meet you. How long are you staying in Manly?"

"I'm in town for only three days. Unfortunately, I have to leave tomorrow," replied McCord.

"Too bad. Well at least you were here for Australia Day. Always a good party. Please sit down and relax. It's a beautiful evening. Enjoy."

The water taxi pulled away from the wharf and headed out towards Sydney. The driver navigated his way through moored boats and away from shore.

"Great choice," said Dex, turning to Kenny. "It's one of my favorite places."

"You've been there before?"

"Yes, but it was a long time ago," noted McCord.

"I hope you don't mind the location. It's a bit pricy."

"Nah, it's the least I can do."

"Good. I was hoping that I wasn't being too presumptuous," said Kenny.

"You only live once."

The ride from Manly to Watsons Bay wharf was only 15 minutes. Kenny and Dex were fairly quiet on the water taxi ride to the restaurant, no words needing to be said. The enduring sunset provided spectacular harbor views to fill any void of conversation. As they approached Doyles the boat slowed down, passing Watsons' old fishing village and Lady Bay Beach, which permits nude bathing. The pilot searched for a spot to dock, then Kenny and Dex were welcomed at the end of the pier and escorted to the restaurant by a sharply dressed host. McCord was starving and looking forward to a satisfying meal at Doyles. The restaurant with its unique location and spectacular views was one of the most celebrated seafood locations in Sydney, a favorite for locals, as well as international tourists and many visiting celebrities.

The waiter seated the couple at a table outside where they could watch the lights in the harbor. McCord told Kenny that he recalled being at the restaurant four years ago for a fundraising dinner. And that at that time the food was fantastic. As Dex sat down, he snuck a quick look over his shoulder and noticed Mel Gibson sitting just two tables over. McCord's man crush became immediately obvious when he kept glancing behind

Cove to catch a glimpse of the Hollywood star. Gibson who was born in Peekskill, New York but was thought of as Australian since he moved there when he was 12 years old. After Gibson's success in the Mad Max films, he started a typical large Aussie family with his now ex-wife. He was seated with two of his six sons; they were feasting on a six-layer seafood tower.

"Do you see who that is sitting behind me?" asked Dex.

"Yeah, that's Mel Gibson. No bother," replied Kenny.

"That was my dad's favorite actor."

"He's just a normal bloke. No different than you and me."

"Can you take a quick photo of me with him in the background. Pops will get a kick out of that."

"That's not what we normally do here in Australia, mate, but hand me your phone." McCord handed Kenny his cell and she discreetly snapped a photo, making believe the focus was on Dex.

"This one's for you father."

During dinner Cove reminded McCord that Australians have a welcoming and laid-back culture and a general lack of interest in what others do for a living. If people elevate themselves too highly, they are likely to be cut down. If a celebrity expects to be treated as exceptional, many Australians will just not oblige. She believed that the Australian psyche was a direct result of an eclectic melting pot of descendants—from petty crime convicts to gold prospectors and people fleeing oppressive social hierarchies. The Aussies and Kenny didn't put a lot of value on the class system. She explained that in America one might call a guy to have something fixed, but in Australia that person is a tradesman.

The couple's delectable dinner selections were choreographed to perfection. They started with a dozen oysters. Kenny then had John Dory served with the head on and McCord the Tasmanian salmon fillet. For dessert they shared a fresh fruit platter and meringue-based pavlova. They also drank three bottles of Hunter Valley chardonnay. Kenny spoke about her earlier dive in the harbor and how she had students feed the barracuda sea urchins from their hands. McCord recounted his visit to the office and review of the internal control workpapers, highlighting Abbot's notation of Barbados in the XML flowchart. Kenny had no idea what he was talking about but smiled and nodded. They both avoided any conversation about boyfriends and girlfriends.

"Thanks again for helping me with everything Kenny," acknowledged McCord. "You really saved me from drowning out there."

"Oh, you were good, mate. It was a little shocking seeing you off Shelly but all good."

"Yeah, your class certainly has a great story tell."

"I just wish I could have done more to help you convince officer Beveridge about your friend," stated Cove.

"You've already done more than enough. Besides she already had her mind made up."

"Perhaps if I sent today's dive class to North Head's inlet, we could have found something."

"Like Abbot's body? I don't think that would've been a pleasant sight. Plus, the rip current is way too dangerous. Last night's undertow was extremely strong," recalled Dex.

"But maybe it would have been OK. The ocean currents by the Heads are density-driven and differ down low compared to the surface currents. Some areas even develop whirlpools," explained Kenny.

"Even so, it wouldn't have been safe. So please don't think twice about it. There's nothing anybody could have done."

"Well, I'm really sorry about your colleague. Also, your mate from Manly. It sounds like you two were really close."

"Yeah, Tony was a great guy. It's all just very sad and confusing," said McCord while shaking his head.

"Hang in there, Derek. Sometimes things just don't make sense and get really hard. But as my mother used to tell me, no one has a rainbow until they've had the rain," smiled Kenny.

"Yeah, I guess brighter days are ahead."

~~~

The two new friends finished up their last bottle of wine and headed over to the water taxi. The boat trip back to Manly Beach from Watsons Bay was calm and swift. After returning to the wharf, they exited the vessel and slowly strolled down Fairlight Walk towards the Manly Art Gallery. Both were enjoying the evening view of the starlit harbor, appreciating their time together and the earlier dining experience. Kenny's Jeep was parked a few blocks from the wharf in front of her dive shop, a short five-minute walk. Once the couple reached the Jeep they slowly climbed in and drove off to Balgowlah. They were both ready for a restful night's sleep, tired and a little tipsy from the steady flow of wine.

They arrived back at Cove's flat shortly after 11:30pm. It had been a productive day for both of them. Before leaving for the evening Kendall had put clean sheets and a large pillow on the couch. It looked very inviting to McCord, and he was eager for some rest. Before leaving Dex alone, Kenny thanked him for a memorable night with a shy smile. She had put on her silky pajama pants and white sports bikini top, the definition of her midsection caught his eyes, and it was hard to stop looking. Her body was nothing short of spectacular. There was a little bit of an uncomfortable silence between the two before Kendall stepped into her bedroom. McCord pulled out a clean pair of gym shorts and t-shirt from his luggage, brushed his teeth and tumbled onto the couch. He was still reflecting on the evening and tried to go to sleep, but the thought of Kenny on the other side of the wall was keeping him wide awake.

Kenny was in her bedroom lying in bed, thinking about Dex alone on the couch. It was starting to drive her crazy. Two grown adults attracted to each other should be able to sleep together, she thought. It felt like a silent conversation, where, if she listened closely enough, she could imagine Dex thinking the same. That some warm, fun lovemaking with the new friendship they had formed would be a whole lot better than sleeping alone tonight. Just the thought and hope of McCord exploring her and loving the taste and scent of her started to push Kenny to the edge. She thought and thought, "I don't think I can wait."

Kendall got up from her bed and peeked out the door. She saw McCord awake as well, maybe thinking about her. He smiled at her as she moved across the room and very smoothly slipped under his covers to snuggle up next to him. No words were spoken at first, then they started to kiss. Cove felt both exposed and at home in her body. Getting to experience an encounter with this stranger, even if it is a casual encounter, would be remarkable.

"You didn't think I could leave you alone tonight, did you?" asked Kenny as she moved in still closer. "I knew it would be hard," kidded Dex. Kenny felt a kind of warmth from McCord that only his tongue could bring. She went through a wide range of emotions from lust and pleasure to helplessness and fear to excitement and gratitude. But it was more than just the physical warmth that excited Kenny. It was how all they had been through the previous day seemed somehow to be wrapped up in his touch, which now lifted her to sheer pleasure. She was no longer thinking, just reacting in kind to bring her partner along with her for this impassioned ride. It felt like an otherworldly experience, her body reacting to his touch. She started to imagine how to enact that kind of pleasure onto him, over and over again.

Their connection continued on through the night, their bodies intermittently tangled in the covers, mastering the art of lovemaking on the couch—two bodies becoming one, where one's pleasure became the other's pleasure, too. Their souls were colliding, pure delight rushing through their organisms, if only for a few moments in time. At the end both were completely satisfied as they took nice long deep breaths, fully exhausted, and elated. McCord put his muscular arm around her and pulled her naked body close to his warm chest, where she was perfectly happy to snuggle in. Cove fell blissfully off to sleep. "What a three days," Dex thought as he settled into the most restful sleep a man could ever want.

The morning came quickly, and McCord had overslept after a memorable night. He was still asleep when the Uber arrived to take him to the airport. Kenny had to use all her strength to shake and wake up McCord. He had been totally wiped out from his eventful three-day visit to OZ.

"Wake up. Your car is here." McCord quickly got dressed, clumsily finished packing his luggage and kissed Kenny.

Then Dex gave her a big warm hug and said, "Thank you for all the help and the great evening. You are an extraordinary woman." And said goodbye.

~~~

McCord's Uber ride to the airport took longer than normal due to heavy traffic after the long holiday weekend. He arrived at the international air terminal and passed through security with an hour to spare, time to buy coffee, a breakfast sandwich, and a newspaper. After boarding McCord found his seat in United business class and readied himself for the long 17-hour intercontinental flight to Los Angeles. He settled in and started reading the *Sydney Morning Herald* from back to front. Like the *New York Post* he enjoyed reading their sports section first. He noticed that the Australian Cricket team was playing test matches next week against the West Indies team in Barbados and thought, "That's a strange coincidence."

The direct flight from Sydney to Los Angeles would fly though all seven Pacific Ocean time zones and arrive around lunchtime Pacific Standard Time. McCord wasn't happy he had to fly United Airlines home, as they didn't have the extra amenities that Virgin had. The plane food wasn't as good as the trip to Australia, but he was able to sweet talk the flight attendant into giving him two dinners.

After McCord fueled up on the two courses he went back to thinking. First he thought about his night with Kendall Cove, but then his mind went to his friend Tony Young. He felt responsible for Tony's death. McCord was the one who sent him to India, there was no questioning that. He also had no doubt at all that Youngy's trip to India was connected to his "accident," no matter what Officer Beveridge thought. She was convinced his death was a drowning, "Leave it alone mate, it was a surfing accident." McCord was not convinced. He felt a flood of anger, it raged through him, something he hadn't felt since playing football back in college.

Somewhere over the Pacific Ocean McCord called Steve Walsh at EDGAR Data & Intelligence. McCord wanted to inform Steve of his near-death experience but opted to hold back the story of his brush with death and just update Walsh on the internal control findings at NSG. He thought it may be better to tell him about the assassinated senior accountant later, as the Aussie passengers around him may think he had "a few roos loose."

In a hushed plane voice McCord told Walsh what his colleagues uncovered in India, the lack of cooperation by apprehensive employees, the movement of EDGAR documents, an unexplained reporting line to Barbados, and an obstinate Managing Director. He went on to describe events surrounding the suspicious drowning death of his friend after arriving back from Bengaluru. McCord left out details of Abbot's murder and his own leap of faith from North Head. Walsh listened and said little, but he had one piece of advice: "Dex if you want to know what happened to your Australian friend, follow the cash, that will lead you to the facts."

McCord still had a full day ahead of him on the plane, plenty of time to think about Walsh's advice. "Follow the cash," he thought to himself. "How is NSG moving cash to or out of Australia, India, and Barbados?" The light bulb went off—wire transfers that would avoid questions from the tax authorities. McCord was not an international tax expert, so he'd need to speak with a specialist. He pulled out his cell phone and called ahead to Los Angeles.

After his phone call and a third beer, McCord fell asleep while watching *Sopranos* re-runs on the seat's small screen. He woke up seven hours later but was still five hours away from Los Angeles. The final third of any intercontinental flight is the longest leg, as the anticipation of arrival seems to slow down time. The formulation for flight travel, Time = Distance divided by Speed adjusted for Direction ($t = d/s$), sure doesn't factor in boredom.

~~~

LOS ANGELES, CALIFORNIA

The international flight eventually arrived in Los Angeles at 2:00pm. McCord's connecting flight was not until 10:50pm, so he had eight hours to kill before his flight to New York. While on the plane he had called an old friend to join him for lunch in Los Angeles, a tax accountant from KPMG he met six years ago in Australia. She had recently left the Big Four to open her own high-net-worth tax practice.

~~~

Sally Sasso was a talkative tax accountant, a rarity in the profession. Most tax accountants are introverted and extremely focused, Sally was the opposite. After receiving a BBA in Accounting at Stanford University, Ms. Sasso went to San Diego State law school. She had her sights on being a tax lawyer, but after graduating law school she didn't want to study and sit for the bar as she had too busy a social life. For Sasso attending prep courses for a legal diploma was not a high priority. Instead, she joined KPMG's LA office working in their high-net-worth tax practice, where she loved hob-knobbing with celebrities and the elites.

Two years into Sasso's career, after completing hundreds of individual tax returns and advising high maintenance clients, she was offered an assignment in Sydney for a year. McCord was not sure if it was Sally's request or if the partners just needed her to leave the office for a while. Sasso's gift of gab, while an asset, was sometimes annoying. If you ask Sally, her story was that she wanted to leave California to be near a wealthy Aussie stud she met on the Los Angeles night circuit.

When Sasso arrived in Australia, she discovered that her prince charming was not only married, but also had a small child. Sally was heartbroken, and the bloke received quit a lengthy lecture, but in the end, she was happy to stay in Sydney for a change of scenery and Down Under escapades. At KPMG's Asia-Pacific tax practice, she was assigned to consult on international transfer pricing, not as exciting as mingling with wealthy LA movie stars, but interesting, nonetheless.

When McCord first arrived in OZ he stumbled upon Sally and her expatriate friends. At the time he didn't know many people and hanging out with U.S. nationals was as close to home as he could get. He enjoyed their company, although a few were quirky, but he made some good friends. The group helped him find his flat in Manly Beach as well as his furniture. Sally would tell McCord, "The beach is the only place to live," and she was with him when he bought his first Speedo, but he did his best to ignore the innuendos and keep their friendship at a distance.

After Sasso completed her required one year of service in Australia she returned to Los Angeles. Upon her return, the KPMG partners assigned her to their international tax practice, not Sasso's first choice. Sally didn't like corporate taxes or documenting sophisticated tax schemes, she loved socializing and interacting with eccentric high-net-worth people. After just five months back in the U.S. Sasso started her own tax practice, capitalizing on her bubbly personality and social contacts. Within a year she was able to scale her start-up. Sally's clients loved her, and the demand for her tax services and friendship was so great that she had to hire five full-time employees almost immediately. She was now her own boss and manager of her busy social schedule.

~~~

McCord texted Sally as soon as the planes wheels were down at LAX. He quickly passed through customs and headed out to the curb for pick up. Outside it was a typical sunny California day. Sally pulled up to the arrivals curb 25 minutes later in a red convertible Mustang, wearing a Hermes scarf around her head of auburn hair and oversized Dior sunglasses. Sally was freely engaged on her iPhone, pointing her finger up in the air to signal McCord to wait a second while she finishes up a call. McCord overheard the conversation.

"Yes, Doris, she is a little bitch. But there is a lot of money at stake, and she's concerned that her inheritance will disappear," Sally said while smiling at Dex.

"OK…OK. I'll pick you up tomorrow for lunch and we can discuss it in more detail. I've got to run. Bye-bye, sweetie."

Sally jumped out of the car and gave McCord a big hug. The last time they saw each other was two years ago when McCord was in LA for a conference. She was happy to see him.

"How are you, Dexter darling?"

"Hanging in there. Thanks for picking me up."

"Anytime for you!"

"How's your company doing?" McCord asked politely.

"I'll have to tell you all about it. I'm having so much fun! Jump in, I'm going to take you to a great little spot overlooking the marina in Santa Monica," Sally said excitingly.

McCord awkwardly got into the small Mustang, grateful that the top was down so he didn't have to hunch over during the drive. Sally pulled away from the curb while changing her playlist to a Tom Petty song. Sally loved Tom Petty. After weaving in and out of midday LA traffic the Mustang pulled up to a fancy bistro. The valets appeared to know Sally well. She must be a regular, Dex thought. The host promptly seated the couple at a table outside overlooking a marina. Sasso loved showing off the view and counting all the sailboats and yachts, future clients she thought.

"I come here all the time. The food is wonderful," touted Sally.

"Great, I'm starving. The meals on the plane were very average."

"I know. I always bring my own food onboard when I travel."

"Thanks again for picking me up. What've you been up to lately?" asked McCord, knowing it may be a lengthy conversation.

"Well. I have a client whose 85-year-old husband passed away and my 65-year-old widow friend has now inherited a number of significant IRAs. The bank told her she cannot roll over the IRAs into her name. I come in and say they're wrong. She absolutely can roll over the IRAs. Such idiots."

Sally continued without taking a breath, "I mean, strictly speaking, she can't roll the old IRA over into her own name. However, she most definitely has the option to elect to make the IRA her own IRA. The real issue is, does my 65-year-old widow friend get to reset the required minimum distribution based on her current age? The answer, Dex, is yes. A widower can roll over the funds into her own name, but she will not be able to take required distributions until she reaches age 72. Exciting stuff, Dex."

"Yeah, real exciting Sally. Sounds like you found a nice little niche for yourself," replied an uninterested McCord.

"It's crazy at times, and I sure meet a lot of wacky characters. And when you throw in disappointed stepchildren that believe the inheritance belongs to them, it starts getting really interesting," continued Sasso.

McCord let Sally finish her crab cocktail and go on about the benefits of tax planning and the excitement of owning her own firm. After 45 minutes she finally took time off from speaking. There was a brief moment of silence for McCord to ask a question. "What do you know about international tax treaties?"

"Treaties and transfer pricing were my expertise when I was in Australia," declared Sally. "What do you want to know?"

"Do you know if Australia has any tax treaties with Barbados?"

"That's an odd question but I believe most likely yes. I know they recently moved away from the monarchy and are now an independent republic, but they are still part of the Commonwealth. The Commonwealth honors tax treaties that allows cash to move freely back and forth between countries," lectured Sally.

Sasso continued to explain that tax treaties are essentially agreements between two countries that allow individuals and corporations to avoid double taxation of income. The treaties permit organizations to freely exchange money and exclude all amounts of income on an individual or corporation's local tax return. This in turn would reduce the tax liability because you do not have to pay taxes in every country on the amounts being transferred. Sally went on to say that Australia and the United States had tax treaties with many countries throughout the world. She noted that the British Commonwealth has the largest network of tax treaties that reflect its long economic and political history of global trade and investment. Sally pointed out that many countries can move around cash freely without questions, especially in developed countries, like Barbados, which leveraged their tax treaties with the intention of boosting economic growth.

McCord and Sasso stayed at the bistro chatting and reminiscing until 7:00pm. The sun was starting to set, and the dinner crowd was arriving, which indicated it was time to leave the restaurant and head back to the airport for his flight. Sasso dropped McCord off three hours before his 10:50pm United Airlines red eye. It was more time than he needed for a domestic flight, but Dex could use an escape from the nonstop conversation. Although he appreciated the captivating time listening to Sasso and her latest escapades, she was a real LA girl.

"Thanks again for taking care of me during the layover. It would have been extremely boring sitting in the terminal."

Sally looked at him and winked, "I just wished you could have stayed overnight."

"Maybe next time."

"Oh, I hope so."

"See you later, Mustang Sally." McCord got out of the car and waved goodbye.

Sasso's car pulled away as she turned up the volume to Tom Petty's *American Girl*.

Chapter 9

"In the business world, the rearview mirror is always clearer than the windshield."
—*Warren Buffett*

- Change of Control
- XBRL – eXtensible Business Reporting Language
- MoMath
- Liv Watson

Stamford, Connecticut

THE 5-AND-A-HALF-HOUR red-eye flight back to New York was an easy one, especially after spending 17 hours on the plane from Sydney. McCord slept most of the way and felt surprisingly energized when he arrived at JFK. It was 7:00am and he wanted to see Steve Walsh right away. He ordered an Uber to take him directly to Stamford, CT.

While McCord was in Australia a significant event had occurred with his client. Falcone Capital had orchestrated a bid to sell EDGAR Data & Intelligence to MA Barton Financial Printers, and Walsh had just been informed that there was no room for two CFOs. McCord expected Walsh to be upset, but he wasn't, it was just the opposite.

"Dex, you won't always be a public accountant," Walsh lectured. "Make certain you have a bulletproof employment agreement. After your house the most important asset you have is your change of control clause. Walsh pulled out his agreement and handed it over to McCord to read the termination clause out loud:

> Termination provision: In the event that (i) there is a change of control of the Company or the Agreement is terminated by either the Employee or the Company for whatever reason the Company shall pay to the Employee**,** in addition to the payment of unpaid base salary, and accrued bonus and benefits payable to the Employee through the date of termination of employment, **an amount equal to 2.99 years worth of the Employee's base salary as in effect immediately prior to such termination.** In addition, the Company shall also, during the 2.99 years following Employee's termination (i) maintain health benefits for the Employee and his dependents for such period or until Employee

obtains full-time employment with an employer that provides comparable health coverage; (ii) continue other benefit payments for such period; (iii) allow the Employee to elect to make contributions to the Company's 401k Plan, and (iv) allow Employee's stock options and other stock awards under the Company's stock option plans to immediately vest and remain exercisable for the period of the lesser of (i) the original term of the stock option or (ii) five years.

"Wow, that doesn't suck," noted McCord.

"Ensure you have that change of control provision, Dex. Not only does it provide you with a nice fat check, but it also keeps you from accepting a stupid and undesirable job. You can be patient with your job search." explained Walsh, "It also gives you a little time to work on your golf game."

"I guess you can practice your drive and putting for a while," commented Dex.

"Yep. I think I'll be OK, Dex," said Walsh smiling. "The stock price and valuation for the purchase is fairly high. These guys are going to owe me a lot of money."

"Must be nice."

"Getting my handicap down to single digits, baby. Let me know when you're ready to take me on."

"Sure will," replied Dex.

Walsh and McCord turned their attention back to Tony and Jiemba's discoveries in India. McCord told Walsh about the attack on him at North Head and what he found in the audit workpapers. Walsh had a tough time comprehending the events surrounding McCord's visit to Australia but was happy to hear Dex wasn't hurt or worse. McCord continued the conversation by showing Steve the flowchart Abbot had prepared, and the narrative included in his internal control report. Pointing out the "?" affixed next to Barbados, with the open question:

"Final 3rd party Quality Review?" Walsh was not aware of this third-party process.

"Dex, you need to track down where the XBRL statements are sent after being completed by NSG."

McCord wasn't completely sure what Walsh meant. He had heard about XBRL but wasn't proficient in the topic.

"XBRL?"

"The XML tagged numbers that we send to the SEC on behalf of our customers," explained Steve.

"Oh, that's right, your clients' 10Ks and 10Qs that are being converted into machine readable records," responded McCord.

"That's correct, Sherlock. Not only their annual and quarterly reports but also their Form 8K earnings releases and material news events."

"Confidential documents."

"Very confidential. Dex, as you know our customers rely on us to file their SEC reports in a timely manner, it's critical that we do. Our operations here in the United States and at the partner's facility in India need to function flawlessly. Find out where and why these files are being sent to in Barbados. And let's hope this is just NSG completing a final QA process. If not, and if someone is receiving the XBRL tagged documents from our Indian friends, then what the hell are they doing with them?"

"OK, I'll find out. I'm on it," confirmed McCord.

"Our clients' information is extremely valuable, Dex. I hate to think what a trader or broker could do with a sneak peek of their information."

"Steve, didn't you say if you control information, you control the world?"

"Yes, smart ass, but our clients' information can only be disclosed to the public at the same time. If it gets into the wrongs hands it would be an extremely costly mistake. It would cost us millions."

"I understand."

"Dex, I need you go to Barbados. Complete a little research on companies down there before you go, see if you can find this partner of NSG's before everything blows up!"

McCord was one step ahead of Walsh. He had opened his laptop and googled "Barbados + SEC filings + financial statements."

"The Barbados government's budget," McCord read aloud.

"That's not it," replied Walsh. "See if there are any technology firms in Barbados."

McCord typed in "Barbados + technology + software development." The first page of search results listed an article about a software development company bringing workers in from India and training the local population. The news clip was dated from over 15 years ago. McCord looked further at the Google results located at the bottom of the page and saw the company name and city of a local technology company.

McCord read the name out loud, "Green Shade$ LLC, Bridgetown, Barbados."

"How about this company, Steve?" said Dex as he turned his laptop around.

"Never heard of them."

"There's not a lot of information on their website. It's privately held, and it looks like they focus on software development, but they also have an investment division for retirement funds."

"Well, get your ass down there and see if they know anything about XBRL or SEC filings or NSG in India. Perhaps there's a connection," noted Walsh.

"OK. I'm not 100% versed on XBRL but I'll do some research," confessed McCord.

"I suggest you learn something quick. Basically, think of it like bar coding financial statements. A universal standard, like the adoption of UPC product codes."

McCord googled the history of bar coding and noted his results to Walsh: "It says here that bar codes began appearing on products in the

1970s. Shortly thereafter congestion in the supermarket check-out lines disappeared." Dex went on, "According to PwC, bar codes saved $17 billion annually in the domestic retail industry alone."

[barcode image: 0 123456 789012, labeled U.P.C. Company Prefix and Item Reference Number]

"You got the idea. But learn about XBRL, not bar codes!"

"Yes. OK."

"Good. You need to get your ass on a plane as soon as possible, I'll arrange for my assistant to book the flight and hotel."

"Happy to do so, Steve. I'll find out who these guys are."

"Please do. We need to know what the fuck is going on, and one more thing," continued Walsh. "Have you read MA Barton's risk factor in their 10K?"

"The company that's going to acquire you? No, I haven't," replied McCord.

"Well, what's happening in Barbados may be a big problem. It could de-rail the acquisition of ED&I. Read this…"

Walsh turned around his computer screen and showed McCord the latest MA Barton Form 10K filing. He pointed to the section titled Company Risk Factors, the disclosure Walsh identified read:

> *Our failure to maintain the confidentiality, integrity, and availability of our systems, software, and solutions could seriously damage our reputation and affect our ability to retain clients and attract new business.*

Maintaining the confidentiality, integrity, and availability of our systems, software, and solutions is an issue of critical importance for us and for our clients and users who rely on our systems to prepare regulatory filings and store and exchange large volumes of information, much of which is proprietary, confidential, and may constitute material nonpublic information for our clients. Inadvertent disclosure of the information maintained on our systems (or on the systems of the vendors on which we rely) due to human error, breach of our systems through hacking or cybercrime, or a leak of confidential information due to employee misconduct could seriously damage our reputation and could cause significant reputational harm for our clients.

"That's not good," noted McCord.

"Yes, it's fucked up!" grumbled a concerned Walsh. "Companies hate any type of reputation risk, an issue like this may blow up the entire sale. Dex, get on a plane to Barbados as soon as you can. Find out what the hell is happening down there."

"I'm on it!"

McCord left Walsh's office in a hurry. He knew it was time to leave. The door slammed behind him. Dex could hear the constant stream of vulgarities behind the glass door as he walked down the hall. Walsh wanted his company, EDGAR Data & Intelligence, sale to go through. He had an airtight employment agreement that would pay him handsomely. McCord was well aware that Steve also had other important and lucrative components in his agreement such as equity awards, benefit plans, bonuses due, and tax equalization for significant cash payouts. Tony's and Jiemba's discovery could jeopardize Walsh's millions from exchanging hands.

For something provocative see Exhibit 6: Common Compensation Terms in a CFO Employment Agreement

~~~

NEW YORK, NEW YORK

McCord left EDGAR Data & Intelligence at approximately 1:00pm, transported to the Stamford Metro North train station by the office facility manager. He caught the next train to 125th street in Harlem. While on the train McCord called Stacy Atchinson and asked if it was OK to come over for a visit. She enthusiastically said yes and told Dex she wanted to hear all about his trip, but only had a few hours before heading to LaGuardia for an early evening flight to Chicago. McCord wanted to spend more time with Stacy but understood the demands of the accounting professions. He wanted to cuddle up with her, he also needed to share his quest with someone.

The ride from Stamford to New York arrived in the city later than McCord intended. Shortly after his arrival in Manhattan he hailed a yellow taxi to a corner bodega near Stacy's apartment on 74th Street, where he purchased a bouquet of flowers. McCord was still feeling a little guilty about his encounter with Kendall Cove in Balgowlah. Also, he had missed Stacy while he was away. It was a new feeling for him, he couldn't get out of his head her PB&J: Passion, Beauty, and Joy.

After arriving at the brownstone, McCord nonchalantly waited for someone to open the outside door. He wanted to surprise Stacy. Within seconds one of the residents came strolling out the door. He knew that if you look nice and pretend you are fidgeting for a key most NYC residents living in secure apartments hold the door open when they walk out, and it worked.

McCord entered the apartment building and walked up three flights of stairs, still carrying luggage from his Australia trip. He knocked on Stacy's door, and the peep hole went light and dark again. The door opened with Stacy smiling, wearing yoga pants and a U Penn t-shirt. She looked fantastic, tall, slim, and essential. Stacy was happy to see Dex.

"I'm back," said McCord holding his bouquet of flowers.

"About time, I thought you were going to stay in Australia forever."

"Not this time," replied McCord.

"Are these for me?" Stacy said excitedly.

"Of course, I handpicked them myself."

"Sure you did. I'll put them in a vase. Come in, come in."

McCord followed her into the apartment.

"These are beautiful, you're such a player," Stacy exclaimed as she pulled Dex into her arms and kissed him on the lips.

The couple moved past the alley kitchen and into the living room, still kissing. Her friend from EY was standing in front of them, guzzling from a water bottle, recognizing it was time to go for a run. McCord had met her at The Five Lamps on trivia night just over a week ago. The young accountant was wearing oversized running shorts, a tank top over a sports bra, and cross-trainers. The couple didn't notice she was standing there.

"Uh hum. Uh hum. Good seeing you again, Derek," said Stacy's friend.

The lovers stopped making out.

"Nice to see you as well," McCord forgot her name.

"I was just leaving, you two probably want to be alone."

"Thanks," the couple said in unison.

"I'll see you later, Stace. Enjoy your trip to Chi town."

"Yeah, girlfriend. Have a great run," replied Stacy.

"Goodbye, you guys," she said as she walked out the door, excited for her friend.

Stacy's friend left the apartment in a hurry. McCord embraced Stacy with a tight hug, leaned down, and gave her a long passionate kiss. He loved being with Stacy and wanted to release the guilt from the opportunity that presented itself just 40 hours earlier. McCord wasn't a guy who was usually in touch with his feelings, however this time he was. He knew their relationship was by no means exclusive, but it seemed to be heading that way.

"Well, that's a nice welcome, I missed you, too. Tell me what happen Down Under."

"It's a long story and you're not going to believe half of it."

"I have two hours before I head to the airport, join me while I'm packing and start from the beginning," Stacy said eagerly.

McCord started with meeting his old friends, Warbo and Austen, at the airport on Australia Day. He then went on to describe his visit to Harry's Café de Wheels, the band playing music in front of the Opera House, and the barbie on the beach. He left out details of the volleyball game. He then described the magnificent church where Youngy's funeral was held, the reception at the Museum of Contemporary Art, the embrace from Tony's father, and being approached by Jiemba.

Dex's voice then started to change, he began speaking softer and became more serious. Stacy stopped packing and sat next to McCord. He continued with describing his jog up to North Head, meeting Jiemba, and then getting shot at by two guys with Caribbean accents. Stacy gasped. He then told Stacy that after Abbot fell into his arms, he had no other option but to jump from the cliffs. McCord noted it hurt some when he hit the ocean but, "I went into survival mode." He described his night swim with sharks, seeing the dive class, and speaking with the police. He left out meeting Kendall Cove.

"Are you OK?" asked a concerned Stacy.

"Just a few sore ribs. But I feel fine."

"What did the police do?"

"Nothing. They thought I was some lunatic from the States sending them off on a wild goose chase."

"It does sound a little crazy. Did you take the police back up to where your friend was shot?"

"Not until the morning. They sent a team that night but found nothing. There wasn't a trace of anything."

"Well, the important thing is you're OK."

"Yes, I guess so," said Dex somberly.

McCord went on to discuss his visit to KGO's office and the review of internal control workpapers, including the strange reference to Barbados.

He told Stacy that Walsh wanted him to make a visit to a technology facility in Barbados immediately.

"Barbados? As in the island?" asked Stacy.

"Yes. They've already bought my tickets and reserved a hotel. I leave in two days."

"That's good, I guess, but crazy. You just got back from halfway around the world."

"Yeah, it is, but I want to go. I need to find out what the hell is going on down there. I believe somehow that facility is connected to Tony and Abbot's deaths."

"You think so?"

"Yes."

"Well, watch out for yourself."

"Walsh told me to look into it. He also said I'd better brush up on my knowledge of XBRL. I'll have to do some research."

"Derek, remember when we met down in DC last fall?"

"Yes, how can I forget?" replied McCord with a smile.

"At the conference was a woman speaking about XBRL, and she gave me her card." Stacy went over to her backpack and pulled out a business card.

"Here. Her name is Liv Watson. Give her a call, she works in New York."

"That would definitely save me some time with research. I'll see if she's available."

"Good plan."

McCord needed a crash course on XBRL. It had slipped his mind that just five months ago he and Stacy had attended a two-day AICPA conference in Washington, DC where the new reporting language was being presented. He must have been too distracted by Ms. Atchinson's presence to recall the topic. Stacy went on to remind McCord that during one of the sessions there was a presentation on XBRL or eXtensible Business Reporting Language. The future reporting standard was introduced as "bar coding" financial statements. The presenter was Liv Watson, Vice Chairman of XBRL International. McCord did not remember Ms. Watson's presentation, but Stacy did.

Dex's time at Stacy's apartment flew by, his play-by-play of his Australian adventure took up Stacy's allotted two hours. She was now frantically running around the apartment grabbing a few last-minute items. They embraced for another long passionate kiss and hug; time didn't permit more than that. The couple walked out of the apartment together and said goodbye, promising to see each other again as soon as they are both back in New York City. Stacy jumped in an Uber and left for the airport. McCord walked west towards the subway and caught the downtown #4 train to head back to his apartment in Murray Hill for some much-needed rest. During his walk he called Liv Watson.

~~~

Liv (pronounced "Liev") Watson was a technology-driven accountant. McCord recalled that Watson was literally a larger-than-life character; her six-foot frame and Norwegian background made her an imposing public speaker, she was known as the Scandinavian Queen of XBRL. Prior to Dex's meeting he got his hands on the book *XBRL for Dummies* which Watson had co-authored with Charles Hoffman, the self-proclaimed Father of XBRL. Her bio stated that prior to her finance and technology career, Liv was a skateboarding champion and MTV video coordinator, traveling back and forth from Oslo to Los Angeles. McCord found it interesting that she highlighted that during an MTV filming in LA she met her husband, fell in love, and shortly thereafter gave birth to twin girls. Watson went on to note that after three years of marriage, she separated from her husband and embraced the role of single mom and that she went back to university and earned a degree in accounting with a minor in finance information systems.

McCord read that Ms. Watson declared herself as a global spokesperson for technology in accounting and one of the original evangelists of the SEC's new XML reporting standard, ultimately becoming one of the founders of the XBRL International consortium. Her role was to travel the world spreading the XBRL gospel. McCord was lucky to get Liv in New York for an education on XBRL and Watson was happy to help her accounting comrade. They agreed to meet at MoMath, the Museum of Mathematics on 26th street between Fifth and Madison. MoMath was Liv's home field, her playground, the theater of geometry, art, and algorithms. It was her way of sending a message to McCord: I'm technological, hip, and it's cool to love math.

For Ms. Watson, the MoMath museum stimulated inquiry, sparked her curiosity, and revealed the wonder of solutions. She would sometimes preach that math is everywhere—a part of our daily lives, from the time you get out of bed, to making breakfast, to knotting your tie. Her mantra was that math touches on so many things in the world around us. There's a connection between mathematics and music, between mathematics and business, between mathematics and art. The museum showed all those parts of mathematics. And that was her point: math may not be as easy as Pi, but it isn't so square, either. Liv certainly was a testament to that philosophy.

McCord shared the same connection to math as Liv, understanding math to be something fun and exciting. At an early age he understood its magic and thought chicks would dig it, too. He believed if he portrayed himself as a math geek, girls would perceive him to be smart and more sensitive than most other large-framed athletes. Sometimes it worked.

~~~

Liv approached McCord crisscrossing the MoMath lobby. "Liv, good seeing you again," said Dex, pretending he remembered meeting her at the conference in Washington, DC. "Thank you for meeting me on such short notice."

"No problem. I appreciate that someone from KGO is interested in XBRL. How can I help you?"

"I'm visiting a client tomorrow and need a quick crash course on how XBRL works."

"You want an answer to the big question, Why XBRL?" suggested Ms. Watson.

"Yes, let's start there."

Liv was gentle with McCord and started walking him through the basics of XBRL while making references to her book *XBRL for Dummies*:

- ✓ A freely available, market-driven, open global standard for exchanging business information
- ✓ An XML language
- ✓ A means of modeling the meaning of business information in a form comprehendible by computer applications
- ✓ A mandate from regulators around the world
- ✓ A global agreement on business information concepts, relationships, and business rules
- ✓ A better approach to exchange information

Watson went on to explain that XBRL was first envisioned in 1997 to assist with corporate financial reporting. The standard was based on eXtensible Markup Language (XML), a technology protocol for transmitting and consuming data across the Internet. It was developed by a few technology and accounting geeks working in Seattle's Microsoft region. Since the early 2000s it had been driven and unceasingly developed by XBRL International Inc., a not-for-profit consortium of over 750 companies involved in providing or using business information.

XBRL was positioned to be the solution that would bring the SEC's EDGAR system into the 21st century. Watson highlighted the fact that traditionally reporting on publicly traded assets had been a labor-intensive process involving the compilation of data from a variety of sources and formats. Data that was manually inputted into spreadsheets and reports prepared by accountants and finance professionals, the final result being a document prone to error that had financial tables and substantial amounts of text explaining the underlying information.

Public companies, research analysts, investment banks, and the Securities and Exchange Commission needed a new solution, so they turned to XBRL. After 10 years of development the new technology became an internationally agreed upon reporting standard by members of the accounting, financial, regulatory, academic, and technology professions—achieving the consortium's ultimate goal of making financial information more standardized and machine readable.

Early on Christopher Cox, the SEC Chairman at the time, embraced XBRL and put his weight behind the movement. His altruistic mission was to level the playing field between institutional investors and the individual investor, and he believed XBRL would accomplish the task. He also desired to become a Republican presidential candidate, which unfortunately ended when he was diagnosed with thymoma, a rare form of cancer. In 2006 COX underwent surgery to remove a tumor from his chest and made a full recovery. But the political damage was done, with too many question marks remaining about his health to be considered a serious candidate.

"You see, Derek, the widespread global adoption of an XBRL standard was being driven by increased demand from investors and regulators," Watson explained. "They were requesting transparency and more sophisticated analytics on investments in stocks, mutual funds, and bonds. So, in 2007, after a lot of arduous work by my consortium, the SEC mandated that public companies will be required to furnish XBRL data in their related EDGAR filings."

"I can see how that started leveling the playing field," noted McCord.

"Yes, it achieved the SEC's primary purpose for stakeholders and companies to use tagged data for analysis. Now individual investors as well as professional traders could compare companies against each other on a apples-to-apples basis in real time."

Watson went on to educate McCord about the substantial benefits of the new machine-readable documents, highlighting that now with substantial amounts of XBRL data tags the analysis and communication of financial information, from software based on standardized accounting industry definitions, would provide uniformity that was otherwise lacking in financial reporting. She also noted that, at the end of the day, the XBRL solution delivered on its promise to provide instant comparability between companies and publicly held financial assets.

"The SEC continues to develop tools that use XBRL Data to discover accounting anomalies. A sort of SEC RoboCop," stated Liv who was more than happy to continue the lecture.

"So how did EDGAR Data & Intelligence get involved?" asked Dex.

"After ED&I raised significant cash from their IPO, they purchased a technology company specializing in data extraction."

"Their northern Virginia facility," answered McCord who knew a little about the history of EDGAR Data & Intelligence.

"Correct. They were a small private company working with NASDAQ on reporting systems, which led to them becoming experts in building software to data mine the SEC's EDGAR system. Then after EDGAR's acquisition they invested millions of dollars in software development. Creating tools to automatically data tag historical and current financial statements into XBRL."

"Seems like a good business plan," added McCord.

"Yes, exceptionally good. But data tagging 10 years of historical information wasn't a trivial task. It took their programmers years to perfect the data mapping software. And not until they completed that task was the SEC feeling comfortable with a mandate. That's when your friends at EDGAR Data & Intelligence became known as the XBRL experts," noted Watson.

"A lot of double-checking numbers, I bet."

"Exactly. Their tools were groundbreaking, but they still required a significant amount of human intervention. The quality assurance process was critical."

"Is that when they started sending public company filings to India to be XBRLized?" asked McCord.

"That's what I heard. The team at ED&I was looking for a low-cost solution," confirmed Liv as she smiled at Dex.

~~~

Watson went on to provide McCord with more details on the history and benefits of XBRL. Highlighting points in her book that businesses now had a compelling reason to adopt XBRL:

- ✓ Making their business information exchange better, faster, cheaper
- ✓ Making financial reporting more transparent and discoverable
- ✓ Improving data integrity
- ✓ Integrating business systems
- ✓ Saving government agencies time and money and making them more efficient

"As Christopher Cox preached, no longer is your company information locked into a single format on a piece of paper, word processing document, or spreadsheet." Liv pulled out of her backpack a simple example of current assets being tagged in XBRL to show McCord.

What is XBRL?

```
<us-gaap: CashAndCashEquivalents contextRef="Current_AsOF" unitRef= "U-USD"
Decimals="0">50000</ us-gaap: CashAndCashEquivalents>
<us-gaap: TradeOtherReceivablesNetCurrent contextRef="Current_AsOF" unitRef=
"U-USD"
Decimals="0">35000</ us-gaap: TradeOtherReceivablesNetCurrent >
<us-gaap: Inventories contextRef="Current_AsOF" unitRef= "U-USD"
Decimals="0">125000</ us-gaap: Inventories >
<us-gaap: PrepaymentsCurrent contextRef="Current_AsOF" unitRef= "U-USD"
Decimals="0">20000</ us-gaap: Prepayments Current >
<us-gaap: OtherAssetsCurrent contextRef="Current_AsOF" unitRef= "U-USD"
Decimals="0">45000</ us-gaap: OtherAssetsCurrent >
<us-gaap: AssetsCurrentTotal contextRef="Current_AsOF" unitRef= "U-USD"
Decimals="0">275000</ us-gaap: AssetsCurrentTotal >
```

Sample XBRL Program Code in
Computer Readable Form

CURRENT ASSETS	
Cash and Cash Equivalents	$ 50,000
Trade and Other Receivables, Net Current	35,000
Inventories	125,000
Prepayments, Current	20,000
Other Assets, Current	45,000
Current Assets, Total	$275,000

Sample XBRL Report in
Human Readable Form

"See, Derek. XBRL tags make the numbers and their related footnotes completely machine readable," pointed Liv.

"I imagine a zero-error rate is required for SEC filings," recognized McCord the auditor.

"Yes. It became an issue for EDGAR. Their demand from new clients and volume of work grew so quickly that their quality assurance process was slowing down delivery. It just wasn't cost effective hiring more quality assurance employees in the U.S to validate the XBRL tags. I believe that's when they started sending their clients' financial statements and press releases offshore to India."

"So much for keeping jobs in America," said McCord.

"It was just too expensive to hire an army of financial analysts and programmers in Virginia." Watson continued, "When the SEC mandated that all public companies file their 8Ks, 10Qs and 10Ks in XBRL, everybody was playing catch-up. The financial printing industry's cheese had been moved."

"I see, companies like MA Barton, DFIN, Vintage Filings and Merrill Corp, the largest SEC filing agents, must have been years behind EDGAR Data & Intelligence in building an automated XBRL mapping technology."

"That's right. SEC filing agents who didn't build out a specialized XBRL software had to outsource the process to third party data taggers, like ED&I."

"So, it would be a build or buy decision for the larger EDGAR filing agents," added McCord.

"I wouldn't be surprised if MA Barton acquired ED&I," stated Watson.

McCord stayed silent. He knew from Walsh that Falcone Capital was coordinating a purchase transaction. Liv continued, "Writing XBRL data extraction software is not easy and companies like MA Barton sure don't have the expertise or time."

"Yeah. It would be a smart acquisition," confirmed Dex.

"MA Barton can probably purchase them for a steal. I heard from a contact that the company is bleeding cash. Barton's latest SEC filing disclosed that they are developing an XBRL capability but are always on the lookout for acquisitions."

"I'll have to take a look at that," replied McCord.

"They also stated that a potential future acquisition may be required due to the effects of market evolution," disclosed Liv. "Hey, didn't Falcone

Capital enter into a voting agreement with EDGAR to be appointed as its proxy to vote all their shares?"

"I believe that information is included in their public filings," said McCord trying not to disclose anything that would be considered confidential information about his client.

"If they do I bet they'll lock in the sale at a great purchase price. I'm sure Falcone would double their money from the investment they made in them a few years ago," reflected Watson.

"It will be interesting to see what happens."

"Very."

"Liv, I really appreciate the help."

"No problem. I hope I didn't bore you with details. I can get passionate about the power of XBRL sometimes."

"Not at all. This was great. I owe you one, Ms. Watson," said Dex smiling.

"Any time for my friends at KGO and you, of course," Watson blushed.

"One more question. Do you know anything about a company in Barbados that is connected to XBRL?"

"There's only one possible connection to Barbados that I know of. A former regulator and developer of the SEC's RoboCop tools, Eric Fromm, left DC a few years ago and joined a firm down there. I don't know the name of the company. But supposedly he was paid big bucks to create a set of quantitative analytic tools designed to review earnings releases, 10Ks and 10Qs," said Watson.

"Interesting move," replied McCord.

"Yes, nice lifestyle change moving to Barbados. I'll have to pay him a visit one day."

"True dat. Thanks again for the help, Liv. When I'm back in New York, let me buy you dinner."

"I'll take you up on that. And Derek, if you want to find an answer to something, solve for the unknown: $A+B=X$."

"X being?" asked McCord.

"X is the unknown," said Liv while pointing at the wall littered with mathematical equations.

"That's the plan."

Liv gave Dex a juicy European goodbye kiss on each cheek and walked out of MoMath. McCord remained behind, staring at Euclid's algorithm painted on the wall, studying the formula for reducing a common fraction to its lowest terms. He was glad he'd reached out to the Scandinavian Queen of XBRL. It was a productive meeting.

~~~

An Australian man and two outsiders on temporary work visas moved quickly through security at Kingsford Smith airport. There were heading to the boarding gate for a Qantas flight to commence their journey from Sydney, Australia to Georgetown, Barbados. The flight time was 26 hours: Sydney (SYD) to Los Angeles (LAX) 17 hours + LAX to Miami (MIA) six hours + MIA to Bridgetown (BGI) three hours. However, with flight changes and layovers the trip would take them over 32 hours.

Metcalf went to Barbados often, but this time he was not alone. Making the trip with him were his two West Indies rugby players who needed to get out of Australia. Metcalf was flying first class in the sleeper cabin. Carroll and Frazier were in the back of the plane in economy. Before boarding, Metcalf purchased three newspapers, *The Sydney Morning Herald, The Daily Telegraph* and *The Manly Daily*. He wanted to see if there was any reference to unidentified bodies washing ashore or discoveries of wrongdoing in North Head. There was no mention. Nauti was going to be able to sleep tight on the long trip to the other side of the world.

If asked the two men in the back of the plane would say they are flying to Barbados to attend the upcoming West Indies test match and to see relatives. Metcalf was going there for different reasons. A year earlier, a few months after the country's move away from the English monarchy and to an independent republic, Nauti's gentlemen friend from the Darden School of Business, Master Teague, had been appointed Prime Minister of Barbados. The powerful position was awarded by the current president and congress shortly after the Bajan independence movement.

Teague and his wife were throwing a huge commemoration event. Nauti was looking forward to enjoying the anniversary with his close business school friend. The trip also gave Metcalf a chance to get his assassins out of Australia and obtain an update on one of his acquisitions, a back-office investment and administration services company whose primary purpose was to manage people's retirement funds.

Prior to Master Teague being named prime minister, Metcalf contributed funds to a lobbyist working with the Barbadian National Congress in a breakaway effort from the English Commonwealth. The then Senator Teague, along with his wife and other government officials, pushed the idea of becoming a self-ruling republic. The separation would require a referendum and two-thirds majority vote. After a couple years of debate, and financial inducements made by Metcalf and the prime minister's wife to several influential members of congress, the citizens of Barbados passed the resolution.

On November 30, 2021, after 55 years under Commonwealth control, the island country separated, declaring their independence. The existing Barbadian monarchy was abolished. Based on the approved breakaway referendum a senior government representative would be appointed president by the existing congress. As its head of state, he or she would appoint the prime minister. Teague's closest ally in congress was awarded the position of president. Teague would later be named prime minister of the new independent country. In this role, he would advise the president, appoint ministers, and have the authority to name 12 senators. A very influential position on a very small island.

A few years before Teague was named prime minister he had notified his good friend in Australia about a state-of-the-art technology facility that was up for sale by the Bajan government. Like most of Nigel's purchases it was an undervalued distressed property. From his education at Darden and experience as an entrepreneur Metcalf recognized the benefits of infrastructure, technology, and outsourcing. Nauti's purchase proposal included a provision to retain the local administrative employees and leverage the facility's current software engineers. Thus, saving and adding jobs to the island. The purchase of the Barbados facility would satisfy the government's need for jobs and economic growth. It would also fill Metcalf's desire to leverage local inexpensive resources and business activities under one roof.

After significant contributions to undisclosed political campaign funds, the then Senator Teague and other congressional beneficiaries ensured that Metcalf Consulting Ltd. became the only bidder. However, in accordance with Bajan law, there was a requirement for local ownership of no less than 25%. At the last minute, the senator's wife was discretely added to the paperwork via a Caymen Islands holding company to keep the potential conflict of interest confidential. After the ink dried on the paperwork, Metcalf's "fair" offer for the undervalued property was promptly approved by the House of Assembly. The purchase transaction was completed without objection. Metcalf renamed the facility Green Shade$ in homage to his accounting background.

Chapter 10

"If computers get too powerful, we can organize them into a committee—that will do them in."
—Bradley's Bromide

- Albert Finn
- Near-Shore Software Development in Barbados
- The IPO Process
- Quantitative Trading

BRIDGETOWN, BARBADOS

McCORD WOKE UP before sunrise to catch the first plane out of New York (JFK) to Bridgetown, Barbados (BGI). He hated the task of getting up at Zero Dark 30 to catch early flights. He ordered an UberX and packed his bag with a few last-minute summer clothes that were in a bin under his bed. The drive to the airport at 5:30am took only 30 minutes instead of the stressful hour and a half with traffic. The VanWyk Expressway was lighter than typical due to the morning hours and the new normal of flexible workday schedules. The post-pandemic office policies had their benefits and unintended consequences. It was also a Friday.

The flight to Barbados on JetBlue was four hours and 45 minutes, a short trip compared to what McCord endured just a few days earlier. The plane was surprisingly full of families eager to start their winter vacations.

Since his ticket was at the last minute, Walsh's assistant was not able to book business class. Dex had to sit in the back of the plane. In front of and behind him were obnoxiously loud and fidgety children. His headphones didn't work. McCord's plan of getting a good nap before landing in Bridgetown was not going to happen.

The flight from New York arrived early at BGI airport at 10:45am to the applause of its young passengers. McCord opened his shade and squinted out the window. It was a beautiful sunny day with deep blue skies. A billboard on top of the terminal read:

Welcome to Barbados
The Blissful Island

The crowded JetBlue flight emptied slowly. Walking hunched over McCord finally got to the front of the plane and moved out onto a platform before looking down at 12 steps of stairs. The first thing he noticed was the heat. The Bajan sun felt like walking into an oven, a big change from the bitter cold of New York in early February. McCord had forgotten sunglasses, his eyes had to quickly adjust like they did when he played softball on the open fields in Central Park. He waited with the other passengers for his luggage on the hot asphalt tarmac, warm sweat dripping down the back of his polo shirt.

After gathering his bags, he crisscrossed patiently through the slow-moving customs line. He was asked three times, "What is the nature of your visit?" Clearly he didn't look like the tourists there for vacation. After 50 minutes McCord made it out of the terminal to the pick-up area. Waiting for him was a large Bajan man in a white short-sleeve dress shirt, turquoise shorts, black socks, and white sneakers. It was Lindsay Arthur, the partner-in-charge of KGO's Bridgetown office. McCord thought he looked like James Earl Jones.

~~~

Lindsay Arthur was a diplomatic and spiritual accountant. He had entered the public accounting world after earning a BBA in Management and Accounting at Toronto University in Canada. Throughout his career McCord met many citizens of the West Indies that had earned degrees north of the U.S. border. It was not surprising to Dex that with a solid education Lindsay flourished in his vocation, he had considerable expertise in international business and an abiding interest in and passion for the art of diplomacy. On the island Lindsay was beloved, a larger-than-life representative of the values of Barbadians, but what McCord found most interesting was that he was a Bible teacher and licensed minister, a very unique competence for an auditor. Arthur's unique temperament and analytical ability to solve problems had made him the natural choice to lead the local firm.

"Welcome to Barbados," said Lindsay in his deep voice while reaching out to shake McCord's hand.

"Thank you. Good to be here."

"How was your flight?"

"Very crowded. A lot of families coming down here for holiday."

"Oh, yes. Our government loves to see tourists," declared Lindsay.

"Thanks for seeing me on such short notice."

"Any time, my friend. How many years has it been?"

"Must be over six years now. Before I left on my expat assignment in Sydney," replied Dex.

"How time flies."

Lindsay pointed towards his Toyota Land Cruiser parked behind him. "Get in, get in. Have you been to Barbados before, Derek?"

"Nope. First time."

"Let me show you our beautiful island."

McCord entered what he thought was the passenger's side only to see the steering wheel. Not realizing that Barbados, as a former British colony, drove on the left side of the road. They both had a laugh as Lindsay was holding the door open on the other side of the car. McCord had met

Lindsay at an AMA management course in New York, *The Voice of Leadership: How Leaders Inspire, Influence, and Achieve Results*. At that time Lyndsay was being groomed to take over the Bridgetown office.

Arthur's car pulled out of Grantley Adams International Airport and headed east on Tom Adams Highway. The two accounting professionals caught up on firm matters while continuing their journey around the island. They were heading towards Bridgetown, the capital of Barbados. The Land Cruiser drove through colorful fishing villages and past several footy fields encircled by wooden bleachers and sponsors' billboards. After driving for 30 minutes, they stopped for lunch in the village of Oistins at Uncle George's Fish Net Grill. Lindsay wanted McCord to enjoy the island's local cuisine and view of the beautiful Caribbean Sea.

"So, how are you doing Derek?" asked Lindsay as the two men sat down at a small wooden table next to a white sandy beach.

"I'm hanging in there. I've had a very busy 10 days."

"You look tired."

"Very. I was in Australia last week for a friend's funeral, then New York for two days, and now I'm here. It's been an extremely taxing journey."

"It sure sounds like it. But now you're in Barbados, mon. All will be better. Revel in the sea," said Lindsay while looking out at the water.

"It's a good start," replied Dex.

"You mentioned on the phone that you wanted to perform due diligence on a local investment and technology firm. And that you have a client who is thinking about moving their retirement plans to a company here in Bridgetown?"

"Yes, that's right."

"You mentioned the name Green Shade$?"

"Yep."

"Well, you're in luck. They are a KGO client. We have been advising the organization for the past few years. Shortly after the facility was acquired. Actually, it was a referral from the Sydney office."

"A good paying client, I assume?"

"Oh yes, one of our better revenue generators. They are doing very well."

"In technology and consulting services?" asked McCord.

"Yes. But I hear that is a very small part of their business now. They're making most of their money from managing pension accounts and trading stocks."

"Interesting. Were you able to arrange a site visit?"

"Yes, of course. The controller at the company is the son of a friend of mine. He will show us around and introduce us to their CEO."

"That's great. Thanks, Lindsay."

"No problem. Our island is small, and most people know each other."

~~~

The two finished their lunch, got back into the car, and continued towards Bridgetown. The technology facility was only 15 kilometers from Oistins, but the drive took the accountants over a half hour due to heavy midday traffic on the Errol Barrow Highway. Lindsay pulled his Land Cruiser into the parking lot in front of a large industrial building around 2:00pm. Loose shells and white stones popped and crunched under the auto's tires. Arthur backed into a space that indicated it was for visitors.

The building was three stories high, long and plain, like a government-owned facility, rectangular except for a one-story square bump added to the front, the reception entrance for acceptable distinguished guests. The double front doors were framed in frosted glass. Next to the entrance was a white sign with green writing:

GREEN SHADE$ LLC
Bridgetown, Barbados

The building had an interesting history. In the early 1990s Albert Finn founded the Bajan 2K Technology Corporation (2K TECH). The Barbados facility was built out by Albert and a group of experienced technologists, courtesy of Year 2000 computer concerns and funding from a successful IPO. Finn was a confident, high-energy entrepreneur. During his days at Boston University, he founded the Young Entrepreneurs Organization (YEO). With Al's outgoing personality and bulldog tenacity, he was able to leverage the YEO and gain access to high profile U.S. CEOs. He was introduced to many executives of the Top 25 corporations in the U.S., his successful group of mentors were happy to help the enthusiastic college kid and the YEO. During that time Albert became friends with a number of legendary business leaders, including Jack Welch at GE and Sandy Weill at Smith Barney.

Finn graduated BU with a degree in Business Information Systems looking to launch an innovative technology company based on future industry trends. His YEO organization, which regularly hosted think tanks, provided Finn with access to important CEO connections. They in turn provided Albert with introductions to some of the smartest and brightest Chief Technology Officers and Chief Information Officers in the world. Finn was looking to parlay those introductions into a business plan.

Every three months the Young Entrepreneurs Organization hosted quarterly roundtables for the big picture IT guys. Finn would throw questions out to the group for debate. He wanted to understand how the technology industry was addressing:

- Worldwide competition
- Deregulation
- Globalization
- Rapid technological advancements

While at the same time gain an understanding into the increased demand at their corporations to:

- Improve the quality of their products and services.
- Improve operating efficiencies and security.
- Reduce costs and time to market of new products and services.

During these sessions Finn discovered a very timely pain point—the potential of a catastrophic technology meltdown due to the quickly approaching Year 2000 changeover from 1999. Firms were scrambling to find talent to correct the problem due to a significant shortage of IT professionals worldwide. Chief Technology Officers were panicking. At the same time, they were all being faced with a convergence of four urgent 21st century issues: a shortfall of specialized IT personnel; an inability to effectively manage mass change issues; the escalating costs of maintaining in-house technology departments; and safely conducting business on the World Wide Web.

Corporations were being faced with an ever-increasing strategic reliance on technology and not enough talent and software engineers to meet the demand. The spiraling costs of IT budgets and the inability to effectively manage the Year 2000 problem created a unique set of challenges for Finn's advisory group. The solution for most was to outsource technology staff somewhere overseas. Corporations were predominately turning to an Indian offshore solution for coding and patch work. At the time India was widely acknowledged as the go to leader in offshore software engineering due to its large numbers of highly educated and English-speaking technology professionals. The country's engineers offered the benefit of lower costs and access to a larger pool of skilled employees. Albert's new technology industry advisors loved the concept of outsourcing but hated the midnight phone calls and long trips to India.

As a child Finn had spent many winter vacations with his family on Barbados. He understood firsthand that the island had an exceptional English-speaking education system. Albert was poised to develop a different solution: near-shore outsourcing. A new near-shore solution at a cost-effective price would save the day for many of his Chief Technology Officer and Chief Information Officer friends.

With a sound business plan and growing customer demand, Finn went out and raised seed money from friends and family. He then hired a team of software engineers and added a group of West Point alumni as project managers. His brother Milo had gone to the academy and believed military graduates were disciplined and hard workers that got the job done. He was not wrong. In just three months 2K TECH opened a small near-shore software development firm in Bridgetown. It met all the technology officers' requirements, including:

A) Access to trained IT professionals from around the world with no governmental limitations on work visas
B) Favorable wage structures and low tax rates
C) Modern communications infrastructure due to a fiber optic ring around the island
D) Stable political and economic system with a currency fixed to the U.S. dollar
E) Convenient location with direct flight access from major United States and European cities (near the same time zone as many U.S. corporations)

2K Technology Corporation checked all the boxes for its technology partners and future Fortune 500 customers. After further investments from friends and family, venture capitalists' private placements, and many customer successes, the vision was fulfilled. Finn proved the business model and was ready to accelerate growth in Barbados to blast off the business. He had one more step to take: raise significant capital to build out a larger facility. Albert and his team of consultants decided to take the 2K TECH company public. He immediately commenced a "beauty contest" or "bake off" of investment bankers to lead the capital raise. There was no competition needed. Albert had built a very solid friendship with the CEO at Smith Barney, who immediately had his investment banking team and research analysts help the young YEO founder with expanding the business, building business models, and deriving valuations. Without delay the Initial Public Offering activity was off to the races.

Finn's handpicked U.S. CFO and finance team were ready to work with the investment bankers. After a few months of around the clock work, the 2K Technology Corporation successfully raised $75 million from an Initial Public Offering (IPO). Finn and his executives were all smiles when ringing the NASDAQ bell.

To learn about the intense experience of an IPO see Exhibit 7.

~~~

Shortly after the IPO, 2K TECH leased 110,000 square feet of space from the Bajan government in Bridgetown. Albert and his investment banking team had leveraged the Year 2000 computer concerns and corporate demand for dot-com initiatives to construct a state-of-the-art technology facility. After obtaining the IPO funds, Milo Finn and his army corps of engineers from West Point were in full attack mode, first assisting the government and Bajan telecom companies with the build out of a modern communications infrastructure, and then constructing a local groundbreaking high-tech facility.

Barbados was proving to be the perfect geographic location for Albert's customers and investors. The island's beautiful beaches, resorts, and weather made it an excellent location to visit and hedge against potential market downturns. It also didn't hurt that as the bird flies the island was 650 miles off the coast of Venezuela and out of the cyclic hurricane path. Almost all storms turned north away from Barbados.

Over the next four years 2K Technology Corporation would report record revenues and profits. The company had become a poster child for success and a sexy Wall Street story. But after business from the Year 2000 computer fixes wore off, the significant demand for routine technology services dwindled. Finn's clients started pulling back on spend, his stock price was cut in half, and 2K TECH was running out of cash to fund the Barbados facility. He had to sell his company. But it wasn't all bad news, Finn was successful in orchestrating a fire sale and walked away with a large multi-million-dollar payment before his thirtieth birthday.

During the following 20 plus years the Bridgetown facility changed ownership three times. Several technology firms tried to make the business work. However, the company couldn't be turned around. The fading excitement of near-shore outsourcing and the impact from a global recession was too much for the technology company to overcome. The facility was shut down and handed over to the Bajan government after the last owner defaulted on tax payments. That was when Master Teague, the then Senator of Barbados, reached out to his friend from UCLA, Nigel Metcalf. Nigel teamed up with Teague's wife and made a low-ball offer for the technology center. It was promptly accepted by the local authorities without negotiation. After finalizing the sale, the company was renamed Green Shade$.

~~~

At first Metcalf converted the Bajan facility into a back-office plan administrator for his actuarial clients. Green Shade$ was being entrusted with handling paperwork on retirement funds for thousands of individuals worldwide. As fiduciaries, Nigel and his team were responsible and liable for the day-to-day management of his clients' pension plans, including handling employee notices, processing distributions, and mailing quarterly statements. Given the extensive list of responsibilities and liability risks, he decided to outsource those services to a third-party administrator. Metcalf wanted to focus his energy on being the investment manager of retirement dollars entrusted to him by his clients, taking on the more lucrative responsibility of investment decisions on his customers' behalf and in the best interest of plan participants. And, of course, to generate significant profits to support his personal investments and lifestyle back in Australia.

Metcalf recruited the best and brightest investment managers from around the world to go to Barbados. He ordered his team of brokers, analysts, and software engineers to work together and build sophisticated trading benchmarks. His algorithmic trading philosophy was going to rely heavily on quantitative analysis and quantitative modeling. Over a relatively short period of time his employees programmed a substantial number of stock algorithms based on financial ratios derived from SEC filings. Metcalf's traders stayed away from trying to predict market emotion. The company's investment strategies would exclude any predictions of a company's fundamental value. They would be based on the occurrence of reported events or trends, which were easy and straightforward to apply through a set of rules without getting into the complexity of predictive analysis. Metcalf believed that utilizing technical indicators was the best way for Green Shade$ to profit from trading stocks.

Nigel categorized trading forces that move stocks up or down into three categories: fundamental factors, technical factors, and market sentiment. A skill that he learned from his statistical days in public accounting. His team of highly paid analysts were able to use financial and fundamental quantitative indicators to try and predict future price movements. They focused on quantitative analysis:

> ➢ Quantitative Analysis analyzes an investment according to easily measured factors, such as earnings, material events, or assets of the company.

They left the rest of the market to trade on qualitative analysis:

> Qualitative Analysis looks at harder to measure factors such as the quality of a company's board, management, or the strength of its brand.

Metcalf's employees were keenly aware that financial figures included in Securities and Exchange Commission filings were the key indicators in determining if a company was properly valued. They understood that reported statements by public companies told a story of profitability and how fast sales and profits are expected to grow or not grow. The information Nigel's team needed was included in company's earnings releases, quarterly and annual reports, and news headlines. This was habitually reported to investors via SEC Form 8K filings and included:

- News releases on sales, profits, and future estimated earnings
- Announcement of dividends
- Introduction of a new product or a product recall
- Securing a large new contract
- Anticipated takeover or merger
- A change of management
- Accounting errors or scandals

Metcalf's team developed numerous trading permutations based on Form 8K filings received directly from NSG Global in India. The reportable events would provide a complete predictive picture of a stock's performance and if a company stock was undervalued or overpriced. The engineers in Barbados understood that the speed of information obtained by a field of programmed gate arrays would generate big investment gains—and that the company's computers and software programs would use machine-readable XBRL information to execute buy and sell orders instantaneously with minimal human intervention.

With a steady flow of confidential SEC filings coming from India, Green Shade$ developed a range of triggering events based on XBRL data tags. Their coders were able to program key financial ratios that allowed their analysts and traders to convert NSG's raw XBRL data reported by public companies on Form 8Ks, 10Ks and 10Qs into concise, actionable information. Their team would now have the advantage of knowing material information before any other trading firm to:

- Evaluate performance.
- Compare target companies to competitors and industry norms.
- Conduct unlawful stock trades.

Green Shade$'s band of brokers and analysts understood that to generate significant gains, they needed to beat other experienced stock traders in the market. Over time they came to appreciate that time sensitive computer-driven data, coupled with knowing the right information, would be the difference between being an investor in the driver's seat or a helpless passenger.

With high frequency trading techniques and confidential information in hand that was not yet in the public domain, the company had the ability to trade thousands of stocks based on inside information. However, while investor returns weren't assured, there was one sure thing: like any Wall Street advantage with bad intentions, Nauti and his financial wizards were going to make serious profits manipulating the market. By the time their competition received company information filed with the SEC, the management at Green Shade$ were already counting their money. Nauti's computers and traders were able to generate millions of dollars in illegal earnings. All thanks to confidential XBRL filings and their colleagues at NSG Global in India.

Chapter 11

"Prediction is very difficult, especially about the future."
—*Niels Bohr*

- The Green Shade$ Trading Floor
- The Controller
- Eric Fromm

McCORD AND ARTHUR were welcomed in the reception area by a young Bajan woman who appeared happy to see them. She was sitting behind a large white semi-circle desk in front of a green wall. Painted on the wall in white was the firm's name – Green Shade$ LLC. There was a large television monitor turned to the U.S. financial news station CNBC. On either side of the desk were stairs leading up to glass doors.

"Welcome, gentlemen. How can I help you?"

"I'm Lindsay Arthur from KGO, here to see Jay Gaucher," replied Lindsay.

"Oh, yes. Mr. Gaucher said he was expecting you. He's in a meeting but I'll let him know you're here."

"That would be great. With me is Mr. Derek McCord."

"Nice to meet you, Mr. McCord. Can I get you some tea or coffee? Or perhaps bottled water?" offered the enthusiastic receptionist.

"No, thank you," Dex and Lindsay replied in unison.

"OK. Please sit down. Make yourselves comfortable. I'm sure Mr. Gaucher will be right out," said the receptionist as she pointed towards a white leather sofa with two matching chairs.

The receptionist sat down and picked up her phone to inform Mr. Gaucher's assistant that his visitors had arrived. Hanging on the wall behind the sofa were old photos of employees standing in front of the building. Most of the personnel looked Indian with a few locals from Barbados entwined. There was also a more recent photo of what looked like an American man standing next to an Indian woman and two Bajans. In the corner of the reception area was a large glass case with an array of colorful opals. A light was shining up from below illuminating the precious stones.

McCord preferred to stand while waiting in reception areas. He liked to stay on the ready for his meetings. He also didn't want to intimidate people by his size when getting up from a chair. Dex was staring at the photo of the five people standing in front of the facility's Green Shade$ sign.

"Who are the people in this photo?" McCord asked.

"Oh yes, it's a very nice picture," said the receptionist from behind her desk. "The tall man in the middle is our CEO, Eric Fromm. He is with the Managing Director of our partner in India and Prime Minister Teague and his wife." She continued, "You know the MD from India was one of the first employees who worked at this facility in the late 1990s. She's the one on the left."

"Hmmm, interesting." McCord replied. "Is she from NSG Global?"

"I'm not sure of the official name of her company. We have quite a few partners around the world. Mr. Gaucher should be able to tell you," replied the receptionist.

After three minutes the door on the right at the top of the stairs opened. A young Bajan man wearing a linen shirt tucked into light green slacks walked down the stairs. He was looking at Lindsay and smiling.

"Mr. Arthur, it's so good to see you," said the man as he stepped off the stairs.

"Good to see you again, Jay," said Lindsay as he reached out to shake hands. "Let me introduce you to Derek McCord. He's from our KGO office in New York. Derek, this is Jay Gaucher, the controller at Green Shade$."

"Nice to meet you, Mr. McCord," said Gaucher as he moved in to shake Dex's hand.

"Good to meet you as well, Jay."

"How do you like our island?" asked Gaucher.

"Well, I just arrived a few hours ago, but from what I see it's a tropical paradise. Quite different from what I left this morning. It was extremely cold in New York."

"Yes, very different. Today is unusually warm for early February. We had to turn up the air conditioning in the building. I hope the temperature is OK."

"Yes, fine, thanks," replied Lindsay. "How's your father doing? I haven't seen him for a while."

"Oh, he's doing great. Living the retired life. Fishing a lot, playing golf, and giving me a hard time. He keeps asking when I am going to move out. But I know he enjoys my company."

"I'm sure he loves being with you, Jay."

"Yeah, mon. He'll miss me when I finally do move out. But I'm in no rush. My mom's cooking is so good," said Jay while rubbing his belly. "Mr. McCord, I was told that you would like to see the facility and get an understanding of our business."

"That's correct. And you can call me Derek."

"OK. Let's head up the stairs and I'll show you our trading floor."

"Sounds good," replied Dex. "Before we go, who is that woman standing with your CEO?"

"Oh, that's Purvi Singh. She is the Managing Director of our partner NSG Global in Bangalore. Ms. Singh comes to our facility quite often. Her company provides us with data feeds and computer programming services. Actually, Derek, she was one of the first employees to work at this facility when it opened up in the late 1990s."

"I heard. It must be a good relationship," replied McCord.

"Yes, very. I understand their service is excellent and we certainly wire them a lot of money. But I don't work too closely with the team over there. Just send the cash." Gaucher motioned the two visitors to follow him up the stairs. "Let's start the tour."

~~~

Jay Gaucher was a compliance accountant. McCord observed that Gaucher was like most controllers—managed the finance team, generated financial reports, completed required regulatory filings, and wanted to make the move to CFO one day. He had graduated from the University of the West Indies in Cave Hill, Barbados, one of five general campuses in the

West Indies university system, earning a BSc in Economics and Accounting. After university Jay joined the finance department at First Caribbean International Bank and became an expert in compliance and regulatory reporting, a very technical controller who was always eager to take on new responsibilities. Gaucher diligently worked at the bank for seven years, traversing his way up the organization chart. His last role before leaving First Caribbean was assistant controller.

Three years previously, shortly after the Green Shade$ acquisition by Metcalf Consulting, Gaucher was recruited to be controller of the new company. His knowledge of the banking industry and reporting regulations made him a perfect recruit for the investment advisory firm. At Green Shade$ his daily focus was primarily on accounting and compliance. While honing these skills was important, he had to change from a look-back controller to look-ahead if he wanted to be on the CFO track. Green Shade$ did not have a local CFO.

In organizations most controllers find comfort with being hands-on and detail-oriented. The biggest challenge Jay had was extricating himself from the details. While his concerns about month-end close should not be forgotten, they should be accompanied by thoughts such as, "How can our company effectively grow in the coming months?" and "What is our greatest area of spend where there is a lot of uncertainty about return?" Not everyone has the risk appetite or strategic skills to become a CFO. Some people are just very skilled staff accountants, and that's all they want to be, and that's OK. Jay had the willingness to learn the language of the executive suite and make the move from being a tactical engineer of accounting information at Green Shade$. However, if Gaucher wanted to go for the C-suite office he would need confidence and vision to get him through the doubt and hurdles in front of him, to be the designer of what goes on, the architect, the CFO. With the seat at the company being empty the role was in his sights, there for the taking.

~~~

The three accounting professionals walked past the reception desk and up the stairs. After reaching the top, they pushed a door open and walked onto an indoor terrace. The terrace continued around three large rectangular rooms that were located below. Each room was the size of a tennis court, built out as individual trading floors separated by retractable walls and surrounded by small glass meeting rooms under a long terrace. The men stopped above the first trading room. The floor was a large open area with numerous desks, computer screens, and phones. There were multiple electronic boards at the front of the room hanging off the terrace, flashing green and red stock prices. In front of the dividing walls stood television monitors turned to business news channels.

There were no employees in the first room. Playing on the televisions were CNBC Asia, BTVI India, and Sky News Australia. The men slowly continued walking on the terrace and stopped above a second large room, similar in size to the first room. The second room was filled with people tapping on their keyboards while staring at monitors. All were focused. Playing on the television sets were Bloomberg Business News, CNBC, and Fox Business Network.

"This is where the magic happens," said Gaucher proudly while pointing down at the three rooms. "The trading floors are segregated by territory. Right now, we are standing above the APAC (Asia Pacific) room. The team is home getting rest and will return to the office after dinner, around 8:00pm, ready to execute trades when the Asian markets open. The middle area is referred to as the NAM (North America) trading room. As you can see the room is packed with traders. Everyone is focused, doing what they do best. Making us money."

McCord interrupted Jay while looking ahead towards the third room. "Let me guess what the far room is for."

"Go ahead," replied Gaucher.

"I assume it's for trading stocks in the EMEA region (Europe, Middle East and Africa)."

"Correct. The team just left before you got here. Their market is closed. They come back very early in the morning."

"So, you have investment managers for each territory?" asked McCord.

"Yes. They are experts from all over the world. Traders teamed up with analysts and everyone working together."

"Even the local Bajans. Particularly good to see," added Lindsay.

Jay continued speaking. "Our support departments are all on the second floor in offices around the terrace. Primarily finance, human resources, and technology." Gaucher pointed across the pit to the second-floor offices. "Over there is the finance group. The HR staff is over there, and we are standing in front of the IT offices."

"Impressive facilities," commented McCord.

"Yes very, we are fortunate to work in a place like this. Derek, my CEO said he wants to meet you. He is in the corner office over there. Between the two of us we can answer all your questions."

"That would be great, thanks," replied Dex.

Moving forward towards the corner office, the men briefly stopped above the third trading floor. The third room was quiet, no employees working at their desks and no screens flashing green and red. Just the faint sound of the televisions tuned to CNBC Europe, Al Jazeera, and CNBC Africa. The three men continued their tour moving towards the corner office on the far-left side of the terrace.

Early on in McCord's career he had several banks, and hedge funds as clients. The activity and noise on their trading floors was a constant. Men and women yelling at screens and cursing at speaker phones, objects thrown in the air without a worry of where they landed. It was a fast-paced, frantic environment, but this trading floor was different. The equity traders were quiet, nobody was yelling and screaming, just polite conversation between money makers, everyone looking confident while watching their computer screens. When McCord was standing above the NAM trading floor; he could hear employees speaking in various accents. It appeared that the Green Shade$'s employees were from the U.S., India, Australia, and

Barbados, all trading in U.S. stocks. McCord was not sure that strategy made sense or if it was even legal. It was his understanding that traders and stockbrokers, executing trades in U.S. stocks, would fall under the auspices of The Financial Industry Regulatory Authority (FINRA).

Dex was keenly aware that most individuals do not have the expertise to make sound investment decisions on their own and could be taken advantage of if not for FINRA's regulations. The rules were necessary because they helped level the playing field between firms and their customers, ensuring that everyone is treated fairly. Millions of Americans were using professional fund managers to invest for their retirement, their children's educations, and other important financial goals. FINRA's responsibility was to make sure that brokers had passed their examinations and had the right qualifications.

McCord was also aware that investment advisers registered by the Securities and Exchange Commission were required to adopt a code of ethics that established a standard of conduct in accord with the adviser's fiduciary duties and required that supervised persons comply with all federal securities laws, including restrictions on insider trading. Dex wasn't sure how the foreign traders below him were staying in compliance with U.S. SEC and FINRA regulations.

The three men finished their walk down the terrace and stopped in front of a large corner office. The glass door entering the office was closed. Inside was the Green Shade$ CEO, Eric Fromm, looking at his computer monitors.

~~~

Eric Fromm was a statistical and regulatory accountant. After meeting with the Scandinavian Queen of XBRL, McCord did a little research on Fromm, he had joined the Washington, DC audit practice of Ernst & Whinny (now called EY or Ernst & Young), after seven years at EY, including an 18-month rotation at their corporate headquarters in London, he left them to join the SEC Office of Corporate Finance in Washington, DC. At the Commission he conducted examinations of issuers' securities, including IPOs, corporate mergers and acquisitions, executive compensation, and cross border transactions. McCord noted that after nine years of reviewing corporate filings, Fromm transferred to The Division of Enforcement (DEO), the police force of the SEC.

On the corner office wall were degrees in accounting from Georgetown University and a master's in finance from The McDonough School of Business. McCord thought Fromm's education at a liberal arts school and extensive experience writing SEC comment letters must have served him well while pursuing white collar criminals and violators of exchange regulations. At the DEO Fromm was able to leverage his Ernst & Young statistical accounting background to create a set of automated analytical tools to crack down on financial reporting fraud, and as Liv Watson noted the technology-based red flag indicators were reliant on machine readable XBRL filings from public companies.

McCord discovered that Fromm had such great success issuing fines for the SEC, he was named director of a newly created task force: Center for Risk and Quantitative Analytics (CRQA). Over time he became known as the SEC's RoboCop. His team were experts at putting financial reports under the microscope and corrupt executives in jail. His capability of discovering corporate wrongdoing led to the SEC collecting hefty seven-figure fines. In addition, Eric's CRQA team was in charge of investigating dozens of daily whistleblower tips of corporate wrongdoing. On an annual basis the SEC awarded over $500 million to an average of 120 whistleblowers, at about $4.5 million per blower. CRQA's efforts resulted in hundreds of whistleblowers receiving substantial cash payouts, this statistic must have bothered Fromm.

As a government employee the maximum pay scale for his SK-16 grade was capped at $195,000, well below market rate for his unique skillset and multiples below whistleblower rewards and his former colleagues who left the Commission for significantly higher salaries. McCord understood that after years of uncovering criminal activities at the CRQA task force, Fromm must have been very frustrated. The timing of his frustration was perfect timing for Nigel Metcalf.

Eric was disgruntled and Metcalf was looking for a numbers guy to run his facility in Barbados. He had heard about the ruthless technology RoboCop at the SEC through an old friend from the UCLA business school that had been the target of one of Eric's investigations. His new quantitative technology driven investment company, Green Shade$ LLC, needed a CEO that was an expert in understanding the power of financial information. And Eric was ready to leave Washington, DC. He had just caught his wife cheating on him with a Capitol Hill congressman, his marriage was in shambles, and he was underpaid by the SEC. He knew that he needed to make a life change, so why not move to Barbados and live like a king? A week after Metcalf's generous offer, Fromm was looking at waterfront property.

~~~

The corner office had a view of the Caribbean Sea, and the aquamarine color of the water was the perfect backdrop for a man who needed a change. Fromm was sitting behind a glass desk on the left side of the office, enabling him to see the spectacular view. On his desk were two computer monitors scrolling with green and red numeric tables and charts, behind him was a long credenza made of mahogany wood from the local baobab tree. On top of the credenza there were pictures of Fromm with former U.S. presidents, a framed Securities and Exchange Commission award, and his CPA certificate. In the corner of the office was a glass table and Tiffany lamp, and under the lamp were several large colorful opals.

Fromm was watching Jim Cramer's *Mad Money* on the wall across from his desk. Eric had become a big fan of Cramer after reading his book *Confessions of a Street Addict*. In the book Cramer described activities used by hedge fund managers to manipulate stock prices—some with debatable legality and others outright illegal. Fromm appreciated Jim's knowledge of hedge funds and quant trading.

As he led the way into the office, Jay introduced Lindsay and McCord. "Hi, Eric. This is Lindsay Arthur, the managing partner from KGO's Bridgetown office and his colleague Derek McCord, visiting from New York."

"Hello, gentlemen. How are you doing?" said Fromm as he got up from his desk to shake their hands.

"We're doing great," replied Arthur. "Jay has been taking care of us."

"I wouldn't expect anything different. He's an excellent tour guide and controller, of course," said Eric with a smile. "Please sit down." The two visitors sat down in front of Fromm's desk. "How can we help you?"

"First, let me thank your company for the business. You are a very important client to us, and we look forward to growing with you," said Lindsay.

"No problem, Mr. Arthur. Jay tells me you have an excellent engagement team. Very responsive."

"Dat shot. Only the best for Green Shade$," noted Arthur. "We appreciate you taking the time today to meet with us. Derek is down from the States to perform a little due diligence. He has a client that may want to move their retirement plans to your company."

"That's fantastic. I can't think of a better place for them to park their investments," confirmed Fromm.

"Yes, Mr. Fromm. I hear your returns are very impressive," added McCord.

"Call me Eric, please. What would you like to know?"

"I guess, first, why do you think Green Shade$ is so successful?"

"Well, there are many factors that contribute to successful trading, Derek. Over the last two years I've learned that the most important thing for profitable investing is the psychological well-being of our traders and the overall space they work in. As you can see, we have made considerable investments in our facility," stated Eric.

"Yes, very impressive. I have never seen a trading environment like this," noted McCord.

"Our team all work together for a common cause: yield high returns for our clients. We've hired some of the best traders and analysts in the business." Fromm turned around one of his monitors and pointed out the Year-to-Date, One-Year and Two-Year investment performance of the Green Shade$ funds:

Green Shade$ Market Performance

Asset Class/Index	YTD Market	YTD GS$	Year 1 Market	Year 1 GS$	Year 2 Market	Year 2 GS$
U.S. Equities:						
S&P 500	-8.1%	12.3%	12.3%	33.4%	16.1%	38.1%
Russell 2000	-8.6%	7.6%	6.1%	24.3%	10.2%	27.3%
Foreign Equities:						
MSCI EAFE	-6.5%	9.7%	2.8%	16.8%	7.6%	15.7%
MSCI EM	-4.8%	5.1%	-5.7%	4.1%	3.4%	7.7%
Alternatives:						
FTSE EPRA NAREIT Global	-7.3%	2.3%	10.6%	24.9%	4.9%	12.5%
Bloomberg Commodity	15.5%	26.3%	19.4%	31.3%	12.7%	20.3%

"As you can see, gentlemen, our performance speaks for itself. A lot of green. Over the last two years we have consistently beaten the general market. I think your client would be happy to generate those type of returns for their employees."

"Yes, very impressive indeed," noted Arthur.

"What do you attribute these returns to?" asked McCord.

"We have analysts and subject matter experts who program trades based on fundamental factors. Specifically, our team understands the financial components that drive stock performance. For example, a company's earnings and profitability will almost always impact stock price," noted Fromm.

"So, nearly all trades are based on financial information?"

"For the most part but not all trades, Derek. While financials are typically the first and foremost measure of performance, related news is just as important. At times it may be more important."

"Thus, all the financial news stations on the monitors," confirmed Lindsay.

"Correct. Immediate access to financial media like Bloomberg and CNBC is an added advantage. A stock's price could go up or down based on the news and emotions like fear. You need to have the latest information from the most credible sources," explained Fromm.

"How about trading methods?" asked McCord.

"We rely heavily on analytics and quantitative trading. We developed a proprietary rating system for each stock based on objective data, optimized for predictive value."

"A sort of black box?"

"Yes, but not exactly. Our trading tools are a little different. We created frequency trading techniques that link to a stock's price history based on chart patterns and financial momentum." Fromm continued, "For example the release of a company's earnings report will influence the price of a stock. A strong earnings report beating analyst estimates generally results in the stock price moving up. Conversely, if the company posted a bad quarter the stock will go down."

"Sounds very simple," said McCord.

"It's a little more complicated than that. Our quantitative stock rating system is based on financial ratios that delivers an objective, data-driven approach to evaluate individual stocks, and how they rank compared to their industry peers. We utilize and compare over 100 metrics and rank the investment accordingly."

"What metrics do you use in the rating system?" asked McCord.

"Our programmers and analysts have developed a proprietary system that evaluates stocks along five dimensions:

- Market Value
- Industry Quality
- Stock Momentum
- Company Estimates
- Financial Results

"These five-dimension ratings are then combined into an overall score that is used to rank the stock," lectured Fromm.

"I can see how you guys perform very well," confirmed McCord.

"Yes, we do. We're no D.E. Shaw, Two Sigma, or Citadel, but yes, we do pretty well."

"Where do you get your financial information?"

"Multiple sources. We leverage news feeds and extract financial data from SEC filings," added Eric.

"Extract?"

"Yes. After a filing is received from the SEC our Indian affiliate cuts it into chunks and sends it to us."

"So, public information?"

"Yes. They XML tag sections of public company 10Ks, 10Qs and 8Ks which are then downloaded into our customized application programming interface. The parsed EDGAR filings feed right into our trading models."

"Do the financial statements' footnotes factor into your rating system?"

"They're the highest rated element."

"Are they derived from XBRL data?"

"Yes, our programs read XML and XBRL tags."

"So, the tagged data goes right into your black box?" asked McCord.

"We don't have a black box," corrected Fromm.

"Oh, I meant to say into your stock rating system. Sorry," replied Dex.

"Correct. All computer-generated data is compiled. However, Mr. McCord, having an accurate information feed into a technical and fundamental analysis is a good thing but it is not the only factor. You still need to program a little bit of common sense into your trading tools."

"That is what your teams are doing on the trading floor," commented Arthur.

"Yes. They watch every trade very carefully using our proprietary indicators. From my days at the SEC, we developed red flags for bad stocks and checkered flags for stock winners. The trading indicators and our rating system are the primary factors in making profitable timely trades," declared Fromm.

"Speaking of timely. How fast do these trades execute after you receive the public information?" asked McCord.

"Our quantitative analysis and execution are measured in nanoseconds. A nanosecond is one billionth of a second. This allows us to beat the market."

"Wow. That kind of speed is difficult to even comprehend," said Arthur.

"A clever way to think about it is to visualize traveling 300 feet versus traveling five miles. If you were traveling in nanoseconds, it would take you 300 billionths of a second to cover five miles. You can imagine the importance this speed is to our traders."

"Thus, the fiber optic ring around our island," added Arthur.

"Correct, Lindsay. It's a necessity. Everything is getting faster in our world. Things have become instant like downloading a movie or music. Nowhere is this acceleration more evident than in the financial markets," preached Fromm.

"It sure has. My office and workpapers are connected to my hip," said McCord, seeking to earn Eric's trust.

"During my days in public accounting, Derek, I distinctly remember my clients calling in stock orders via telephone. The trading process has certainly changed since then," reminisced Fromm. There was a slight pause. "Have I answered all of your questions, gentlemen?"

"Yes. Those are all the questions I have. This has been very helpful. My client will be extremely impressed by what you are doing here. And I'm sure they'll want to make a visit to the island as well."

"Who wouldn't, Derek?"

The four men got up from their chairs and started to walk out of the office. McCord stopped and looked out the window.

"Such a magnificent view. I can see why you moved down here."

"Yes, you never get tired of it."

McCord then looked over to the credenza, "Where are these opals from?"

"Oh, these are from Australia. We have a very generous owner."

McCord nodded and smiled.

Fromm walked the men down the terrace overlooking the trading floors. He shook hands with Arthur and McCord and said good luck as they exited through the door at the end of the balcony. Fromm was amped up, and a guy like McCord was not going to get in his way. He was on to something huge. The pieces of his local fiefdom were falling into place like never before. He was going to be one of the most influential men in the West Indies. His business skills, SEC knowledge, and creative thinking were bringing him to places that his former colleagues had never dreamed of. He had a desire and a vision, and he didn't have to have any more boundaries.

As the visitors from KGO were led by Gaucher down the stairs back into the reception area, McCord looked back before the door closed and noted his host proudly standing on the terrace, watching his traders in action battling for ungodly sums of money.

"Thank you for the tour, Jay," said Lindsay.

"My pleasure, Mr. Arthur. I'll tell my dad you said hello."

"Please do."

"I hope we were able to answer all your questions, Mr. McCord," Jay said with a smile.

"Yes. Extremely helpful. Please convey my thanks to Mr. Fromm again. It was good of him to take time out of his busy day."

"Sure will," said Jay.

"One question I forgot to ask. Who owns Green Shade$?" asked McCord.

"We have two owners. The minority owner is an investment fund in the Cayman Islands. We send dividend checks down to them often."

"A private investment firm?"

"Sort of. It's not public information but the owner of the Cayman fund is the prime minister's wife."

"That's interesting," commented McCord.

"She comes to our facility fairly often and spends a lot of time with Mr. Fromm. They seem to have a very good relationship. But our largest shareholder is a company located in Australia. The owner usually visits us five or six times a year. Actually, he arrived on the island yesterday."

"From Australia?"

"I believe so."

"Do you know where he is now?"

"I think he's attending an exhibition polo match in Saint James Parish." What's his name?"

"His name is Nigel Metcalf."

If you like fun with math, see Exhibit 8: Key Financial Ratios

Chapter 12

*"You have to choose the voice you are going to trust.
You can't listen to everyone."*
—Alice Hoffman

- The Prime Minister
- Polo Field
- Villa Balmoral
- Bolanlé Teague

"NIGEL METCALF. HOW do I know that name?" thought McCord. He had heard the name Metcalf before but could not place it. McCord's brain was tired, and he was desperate for a little rest, but he needed to meet this Nigel Metcalf. Lindsay and Dex agreed to make a visit to the polo field. The Land Rover departed the Green Shade$ parking lot of loose shells and white stones turning left towards the north end of the island. Once Arthur navigated his way out of the busy Bridgetown streets his Rover accelerated onto the coastal Spring Garden Highway. The Barbados Polo Club was 30 kilometers north in the Parish of Saint James.

"Impressive facility," stated Arthur while keeping his eye on the road.

"I've never seen a trading environment like theirs," added McCord.

"Their investment returns are impressive, too. It appears they have the right stuff, mon. I'm happy for my friends son, it looks like he landed a good job."

"I agree, it's a nice office and their rating system seems to work. Their two-year investment performance is extraordinary considering the current market conditions."

"It's unfortunate we can't put our firm's retirement plan with them. Our conflict-of-interest requirements prohibit that," stated Lindsay.

"That's too bad. You could have been able to retire early."

"Not yet, my friend. Our *Blissful Island* is too expensive," protested Arthur. "I still have a few mortgage payments left and need to tuck away more for retirement, and my wife's lifestyle."

"Ha yes, nowadays it seems to be expensive everywhere. I mean, I like New York, but what I pay in rent and taxes is ridiculous. I could live large down here."

"We'd be happy to welcome you."

"Thanks. I can see why Fromm came to Barbados. Warm climate, casual lifestyle, and I am sure he is paid much more than what he was making at the Securities and Exchange Commission," McCord sensed.

"Eric seems to be a good man. He has given back to the island," noted Lindsay. "I hear he is working with the prime minister's wife on several causes: Hope for Children, Barbados Cancer Society, and Community Tourism Foundation, to name a few."

"It's nice to see he's supporting the community," agreed McCord.

The polo field was a 20-minute drive from the Green Shade$ facility and was located just up the hill from McCord's hotel, the Sandy Lane Luxury Beach Resort. The hotel was regarded as the premier address in the Caribbean, a preferred resort for luxury travelers from around the world. McCord normally wouldn't stay at a place like Sandy Lane, but Walsh's assistant booked it for him. EDGAR Data & Intelligence was buying, as long as McCord returned with answers.

The polo club was set back from Spring Garden Highway down a long tree-lined driveway. At the end was a gabled wooden clubhouse painted white with green shutters. A large overhang created a shady patio area for its guests. Near the pitch under the veranda were tables full of crackers, cheese spreads, mango, tasty looking cakes, and multiple bouquets of flowers. Wine and local Bajan rum were also being served. The adjoining grassy field made it an exceptional venue for the game of kings.

Polo etiquette for the audience falls more in line with a golf match than a football game. The attendees in chic attire enjoy the thrill of watching 1,000+ pound horses moving gracefully under the hand of their riders. These were men and women dressed to impress and to be seen. The men in their sear-sucker blue blazers, Ralph Lauren collared shirts. and pastel shorts. The women wearing wide-brimmed, dramatic hats, sophisticated sundresses, and pretty shoes with no heels. All were trying to keep cool under the hot Barbadian sun.

McCord and Arthur exited the Land Rover and moved towards the playing field. The field was 300 yards long and 160 yards wide. On the end lines were goal posts 24 feet apart. In front of them horses were galloping at full speed. Arthur led the way towards a group of gentlemen looking out towards the horses, pretending to be paying attention to the match while having a social discussion. A tall man in the middle of the party was holding a decorative long-handled mallet. He appeared to be getting most of the attention. Lindsay walked over to the man with the stick and entered the semi-circle. McCord stood behind his friend.

"Good afternoon, Mr. Prime Minister."

"Lindsay! How are you, my friend?" replied the distinguished man in a powerful voice.

"Very well, very well. Apologies for the interruption. I wanted to introduce you to my associate from New York," said Arthur while stepping to the side. "Prime Minister Teague, this is Mr. Derek McCord."

The prime minister extended his large hand to Dex. "Nice to meet you, Derek. Welcome to Barbados."

"Thank you," replied McCord.

"How are things in New York?"

"Very cold, sir. Much different than your beautiful island."

"Oh yes. We are truly fortunate and appreciate our visitors," replied the politician. "What are you doing on the island?"

"I'm here to perform a little due diligence for a client of mine."

"We welcome any and all commerce to Barbados. You'll find our workforce and infrastructure second to none in the Caribbean."

"I agree, sir. So far what I've seen has been very impressive."

"Excellent. Are you staying long?"

"I'm not sure yet but hopefully long enough to enjoy the sand and water."

"Ah, you must enjoy our restaurants, too. We appreciate our service sector on the island. Considerable attention is given to our guests."

"I can sense that. A lot of pride is in the air."

"Do you know much about polo?" asked Teague.

"I have to admit that this is the first time I've been to a polo match," confessed McCord.

"I think you are not alone," said the Prime Minister with a big smile.

Teague introduced McCord to a few other men in the group. Others introduced themselves. Most of the men were either local businesspeople or politicians. Dex noticed that the majority of spectators had no idea how the match was played, who was playing, or what the score was. It seemed that no one understood the rules of polo. Everyone was bluffing their way through, trying to convince everyone else they understood what was happening and that they were enjoying it. Horses ran back and forth. Balls were hit, sometimes the scoreboard changed. McCord was no different, he didn't even know which end of the stick the ball was hit with.

~~~

Master Teague is a savvy political technocrat. When he was a young senator, Teague was instrumental in bringing technology and IT businesses to Barbados. He became the primary supporter of building a high-speed fiber optic ring around the island. The then senator preached that the investment would bring long-term economic stability and attract international businesses with a secure and profitable infrastructure. More importantly, Teague believed that technology, along with tax incentives, would bring a global skilled work force to the island to train locals.

The future prime minister supported the initiative by sponsoring numerous incentives for information technology businesses and their skilled expatriates, including relief programs that permitted tax-free payments to foreign employees, such as allowances for housing, food, and travel. It was an ideal opportunity for companies like 2K TECH Corporation and their young software engineers around the world, for example Purvi Singh of NSG Global.

At its peak, the technology company employed over 750 people, primarily from India and other tech-savvy countries. Starting wages for the new residents were $15,000 per year. This was the equivalent of making 100,000 rupees in India, very wealthy by Indian standards. Many of the employees sent a portion of their earnings back home to their families in India, but most spent their well-earned salary on the island's holiday activities and Bajan nightlife.

On most evenings technology companies would open their facilities to provide training to locals on project management and software engineering. After years of knowledge transfer, Teague and his fellow politicians were able to leverage the intellectual capital of the imported multi-nationals for the benefit of the island's long-term economic growth. For years the local policymakers publicized their great relationships with the new foreign corporations, highlighting the financial stimulus the global workforce provided. The arrangement was a win-win for everyone.

After years of economic success from riding the tailwinds of the dot-com boom and post Y2K solutions, it all abruptly ended. New business that was being sent to the island slowed down and companies like 2K TECH Corporation, with its large infrastructure and reliance on foreign revenues, couldn't stop the financial bleeding. After a few decades of ownership changes, amongst numerous international IT services firms, the enterprise and their employees could no longer be supported. The last company that gave it go had to sell the facility and lay off workers. Indian programmers were sent back to their homeland and the building was handed over to the Bajan government. However, the years of training local Barbadians on project management and technology was not lost. That was when, on the urging of then senator Master Teague, Australia's Metcalf Consulting Ltd. came to the island to leverage and utilize the educated workforce.

~~~

Prime Minister Teague, McCord, and Arthur were having polo-themed conversations while chewing their humidity-infested crackers and sipping lukewarm wine. The polo match was a hot, thirst-inducing, classy, confusing affair. Sweat was rolling down all the attendees' faces on account of the steamy 96-degree heat wave. Lindsay had just accepted an invitation to the prime minister's villa that evening to celebrate the one-year anniversary of his appointment and the island's independence.

While looking at McCord, Prime Minister Teague requested, "I hope you will also join us tonight, Derek."

"I would be honored, sir," replied McCord.

"Good. We start at 7:00pm. It's going to be a special event. My wife has been planning it for months. That's why I am here this afternoon. Better I get out of the way."

"I know what you mean," answered Arthur laughing. "It's best for us men to just let the women take over."

"So true."

"Knowing your wife, Mr. Prime Minister, it will be first-class all the way."

"Amen, Amen," replied Teague.

McCord looked out towards the field. He noticed a sharped dressed man standing on the sidelines of the grassy field. The man was intently observing the eight massive horses thundering in front of him.

"Who is that over there?" asked McCord.

"That is one of our most important financiers," replied Teague. "Mr. Nigel Metcalf from Australia. He is the co-owner of our largest technology and investment house on the island."

"The Green Shade$ facility?"

"Yes, correct. They have been instrumental in the economic success of Barbados."

"How long has Mr. Metcalf been here?"

"Came in yesterday for the celebration. Nigel and I go back many years. All the way to university at UCLA."

"He must be a good friend to travel all the way here."

"Yes, we are very good friends," replied Teague.

As the horses stopped and riders dismounted McCord left the group and walked over to the man on the sidelines. Attendees at the match were on the ready to participate in the traditional stomping of the divots. Parties started running onto the field. Metcalf followed the enthusiastic participants. McCord walked on the field to join Metcalf who was pushing grass back in place that the horses had ripped up. Nigel first saw McCord's shadow, then he looked up. A feeling of disbelief shocked him to the core, he thought he had seen a ghost. His emotions quickly turned to fear, then anger, which he immediately tried to squelch. Metcalf was clearly surprised to see the large man he had met less than a week ago in Sydney.

Earlier McCord couldn't remember how he knew the name Nigel Metcalf, but that changed when he saw his face. Dex immediately recognized Nigel as the older, distinguished man that Warren Young had introduced at Tony's funeral reception. He knew meeting him in Barbados was not happenstance. It had to be something else.

"Derek McCord?" asked Nigel.

"Yes, Mr. Metcalf. You remembered my name."

"Uh hum, yes. What are you doing in Barbados, mate?"

"On business," said McCord not wanting to disclose that he had visited his facility earlier.

"Well, that's an interesting coincidence. Do you come here often?" asked Metcalf.

"First time. I'll probably visit more often now. It's a beautiful island."

"I agree, Derek. And you have come at a great time. The weather is perfect during February. Although today is a little hot," Metcalf highlighted while trying to stay unfazed by McCord's appearance.

"Extremely. I'm not used to this high temperature."

"Better than New York, I imagine."

"Yes, I am very lucky to be here."

The two ended their brief conversation and remained silent in their thoughts. McCord and Metcalf continued walking around in unison, stomping divots in the field until it was time to return to the sidelines. The final two chuckkers of seven and a half minutes each were about to begin. Metcalf walked ahead of McCord, back towards the group where Prime Minister Teague was standing. Lindsay had left that group and was standing with three women and a man. McCord left Metcalf and joined his friend.

"Did you stomp the divots, Derek?" asked Lindsay.

"Absolutely. It was good fun," replied McCord pointing at his dirty docksiders. "I also met Nigel Metcalf."

"The co-owner of GreenShade$?"

"Yes. What's crazy was that I knew him, and he remembered me. We met last week when I was in Australia at my friend's funeral."

"No kidding, mon. It's a small world, my friend. Small world. Did you ask him about his facility?"

"No, I didn't. There really wasn't a chance to. Plus, I was still trying to figure out why he's down here," commented McCord.

"Perhaps you'll see him at the celebration tonight," replied Lindsay. "You can gather more information for your client there. I'm sure he'll be able to elaborate on the investment performance Eric Fromm spoke about."

"Good idea. We'll double check the facts."

"Yes, like a good auditor," laughed Lindsay.

McCord and Arthur stayed at the field speaking with locals until a loud bell rang indicating that six chukkers had been played and the game was over. The players in white and blue helmets dismounted their exhausted horses and began hugging and shaking hands. The home team Barbados Polo Club had defeated Apes Hill Club in the exhibition match. The men and their guests headed towards a fiery barbeque set up next to the club house. A selection of chicken and barbequed pork were being grilled. It was now late afternoon, and the wine was being replaced by spiced rum and beer. The players were ready for a bashment bawl-out. Lindsay asked Dex if he wanted to grab a bite before heading to the hotel. McCord declined. He was tired and sweaty. He needed a shower and a change of clothes before going to Prime Minister Teague's celebration.

The two men returned to the Land Rover and drove down the grassy driveway towards Sandy Lane Hotel. They were at the resort's grand reception entrance in less than three minutes. It was 5:00.

"I'll see you in an hour and a half," stated Lindsay. "The prime minister's villa is a 30-minute drive. We should be there by 7:00."

"Sounds good," replied McCord. "It was a productive day. Thanks for helping me out."

"No problems, my friend. It was fun. And it should be a great night."

"I hope so."

Walsh's executive assistant up north at ED&I headquarters didn't disappoint when reserving a room for McCord's visit. Sandy Lane was perfectly set on the western coast of Barbados, frequently called the "platinum coast" for the beauty of its beaches and sparkling waters. The resort had it all, the classic elegance of Palladian buildings mirrored by the spacious comfort of the hotel rooms and suites, many shaded by mature mahogany trees. The main building overlooked the sea and tranquil coral sand beach. The resort also included stunning private villas, a PGA golf course, an outstanding spa, and an exceptional level of warm Barbadian hospitality.

McCord retrieved his suitcase and backpack from the rear seat. A bellhop in a blue uniform immediately grabbed his bags and escorted Dex past cascading fountains towards check-in. Singing birds and the scent of tropical flowers filled the air of beautifully manicured gardens. Inside he was welcomed by a smiling local behind a reception desk. After presenting identification and a credit card McCord was provided a room key. The clerk noted he was staying in a very fine room, a one-bedroom suite in the Dolphin wing. Walsh must have taken care of me, he thought. McCord was escorted to the second floor and shown his room. He handed the escort a US$10 tip, equivalent to 20 Bajan dollars, and the youthful porter appeared happy.

The Dolphin suite was spacious enough to feature a large living room, outside patio, and brilliant bedroom with an elegant en suite bathroom, the balcony overlooking the azure waters of the Caribbean. McCord had a brief time before he would have to leave. He wanted to spend time looking at Abbot's report but instead went onto the balcony and laid on the chaise lounge. The gentle sound of the waves was hypnotic, and he drowsily closed his eyes.

An hour had passed before McCord woke up to the sound of calypso music at the pool. He was confused for a second, then swiftly got his bearings. He had 20 minutes to get dressed. Dex hung up his pink button-down shirt, blue blazer, and khaki pants on the inside of the shower door; Stacy's steam out the wrinkle's solution was at work. He quickly showered, shaved, and got dressed. The wrinkles weren't completely out of his clothes, but they looked good enough. McCord didn't have time to look at emails or review workpapers but figured he could do that later; he didn't want to keep his host waiting. By the time McCord arrived at the lobby Lindsay was speaking with the resort manager, who was a friend of the Arthur family. Dex thought, "Everyone on this island really does know each other."

~~~

After McCord left the Polo field Nigel Metcalf summoned his hired assassins. Nauti was enraged over seeing McCord alive and well. Carroll and Frazier did not finish the job on North Head. The two men pulled into the Polo field in their rented white Toyota Hiace Van. They weren't sure what they were summoned for, but Metcalf didn't look happy when they arrived.

"I thought you said he was dead," Metcalf said in a furious hushed tone.

"Who?" asked Carroll.

"The American from New York."

"He is. We saw him jump off the cliff. There was no sign of life in the water," explained Frazier.

"Well, mate. He's still alive and fucking on this island."

"How do you know?"

"He was just here speaking with me. That's how I know!"

"The tall Yank, mon?" asked Frazier.

"Yes, idiot. You need to take care of the situation."

"OK, Mr. Metcalf. Sorry. We will make sure the job is finished," replied Carroll.

"You'd better. He's attending the prime minister's celebration tonight. I'll arrange that you work with the valet. Keep an eye on him but do not make any moves at the party."

"But shouldn't we…"

Metcalf interrupted the men, "Let me repeat, nothing happens at the party. You need to take care of it later. Follow him when he leaves and find out where he is staying. Then pick your moment."

"Yes, absolutely. We'll take care of it. Eliminate the American by any means necessary. Correct?" confirmed Carroll.

"Yes, correct. But we don't want a scene on the island. Dispose of the body and ensure it's not found. These are critical times for Master Teague and his wife."

"We will take care of the problem," stated Frazier.

"No shit you will. After you complete your assignment reach out to Fromm at Green Shade$. He will arrange for your return to Australia. Again, take care of your target and leave no trace. Got it?" demanded Metcalf.

"Yes. It will be done, mon."

"It better be. Otherwise, you will not be returning to the Ocean Hawks."

"We will see you in Pittwater, ready for the season," replied Carroll.

"Good. Now drive me to the prime minister's villa and I'll speak with security."

The three men entered the minivan and headed north; further instructions were dictated by Metcalf on the way. This time a gun would not be available. The laws of Barbados prohibit the possession, use, import or export of a firearm by any person. Carroll and Frazier would have to figure out how to complete their assignment without the benefit of a firearm. The two men assured Mr. Metcalf that after tomorrow the American would no longer be a problem; this was their territory, and they knew how to take care of problems. Especially big ones.

VILLA BALMORAL, BARBADOS

The two accountants left Sandy Lane promptly at 6:30pm. The Land Rover headed north through the village of Holetown. A mile past town they turned right towards Mt. Hillaby, the center of the island. The sun was starting to set as Arthur and McCord drove through the mango fields in the north, the colors of the pink and orange sky complimenting the sweet scent of the mangos. As Lindsay's Rover sliced through the air, they passed a group of dust covered workers happily walking home after a day of picking.

Arthur pointed out that the mango was an economically important crop to Barbados and the harvest was currently in full swing. That it was still one of the few fruits in the world that needs to be picked by hand. The mango pickers were considered artists on the island as the greatest possible care had to be taken when picking, even the smallest cracks in a mango would result in rapid spoilage by rotting, a serious loss of value in the lucrative global market.

"The scent is very seductive, isn't it?" Lindsay said while driving.

"Surprisingly intense, I can almost feel it on my skin. Who do all these guys work for?" asked McCord while gazing out the window.

"The workers are employees of the prime minister and his family. They own over five acres of these fruit trees."

"Not a bad cash crop," mused McCord.

"Not bad at all, and don't worry, they'll give you a bushel to take home."

The aroma emanating from the rows and rows of mango trees was an intoxicating reminder of the beauty that surrounded them. A magnificent place to live, McCord thought.

The entrance to the compound had two guardhouses securing the property. A sign read Villa Balmoral. McCord found this ironic considering the connection of the name to the British monarchy. Serious looking men with decorative uniforms and large wooden batons were welcoming visitors. The heavy metal gates opened and closed as guests were cleared. The guards recognized Lindsay right away and waved the auto through into the long driveway. On either side of the private road were mature bay leaf trees with large leaves that cast massive shadows down the long straight driveway. White crushed seashells provided the echo of paradise as Lindsay's Rover left behind a mysterious dust. At the end of the majestic drive was a roundabout featuring a water fountain with a sculpture of flying fish skimming on top of curling waves.

Valet with welcoming smiles greeted Arthur and McCord. Dex saw out of the corner of his eye two uniformed men standing next to a white Toyota van who appeared to be staring at him. McCord didn't look back as he didn't want to offend the personnel. The valet who took Arthur's car keys directed the guests to pass through the tropical gardens that shielded the house. On the path, ground lights accentuated the stone walkway and tropical plants. Passing through the entrance of the house, they moved into an open-air courtyard. The men were greeted by a beautiful woman wearing an ornate African head dress flanked by two Royal Standard Poodles. It was the prime minister's wife.

~~~

Bolanlé Teague was a driven and persuasive organizer. Bolanlé means "the one who finds wealth at home," a traditional African girl's first name. It has an eccentric pronunciation and is believed to attract wealth. Bolanlé was raised in the African nation of Uganda in the early 1970s. Her father built his wealth selling opals mined in Uganda and Ethiopia, and he also imported the precious stones from Australia for local trade. Bolanlé's life was joyful until her father, a high-ranking statesman at the time, was brutely murdered when the tyrant Idi Amin overthrew the government in 1972. It was said that the three-year-old had witnessed her father being decapitated by a machete. The genocide that followed in Uganda was even more horrific. Her mother and siblings were enslaved by Amin's troops while thousands of citizens were brutely murdered. Bolanlé was able to escape and go into hiding but never saw her family again. Eventually she left the country with her cousin and went to the West Indies, settling in Jamaica. Two and a half years later she moved to Barbados. Bolanlé was a survivor.

Bolanlé meet Master Teague when she was 24 years old. The young up-and-coming politician caught her eye at a dance club in St. Lawrence Gap. The country was celebrating Crop Over, a day of music and merriment to recognize the final sugarcane harvest of the season. Her confidence and beauty swept Teague off his feet. For three straight months they enjoyed every kind of nightlife venue, from flashy cocktail bars and dance clubs to no-frills rum shops and full-on festivals. They became inextricably devoted to each other. Just four short months after meeting they got engaged.

The couple were married three months later in a themed wedding that paid homage to Bolanlé's side of the family. They planned a colorful African celebration in a Caribbean way, complete with steel pan players, numerous floral displays, and a traditional Bajan buffet dinner with cou cou, flying fish, jerk chicken, and plantains.

The new Mrs. Teague immediately became known as the politician's flamboyant wife from Africa. She was a socialite and enjoyed throwing lavish parties. Bolanlé was also a savvy businessperson. She helped manage the family's mango farms and started her own opal import business, giving honor to her late Ugandan father. The opal business flourished as she opened numerous store fronts in key Caribbean cruise line destination ports, taking advantage of the daily deluge of tourists who were ready to spend money on jewelry that looked tropical. Her major source of opals was from Metcalf Mining Ltd. in Australia, the company owned by her husband's good friend from university. The opal business was just one venture that Bolanlé and Metcalf partnered, she also was his co-owner of the local tech facility that they named Green Shade$.

Over the years Master Teague and Bolanlé became known as the Barbadian power couple. Her elegance and power of persuasion helped her husband get elected as one of the youngest senators on the island. The cash flow from her opal business came in handy when garnering votes for her husband and motivating other politicians. She wanted more. A number of years later Bolanlé and a few senators started a movement for a breakaway from the English Commonwealth. Her funds from the opal business and illicit investment gains as co-owner of Green Shade$ helped make the movement reality. And when the Barbados independence referendum finally passed, and a prime minister had to be named, she was able to motivate members in The House of Assembly and certain influential Senators with sizeable contributions.

~~~

"Lindsay, you beautiful man, we're so glad you could make it," the enchanting women said while kissing him on each check.

"I wouldn't miss such an event and a chance to see such a lovely woman like you," Lindsay gushed. "Let me introduce you to my good friend from America. Mrs. Teague, please meet my colleague Derek McCord from New York."

"Please to meet you," McCord bowed uncomfortably.

"Welcome to Barbados, Mr. McCord. I hope you are finding our island very appealing."

"I have to admit it is extremely intoxicating."

"Yes, truly," she smiled. "It also tends to be seductive but be careful of the temptation. You may never want to leave," she quipped.

"Who are these beauties?" Dex said while cautiously pointing at the black and white poodles standing at Bolanlé's side.

"Oh, these are my closest companions, Athena and Achilles," pointing at Athena, a black female royal standard and then Achilles, a male white royal.

"Do you like dogs, Mr. McCord?"

"Yes, I had a German Shepard growing up in Virginia but unfortunately the paved streets in Manhattan are not conducive to having pets. I'm not a big believer in leashes, Mrs. Teague."

"Neither am I, Mr. McCord. And please call me Bolanlé," she said while casting a seductive smile toward Dex.

"Pardon me, gentlemen, I need to check on my husband. Let's chat later, Mr. McCord. I want to hear all about the latest news in New York."

"You can count on it, and please call me Derek."

The prime minister's wife flowed out of the courtyard while keeping her headdress affixed. McCord watched the African headwrap traveling across the reception area, stopping periodically to greet chosen guests. Dex found it very odd that the dogs were not leaving her side. Clearly they considered her the alpha, not the prime minister.

Arthur and McCord continued walking through the courtyard towards the pool area. The patio was filled with tables of local cuisine and drink stations. Further down guests were fully engaged in conversation, standing around a large swimming pool and eating from small plates while watching a bat show. An army of bats were taking turns skimming mosquitoes off the top of the pool. At the end of the pool stood two 12-foot marmoreal Roman pillars looking out to the valley of mangos. Next to one pillar was Eric Fromm speaking to a sharped dressed Caucasian couple. McCord excused himself to Lindsay, he wanted to hear more about Green Shade$ and its connection to NSG Global in India.

"Hello, Derek," said Fromm as he noticed the bulky man heading towards him. "Come here, come here. There is someone I want you to meet."

"Hello," said McCord as he reached out to shake hands with the gentleman and his partner.

"Derek McCord, this is U.S. Ambassador Kadlec and his wife Kim."

"Nice to meet you, Mr. Ambassador."

"Derek is from KGO New York," explained Eric.

"Good to meet you. And you can call me Dan."

"Nice to meet you Dan."

"This is my wife Kim," said Kadlec as he stepped aside. "She is originally from New York."

"Long Island, actually," noted Kim while shaking McCord's hand.

"What brings you to Barbados, Derek?" Ambassador Kadlec asked.

"I've been requested to perform due diligence on Mr. Fromm's company for a client up north. They are interested in moving their retirement plans to his company for safekeeping and better performance results."

"That is fantastic. The more business and money brought to the Caribbean the better."

"We try to identify, confirm, and advise the best in class for all our clients," stated McCord who used that assertion on frequent occasions.

"What type of business, Derek?" asked the ambassador's wife.

"My client is a technology company with a substantial number of employees worldwide. They want to ensure their retirement funds will be safe at Green Shade$."

"Great to hear Eric's company is on the radar in the states. The Bajans have invested heavily in terms of training and preparing people for the 21st century," replied the diplomat.

"It must be fun being the ambassador to Barbados, sir," said McCord trying to avoid the subject of the real reason for his visit.

"You'll have to ask Kim that question. I have been extremely busy and not with only Barbados. Our diplomatic duties also include eight other eastern Caribbean islands, like Antigua, St. Kitts, and St. Lucia, just to name a few."

"But we love living in Bridgetown," added Kim Kadlec. "Our residence is magnificent."

"Pardon my ignorance but what is your role down here?" asked McCord.

"Good question, son. We represent the U.S. government on behalf of the president in treaty negotiations, immigration, foreign aid, and humanitarian programs," explained the Ambassador.

"Wow. A very big job."

"Indeed. That's why we collaborate closely with companies like Eric's."

"You do indeed," confirmed Fromm. "At Green Shade$ we consider our company integral to the underlying principle of Caribbean culture and its future. Our mission is 'to build a better working Barbados.' That includes a trust between our clients, the public, and private sectors."

"I'd say mission accomplished," added Kadlec.

"As you have seen and heard today, Derek, we're bringing world class standards to the island and our organization in terms of how we operate and how we provide our services," said Fromm.

The conversation continued with Mrs. Kadlec describing the elegance of the diplomat's residence. Rum drinks flowed and toasts were made, acknowledging the great relationship the islands had with the representatives from the United States. McCord attempted to extract more information from Fromm about his company's relationship with NSG Global in India but was unable to do so, Fromm kept changing the subject to the performance of their retirement plans and his days working at the SEC. After a half hour of interesting discussions McCord excused himself from the conversation. He needed to use the restroom. He walked past the pool and back towards the front of the villa, on the left side of the courtyard were French doors leading into a large living room. McCord figured a bathroom would be somewhere in there and entered. The room was decorated with African and West Indies treasures. Moving forward he discovered ornate swords, tribal shields, and colorful flowers that gave way to a beautiful rainforest of plants. The coral tile on the floor changed colors as McCord sauntered around the room. On the left side was an entrance to a small den radiating with light. The den's walls were lined with glass mirrored cabinets full of opals. The interior lighting made each precious stone radiate with a magnificent tint. McCord was mesmerized by the stones. The last time he had seen opals so majestic and colorful was at a display in the Sydney Opera House.

"They are beautiful, aren't they Mr. McCord? I mean Derek," said Mrs. Teague approaching from behind as the two standard poodles stood between them.

"Yes, impressive. I didn't know you could get opals on the island."

"Oh yes, at all my shops. But these are gifts from my home country and all the way from Australia. Precious stones from dear friends," Bolanlé added.

"You have friends in faraway places," McCord quipped.

"Being a civil servant's wife does have its perks. I receive fascinating gifts and meet very interesting people."

"Well, I hope I fall into the category as an interesting person."

"I don't know yet, Derek. Hopefully we'll get to see more of you on the island, then I'll come to a conclusion."

Bolanlé grabbed McCord's hand and showed him the rest of the house. One room was more impressive than the other. The only room she did not show was the master bedroom. Dex was relived, that could have gotten uncomfortable, he thought. After a 10-minute guided tour, the prime minister's wife finally showed McCord where the restroom was located.

"Don't be too long, Derek. We're about to start the fireworks show."

"Thank you for showing me your villa. I will just be a second."

"Great. We'll all be out by the pool," added Bolanlé.

By the time McCord returned to the pool the fireworks had started. The night skies were transformed into pyrotechnic glory, courtesy of Fireworks by Grucci, a company brought to the celebration courtesy of the U.S. government and Ambassador Kadlec. State-of-the-art computer programs orchestrated the show to a choreography of music. Bursting flowers filled the air followed by loud explosions, some of the fireworks shot straight up before exploding, while others quickly shattered into thousands of sparks. The extravagant show lasted 35 minutes. At the grand finale, a rapidly fired barrage of aerial fireworks was followed by an army of drones. The drones displayed the English Union Jack that quickly changed to the ultramarine and gold vertical tricolor flag of Barbados, complete with the black trident in the center. The thunderous applause and boisterous laughter of the crowd was unforgettable.

The Teagues' celebration continued for a few more hours, and the guests were in no hurry to leave, but McCord was tired and eventually convinced Arthur it was time to go. As they were walking through the courtyard Dex noticed a group speaking in the opal room. It was Metcalf, Fromm, and Bolanlé Teague. They looked to be having a serious conversation.

The valet retrieved Arthur's Land Rover shortly after the two men left the villa, but not after receiving a party favor of a bag of freshly handpicked mangos. It was after 11:00pm. The Rover rolled past the flying fish water fountain and down the bay leaf tree-lined driveway, back towards the rows of mango trees. McCord couldn't stop thinking about the room filled with

Australian opals and the group inside. He didn't notice that a white Toyota van was following them. In less than 20 minutes they arrived back at Sandy Lane. McCord got out of the car and thanked Arthur for an entertaining day. A white minivan parked across the street.

~~~

The conversation in Villa Balmoral's opal room between Metcalf, Fromm, and Mrs. Teague was uncomfortable and intense. Metcalf had just finished briefing them about unfortunate events in Australia and McCord's visit. The three were anxious to hear more detail about the auditor from New York. As information was disclosed Eric and Bolanlé started to have serious concerns. Nauti was deep in thought.

"What are we going to do about that auditor?" asked the prime minister's wife.

"He was asking a lot of questions today. Searching for something," added Fromm.

"I'm on it," stated Metcalf. "This time tomorrow you will not have a worry."

"How's that, my friend?"

"Our rugby players are following him as we speak. They will take care of the problem."

"Nauti, my husband, and I have invested a lot of time and money in the success of your company. We need to ensure the American is taken care of."

"And he will be," stated Metcalf.

"I don't have to explain to you what else is at stake. I have been working on our larger plans for years. We do not need any distractions!" insisted Bolanlé.

"You don't need to tell me that! I had my friend's son assassinated for your cause," Metcalf replied angrily. "So yes, I understand the importance of this matter. Where are we with the other islands?"

"I continue to buy influence, but we need more money, Nigel. My contacts are not easily bought. So far, we have assurances from the pension ministers of Antigua, Bahamas, and St. Lucia. It looks like we can get a commitment from Grenada as well."

"Excellent!" said an enthused Fromm listening intently.

"Yes, our new friends are willing to move their island's social security funds to Green Shade$. Managing these assets will get us a step closer to achieving our goal of expanding influence away from the Commonwealth to a united West Indies Federation."

"And a lot more money coming our way," added Fromm.

"How much under management are we looking at?" asked Metcalf.

"Between the four islands we should receive over $1.5 billion of their social security funds. This will add substantial capital to our current investments under management," noted Bolanlé.

"Let's make this happen," stated an enthused Fromm.

For the past 12 months Bolanlé Teague had been spreading her influence and money around the Caribbean with the goal of her husband becoming the leader of a newly formed West Indies coalition. With financial assistance from Bolanlé's hidden Cayman Island funds, many of the other Caribbean islands were starting to garner support and prepare referendums to break away from England. Since Queen Elizabeth II had died and an unpopular King Charles III now sat on the throne, her plans were becoming close to reality.

Bolanlé believed she still needed to buy influence from several more island ministers, who were responsible for the oversight of their citizens' national social security, insurance, and pension funds. Obtaining their commitment was going to require 'unofficial contributions' that would lead to Green Shade$ securing the lucrative business of managing retirement funds that fell under each local minister's control—and their island's workers' organizations. With cash and illegal profits in hand Bolanlé would be able to secure a significant amount of influence. Her plan was already in motion and on the path towards success.

"As you know, gentlemen, we have a lot at stake. I've persuaded the ministers to provide us with a two and a half percent annual management fee on the pension funds. Not counting gains on our investments that will be over $37 million per year in fees alone!" explained Bolanlé.

"Excellent," said an enthusiastic Fromm.

"Yes, a lot at stake," confirmed Metcalf. "Where are we with the Australian ambassador?"

"Since King Charles' coronation bells rang out from Westminster Abby and throughout the Commonwealth, our politicians have been planting the seeds of a succession with your ambassador, who is in contact with your politicians. He will let us know next steps, but it will probably require significant capital, garnering votes for an Australian referendum is going to take significant payments to several high-level officials in Canberra," noted Bolanlé.

"OK. When I get back let me know if I need to speak with any members of Parliament."

Metcalf understood that it would be a heavy lift to persuade members of the Australian Parliament to split away from the Commonwealth but felt the timing was right. He believed his country had been held back as a world power and with King Charles III on the throne their economic position would deteriorate. He needed and wanted to be a big part of a succession—his future political aspirations and financial standing depended on it.

Nigel turned his attention back to the situation of McCord's presence on the island.

"Eric, I told the boys to contact you when the job is done. You'll need to get them out of the country," instructed Metcalf.

"Understood. I'll use our petty cash. It'll be impossible to trace."

"Don't send them back to Australia. Send them to Jamacia. Carroll is from there and will know how to get lost for a while."

"Agreed," confirmed Eric. "We don't want the Green Shade$ name connected in any way to the American."

"Let me know if I need to call in any other favors on or off the island," added the prime minister's wife.

"Understood, Bolanlé. But the matter should be taken care of. I don't want to involve the prime minister or any of your contacts."

"Good. Thank you, Nigel. Now let me get back to my guests," said Bolanlé as she strode confidently out of the opal room.

Metcalf and Fromm discussed the details of Carroll and Frazier's assignment. Metcalf had concerns that the two men would not properly finish the job, but he had no other options. Nigel provided Fromm with the cell number of Carroll noting he was the more dependable assassin. He was leaving Barbados in the morning and wanted Fromm's personal assurance that the situation would be taken care of, and confirmation when the job was finished. The former SEC official confirmed that he will make sure the auditor will no longer be anyone's concern after tomorrow.

Chapter 13

"We shall not fail or falter; we shall not weaken or tire...
Give us the tools and we will finish the job."
—*Sir Winston Churchill*

- News from Australia
- Thunder Bay Beach Bar
- FBI's International Operations Division
- Metcalf Ownership Structure

McCORD WALKED THROUGH the royal lobby of Sandy Lane and made his way up to the Dolphin suite. He was sitting at the room's desk, wide awake and reviewing the events of the day. Nigel Metcalf and his presence in Barbados was on his mind. McCord booted up his laptop and opened the NSG internal control report. Scrolling down he stopped at the ownership findings. Abbot had noted that NSG Global was privately held, and the co-owners were Metcalf Consulting Ltd. and a Cayman Islands investment company. McCord had missed the connection, but there it was in black and white. Nigel was calling the shots at both NSG Global and Green Shade$.

McCord could not sleep after reviewing Abbot's report. He performed numerous google searches on Metcalf, reading about his personal history and investments. He found only limited details of a former public accountant who had achieved great financial success: a premier championship footy team, board member of several philanthropic organizations, and a self-made millionaire. It all looked good on paper. How could a guy like that want to jeopardize his success by stealing inside information? Or worse, was he the person who hired the assassins to kill Youngy, Abbot, and Dex himself? McCord still had questions but eventually fell asleep.

McCord's cell phone rang at 5:15am. He didn't recognize the number but could see through glassy eyes that it was an international call. Country code 0061.

"Hello, this is Derek," answered a sleepy McCord.

"Mr. McCord, this is Officer Beveridge from the Manly Beach Police Department."

Dex sat up in his bed. "Yes?"

"Sorry for the early wake up call. I wanted to inform you that there have been new developments in your case."

"What do you mean?" asked McCord with a groggy voice.

"Your friend Jiemba Abbot. A nude bather at a beach near Watsons Bay discovered his body. It washed up on shore, found tied up in rope with a few rocks stuffed in his clothes. The killers didn't do a great job of disposing Mr. Abbot's body. Obviously not professionals."

"Are you sure it was him?"

"Forensics is inspecting the corpse now, but we think it's him. The body matched the description you provided us. The tattoo of the lizard on the neck and gunshot wound validates your story," noted Beveridge.

"Have you informed his parents?" asked McCord.

"Yes. They are getting us dental records so we can confirm the identification. I owe you an apology, mate. Kenny was right. You're not a crazy Yank."

"Thanks for the kind words, officer," Dex said sarcastically. "Did you discover anything else about Tony Young's death?"

"That's another matter but we'll be opening up the case again, performing an autopsy, and taking a closer look at the circumstances and evidence surrounding his death."

"I appreciate that. If you need any other information let me know," offered McCord.

"Nothing right now, Mr. McCord, but we'll contact you if needed."

"Thank you, Officer Beveridge."

"No worries, mate. We'll be in touch."

"That would be great."

"The MBPD appreciates your assistance. Good night."

McCord put down his cell phone and looked out his window towards the sea. His conversation with Officer Beveridge made him feel vindicated but not satisfied, he needed to know more. As Liv Watson, the queen of XBRL suggested, solve for X. Why did the killers go after Jiemba Abbot? Who killed Tony Young? Did it relate to what was in the NSG workpapers? How was Nigel Metcalf involved? McCord had work to do.

Out his hotel window the sun was starting to rise over the Caribbean Sea. McCord needed to clear his head and think, fit all the pieces together. He put on board shorts and a muscle shirt to go for a run along the shoreline, determined sneakers wouldn't be necessary on the soft sand. Dex left his room and walked downstairs; the resort was quiet. The front desk was staffed by a white suited older gentleman who had been on duty all night. McCord noted in the lobby sat two men on opposite sides of the room, one a businessman in casual attire reading the paper and sipping coffee, the other looked like a local in teal Bermuda shorts wearing a white Izod collared shirt.

McCord exited the lobby and walked past the pool. Once on the beach he headed north in a slow steady jog. The beach was empty, no guests awake yet to enjoy the morning sunrise. The white coral sands behind the hotel and along the Barbados shoreline made an excellent track for an early morning run. On his left the sun was rising on the aquamarine water, serving as an ideal backdrop.

One of the men sitting in the lobby, the local, got out of his chair and watched McCord as he exited the grounds towards the beach. The man then quickly turned around and marched out the front door, leaving the resort and walking past the outside fountains and onto the main road, where a white minivan was waiting across the street to pick him up. The other man in the lobby put down his newspaper and intently observed the activity. After McCord and the local left the resort, he got up from his chair and went towards the guest's rooms.

~~~

Carroll crossed the road and jumped into the minivan. Frazier, who had been napping in the driver's seat, woke up startled and confused. Shaking his head quickly from side to side, he was ready for action. He hastily turned the key and revved the van's engine.

"He's left the hotel. Turn around," yelled Carroll as he closed the van's door.

"Where's he heading?" asked an excited Frazier.

"He's running on the beach. That way!"

"Let's get him!" Frazier turned the steering wheel 360 degrees. The van's tires spun forward on the sandy highway.

"Take I easy, take it easy. Not too fast, let's make sure he's away from the hotel."

"OK, mon."

The assassins slowly drove down the H1B highway eagerly looking for their target. The two-lane road was running parallel to the Caribbean Sea, there were no other vehicles on the road due to the early Saturday morning hour and late-night Saint Parish celebrations. In the east a bright sun was starting to rise. As the hired assassins drove north, colorful two-story apartments, small motels, and beach bars were intermittently blocking their view of the beach's shoreline, the men were on the lookout for McCord. After driving a few kilometers, they spotted the large American jogging on the beach near the intersection of Cemetery Lane and the H1B, one and a half kilometers before the village of Holetown.

"There he is! Slow down," instructed Carroll.

"I see him, mon. Let's take him out now."

"Not yet. We need to pick the right location. Somewhere away from all these motels."

"Got it. We're going to lose him again when he gets to Holetown," noted Frazier.

"How far until Holetown?" asked Carroll.

"Just down the road some. After the village it's only beach for a few kilometers that could be a good spot. He's in my territory now," proclaimed a proud Frazier.

"Did you get in touch with your cousin?"

"Yes. I went to his house while you were in the hotel. He lives right here in Holetown, around the corner."

"How about a weapon? Did you get one?"

"He didn't have a gun; you can't find one on the island. But he did give me his old cricket bat, it will do the trick."

"All we have is a cricket bat?" asked Carroll.

Shortly past midnight, while Carroll was waiting in the Sandy Lane lobby, Frazier made a visit to his younger and bigger cousin in Holetown. He had called him earlier from the Teague villa asking for a weapon that would neutralize McCord. Frazier's cousin did not have a firearm, nor did he know anyone that could get one, but he wanted to help his rugby idol any way he could. The two large men decided that an old wooden cricket bat stored in his backyard shack would be good enough to get the job done, at least until Frazier's eager cousin was able to arrive and help finish the task. Both men were confident locals believing that they will be able to easily take care of the big American. After all, it wasn't the first time the two of them had to take care of problems on their island.

"Yes, I'll knock him silly, mon. Don't worry 'bout that. I also got you something," said Frazier as he reached back and handed Carroll a heavy metal crowbar that was lying on the floor.

"Where did you get this?" asked Carroll while looking at the weapon.

"I found it beneath the back seat of the van. It was with the spare tire."

"Is that all we have?"

"Yeah, but I told my cousin to be on the ready to help us. He's a good fighter and we can use his fishing boat. It's over there some," explained Frazier while pointing towards the town's marina. "We can drop him in the sea. Like we did with the Australian."

"OK, call him now. Tell him to meet us down at the beach some," ordered Carroll.

"All right, mon. All right."

Frazier called his cousin and told him their target was on the run. He instructed him to drive his wooden fishing boat along the shoreline north of Holetown, and to bring plenty of rope and an anchor. Carroll could hear the enthusiasm on the other end of the phone. Frazier finished the call by telling his cousin he'd provide him with an exact location shortly.

"He's ready to go," said Frazier.

"Good. We will need his help with making the American disappear. No mistakes this time, we finish the job or else our Ocean Hawks career is over."

As predicted by Frazier, McCord came into view on the sandy beach past Holetown. His stride was steady with purpose as the sun was rising over the sea behind him.

"There he is. What's up ahead of us?" asked Carroll.

"Only a few small houses and beach bars."

"OK. We're going to have to make our move soon."

"How 'bout Thunder Bay Beach Bar? It's down the road some past Carton Road," noted Frazier.

"Hmmm, behind a beach bar. That might work. No witnesses," confirmed Carroll.

"The bar is another 1 and a half kilometers or so, mon."

"OK, that's the spot. Speed up. Let's get ahead of him."

"Dat Shot!"

"Call your cousin back and tell him to bring his boat around to the bar," ordered Carroll.

"I'll call him now, mon."

Frazier accelerated the minivan past McCord on the H1B. They passed the Millie Ifill Fish Market and pulled into the sandy parking lot of Thunder Bay Beach Bar. Both men exited the van with their weapons in hand. They swiftly walked past the tiki bar towards the beach and waited at the shoreline. They could see McCord heading towards them in the distance.

~~~

McCord's intended destination from Sandy Lane was Gibbes Beach, his Google Maps had indicated that it was seven kilometers away from the hotel. From the start McCord was able to maintain a lengthy stride along the Caribbean shoreline. His focus was on the rising sun until his thoughts turned to Tony Young. Looking out to the water he wondered if his late friend enjoyed the sunrise during his final hours. McCord had been running at a good pace, deep in thought for over a half an hour now, passing by several shops and small beach resorts. He recognized that none of the motels or resorts were grander than Sandy Lane, he would have to thank Walsh's assistant when he got back to Stamford. McCord looked at his watch and believed he was getting closer to reaching his landmark.

The H1 highway on the right was nearly empty except for a white minivan that McCord noticed was driving swiftly north. "Dayworkers," he thought. In a few minutes he would reach his landmark with the plan of turning around and heading back to his hotel. As he got closer to his destination, he noticed two men standing by the surf in front of a tiki bar, blocking his path. Both appeared to be holding something in their hands. As McCord approached the men, they started moving towards him with purpose, and he thought, "Should I turn around and go in the opposite direction or pass by the locals?" He decided not to slow down or break his stride but respectfully wave hello instead. The men were intent on stopping him. They stayed in front of McCord, put their hands up, and motioned him to stop.

McCord wasn't one to run away from an uncomfortable situation. Perhaps these guys just had a question, although it didn't appear to be the case. He knew it was probably smarter to ignore the men in front of him and go the other way, as his brother often told him, "Even though you may be a good fighter, sometimes it's best not to fight if you don't have to." But McCord never claimed to be smart. He was always a tad pigheaded and occasionally combative if backed into a corner. Dex ran straight at the two men and stopped in front of them, ready for either a friendly hello or a confrontation. He studied their faces with a puffed-out chest and a bad ass look as if he was saying, "If you fuck with me you are going to need more guys."

One of the men was wearing a white Izod shirt similar to the local in the lobby of Sandy Lane. The other wore a blue muscle shirt that had been faded by the sun. The men inside the shirts looked athletic enough, like wrestlers. The bigger guy held a cricket bat, the smaller guy had a metal crowbar in his hand. They looked like competitors who would not stand down.

"Can I help you?" asked McCord.

"Are you American?" said the smaller man.

"Yes. Who wants to know?"

"You don't remember us do ya, mon?"

"I can't say I do. Listen I don't want trouble and I don't have my wallet on me. So, I suggest you wait for somebody else," McCord replied, intending to buy time to plan a strategy.

"Perhaps your Aboriginal friend would remember us. Oh, wait. He can't, mon. I think he's dead," taunted the larger man in the muscle shirt.

At that point McCord recognized the voices and remembered the size of the shadows that were approaching him on North Head a week ago. One tall shadow and one short. Anger started to rise inside McCord. He had to keep his cool, both had weapons but no gun this time.

"Now I remember. You two wanted to join me for a swim," mocked McCord.

"You were doing the swimming, my friend. I guess you'll try to do the same this time?" asked the Jamaican.

"No. I don't feel like getting wet," replied McCord.

McCord was a good fighter. His ability was painfully cultured at an early age from lost battles with his older brother Brad. Growing up, he always wanted to beat the older McCord in everything from Battleship to wiffleball to wrestling. Their battles were always close but when it came to backyard fighting, Brad was unbeatable. Dex had endured some painful lessons from his older brother. As a 16-year-old Brad had left home to formally train in mixed martial arts and UFC fighting. After earning his blackbelt the older McCord entered and won several local cage-fighting exhibition bouts, but a shoulder injury kept him from pursuing a professional career. That didn't stop him from practicing on his younger brother, Dex had been schooled by the best.

The two men were advancing closer to their target with a mad look in their bloodshot eyes. McCord started moving to his right towards the parking lot. He wanted to draw the men away from shore and into soft sand, he thought, less leverage for their weapons. McCord understood velocity ratios, and he needed to reduce his attacker's velocity ratio and lower the speed of the lever. The length of out-lever to length of resistance arm would matter, which meant getting closer to the fulcrum of your opponent. The two locals followed him into the softer beach sand towards the tiki bar.

In most lopsided fights McCord knew that you should take down the biggest guy first. In this case the weapon dictated his first move. McCord headed for the shorter man with the more dangerous weapon. The smaller man was standing to his left with the crowbar raised in his hand.

But McCord's plan had to be quickly changed, as he did not have to decide who to take down first. The man more his size with the cricket bat moved forward first, awkwardly approaching in the sand from the right. The local Bajan shifted his weight on his right back foot and started a short compact backswing with the cricket bat, aiming to break his target's head. The swing was lengthy and clumsy, too slow a velocity ratio as a result from standing in sand. McCord ducked as the guy in the muscle shirt swung the bat over his intended target's head. The attempted blow missed the wicket. It was a decent enough swing to maybe hit a cricket ball but not in combat.

The big guy's body and head followed through to McCord's right side. Dex accurately planted his right elbow into the side of the Bajan's head, "Target the soft spot of the skull," thought McCord. He was trained by his brother that the elbow plant in the head works best. The fist-to-skull impact could severely damage a hand but not an elbow, and the side of the head is better than the front or back. It was a solid pile-driver delivered fast by McCord. The large man in the muscle shirt went down like a ton of bricks as the bat released out of his hands. McCord was already stepping past the concussed body in the sand and was now focused on the other threat.

The guy with the crowbar was surprised to see his partner go down so easily. He promptly charged McCord but made the same mistake most people make—he lunged forward too quickly without thinking. He had his crowbar pulled back to the side ready to swing, trying to catch McCord with a swift blow to the ribs. Three things are wrong with that. A short swing doesn't hold a lot of power, especially against a big guy like McCord. Second, a blow aimed at the mid-section is too easy to defend against, better to aim high at the head. And third, swinging at someone in sand while lunging forward slows down the speed impact. The force of the blow comes from the weight of a man's weapon multiplied by the speed of his swing. *Mass times velocity equals momentum.* Nothing the smaller Jamaican could do about the weight of his crowbar; it's going to weigh the same all the time and standing in the sand was going to reduce his velocity. The only chance he had was to swing hard enough to damage McCord's face, but at six foot five that wasn't going to be an option for the shorter man. McCord laughed at the undersized man as he kept swinging his weapon back and forth. After four attempted body blows, he kicked the legs out from under the local and held his face down into the sand, just like his brother Brad had done to him in their backyard at home.

The smaller man continued to struggle, McCord drove the heel of his hand into the knob of his aggressor's elbow, the joint cracked as the wrist was overextending, and the crowbar was immediately released. His attacker was screaming out in severe pain.

"Give up yet?" McCord yelled. "You can do better."

Still resisting, the smaller local tried to get up. McCord grabbed him by the hair and kneed him in the side of his head. The man immediately collapsed in the sand.

Standing over him, Dex demanded, "Who sent you after me?"

The man in the Izod shirt didn't answer. McCord screamed out another question.

"Did you kill Tony Young?"

Sill no answer, just shrill moaning. He felt anger and rage building up inside.

McCord noticed the larger man lying in the sand was starting to gain consciousness and trying to get his bearings. He was slowly getting back on his feet, his eyes were unfocused, not a whole lot of thought going on in his head. McCord walked over to the big man, grabbed his hands and arms, and crashed a left hook into the triangle between the pectorals and above his six-pack abs. Another tactical blow taught by McCord's older brother and delivered to perfection. The guy went into all kinds of distress and slumped forward and down. He then delivered a finishing knee to the face that displaced the guy's teeth. McCord was showing no mercy. He wanted revenge.

Dex then turned back to the smaller guy with the broken elbow. He thought about showing restraint, but it was just a passing thought. These guys were responsible for Abbot's death, and probably Tony's, too. The two men were somebody's goons, knowingly deployed and he was going to make sure they didn't return. He kicked crowbar man in the groin and broke his nose with a powerful punch. Then he picked up the crowbar, looked at it, and went over to the larger man. McCord knew he was good at swinging a softball bat. His cylindrical bat always connected with the spherical ball, so he figured he would be just as good with a crowbar. He declared out loud, "Hmmm, this should work." With one swing he broke the bigger guy's left wrist with the metal crowbar, and then he decided to break the other wrist. There goes his athletic career, Dex thought. He turned back to the smaller attacker who was lying in the sand still dazed from the punch in face. McCord broke both his wrists.

Damaged goods. Four broken wrists: *1+1+1+1 =4.*

Dex liked math. Most accountants like math.

~~~

McCord looked up towards the Thunder Bay Beach Bar entrance. A small Suzuki Swift was skidding into the parking lot. The car came to an abrupt halt as the driver's side door flew open. A Caucasian man in casual business attire struggled to get out of the small car. He started running towards McCord and the bodies sprawled on the beach, a gun was in his hand. McCord was frozen, he wasn't sure what his next move would be. He thought about his options—start running, swimming, or accept the outcome.

The man with gun yelled out, "Are you OK?"

McCord was surprised by the question. "Yes, I'm good."

"Looks like you didn't need my help," said the man as he got closer.

"Who are you?"

"Doug Borden, FBI International Ops Unit."

"I'm happy to see you," said a relieved McCord. "How did you know I was here?"

"I was following that white minivan after you left the hotel," stated Borden, pointing over to the parking lot.

"What made you follow them?"

"Your friend Steve Walsh from EDGAR. He told me to keep an eye on you."

"Thanks. I could have used your help a little earlier, but I think we're good," replied McCord as he glanced over to the two men trying to get up.

"Sorry about that. Left my rental keys in the room."

"FBI, huh?"

"Yep," said Borden as he pulled out his badge from under his shirt. "We better clean up this mess. I'll call the Barbados police and my friends at the FBI Caribbean desk."

"I'd appreciate that," replied McCord.

The West Indies men were struggling to get up. Borden went over to the bigger man and kicked him down into the beach sand. He showed them his badge and waved his gun at the suspects, telling them to stay down and that he had the authority under the laws of the United States government to shoot them on sight. Borden didn't really have the authority, but it sounded good. He asked the offenders if they understood, they both nodded and remained seated in the sand. At that moment, a green and yellow fishing boat slowed its engines 20 meters from shore in front of the group. A local was at the helm looking intently at the action on the beach and the men lying in the sand. McCord waved to the fisherman; no response was received from the large man at the wheel. The idling boat revved its engines and quickly cruised away.

While McCord and Borden were waiting for the police to arrive, Dex informed his new friend that the men were responsible for the murder of his coworkers in Australia, and that they were also sent to kill him. He went on to explain the shooting of Abbot on the cliffs of Manly and that he believed they were responsible for the drowning death of his friend Tony Young.

"These guys followed you from Australia?" asked Borden.

"We didn't do anything, mon!" yelled Frazier from the sand.

"Shut up and stay down," replied Borden while waving his gun.

"I don't think they followed me from Australia. But it's not a coincidence they are here," explained McCord.

"Why's that?"

"I think they were ordered to come to Barbados by their boss, Nigel Metcalf. He probably wanted to get them out of the country."

"Go on."

"Metcalf owns a company in India that prepares SEC filings, and he is also co-owner of a local investment house here on the island. My colleague in Australia, who was with me when those guys over there shot him, discovered that confidential SEC filings were being sent to his company in Barbados before they went back to the U.S," explained McCord. "I believe

Metcalf's traders in Bridgetown are using inside information to make illegal trades in stocks."

"What's the name of the company?" asked Borden.

"Green Shade$. Metcalf from Australia along with the Prime Minister of Barbados' wife own the company."

"The prime minister's wife? How do you know this?"

"My local auditor gave me a brief on Green Shade$, his report specified who the owners were."

"Have you seen this guy Metcalf?" asked Borden.

"Yes. Yesterday afternoon and last night at Villa Balmoral."

"Prime Minister Teague's villa?"

"He and his wife were hosting a party celebrating the anniversary of his appointment as prime minister," replied McCord.

"OK, this is getting interesting."

The conversation was interrupted by a white, blue, and yellow police car pulling into the parking lot of the beach bar. The Barbados Police Service had arrived on the scene. Two St. James police officers jumped out of their vehicle and ran towards the men with tasers in hand; they were not armed with guns in accordance with the Constitution of Barbados, Section 12. Borden waived his FBI badge so as not to alarm the local officers. The suspects were sitting crouched over in the sand, their heads bent down between their knees while supporting their damaged wrists.

For the next 10 minutes Borden explained the situation to the police officers, and McCord added details when he was called upon. It was evident that Borden, the FBI International Operations agent, had been to many foreign crime scenes and knew protocol. He said all the right things so as not to alarm the local officials. As the conversations continued the local police came to realize that McCord had inflicted considerable damage on the two men sitting in the sand. They were going to need medical attention. A short time later an ambulance arrived at the beach to take the wounded assassins to the hospital. It was going to take a lot of plaster to set their arms and wrists. The police assured Borden that they would be held for attempted murder and brought to the police station after they were "fixed up."

While Carroll and Frazier were being escorted to the ambulance, a local FBI agent arrived on the scene. Borden knew the woman, Jennifer Kilgore, from an assignment they had together in Belgium. McCord along with Borden quickly filled her in on the sequence of events that had occurred earlier in the morning and over the past few weeks. Kilgore had been on the island for six months and was very familiar with Green Shade$, she noted that she recently met Eric Fromm at a Barbados Chamber of Commerce event. She had been impressed by his extensive experience at the SEC and in Washington, DC. Borden and McCord continued to tell the local agent what had transpired on the beach and provided theories on who sent the suspects. Kilgore understood that she was going to need a strong investigative team to unravel all the facts.

~~~

Douglas Borden was a forensic accountant. Borden graduated from the University of Chicago with a Master of Science in Accounting, and the Federal Bureau of Investigation recruited him right out of college. Doug wanted to join the fight against crime, and he liked carrying a gun. Shortly after starting his career, he sat for the Certified Fraud Exam (CFE), passing the tough test on his first sitting. On the job he developed a unique set of diverse skills in detecting and investigating fraudulent financial activities. Borden had spent his entire 32-year career at the FBI, including 15 years at legal attaché offices in various European cities. After his successful tenures overseas, he returned to the U.S. to be director of the FBI's International Operations Division at FBI Headquarters in Washington, DC.

It was two days ago, after McCord's visit to EDGAR Data & Intelligence in Stamford, that Steve Walsh contacted the FBI. The call was directed to Borden. Walsh expressed concerns that McCord may be on to something that could put him in danger. On that same day, Borden left DC on the first plane to Barbados and checked into the Sandy Lane hotel. After contacting Kilgore and a late-night dinner at the resort, Borden made himself comfortable in the hotel lobby waiting for McCord to appear. He was there almost all night until he observed McCord exiting the hotel in the early morning hour, promptly followed by a local who was also waiting in the lobby. That was when he went up to his room, retrieved his car rental keys, and drove north on the M-1 highway.

Kilgore's local FBI team arrived at Thunder Bay Beach Bar shortly after the hired killers were taken to Queen Elizabeth Hospital in Bridgetown. On the beach McCord could hear Borden providing further details to Kilgore and her local agents that the offenses committed at Green Shade$ may have been around transactions involving international money-laundering and transnational crime. He added that the organized schemes could have included individuals who operated globally with the intent of obtaining power, influence, and monetary gains, while protecting their activities through corruption and violence by any illegal means. Men like Metcalf and women like Bolanlé Teague.

Shortly after arriving at the hospital the suspects were identified by one of the nurses who was a big fan of the rugby league. She recalled that Carroll and Frazier had left the West Indies seven-a-side team to join a club in New South Wales, Australia, the Manly-Warringah Ocean Hawks. While in custody the two athletes continued to be questioned by police but were not giving up any details, including an explanation for the attempted assault on McCord or why they were back in Barbados. The injured men claimed McCord attacked them. The Barbadian police didn't believe them, but they were having difficulty finding eyewitnesses to support the charges.

The suspects stayed silent until McCord made a call to Manly Beach Police Department Officer Beveridge. At the direction of Borden, McCord requested that the officer along with an Australian FBI representative visit the players' team facility. Within hours Beveridge and a local FBI agent arrived at the rugby facility halfway around the world and demanded the employment files of Carroll and Frazier. The front office complied and gave the address of the Pittwater flat where the two suspects were living. The manager of the Ocean Hawks facility was unable to inform his boss, Nigel Metcalf, of the policemen's inquiry as he was in transit on a plane somewhere over the Pacific Ocean.

While searching Carroll and Frazier's apartment the Australian police discovered Tony Young's blue Mazda Miata and surfboard stored in the garage, with a Glock handgun in the glove box. Three hours later the local forensic team confirmed that the bullets in the gun matched the one discovered from the autopsy of Jiemba Abbot. The gun had been registered in the name of Nigel Metcalf. Shortly after the weapons match, the Aussie investigators notified the team in Barbados of the findings. Assault and attempted murder charges were going to be made against Carroll and Fraizer.

Back in the hospital in Bridgetown, Carroll and Frazier were still not cooperating with the local authorities. It was not until new evidence from the Australian police force was presented that the two rugby league players started to talk. They were no longer going to be loyal to Metcalf who had limited their playing time and made them sit in the back of the plane on the long flight to Barbados. Errol Frazier, the local Bajan, was the first to crack. He admitted that they were involved with the murder of Tony Young and the shooting of Jiemba Abbot, quick to declare that he didn't pull the trigger and was just following Metcalf's and his Jamaican partner's orders. After confessing Frazier was expecting to get preferential treatment from the local police due to his family ties in Barbados. It was not going to happen.

Carroll was not as forthright with the legal authorities. He claimed that since he was from Jamaica he would not be subject to the Barbadian laws, citing that the local government cannot force someone to provide testimonial evidence against himself in a criminal case. And that he is not required to answer any questions that would incriminate him. Carroll surprised the investigators with his understanding of Caribbean law, knowledge he obtained while listening to Jamaican lawyers defending his brothers. In the end, though, there was enough evidence back in Australia that a confession was not needed.

Shortly after the plaster dried, the extradition process began for the two Caribbean men. The Australian authorities had requested an immediate return of the criminals. The Bajan police had no problem agreeing to the prompt deportation of the West Indies players, as they wanted to keep the attempted murder charges quiet to avoid any unwanted attention that could hurt the tourism industry.

The duo's international crime would fall under the Barbados Extradition Act of 1979, which involved three steps: a demand from the authorities in NSW Australia, the issuance of an extradition warrant, and a proof of probable cause. In addition, the principle of double criminality had to be proved, which meant the accused men had to commit a crime in Australia that constituted a crime in Barbados. A case of murder as a probable cause was all that was necessary. The extradition hearing and deportation was completed swiftly and with no appeal. Within days the judge had the men off the island and on a plane headed to Australia.

One week after the attack on McCord, the two West Indies rugby players were welcomed back to Sydney's International Airport by the New South Wales police force and MBPD Officer Beveridge. The murder investigation against Carroll and Frazier would be the responsibility of Beveridge and the NSW authorities. The cases against the assailants were straightforward. The murder weapon was found, the Bajan had confessed, and additional video evidence from street cameras were backing up statements. Nigel Metcalf's charges, however, would take a larger team and a little longer to construct.

~~~

During the day of the assailants' attack, McCord, Borden, along with the local FBI legates, visited the Green Shade$ office to speak with Fromm.

The FBI and other agencies were searching for further facts on the money trail and the defendants' motive. On the way to the facility the group stopped at Sandy Lane and waited for McCord to grab the flowchart Abbot had created. The team from the FBI wanted to further understand the movements of confidential SEC documents from the United States to NSG in India to Fromm's band of merry traders in Barbados. While the team waited at the hotel McCord took a desperately needed shower, changed clothes, and put on shoes. He also called Lindsay Arthur and updated him on the situation. He requested that Lindsay get in touch with Jay Gaucher and meet him at the Green Shade$ facility.

By the time the men arrived in Bridgetown, Gaucher and Arthur were waiting for them. Eric Fromm was not there and could not be contacted. McCord and Borden, along with Kilgore's investigative team, sat down with controller Gaucher and his accounting records. Lindsay Arthur was there to assure Jay that he did nothing wrong and to help the authorities. The controller started pulling banking records and wire transfer information that he thought would be useful. Gaucher confirmed that he was instructed to send millions of dollars over the past two years to international accounts in the Cayman Islands, India, and Australia. He provided the names of bank accounts, account numbers, and amounts.

In the Green Shade$ conference room, McCord sketched out the ownership structure of each entity affiliated with Nigel Metcalf. He was able to identify all the organizations in Metcalf's scheme by looking at Abbot's audit workpapers, company bank statements, and by just completing simple Google searches. On the white board of the Green Shade$ conference room the group sketched out the following:

Metcalf Ownership Structure and Green Shade$ Cash Flows

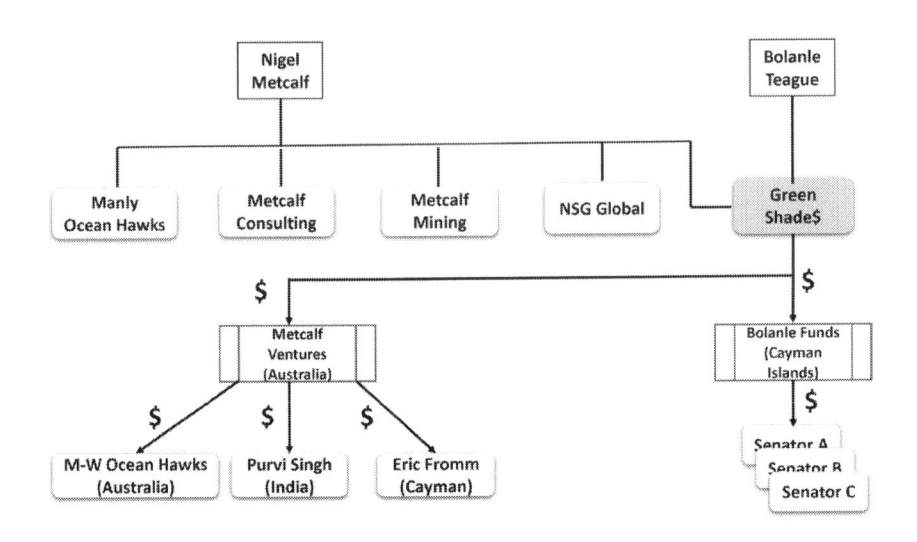

```
         Nigel                                              Bolanle
         Metcalf                                            Teague
    ┌──────┬────────┬────────┬─────────┐                      │
  Manly   Metcalf  Metcalf  NSG Global  ─────────────────  Green
  Ocean   Consulting Mining                                Shade$
  Hawks
              $                                              $
           Metcalf                                        Bolanle Funds
           Ventures                                       (Cayman
           (Australia)                                    Islands)
         $  │  $   $                                         $
    ┌───────┼───────┐                                      Senator A
  M-W      Purvi   Eric                                    Senator B
  Ocean    Singh   Fromm                                   Senator C
  Hawks    (India) (Cayman)
  (Australia)
```

The trail of cash moving around the Metcalf organization was starting to reveal the facts. With the data exposed by McCord and Gaucher the U.S. federal agencies would be able to start their investigation. Borden's team immediately contacted the Cayman Islands Monetary Authority, Reserve Bank of India, and Australian Securities and Investment Commission for assistance. The bank account details provided on Metcalf Ventures, NSG Global, and the Bolanlé Funds had identified in a number of incoming and outgoing transactions that would warrant further investigation by these foreign agencies and the Securities and Exchange Commission.

International Operations Director Doug Borden would lead the investigation into the legality of cash movements and international wire transactions. His team would gather enough facts to direct the Securities and Exchange Commission on unlawful stock trades, amounts, and settlement dates. The SEC and their army of accountants would take over from there. They were going to have plenty of facts to build a case by investigating Green Shade$ trading activities around notable events such as earnings announcements, acquisitions, and other material events that moved stock prices. Ironically, the SEC was going to utilize the same RoboCop tools that Fromm created to detect illegal insider trading.

Borden would also need to coordinate efforts with other local law enforcement agencies and banking regulators in countries where criminal activities took place. The investigation would take months but ultimately the FBI and SEC would uncover a wide range of charges against Metcalf and his partners: money laundering, tax evasion, insider trading, and the list would build as the accounting experts got involved.

Thirteen hours after McCord set out for his morning run, he had exposed a sophisticated scheme of insider trading and political corruption on an international scale. McCord and Borden were satisfied with the outcome and ready to head back to Sandy Lane after a long but very productive day. Walsh from Stamford had called McCord earlier and thanked him for uncovering the facts, and he was happy that his wunderkind didn't get hurt in the process. He told Dex to take his new FBI friend to dinner at the resort and celebrate, the meal and drinks were on him.

The two men arrived at Sandy Lane shortly after 8:00pm. The sun was starting to set when McCord wrestled himself out of Borden's small rental car. They walked through the resort lobby and down a marble staircase to the lower terrace restaurant looking out towards the sea. The colors of the sunset reminded McCord of his recent visit to North Head on the other side of the globe.

"Long day," said Borden as the two men sat down.

"It's been a long few weeks. The last thing I remember is getting caught in a five-man shout."

"What's that?"

"Never mind. I'm just glad we uncovered what was going on," replied McCord.

"Thanks to you, my friend. We appreciate what you went through to get to the facts."

"No problem. It certainly was an adventure."

"Yep. Something you can tell your grandkids."

"Ha. Maybe someday but for now I'm starved," declared McCord. "What are you getting? Our dinner and drinks are on Walsh."

"I'm not sure I can accept the gift but since your client is buying, I'll overlook the Bureau's policy on accepting favors," replied Borden.

"Let's start with the Alaskan king crab legs followed by a 32oz Tomahawk steak. It's the least EDGAR could do considering what we uncovered."

"Sounds good. Let's chase them with a tropical cocktail."

"With an umbrella on top," added McCord.

"Definitely!"

The two men waved down the waiter and provided a lengthy list of cocktails and food.

"So, McCord. What are you going to do after you get back to New York?"

"Well, it's busy season. I have a few public clients that have mid-Feb reporting deadlines. And I'm sure I'll have a few partners bitching about staffing assignments."

"Sounds exciting," commented Borden. "Have you ever thought about working for the FBI?"

"Yes. When I was at William & Mary I interviewed with someone from the bureau."

"I know. I pulled your file."

"You have a file on me?" asked McCord.

"We have a file on most certified public accountants," said Borden with a laugh. "Why didn't you join?"

"I wanted to see what public accounting was like. And living in New York."

"Well, we are a different agency than 10 years ago. Times have changed. New types of criminals," noted Borden.

"Yeah, smart ones," replied McCord.

"Would you be interested in joining the Bureau now?"

"I don't know. Sometimes I think I may stay at KGO and stay on the partnership track. Other times I think of leaving to become a CFO somewhere. But considering what happened here and in Australia, I may be open to anything."

"Hey, I know working at the FBI is not for everyone, but I am guided by the phrase "respice, adspice, prospice."

"Which means?"

"Look to the past, look to the present, look to the future."

"Very prophetic. But OK, I'll consider it."

"Good. I want you to come up to Quantico, Virginia for a visit. It's the FBI's training academy. I'll introduce you to a few important people. Show you the type of interesting investigations we're working on."

"Alright. It's always worth taking a look at something new."

"Cheers to that. See you in Quantico then," said Borden as he raised his glass.

For something impressive see Exhibit 9: Chief Financial Officer Salaries.

Chapter 14

"Finance is the art of passing money from hand to hand until it finally disappears."
—Robert Sarnoff

- Release the Accountants
- Litigation Support Team
- The Charges

BACK IN AUSTRALIA the charges against Carroll and Frazier were sealed tight. There was enough evidence presented that the rugby players would be found guilty without objection. The men were going to serve life sentences. However, the accessory to murder charges against Metcalf were a little more challenging, and, of course, he had hired the best lawyers money could buy. The prosecutors were going to have to prove that he aided and abetted Carroll and Frazier, and that Metcalf was directly complicit in the murder acts.

After months of investigative work and discoveries the prosecution accomplished their job. The facts were brought forward to the local New South Wales tribunal, and it was proven that Metcalf facilitated the offenders to commit the crimes by providing information regarding the victims' whereabouts, all while knowing the assassins intended to kill the victims. In addition, the evidence supported the prosecution's claim that Metcalf provided the murder weapon. Nauti was found guilty and sentenced to life imprisonment in Australia without parole. The families of Young and Abbot would have closure.

The United States criminal and regulatory agencies were pursuing their own legal cases against Metcalf Consulting Ltd. and its subsidiaries. The SEC had obtained emergency court orders to freeze Metcalf's assets worldwide as they retraced the movement of hundreds of XBRL documents. During their investigation it was confirmed that non-public information was being sent to Green Shade$ directly from NSG Global in India.

The authorities took immediate action to ensure that cash accumulated from illegal trading activities could not continue to be siphoned out of the banks while the federal agencies and international regulators completed their analyses. As the facts were uncovered several offshore investment accounts of Metcalf's employees and certain politicians in Australia, Barbados, and other Caribbean nations were frozen.

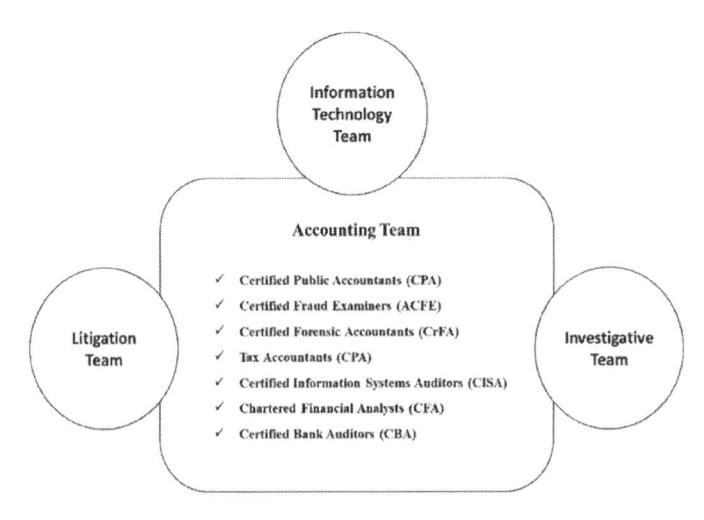

~~~

Metcalf, Fromm, Singh, and Bolanlé Teague were charged with multiple insider trading, tax evasion, bribery, and money laundering crimes, but the cases against them were going to take significant research and involve multiple jurisdictions. To gather all the facts, the local authorities, the SEC, and the FBI needed assistance from foreign agencies and legal attachés. As with most global FBI investigations, a meaningful international nexus would need to be established to balance the local jurisdictions' concerns with the FBI's interest in addressing the transnational aspects of the investigations. The agency would need to lean on the capabilities of the Barbados, Australia, and India law enforcement communities. A substantial worldwide investigative effort would be vital in determining the value of restitution.

Borden and his friends at the FBI would need to activate their teams of accountants. Their criminal investigators and litigation support specialist would depend on specialized accountants for the compilation of financial data and information:

Information Technology Team

Accounting Team
- Certified Public Accountants (CPA)
- Certified Fraud Examiners (ACFE)
- Certified Forensic Accountants (CrFA)
- Tax Accountants (CPA)
- Certified Information Systems Auditors (CISA)
- Chartered Financial Analysts (CFA)
- Certified Bank Auditors (CBA)

Litigation Team

Investigative Team

The legal and regulatory allegations against the four suspects would require a thorough gathering of financial evidence, facts, and motivation. The assembled accountants were going to have to collaborate closely with members of the Bureau, foreign banks, and several global legal teams. Specifically, they would need to quantify the damages and determine how the crimes were executed. The specialized bean counters would include:

- Certified Public Accountants who would bring their technical accounting expertise on: FASB transactions; SEC disclosures; ethics violations; and internal control failures.
- Certified Fraud Examiners who would leverage the Fraud Triangle to explain what motivated the four fraudsters: opportunity; financial pressure; and rationalization.
- Certified Forensic Accountants who would use classic investigative tools: uncover financial evidence; analyze the what and how; and report in detail, laying out the case for the attorneys.
- Tax Accountants who would gather violations of local tax laws; international tax treaties; and tax fraud schemes.
- Certified Information Systems Auditors who would utilize a number of ISACA certifications disciplines: information systems controls; cybersecurity nexus; and enterprise technology governance rules.
- Charted Financial Analyst who would need to quantify the fraudulent security transactions; identify FINRA violations; examine broker compliance; and review technology governance.
- Certified Bank Auditors who would identify violations in money laundering; regulatory banking compliance; illegal cash flow transactions; and regulatory reports.

After 12+ months of discovery the evidence became indisputable. It was determined that insider information was used to reap more than $120 million in illegal profits, primarily obtained from confidential information included in EDGAR filings. The four primary defendants were facing a number of criminal charges and consequences. In addition, despite the SEC's logistical challenges of inspecting wire transfer information and trading activity in offshore Cayman Islands accounts, they, along with other Caribbean agencies, were able to uncover evidence on four Bajan senators and three West Indies politicians. The trail of money confirmed that the politicians were receiving illegal funds from Bolanlé Teague for personal profit and to support an effort to break away from the Commonwealth. All seven politicians were charged with bribery and money laundering.

The primary perpetrators in the Green Shade$ case met different outcomes:

Eric Fromm was picked up by the authorities at his luxury home in Barbados a week after McCord and Borden outlined the movement of cash on the Green Shade$ white board. He was very surprised to the see local Barbadian police being accompanied by the FBI. The charges of insider trading, money laundering, and FINRA violations were made, and he would be sent back to the United States to face additional federal charges.

Bolanlé Teague was visited at her villa by law enforcement officials three weeks after the investigation began. It was uncovered that over a period of four years Bolanlé had been making significant payments to influential senior members in the House of Assembly and to certain influential representatives on other West Indies islands. It was verified that Mrs. Teague's "donations" were made to influence a number of local politicians to bring favor to her husband's political aspirations, contributions that led to the demand of her husband being appointed prime minister. It was also discovered that she had been making sizeable payments to ministers and other influential leaders throughout the Caribbean to push local referendums for the separation from the Commonwealth. Numerous indictments were handed out to ministry officials in Antigua, Bahamas, and St. Lucia for accepting bribes from the offshore accounts of Bolanlé Funds, Cayman Islands. Bolanlé was charged with money laundering and bribing government officials; the details of Mrs. Teague's influence became global headline news. She would be sentenced to a minimum of 10 years in prison.

Prime Minister Master Teague was not aware of his wife's wrongdoings. After the news broke, he resigned from government and focused on his mango farm. As a result of the Teagues' scandal the Barbados referendum for independence became null and void. The referendum would have to go before the citizens a second time. After months of renewed debate, the breakaway from the Commonwealth was passed once again by the Bajan citizens with over two-thirds majority vote.

Purvi Singh was questioned by the Indian authorities, including the Reserve Bank of India and Securities and Exchange Board of India. She was accused of tax evasion, wire transfer fraud, and the illegal distribution of confidential foreign documents. Ms. Singh was found guilty, but her sentence was light. The jury provided leniency because she was following orders from Metcalf, and she funneled most of her illicit gains to the Chickpet slums and the government's "Gati Shakti" subsidy. She was confined to house arrest for 12 months. Purvi would return to the information technology industry after writing her autobiography.

Nigel "Nauti" Metcalf was surprised to see the Australian Security Intelligence Organization, New South Wales Police Force, and Manly Beach Police Department Officer Beveridge when he got off the plane after his 32-hour flight back from Barbados. A substantial number of events had transpired after he boarded the flight following the night of celebration at Master Teague's villa. He was unaware that while enjoying first-class travel his global organizations were being shut down and under investigation.

Metcalf was arrested at the airport in front of several members of the media on accessory to murder charges. He was looking at a life sentence. Nauti was also facing numerous charges from jurisdictions around the globe for insider trading, tax evasion, and money laundering. He was going to have to liquidate all his businesses, even his Manly-Warringah Ocean Hawks footy team.

Epilogue

"There are some ideas so wrong that only a very intelligent person could believe in them."
—George Orwell

Green Shade$

DEX McCORD'S FORMER colleagues earned their way into every aspect of business, government, not-for-profits, media, banking, and personal finance. He was proud to be part of a finance profession that made a big impact on all segments of our global economy. He loved how *Fortune* magazine once described Certified Public Accountants: "Members of the newest, least-known of the greatest profession, accountants seek truth in an even more complicated corporate world. A race of men nobody knows, they split finer hairs than any lawyer. And on their diagnosis, millions upon millions of dollars may change hands."

The network of accountants that supported McCord on his journey were not surprised by the triumph of their friend, after all Dex was an accountant just like them. His finance friends went on to have phenomenally successful careers:

Steve Walsh the specialist accountant. Steve was able to finalize the sale of EDGAR Data & Intelligence to MA Barton, despite internal control weaknesses at their partner's facility in India. The company was sold at a fair value, and Walsh walked away with his severance package and over $2.5 million in equity profits. He improved his golf game and was on the lookout to find his next *WAVE*.

Don Borovina the competitive accountant. Don went on to win five more softball championships. After serving his time as partner in charge of staffing he was promoted to Managing Partner of KGO's New York Metropolitan Area. He never stopped busting McCord's balls.

Stacy Atchison the scholarly accountant. Stacy remained working at Ernst & Young's consulting group for two more years, until the long hours and travel became too much. Deep down she was a philomath and left EY to pursue a PhD in Finance and Education. Stacy moved to

Washington, DC to continue her studies at Georgetown University. Her relationship with McCord is a lengthy story, to be told at another time.

Austen Perrin the trustworthy accountant. Austen continued his career at a Global Shipping Company in Sydney. With hard work he rose through the ranks at the international conglomerate from Logistics Manager to Chief Financial Officer. He ultimately moved to New Zealand and became Executive Director and owner of a freight company.

Mark "Warbo" Warburton the critical thinking accountant. Warbo became a remarkably successful investment banker at a large investment bank. After being transferred to Singapore for three years and entertaining hundreds of customers, he returned to Sydney. Mark earned a promotion to Executive Director, Head of Equity Capital Markets. He retired early and bought a new boat.

Kendall "Kenny" Cove the energetic accountant. Kenny went on to open three more dive shops in New South Wales. She was able to afford a large flat near her shop in Manly Beach. Kendall and MBPD Officer Beveridge became good friends after the McCord incident. She still thinks about Dex and hopes to see him again.

Sally Sasso the talkative tax accountant. Sally expanded her tax practice. She now employs more than 30 finance professionals in her Los Angeles office. Sally met an executive movie producer and had two children. Sasso's skills in high-net-worth tax planning came in handy.

Liv Watson the technology driven accountant. Liv continued to crisscross the globe as the Queen of XBRL. Her evangelism led to XBRL mandates in many global equity markets and tax jurisdictions. She still skateboards with her twins.

Jay Gaucher the compliance accountant. Jay realized his dream of being promoted to CFO after the Green Shade$ business was sold at auction. The investigation and due diligence on the facility recognized that Jay had always tried to do the right thing. He finally moved out of his parents' house but misses his mom's cooking.

Lindsay Arthur the diplomatic and spiritual accountant. Lindsay remained Managing Partner at KGO Barbados for two more years. He enjoyed spending time with the employees and his clients, but it was not his calling. He completed his biblical studies at a theological seminary and left the firm to be a pastor and teacher. He still encourages his friend from New York to come visit the Island.

~~~

Derek McCord the Manly Accountant had a tough decision to make. Go back to New York and continue his career track towards partner or CFO or join the FBI on the invitation of the federal government. McCord needed advice. After a few more days in Barbados helping Borden and his team uncover additional information and facts, McCord decided to visit his family in Newport News, Virginia. The trip from Barbados to Norfolk took eight hours: Bridgetown (BGI) to Miami (MIA) three hours, plus a two-hour layover, plus MIA to Norfolk (ORF) three hours. McCord's father was there to greet him at the airport.

Jack McCord was a third generation Irish American who left Boston to pursue a career in baseball. Out of high school Jack was drafted by the NY Mets and sent to their minor league Single A affiliate in Florida. He was a good baseball player but never made it to the show' – the major leagues. His last stop was in Triple A playing for the Tidewater Tides in Norfolk. After Jack left organized baseball, he stayed in the Virginia Beach area getting a job at Newport News Shipbuilders (NNS), the largest industrial employer in Virginia. NNS was the sole designer, builder, and refueler of United States Navy aircraft carriers. They also had a highly competitive sandlot baseball team. Jack loved working at NSS and became a respected supervisor on the assembly floor, eventually moving up the ranks to senior management.

Father and son left Norfolk International Airport and headed to their nearby family house in Hampton. Mom was back home getting dinner ready for the family. Derek's mother, Jennifer, was a native Virginian, a mathematics teacher in the Chesapeake Public School District. She was 21 when she met her future husband on nearby Virgina Beach. The future Mrs. McCord was there enjoying a day of body surfing with friends when she crashed into Jack while riding a large curling wave, and it was love at first sight.

The other McCord children, Brad and Carol, came over to see Derek and to enjoy a home-cooked meal. Mom was baking a Virgina Ham and making her famous southern peanut soup. When Derek walked into his childhood home and smelled his mom's cooking, warm memories came flooding in. Dex's mother hustled out of the kitchen in her apron and gave her son a big, long hug. She missed her boy and was looking forward to hearing all about his recent adventures. Dex's brother Brad slapped him on the back and handed him a cold Budweiser. His sister Carol waved from the living room; she was busy finishing up tomorrow's lesson plan for her third-grade class.

The McCord family hadn't all been together since Thanksgiving, and there was a lot of catching up to do. After cups of soup and a belly full of delicious baked ham, Derek filled the family in on what had occurred during the past two weeks. He started with seeing his friends in Sydney and Tony's funeral. The family became more engaged when he told them about his jump off the cliff at North Head, seeing Mel Gibson, his visit to the math museum in New York, and the fight on the beach in Barbados.

McCord's dad was proud of his son, glad that he was able to assist the U.S. Government and local authorities in uncovering a serious criminal matter. His mom was concerned about his physical and emotional well-being. Once Derek assured her that he was fine, Mrs. McCord's interest turned to his visit to MoMath. His brother Brad simply said, "I would have kicked your ass in Barbados." Carol said, "Good for you" and left the dinner table to finish her lesson plan.

The family spent the rest of the evening laughing and getting caught up on each other's personal lives. They loved and supported each other.

Everyone was happy to see Derek back home, even if it was for only one evening. Derek's siblings left the McCord residence after 10:30pm since they all had work the next day and an early wake up time.

After older brother Brad and younger sister Carol left, Dex told his parents about Borden's offer to join the FBI. He told them that he was torn about staying on his career path as a public accountant or changing course. Jack and Jen told their son that they would support whatever decision he made. His father coached him to do what he feels is right and to follow his passion. His mother told him to ensure he was happy with whatever path he decided, but she wasn't too thrilled about her son having a gun.

~~~

Dex woke up in his small childhood bed to the smell of bacon. The morning had arrived way too soon for his liking. He joined his parents for breakfast before they both had to run off to work. Jack wanted to take the day off and drive his son up to FBI Headquarters in Quantico, but Dex insisted that he save his vacation days for his next visit, that he would be fine hitchhiking up to Northern Virginia. Dex also wanted to spend a little time on his own to figure out what career path to follow. The three embraced before departing and went their separate ways.

A male hitchhiker standing six feet five and weighing 225 pounds is on the cusp of acceptability for rides. Generally, women won't stop for him because they see a danger, men can be just as panicky. But McCord had showered and shaved that day, looking preppy in his khakis, button-down shirt, and docksiders that he had retrieved from his closet. He thought his clean appearance would shorten the odds of securing a ride, that and there were enough trucks on the road with confident drivers that he should be able to make it up to Quantico by noon. It only took two rides for McCord to reach Northern Virginia. A young man in a pickup truck took him west for two hours on Route 84 to Richmond, and not long afterwards on the ramp of Route 95, an older man in a Chevy Suburban drove McCord an hour and a half north to Exit 148.

Dex was quiet most of the journey, partly because the transportation was too short for conversation and partly because he wasn't in the mood to discuss inconsequential matters. He got out of the Suburban, thanked the driver, and walked down the exit ramp to the flashing red light. His mind was still not made up. McCord thought a career as an FBI agent sounded challenging and exciting, a journey that could be life changing. However, if he stayed in accounting, he would have the opportunity to help others and learn something new every day, not to mention the potential of significant earnings. McCord needed to make up his mind.

At the bottom of the ramp, McCord stood for five minutes going through the pros and cons. Finally, he made a decision, looked both ways, and took a large step forward and continued walking across the road and up the entrance ramp towards Route 95 North – New York. McCord had decided that it wasn't time to make a move away from public accounting, not just yet. He whole-heartedly believed that dedication to knowledge and continued growth would be his key to personal success and happiness, and there was the thought of Stacy Atchinson, too.

McCord stood on the ramp for five minutes before a driver in a shiny red Ford F150 offered him a ride. He was an older, well-dressed man wearing Ray-Ban aviator sunglasses.

"Where you heading, son?"

"Going up to New York," replied McCord.

"It's in my direction, jump in," said the gray-haired gentleman while placing his soft cooler in the back seat.

"Thank you," said McCord as he climbed onto the F150.

"I'm going as far as Philadelphia to see my daughter and grandchildren. Does that work for you?"

"Sure does."

"Yeah, I try to get up there every two to three months to see the kids. Cute little buggers they are. Are you with the Bureau?"

"No sir."

"I'm 15 years retired from the Agency. Best time of my life working with the men and women of the Bureau. What do you do for a living?"

Dex thought and replied, "I'm an accountant, BUT…"

Letter To The Reader

I'm grateful for your interest and time spent reading Green Shade$. Hopefully you enjoyed this exciting financial thriller and left with a fresh belief in what it's like to be an accounting and finance professional—not boring but intelligent with integrity that is making a difference in people's lives, a most trusted advisor.

Please recommend my book to your friends and continue to spread the word about Dex McCord's adventures. For those who have reviewed my book on Amazon—there is no greater gift to an author. If you have not yet reviewed Green Shade$ please leave a review on the site from which you purchased the book.

I hope to hear from you,

Greg

Index Of Exhibits

Exhibit 1: Purpose of Financial Statements and Double-Entry Accounting

Exhibit 2: The Fall of the Big Eight, Public Accounting Roles and Annual Salaries

Exhibit 3: The New CPA Exam

Exhibit 4: T-Account Finance Education Model—WIDE and DEEP SKILLS

Exhibit 5: The Major Differences Between GAAP and IFRS

Exhibit 6: Common Compensation Terms in a CFO Employment Agreement

Exhibit 7: The 10 Steps in an IPO Process

Exhibit 8: Key Financial Ratios

Exhibit 9: Chief Financial Officer Salaries

Exhibit 1: Purpose of Financial Statements and Double-Entry Accounting

Name of Statement	Purpose	Information Presented
Income Statement	Presents the organization's operating performance during a period of time.	Revenues earned. Expenses incurred. Profit, Income, or Loss, the difference between revenues and expenses
Balance Sheet	Reports the organization's financial condition at a point in time.	Assets, what the organization owns. Liabilities, what the organization owes to others. Stockholders' Equity, the difference between Assets and Liabilities, i.e., what belongs to the shareholders.
Statement of Retained Earnings	Describes what was done with the profits reported on the income statement.	Dividends paid to the shareholders. Retained Earnings, the profits left in the business, i.e., reinvested.
Statement of Cash Flow	Describes how cash came into the business and how it was used.	Operating Cash Flow, the cash generated by the day-to-day operations of the organization. Investing Cash Flow, the cash reinvested in the business or generated by selling off pieces of the business. Financing Cash Flow, the cash generated by borrowing or selling stock to investors and the cash disbursed to pay off debt, buy back stock, or pay dividends.

Business transactions are recorded in a double-entry accounting system that involves the use of debits and credits. This procedure requires that every transaction be recorded two ways: as one or more debit entries and as one or more credit entries. The debit entries <u>must</u> equal the credit entries.

Debit is probably the most misunderstood of all accounting terms. Most people think a debit is always a negative. In reality, a debit entry is merely a left-hand entry in a ledger account, while a credit is a right-hand entry (think of utilizing "T" accounts). Debits can be positive or negative depending on the account type. For example, a debit entry increases an asset account while it decreases a liability or equity account. Likewise, a credit entry can be either positive or negative. A credit decreases an asset account but increases a revenue account. Clear as mud right?

Adding to the confusion is our time spent looking at bank statements. When we receive money our bank lists the receipt of cash as a credit. However, in double-entry accounting receiving cash means it gets posted to the balance sheet as a debit. Your bank statement is prepared from the bank's point of view. Cash is leaving their balance sheet so the asset must be released via a credit. Additionally, when a bank charges service fees it is reported as a debit (expense) to you but for the bank the fee is a credit (revenue). The banks do this to integrate your electronically prepared bank statements with their automated accounting systems.

Practically speaking, for most nonfinancial professionals, it is unimportant to know whether an account is "debited" or "credited." However, it is extremely important to understand the impact of various transactions on the different accounts (i.e., whether an account is increased or decreased). The bottom line is these debits and credits are what make up Journal Entries. These JE's record accounting transactions with respect to time and provide supporting details about all accounting transactions.

An audit involves checking transactions and verifying information. Such checking is done on a statistical sampling basis. In an audit, the CPA or CA also goes outside the company to verify information. In addition, the auditor assesses the accounting systems and methods used and evaluates estimates and assumptions made by management. In the United States and Australia as well as most other countries, all companies whose stock is publicly traded are required to have their statements audited. While an audit is not a requirement for privately held companies, large private companies are usually audited. Lenders often require an audit. Also, if the shareholders are not actively involved in the business, they may want an audit.

Exhibit 2: The Fall of the Big Eight, Public Accounting Roles and Annual Salaries

The world's biggest accounting firms were once known as the Big Eight:

- Arthur Andersen
- Arthur Young & Company
- Coopers & Lybrand
- Ernst & Whinney (formerly Ernst & Ernst)
- Haskins & Sells (merged with European firm to become Deloitte, Haskins and Sells)
- KPMG (formed by merger of Peat Marwick International and KMG Group)
- Price Waterhouse
- Touche Ross

They were initially reduced to the Big Five by a series of mergers starting in the late 1980s, then became the Big Four after the demise of Arthur Andersen, following its involvement in the Enron scandal. In the 1990s Enron Corporation was one of the fastest-growing energy, commodities, and service companies in the United States. However, the entire organization was based on massive accounting and corporate fraud that eventually came to light. Its CFO and other executives orchestrated a scheme to use off-balance-sheet special purposes entities to hide Enron's mountains of debt and toxic assets from investors and creditors. The company's accounting improprieties, fake holdings, and lack of transparency resulted in restatements disclosing billions of dollars of omitted liabilities and losses. In 2001, Enron filed for bankruptcy. It was the largest in U.S. history at the time, ending with a stunning fall from grace.

In 2002 Arthur Andersen was indicted for obstruction of justice on the grounds that it knowingly, intentionally, and corruptly persuaded its employees to shred Enron-related documents related to its audit. The jury found Arthur Andersen guilty, resulting in what infamously became known as the Enron scandal. Since federal regulations do not allow convicted felons to audit public companies, Andersen surrendered its CPA license, effectively putting the firm out of business. The scandal resulted in a wave of new regulations and legislation designed to increase the accuracy of financial reporting for publicly traded companies. The most important of those measures, the Sarbanes-Oxley Act (2002), imposed harsh penalties for destroying, altering, or fabricating financial records.

The roles, responsibilities and salaries of public accountants are:

Staff Auditor (1-3 years) performs the detail work of a financial audit under the supervision of a Senior. These accountants do over 90 percent of the ceaseless grunt work that goes into an audit. Staff Auditors will often start to direct small audits at the two-year level. They become experts in scanning documents, counting inventory and performing research. The salary ranges during your first three years in "public" is $65,000–$75,000.

Senior Auditor (3-6 years) works under the general direction of an Audit Manager. Responsibilities include the direction of audit field work, assignment of detail work to Staff, and review of their working papers. The seniors keep the first-year workers in line, define for them the objective of the audit, and make certain that the engagement is completed on schedule and according to the audit plan. They also prepare financial statements, create corporate tax returns, and suggest improvements to internal controls. By the time you are made senior your salary is in the range of $75,000 to $100,000.

Audit Manager (6-8 years) supervises Seniors and Staff. Their job is to manage the audit on a day-to-day basis, dividing up the workload and checking the progress. Responsible for audit program approval, personnel scheduling, audit working papers review, financial statement disclosure, day-to-day client relationships, determination of billings for engagements, and training and evaluation of staff and seniors. By the time you were made a manager your salary was in the range of $100,000 to $140,000.

Senior Audit Manager (8-13 years) like a new manager supervises young Managers and Seniors. They also have the same audit responsibilities but now the role as a Senior Manager is to become a trusted advisor and create a meaningful impact with their global clients. An important part of their role is to actively establish and strengthen internal and external relationships. They are also expected to lead strategies and identify business opportunities for their own firm. Achievement of this level is critical to long-term success within a CPA firm, since it is awarded only to those with Partner potential. By the time you are made a senior manager your salary will be in the range of $140,000 to $175,000.

Partner level is coveted since only about 2 percent of all persons entering CPA firms will reach this plateau. The financial rewards are significant. The Partner normally purchases equity in the firm and therefore shares in all profits. Typically, a professional must be a CPA to become a Partner. In larger firms, an equivalent position of Principal is available to deserving specialists who are non-CPAs. An Audit, Tax, or Consulting Partner is typically responsible for overall client-related activities. The Partners are there to provide leadership, ensure quality control, protect the firm's reputation, sign the auditor's opinion, and keep the client happy. First year partner salaries typically range from $200,000 to $250,000.

Senior Partner performs all the duties of a Partner. The achievement of Senior Partner is obtained as a result of longevity with a firm and expert handling of instrumental accounts and personalities. The title of Senior Partner may also be attained through participation as a member of the Executive Committee, which is responsible for developing the firm's policies, planning activities, or providing day-to-day management and administration of one or more branch offices or regions. Senior partner salaries start at $250,000 and could go to well over $1,000,000.

Besides financial rewards striving towards a partnership bestowed some advantages. Whereas success at a typical company means climbing to one of just a few top positions, and probably elbowing others aside in the process. Partnerships provide a broader top to the pyramid. The Big Four firms have over 30,000 partners globally. They are consensual in style, which is critical when managing clever, self-regarding people.

One "big" question surrounding Big 4 partner pay is how do they achieve that high end of the salary range? Working your way to $1,000,000+ through longevity can't be that easy. The answer—profit share in fees other than audit. Historically, the Big 4 have made their money servicing large multinational companies. During the late 20th century all the public accounting firms significantly increased their consulting capabilities to deliver non-audit and accountancy services. The non-audit revenues were accelerating until the Arthur Anderson Enron accounting scandal led Congress to direct the SEC to create stronger barriers between auditors and other parts of their firms.

The Big 4 have been gradually rebuilding their non-accountancy services since the scandal and have again massively built up their consulting practices. As time passed, auditor conflicts of interest were repeatedly becoming the norm. With some firms spinning off sections of their consulting practices for significant money in order to stay one step ahead of the SEC. Some large accounting firms are planning IPO's, and the firm's partners will reap millions from splitting consulting practices. Today the U.S. Big 4 firms make only a third of their revenue from their audit function. So, as you can imagine, being a partner in the Big 4, means you are now working at one of the biggest professional service firms in the world. Not just an accounting, tax, and audit firm.

Senior partners, having more experience, serve the larger corporations. Thus, more profit share. You'll be handsomely rewarded but remember that every firm wants its pound of flesh, and the Big 4 partners are expected to work very long hours and continue finding new clients via networking and attending social functions. Also, it's fair to say that every firm puts pressure on you to make your revenue targets. There's no difference there between Big 4 and any other firm. However, the pressure seems to be greater within the Big 4 and other partners are quicker to have tough career conversations if you are not performing and progressing as well as they would like. Every partner is focused on profit share.

The ability for higher profit share at a Big 4 firm is much greater than mid and small tier firms. Accomplished by leveraging employees and charging exorbitant fees. The typical ratio of partners to non-partners in a Big 4 firm is much bigger than a mid-tier firm. For example:

- Big 4 firm—the ratio is 1 partner: 15–20 non-partners.
- Mid-Tier firm—the ratio is 1 partner: 5–10 non-partners.
- Smaller firms—the ratio is 1 partner: < 5 salaried employees.

No wonder the profits are greater at the Big 4 firms. But it's far from easy to maintain that $1M+ salary. The other partners tend to have an 'what have you done for me lately" culture. In other words, if you don't consistently find new clients and progress to the higher ranks of the firm, you are often asked to leave. Those principals of joint ownership help to encourage co-operative behavior amongst the partnership.

Exhibit 3: The New CPA Exam

For years the CPA exam was made up of four parts, graded by the AICPA. The topics tested were:

- Auditing & Attestation: engagement acceptance and planning; entity and internal control; procedures and evidence; reports; accounting and review services and professional responsibilities
- Financial Accounting & Reporting: concepts; accounts and disclosures; transactions; governmental and not-for-profits
- Regulation: ethical and legal responsibilities; business law; federal tax process; gain and loss taxation; individual tax and taxation of entities
- Business Environment & Concepts: corporate governance; economics; finance, information technology; strategic planning and operations management

The examination took two days, and every candidate had to pass all four parts. Each of the parts of the examination were graded on a scale of 0 to 100, the minimum passing score was 75.

Over the past century the CPA exam, and for that matter the accounting profession, has been constantly changing. In fact, from the very first certified public accountancy law passed in 1896 to the present day, the nature of being a CPA is marked by constant evolution and transformation. Recently the current licensure model underwent a change to fit the skills and competencies that new CPAs require today and in the future. The traditional four-part CPA exam that McCord passed was modified. In a joint initiative the National Association of State Boards of Accountancy (NASBA) and the AICPA introduced a new Uniform CPA Examination. The new exam included three core sections that each candidate takes:

- Accounting and Data Analytics
- Audit and Accounting Information Systems
- Tax

These three 'core' sections are supplemented by a candidate selecting one of the three separate discipline sections:

- Business Analysis and Reporting
- Information Systems and Controls
- Tax Compliance and Planning

These budding competencies allow a CPA candidate to expand their knowledge in an area that most directly aligns with a career path. After passing the three core competencies and one of the disciplines sections a person will be eligible to become a CPA, subject to state work experience requirements. A candidate is not required (or permitted) to complete more than one of the three discipline sections. The rationale for the new exams mixed core and discipline structure is that it more accurately reflects the environment in which accountants function.

Exhibit 4: T-Account Finance Education Model—WIDE and DEEP SKILLS

McCord understood that no one becomes a CFO based on technical knowledge alone. That an individual's "soft" or "power" skills are just as important to the job as technical acumen. Steve Walsh, ED&I's CFO, was no different than most leaders. Through his years of experience, he was able to harness a certain amount of 'critical thinking' and 'emotional intelligence' skills. Why does emotional intelligence matter? Because at the core of every outstanding leader are the abilities to connect, achieve, inspire, and act with resilience. McCord was keenly aware that he needed to enhance these management skills.

POWER SKILLS

Communication	Presentation		Decision-Making	Leadership
	US GAAP	T		
		E	IFRS	
	FASB	C		
		H	IAS	
	SEC	N		
		I	GAAS	
	IRS	C		
		A	IBFD	
	SALT	L		

WIDE power skills are vital to a successful career. Great leaders are measured on their ability to motivate teams, deliver exceptional results, and shape the business environment and microcultures. The modern-day rules for an effective CFO have changed. When a CFO transitions from being an individual contributor to managing a large group of people, it is no longer true that technical skills alone will drive desired results. Individual efforts that may have worked in the past will no longer be effective. Your soft skills need to be perfected. In fact, based on a survey reported by the Society for Human Resource Management, 97% of employers stated soft skills were either as important or more important than hard skills. In the AICPA's report, *CPA Horizons 2025* – the six core critical competencies identified were communication skills, critical thinking and problem-solving, leadership skills, anticipating and serving evolving needs, synthesizing intelligence to insight, and integration/collaboration.

DEEP technical skills are mandatory for a finance career. At public accounting firms technical and on-the-job training is given (this may not be the case with soft skills). All public accounting firms require their employees to take a certain amount of technical and ethics training. In fact, once you have earned a Certified Public Accountant (CPA) or Certified Management Accountant (CMA), your education is far from over. You will still need to complete a number of annual continuing professional education (CPE) credits in order to remain licensed.

Accounting has been called the language of business with on-the-job learning occurring almost every single day. For example, you may be requested to look at how your client accounted for leases or joint ventures. However, even if you have in-depth knowledge of GAAP, most don't have the technical transactional rules memorized. At some point you will have to learn how to effectively perform accounting research. However, at larger accounting firms and in most cases, you don't need to be an expert on all technical competences but rather be smart enough to identify complex issues and then reach out to the experts for advice.

The technical skills from the T-Account Finance Education Model are the primary research resources to draw from for rules of accounting, auditing, tax, and reporting:

- Generally Accepted Accounting Principles (GAAP)—A set of practices in the United States that guide accountants in preparing financial statements. Audited statements generally conform with

GAAP since the auditors must disclose any deviations from the principles.
- International Financial Reporting Standards (IFRS)—a set of globally accepted reporting guidelines to ensure uniformity in accounting practices that makes financial records comparable across different reporting entities worldwide.
- Financial Accounting Standards Board (FASB)—The group responsible for establishing generally accepted accounting principles in the United States.
- International Accounting Standards (IAS)—The international version of GAAP; established by the International Accounting Standards Committee and followed by many large multinational corporations.
- Securities and Exchange Commission (SEC)—The U.S. government agency that regulates the sales of stocks and bonds by public companies.
- Generally accepted Auditing Standards (GAAS)—Rules that Chartered Accountants and Certified Public Accountants follow when auditing their clients.
- The Internal Revenue Service (IRS)—The U.S. tax collection agency that administers the Internal Revenue Code enacted by Congress.
- The International Bureau of Fiscal Documentation (IBFD)—in Amsterdam, the Netherlands, provides cross-border tax expertise on treaties and other international tax activities, including transfer pricing.
- State and Local Taxes (SALT)—state corporate income taxes, sales tax, partnership taxes, tax credits or unclaimed property, navigating the compliance process is a major challenge.

Public Accounting firms provide all the required technical training, but most accountants want more than just to be competent in how to account for leases or the latest revenue recognition rules. Take it upon yourself to embark on your own learning journey. Many training experts recommend soft skill education at the American Management Association International. The AMA, a 100-year-old non-for-profit management and leadership training organization, is known for changing behavior. They have a long track record of educating professionals at all levels in business. Providing individuals with the knowledge, skills, and tools to achieve performance excellence. AMA also provides a forum to exchange ideas and best practices with other senior leaders in the corporate world.

The WIDE fundamental skills of CFO's (and accountants) that if mastered will help improve consistency of results:

1) *Communication*—You'll need to boil down complex financial topics into simple messages that non-finance experts can understand, without talking down to them. Recognize the impact your emotionally intelligent communication skills have on your audience.

2) *Presentation*—CFOs and accountants must present to the board of directors, investors, analysts, and when appropriate, the media. They can't be introverted or camera-shy. Modify passionate behaviors that will expand your sphere of credibility and influence.

3) *Decision-Making*—In many meetings, everyone is waiting for the CFO to decide. The ability to assimilate information quickly, weigh the options, and take responsibility are all key. Bring it all together by synthesizing complex issues and challenges. Turn them into opportunities.

4) *Leadership*—A command and control leadership approach may have worked well in the past but in nearly all corporate cultures today workers require inspiration and a more collaborative approach. Leverage your teams technical, social, and emotional intelligence to produce results.

The span of responsibilities for accountants continues to increase in a flatter, global, more matrixed business environment. It is not easy being a great Chief Financial Officer. You must own a broad range of technical and soft skills while also understanding the use of technology in a digital landscape. A must-have to manage and scale operations. CFOs will always be in the front lines leading the tactical transformation of their company's operations.

Steve Walsh had WIDE power skills. He was a common sense and "right time / right place" opportunistic accountant. His salary package and employment agreement were certainly evidence. He had made an investment in himself and mastered the art of building a network, two of the most important things an accountant can do when progressing in his vocation and essential for all professionals as their careers progress and roles transform. Particularly building out strong internal and external relationships with key individuals along the way. McCord understood, more than others, the value of his accounting and auditing experience, his extensive network, and the dedication it took to get to the top of the pyramid.

Exhibit 5: The Major Differences Between GAAP and IFRS[1]:

During the first decade of the 21st century academics made large strides converging U.S. Generally Accepted Accounting Principles (GAAP) and International Financial Reporting Standards (IFRS) but that progress stalled. Despite numerous joint convergence efforts, the accounting standards setters could not agree on one set of global financial reporting standards.

The following are some of the major differences between GAAP and IFRS:

Consolidation. US GAAP has a two-tier consolidation model: based on voting rights and decision making over significant activities. IFRS favors a single control model centered on indicators of control.

Inventory Costing. US GAAP utilizes several inventory costings models such as LIFO (last-in-first-out) and FIFO (first-in-first-out). Under IFRS the LIFO method of accounting is prohibited. Under both frameworks inventories should be written down to market value; however, if market value later increases, only IFRS allows the earlier write-down to be reversed.

Revaluation Model for Property, Plant &Equipment (PP&E). US GAPP tends to follow a conservative approach, where market price reductions are recognized but increases are not (except for marketable securities). Under IFRS assets are accounted at fair value, using the revaluation model. So, both market value increases and decreases are recognized.

Capitalization of Development Costs. US GAAP prohibits the capitalization of development costs, with limited exceptions for website and software development. The requirement that all Research and Development (R&D)

---

[1] *Journal of Accountancy*

costs incurred internally be expensed immediately is a conservative approach. Under IFRS, development costs are capitalized if the technical and economic feasibility of the project can be demonstrated in accordance with certain criteria.

Post-Employment Benefits. Under US GAAP companies use the expected rate of return on plan assets reflecting changes in the fair value over and up to five years in determining the expected returns in the retirement plans. It also separately calculates the interest costs on the benefit obligations. This is why Actuaries make so much money. Under IFRS, companies simply calculate a net interest cost (or income) of the plan assets by applying the discount rate to the net defined benefit liability (or asset).

Certain Nonfinancial Liabilities. Under US GAPP the recognition of certain nonfinancial liabilities, such as contingencies, depends upon the probability that a liability has been incurred. It defines probability as an event that is likely to occur (i.e., about 75%). Under IFRS, probable is defined as more likely than not to occur (i.e., greater than 50%). As a result, IFRS has a lower accounting recognition threshold, resulting in a liability being recognized earlier.

Exhibit 6: Common Compensation Terms in a CFO Employment Agreement

A CFO's employment agreement is why most can sleep at night. It's the only security that the top finance chief and his family have. Below are extracts of Bed, Bath & Beyond's late CFO's employment agreement that was filed with the Security and Exchange Commission. Unfortunately, he committed suicide purportedly due to pressure at work, 18-hour days and a depressed stock price.

Source: BED BATH & BEYOND INC (BBBY) 8-K filed 4/30/2020

Section 3. <u>Compensation and Reimbursement of Expenses</u>.

(a) Base Salary. During the Term, Executive's annual base salary (the "<u>Base Salary</u>") shall be **$775,000.00**, payable in accordance with the Company's regular payroll practices in effect from time to time and subject to all applicable taxes and withholdings, but no less frequently than in semi-monthly installments.

(b) Annual Bonus. Beginning with respect to fiscal year 2020 and for each completed fiscal year thereafter during the Term, Executive shall be eligible to receive an annual cash performance bonus (the "Annual Bonus"), with a target Annual Bonus opportunity equal to eighty-five percent (85%) of his Base Salary. The target Annual Bonus opportunity may be increased by the Compensation Committee in its sole discretion. The Annual Bonus earned, if any, with respect to a fiscal year will be subject to the performance of Executive and the Company during such year, relative to performance goals established for such fiscal year by the Compensation Committee… and the Company shall pay the Annual Bonus, to the extent payable in accordance with this Section

3(b), on or before the date that is two and one-half (2½) months following the end of the fiscal year with respect to which it is earned…

(c) Sign-on RSU Award.

(i) On the Start Date, as an inducement material to Executive entering into this Agreement and commencing employment with the Company, the Company shall grant to Executive, and Executive shall receive, a one-time, sign-on award of time-vesting restricted stock units ("RSUs") pursuant to, as determined by the Compensation Committee in its sole discretion, (x) the inducement grant exception to shareholder approval of equity plans set forth in Nasdaq Listing Rule 5635(c)(4), (y) the Company's 2012 Incentive Compensation Plan, as amended from time to time or any successor plan (the "2012 Plan"), or (z) the Company's 2018 Incentive Compensation Plan, as amended from time to time or any successor plan (the "2018 Plan") (the "Sign-on RSU Award"). The Sign-on RSU Award will have an aggregate value at grant equal to **$775,000.00** and will vest in substantially equal installments on each of the first, second, and third anniversaries of the Start Date…

(d) Long-Term Equity Incentive Awards. In spring 2020, at the same time as such awards are granted to other members of the Company's senior management team, the Company shall grant Executive a long-term equity incentive award(s) under the 2012 Plan or the 2018 Plan, as determined by the Compensation Committee in its sole discretion (the "2020 Equity Award"). The 2020 Equity Award will have a target value at grant equal to **$1,937,500.00**…

(e) Relocation Benefits. In connection with the commencement of the Executive's employment and Executive's relocation to the New

York metropolitan area, the Company shall provide Executive with the relocation benefits summarized on Exhibit A hereto.

(f) Reimbursement of Legal Expenses. The Company shall pay or reimburse Executive for his reasonable out-of-pocket legal expenses incurred in connection with the negotiation and execution of this Agreement, up to a maximum of $10,000.00. Executive shall provide the Company with such receipts or invoices as the Company deems reasonably necessary to verify the amount of such expenses.

(g) Reimbursement of Business Expenses. Executive is authorized to incur reasonable expenses in carrying out his duties hereunder and shall, upon receipt by the Company of proper documentation with respect thereto (setting forth the amount, business purpose and establishing payment) be reimbursed for all such reasonable business expenses incurred during the Term, subject to the Company's written expense reimbursement policies and any written pre-approval policies in effect from time to time.

Section 4. Employee Benefits.

(a) Company Employee Benefit Plans. During the Term, Executive shall be provided the opportunity to participate in all standard employee benefit programs made available by the Company to the Company's senior executive employees generally, in accordance with the terms and conditions of such plans, including the eligibility and participation provisions of such plans and programs, as such plans or programs may be in effect from time to time…

(b) Financial Planning Benefit. During the Term, upon presentation of appropriate documentation, the Company will reimburse Executive for up to $10,000.00 annually for assistance with tax preparation and financial planning.

(c) Automobile Allowance. During the Term, the Company will provide Executive with an automobile allowance of $1,000.00 per month on a net after-tax basis, which may be applied toward the cost of leasing or purchasing an automobile, or toward the cost of a car service or other similar transportation service.

(d) Vacation and Other Leave. During the Term, Executive shall be entitled to take up to four (4) weeks of paid vacation time per calendar year, or such greater amount as may be provided pursuant to the Company's vacation policies in effect from time to time, provided that such time will not carry over from one year to the next…

Not too shabby compensation and benefits clauses if you can get them. Sadly, the late CFO of Bed Bath and Beyond was not able to enjoy all the hard work he put into his career before his passing.

Exhibit 7: The 10 Steps in an IPO Process

Few experiences are as tricky and exhausting for a finance chief as taking a company public. As Dale Buss of the StrategicCFO360 confirmed, "IPOs are like black holes for CFOs: an intense experience that compels them gravitationally into the singularity of the offering day, where they explode on the other side into a whole new universe of experiences, responsibilities, stresses and paybacks." Below are the 10 steps in a company completing a successful IPO:

1) Select the Working Group
    - Investment bankers, law firm, accounting firm, financial printer, insurance broker
2) Complete Due Diligence
    - US GAAP financial statements, internal control review, SOX compliance, virtual data room
3) Draft the Initial Public Offering Prospectus
    - Form S-1, growth strategy plans, EDGARization of documents
4) Submit Required Applications for Listings
    - NYSE or NASDAQ, CIK public number, CIK confirmation code
5) File the IPO Registration Statement with the SEC
    - S-1 filed (red herring), underwriting agreement to FINRA
6) Respond to Securities and Exchange Commission Comments
    - SEC 30-day review, clear comments
7) Prepare IPO Marketing Materials
    - A compelling story, vision and growth goals, IPO goals established

8) Conduct the IPO Roadshow
    - Sales pitch, maximize number of presentations, build buzz, fill the order book
9) Complete the Initial Listing Application and Filing with FINRA
    - SEC to declare effective, application to exchange, underwriters' compensation information to FINRA
10) Set the Share Price and Allocate Shares
    - Assess investor interest and release shares to underwriters

Exhibit 8: Key Financial Ratios

While there are different ways to acquire information to assess the value and growth potential of a stock, fundamental financial analysis from reported results remains one of the best ways to establish a benchmark of a stock's performance. Metcalf's equity traders focused on growth, earnings, and market value. Making actionable trading decisions on a security's intrinsic value based on financial data. The two most profitable trading metrics are the price-to-earnings (or P/E) ratio and price-to-book (P/B) ratio.

A P/E ratio is the ratio of a company's share price to its earnings per share. Investors use this ratio to compare the performances of similar companies against one company's records, both historical and projected earnings. In other words, it is the amount an investor must pay for each dollar of earnings. It indicates whether the market price of a stock reflects the company's earnings potential or true value, and helps investors determine if it is under or overvalued. P/E ratio is calculated by dividing a company's price per share by its earnings per share.

Financial Information	Price to Earnings Ratio Formula
> Income Statement > Most Recent Stock Price	$\text{P/E Ratio} = \dfrac{\text{Share Price}}{\text{Earnings Per Share}}$

Since this metric varies between industries, there is no benchmark for what makes a "good" P/E ratio. That said, a relatively high price-to-earnings ratio can indicate that the stock is overvalued or that it is expected to have significant future earnings growth. On the other hand, a low P/E ratio can indicate that either the stock is undervalued, or expectations are low. For example, if the industry average price-to-earnings ratio is 25, a calculated P/E ratio of 50 could suggest that the stock is overvalued.

A P/B ratio is a measure of a company's share price in relation to its book value of shareholders' equity, indicating the price investors must pay for each dollar of book value. This relative metric is better suited for comparisons against other companies and industries. Price-to-book ratio is calculated by dividing the company's current share price by its book value per share.

Financial Information	Price to Book Ratio Formula
> Balance Sheet > Most Recent Stock Price	$\text{P/B Ratio} = \dfrac{\text{Share Price}}{\text{Book Value Per Share}}$

Price-to-book ratios vary between industries, making it difficult to set a benchmark for what makes a "good" price-to-book ratio. However, if the value falls below the industry average, it may indicate that the stock is undervalued. If the value is above the industry average, it may indicate that the stock is overvalued.

Green Shade$ also made use of a number of other important financial ratios and key performance indicators (KPI's) that accountants and management use almost every day. The handful of ratios that the company's technical traders utilized for financial analysis were:

1. <u>Profitability Ratios</u>

Profitability ratios measure a company's ability to generate earnings and profits in relation to its revenue, operating costs, shareholders' equity, and balance sheet assets. In other words, these useful financial ratios reflect how well a company can convert its resources and assets into income:

a) Return on Assets (ROA)

Financial Information	Return on Assets Formula
> Income Statement > Balance Sheet	$ROA = \dfrac{Net\ Income}{Total\ Assets} \times 100$

In general, an ROA above 5% is considered good. A higher ROA is better, as it indicates that the company can generate more income from each dollar of assets.

b) Return on Equity (ROE)

Financial Information	Return on Equity Formula
> Income Statement > Balance Sheet	$ROE = \dfrac{Net\ Income}{Shareholder's\ Equity} \times 100$

While averages can vary depending on the industry, an ROE above 10% is generally considered good. A higher number is better, as it indicates that the company can generate more income from each dollar of shareholders' equity.

c) Profit Margin

For profit margin, a higher number is better, as it indicates that the company makes more profit from each sale. Averages vary significantly between industries, but generally speaking: A profit margin of 5% is low, 10% is average, and above 20% is good.

Financial Information	Profit Margin Formula
> Income Statement	$Profit\ Margin = \dfrac{Profit}{Revenue} \times 100$

2. Liquidity Ratios

Liquidity ratios measure a company's ability to meet short-term debt obligations without raising additional capital. These important financial ratios can be used for internal analysis to gauge economic health. They can also be used for external analysis to compare against other companies or industries.

a) Current Ratio

Financial Information	Current Ratio Formula		
> Balance Sheet	Current Ratio =	$\dfrac{Profit}{Revenue}$	x 100

Industry averages vary for what is a good current ratio. However, a ratio above 1 indicates that the company has more current assets than current liabilities, whereas a ratio below 1 indicates that the company has more current liabilities than current assets.

b) Quick Ratio (acid-test ratio)

Financial Information	Quick Ratio Formula	
> Balance Sheet	Quick Ratio =	$\dfrac{Liquid\ Assets}{Current\ Liabilities}$

A value above 1 indicates that the company can immediately pay off its current liabilities using its liquid assets. A value below 1 indicates that it cannot.

c) Cash Ratio

Financial Information	Cash Ratio Formula
> Balance Sheet	Cash Ratio = $\dfrac{\text{Cash and Cash Equivalents}}{\text{Current Liabilities}}$

A cash ratio above 1 indicates that the company can immediately pay its current liabilities in cash. A cash ratio below 1 indicates that the company cannot.

3. Leverage Ratios

Leverage ratios measure the amount of debt a company incurs in relation to its equity and assets. These are some of the most important ratios for financial analysis and provide important information about the company's capital structure, its ability to meet financial obligations, and how it uses debt to finance its operations.

a) Debt Ratio

Financial Information	Debt Ratio Formula
> Balance Sheet	Debt Ratio = $\dfrac{\text{Total Liabilities}}{\text{Total Assets}}$

For the debt ratio, a lower number is generally better and indicates that the company has more assets than debts (i.e., is less leveraged). Since cash flows, capital structures, and financing methods vary between industries, it can be difficult to set a benchmark for what makes a "good" debt ratio.

b) Debt to Equity Ratio (D/E)

Financial Information	Debt to Equity Ratio Formula
> Balance Sheet	Debt to Equity Ratio = $\dfrac{\text{Total Liabilities}}{\text{Total Shareholder's Equity}}$

Because capital structures and other variables can all influence the interpretation of the debt-to-equity ratio, a higher value isn't always a bad sign. Debt can actually help companies increase their growth potential, so this important financial ratio should be used in conjunction with other metrics to gauge a company's financial health.

c) Interest Coverage Ratio

Financial Information	Interest Coverage Ratio Formula
> Income Statement	Interest Coverage Ratio = $\dfrac{\text{EBIT}}{\text{Interest Expense}}$

A value above 1 indicates that a company's EBIT can cover its interest payments, whereas a value below 1 indicates that it cannot. A higher number is better because it reflects a greater ability to repay debt.

4. **Market Ratios**

Market ratios (also called price ratios and valuation ratios) are some of the most important financial ratios for investors and are used to evaluate the share price of a company. For instance, they can be used to determine whether share prices are overvalued, undervalued, or priced fairly. They are often used by investors to evaluate stocks as potential investments, analyze stock trends, and more. Besides P/E and P/B ratio's other commonly used market ratios include:

a) Price/Earnings-to-Growth (PEG) Ratio

Financial Information	PEG Ratio Formula
> Income Statement > Most Recent Stock Price	PEG Ratio = $\dfrac{\text{P/E Ratio}}{\text{EPS Growth}}$

In general, a value below 1 may indicate that the stock is undervalued, whereas a value above 1 may indicate that it is overvalued.

b) Dividend Payout Ratio

Financial Information	Dividend Payout Ratio Formula
> Income Statement	Dividend Payout Ratio = $\dfrac{\text{Dividend Paid}}{\text{Net Income}}$ x 100

Typically, 40% is considered a "good" dividend payout ratio, but averages vary depending on the company, industry, and a multitude of other factors. Generally speaking, a higher value indicates that more of the company's earnings are paid as dividends, whereas a lower ratio indicates that more of its earnings are reinvested back into the company.

5. Activity Ratios

Activity ratios (also called operating ratios and efficiency ratios) measure how a company uses its resources to generate sales. These important financial ratios are often used by investors to gauge the efficiency of an operation, the speed at which cash is collected, the rate at which inventory is turned over, and so on. These fundamental analysis ratios are most effective when used as comparisons over time, either to measure an improvement in company performance or see how it stacks up to its industry peers.

a) Inventory Turnover Ratio

Financial Information	Inventory Turnover Ratio Formula
> Income Statement > Balance Sheet	Inventory Turnover Ratio = $\dfrac{COGS}{Average\ Inventory}$

A higher value can indicate that products are being sold quickly or that inventory levels are insufficient. A lower value can indicate that products are being sold slowly, inventory is becoming obsolete, or inventory levels are in excess.

b) Receivables Turnover Ratio

Financial Information	Receivables Turnover Ratio Formula
> Income Statement > Balance Sheet	Receivables Turnover Ratio = $\dfrac{Net\ Credit\ Sales}{Average\ Receivables}$

A higher receivable turnover ratio may indicate that the company is efficient at collecting money owed or that it has a conservative credit policy (e.g., issues less credit, has short payment terms). A lower value can indicate that the company is inefficient at collecting money owed or that it issues credit too generously to customers that are unable to make payments.

c) Payables Turnover Ratio

Financial Information	Payables Turnover Ratio Formula
> Income Statement > Balance Sheet	Payables Turnover Ratio = $\dfrac{Net\ Credit\ Purchases}{Average\ Accounts\ Payable}$

A higher value indicates that the company is more efficient at managing its cash flows and paying its creditors, while a lower value indicates that it is less efficient.

Exhibit 9: Chief Financial Officer Salaries

A significant number of accountants ultimately become CFO's or Controllers, however more importantly many come to be—*Quiet Millionaires*—the behind-the-scenes guys at successful companies. Most CFOs are paid very well. Based on a 2024 study by Salary.com the average Chief Financial Officer fully loaded salary in the United States is approximately $437,000 with a range of typically $331,000 to $561,000. According to CFO Search Inc. the Average CFO Base Salary Range by Company Size is:

Company Size	Private Company	Public Company
$10 – $100 Million	$161,000 – $284,000	$176,000 – $304,000
$101 – $300 Million	$207,000 – $325,000	$224,000 – $342,000
$301 – $500 Million	$235,000 – $384,000	$256,000 – $410,000
$501 – $999 Million	$264,000 – $487,000	$275,000 – $507,000
$1 Billion – $5 Billion	$271,9000 – $536,000	$293,000 – $567,000

The above is just the average <u>base</u> salary. When you start adding bonuses and equity awards the numbers get astronomically high. Based on a Willis Towers Watson study of CFO median pay with incentives at largest companies were over $3.7 million, $2.1 million for mid-cap companies and $1.4 million for small cap companies. On average, CFOs make about eight times as much as their company's average employee.

It's true that a very small percentage of CFO's end up on the top earners list, however many quickly become millionaires based on hard work, timing, and patience. For example, take a look at Joe Ianniello, a former public accountant. After graduating from Pace University with a major in accounting and a minor in baseball he started his career at KPMG. He was one of the firm's prize softball players. Joe spent seven years with KPMG and then joined CBS Corporation. Over two decades at CBS he climbed the accountant corporate ladder spending time in various roles including that of internal auditor, financial planning analyst, investor relations director, Treasurer and head of Corporate Development, a role in which he identified and assessed potential mergers and acquisitions. He gained a reputation for being one of the hardest working and most disciplined financial executives in the media and entertainment business. He became the CFO of CBS after 12 years at the company.

After 4 years as CFO, Joe became the Chief Operating Officer and was being groomed to succeed the then current CEO Les Moonves, who was later ousted from his position after he was accused of sexual misconduct. The #metoo movement was not going to make any exceptions. Joe was immediately named President and acting CEO of the CBS Corporation.

Shortly afterwards, CBS and Viacom boards began discussing a possible merger. If the merger happened, Ianniello was likely the odd man out since the controlling shareholder, Shari Redstone, handpicked the Viacom CEO. If Ianniello was not appointed the CEO of the combined company he would be entitled to his exit package which was 3 years of compensation.

During the negotiations, the CBS directors wanted Joe's stewardship over the CBS assets post deal even if they still had to pay him, Joe agreed to stay on after the merger and became the Chairman and CEO of all the CBS assets. Joe was subsequently replaced after the merger and according to the company's proxy of that year received a total of $125 million in compensation making him the 3rd highest paid executive in the country.

Joes' financial success was an agglomerate of an accountant's journey. At CBS he had been involved in almost every financial aspect of the business and toward the end of his tenure every major financial decision. Fred Reynolds, a serial corporate CFO and former CEO of Viacom, described Joe as someone who "can play at every level of the corporation and is always ready to step into vitally important positions, he has my complete trust." Ethics and trust is what set Joe and most accountants apart.

~~~

McCord understood that today's Chief Financial Officers are expected to have strong leadership skills, ethics, and work toward a bigger picture. During his adventure he had to quickly engage in tactical problem solving, make crucial decisions, and build relationships (even romantic ones). I think we can all agree that Dex's level of foresight, vision and critical thinking will lead him to executive stardom, plus timing and a little luck always helps.

About the Author

Greg D. Adams, CPA is currently SVP and CFO of American Management Association International, a nonprofit educational organization. He has held senior financial positions (CFO, COO & Director) for over 25 years in both public and private sectors. Greg's leadership mission to help employees and business leaders achieve corporate excellence has given him firsthand insight into corporate players of all types and ranks, both inside and outside the global business world. For three of the 11 years he spent in public accounting at KPMG, Greg lived in Sydney, Australia, a key setting for Dex McCord's adventures in *GREEN SHADE$*. Greg graduated from the college of William and Mary with a BBA in accounting. He has a daughter named Olivia and resides in Westchester County, New York with his wife Kristine.

Follow Greg on:
LinkedIN
http://wwwCPA-Author.com
Email me at: greg@cpa-author.com

Greg D. Adams, "CPA" Account of the Amazons

Made in the USA
Middletown, DE
20 June 2024